**Sa** Metropoli

Please return this item to any the ret

You may renew the item unless it has been reserved by another borrower.

You can renew your library items by using the 24/7 renewal hotline number - 0845 352 4949 or FREE online at opac-lib.sandwell.gov.uk *HT*

THANK YOU FOR USING YOUR LIBRARY

Moore
evans
24|7|19

# The Billionaire's Club

*Meet the world's most eligible bachelors...*

by

Rebecca Winters

**For tycoons Vincenzo Gagliardi,
Takis Manolis and Cesare Donati,
transforming the Castello di Lombardi into
one of Europe's most highly sought-after hotels
will be more than just a business venture—
it's a challenge to be relished!**

**But these three men,
bound by a friendship as strong as blood,
are about to discover that the chase is only half
the fun as three women conquer their hearts
and change their lives for ever...**

*Return of Her Italian Duke*
*Bound to Her Greek Billionaire*
*Whisked Away by Her Sicilian Boss*

Available now!

# WHISKED AWAY
# BY HER
# SICILIAN BOSS

BY
REBECCA WINTERS

First Published in Great Britain 2017
By Mills & Boon, an imprint of HarperCollins*Publishers*
1 London Bridge Street, London, SE1 9GF

© 2017 Rebecca Winters

ISBN: 978-0-263-92335-3

23-1017

Our policy is to use papers that are natural, renewable and recyclable products and made from wood grown in sustainable forests. The logging and manufacturing processes conform to the legal environmental regulations of the country of origin.

Printed and bound in Spain
by CPI, Barcelona

**Rebecca Winters** lives in Salt Lake City, Utah. With canyons and high alpine meadows full of wildflowers, she never runs out of places to explore. They, plus her favourite holiday spots in Europe, often end up as backgrounds for her romance novels—because writing is her passion, along with her family and church. Rebecca loves to hear from readers. If you wish to email her, please visit her website at www.cleanromances.com.

To all of you readers who have read my books
and let me know you enjoy them.

You'll never know what your kind, encouraging
words do to make this author's job a pure delight!

Thank you from the bottom of my heart.

# CHAPTER ONE

*Salon des Reines, Paris, France*

THE CHAUFFEUR OF Le Comte Jean-Michel Ardois pulled the limousine up in front of the bridal salon on the Rue de L'Echelle. In the last two weeks Princess Tuccianna Falcone Leonardi of Sicily had been here with her mother three times for the bridal dress fitting. Each time they'd come, she'd made excuses to visit the bathroom in order to study the layout of the exclusive shop.

This morning was her final fitting to make sure everything was perfect for the wedding ceremony tomorrow. Only Tuccia had no intention of showing up for the elaborate nuptials arranged by her parents and Comte Ardois ten years ago in a horrifying, iron-clad betrothal forced upon her. She'd dreamed of her freedom forever. Now had come the moment for her escape.

Madame Dufy, the owner, welcomed them inside. After fussing over Tuccia and telling her how excited she was for her forthcoming marriage to the *comte*, she took them back to the dressing room befitting a queen.

"Delphine will be with you in just a moment with your gown. It's as exquisite as you are, Princess."

The second she left, Tuccia turned to her mother, the Marchesa di Trabia of Sicily. "I need to go to the restroom."

"Surely not!"

"I can't help it. You know how I get when I'm nervous."

"You are impossible, Tuccia!"

"If I don't go, it might happen in here."

Her mother's hands flew up in the air. "All right! But don't take too long. We have a long list of things that must be done today."

"I'll hurry, Mamma."

*Yes, she'd hurry.* Right out of the clutches of the *comte*!

She knew he planned to assign her a bodyguard the moment they were married and never let her out of his sight for the rest of their lives. After overhearing him discuss it with her parents, who'd said she needed a strong hand, she'd been planning how to disappear.

Tuccia opened the door and walked down the hall to the door of the bathroom. But she only went inside to leave her betrothal ring on the floor near the sink. Whoever found it could think what they wanted. After looking around to make sure no one had seen her, she rushed down another hallway straight out the back door of the shop.

From there it was only a short run down the alley used for delivery trucks to the street where she climbed in a taxi.

"Le Bourget Aeroport, *s'il vous plaît*."

Her heart refused to stop thudding as they drove

off. She looked behind her. No one had come running out of the alley chasing after her yet. Tuccia prayed all the way to the airport where she boarded an Eljet chartered for her under a fake name and paid for her by her aunt Bertina. Once it landed in Palermo, Sicily, she'd take a taxi to her aunt's palazzo.

Before long Tuccia's favorite person in the whole world would be offering her sanctuary. Her life would continue to depend on Bertina's help, or all was lost.

*The next day, Milan, Italy*

Dinner had concluded in the private dining room of the legendary fourteenth-century *castello*, the home of the former first Duc di Lombardi in Milan, Italy.

Vincenzo Gagliardi, the present-day *duc*, lifted his goblet with the insignia of the Gagliardi coat of arms. "*Buona fortuna* this trip, Cesare. Our business is depending on you. May you return with my wife's replacement soon. The baby will be here in two months. I want Gemma off her feet ASAP."

"Amen," Takis declared, raising his glass. "You're going to have to be quick, *amico*." He touched his goblet to Cesare's, and they sipped the local vintage Lombardia that Vincenzo had produced from the vast wine cellar for his send-off.

Cesare Donati eyed his two best friends with a smile. They'd been like brothers to him for more than a decade. Together they'd turned the former fortress palace of Vincenzo's family into the five-star Castello Supremo Hotel and Ristorante di Lombardi, Europe's most sought-after resort.

"I have a surprise for you. I'll be back in two days

with our new pastry chef. I told Gemma as much this morning."

"That soon?" they said in unison.

"It's been arranged for a while, so have no concerns."

His friends smiled in relief. For Cesare's contribution to their successful enterprise, he'd already found the perfect person to replace Gemma as the *castello*'s new executive pastry chef.

But he'd been keeping the identity of his choice a secret until he could present Ciro Fragala in person with one of his many specialties for their delectation.

Vincenzo's wife had learned to make Florentine pastry from her mother who'd cooked for the last *duc*. Though her cooking was perfection and drew the elite clientele that came to the *castello*, in Cesare's opinion the best cook in the world was his own Sicilian mother.

She'd learned from the nuns who made divine pastries and ran the orphanage where she'd been raised until she turned eighteen. On her say-so—and she would know better than anyone else—Cesare had done the necessary research on Signor Fragala, the pastry cook she'd declared to be the finest in all Sicily. After a visit to the Palermo restaurant with his mother two months ago, he'd agreed totally with her assessment.

Hiring Ciro meant sensational new desserts for their business enterprise in Milan. The two of them had met with the fifty-five-year-old widower several times in the last few weeks. The chef had said he would leap at the chance to work at the famous *castello* restaurant.

Since he didn't have children, it wouldn't be a problem to move. He'd given his notice and Cesare planned to fly him to Milan. The new chef would work well with their executive French chef at the *castello*. Most of all, the guys would be pleased by the man's amiable personality.

"We'll drive you to the airport," Vincenzo stated.

Cesare shook his head. "Thanks, but you've done enough by surprising me with this dinner. You've both got pregnant wives who've been generous enough to let us have this meal together. By now they'll be wondering where you are. The limo is waiting as we speak."

"Then we'll walk you out," Vincenzo murmured.

*"Grazie."*

He drained the rest of his wine and got to his feet. Reaching for the suitcase he'd left by the double doors, he moved ahead of them to the portrait-lined corridor of the former *ducs* with their legendary silvery eyes.

"Stay safe," Takis said as Cesare climbed in the rear of the limo.

"Always."

Vincenzo smiled. "We can't wait to meet this mystery paragon of pastry chefs." He patted Cesare's shoulder and shut the door before it drove away from the *castello*.

Two hours later, the Lombardi ducal jet arrived at Palermo International Airport, where another limousine waited for him on the tarmac. Cesare told the driver to take him to the posh Mondello borough. It was there he'd bought a villa in the famed *art nouveau* style for his mother and sister who was now married and lived in the city with her husband and their toddler.

He'd wanted nothing but the best for his wonderful mamma, Lina Donati.

She would never leave Palermo. After being raised by the nuns and learning how to cook from them, she'd started out working in a local restaurant after leaving the orphanage.

Her subsequent marriage was short-lived. Abandoned by her husband, she'd cooked her way through life to support their little family and had made a name for herself. Cesare believed she made the best food on earth. In her honor he'd had a state-of-the-art kitchen installed because he couldn't do enough for her.

Thanks to a bad back from being on her feet all the time, she now cooked exclusively for Bertina Spadaro, who wasn't a demanding employer. Cesare had begged her to retire. He would take care of her forever. But his mother said she couldn't imagine not having work to do and she loved Bertina. The aristocratic older sister of the Marchesa di Leonardi di Trabia had become her friend.

The Leonardi family descended from the royal Sicilian family of the commune of Trabia, thirty miles from Palermo, and could trace their roots back to the 1400s, when the land and castle were granted them by Frederick III. The present *marchese* and *marchesa* had established their own *palazzo* in the heart of Palermo.

Bertina and Lina had become fast friends over the years and were in each other's confidence. The rest of the time his mother spent with Cesare's family, or tended her spectacular herb garden.

The elite area of Mondello had everything: exclusive yachting clubs dotting its sandy beach, restaurants, shops and a marina with numerous yachts, including the *marchese*'s gleaming white royal yacht that stood out from the others.

Before buying the villa for her, Cesare, too, had been captivated as he'd walked through the sand of its private beach front, inhaling the air filled with the heady scent of orange blossoms and jasmine. Whenever he flew to Palermo, Cesare was reminded that with all its rich history, there was nowhere else in the world he found more fascinating.

But tonight as they drove into the ancient, colorful city, he was met with the strong smells of fish and spices that always brought back memories of his youth. There was a hint of the old Arab souks, taking him back to his childhood. As a boy, these streets with their subtle niches and labyrinths had been his backyard.

His father had been in the merchant marines, but ran off before Cesare was a year old, leaving his mother to work in a trattoria and support him and his older sister Isabella. They'd lived in the apartment above it in a rougher neighborhood of Palermo. Cesare's world had been filled with lots of purse snatchers, few showers that usually didn't work, grueling heat. Everything had been run-down and chaotic.

Since he'd been too young to remember his father, he didn't miss him, only the idea of him. Cesare had envied his friends who had fathers and taught them things. Early in life he'd felt embarrassed at times that he was the only one who went to mass unaccompanied while the other boys walked in the church with their own fathers.

As he grew up, the embarrassment went away, but he lacked the confidence he saw in his friends whose sense of belonging seemed to give them an extra layer of it.

Cesare couldn't comprehend a man abandoning his wife and children, never caring about them again. Sometimes in his teens he'd dreamed about meeting his father, but those dreams were unsatisfactory because his father always turned away from him. The dreams eventually stopped, but not the feeling that there was something lacking in him.

At the age of thirty, Cesare was living a different life. Thanks to the college mentor who'd taught him and his partners how to invest, his worth now figured in the billions. But the past could never be forgotten and had formed him into the man he'd become.

Over time he'd seen enough to decide romantic love was transitory at most. Of course there were exceptions, like his partners' marriages. But at this stage in his life Cesare wasn't that confident that he was marriage material. He hadn't witnessed two parents loving each other. So far he felt he was better off alone like his mother. With a sister and brother-in-law and their daughter Elana, Cesare was happy enough with the family he loved.

In fact he had all he needed, including the occasional relationship with a woman. There was no guarantee that one would stay with him if he did get married, or that it would last.

*Or that he might not be more like his father than he thought...*

From time to time that thought haunted him because he hadn't met a woman who meant everything

to him. Maybe he'd subconsciously pushed them away
so he didn't have to deal with commitment. Though
he didn't want to bring up past pain to his mother,
one of these days he would have a talk with her about
the man who'd disappeared on their family, on *him*.

When the limo finally reached the villa, Cesare
put his darker thoughts away and paid the driver before getting out. His mother was expecting him, and
knew he'd be flying Ciro Fragala back to Milan with
him the next day. But it was close to one o'clock. She
always went to bed early.

He'd told her not to wait up and they'd talk in the
morning before Ciro arrived at the villa in a limo Cesare had arranged for ahead of time. The man would
be shipping his belongings to Milan and he'd stay
in a room at the *castello* until he decided where he
wanted to live.

Every time Cesare came to Palermo, he was
charmed by the large ochre-colored villa spread over
two floors with three beautiful terraces and a Mediter-
ranean garden. The small pool was lined with glazed
tiles of North African origin.

From the terrace off the dining room he was met
with a glorious view of the Gulf front. It was a sight
he'd always loved after climbing the bluff called
Mount Pellegrino many times in his youth. From
there he could imagine himself escaping the suffocating heat and madness of the city and sailing away
to America. Incredibly that dream had come true.

Once he'd entered the foyer, he turned off the outside light and moved across the stone tiles of the villa
in the dark to the kitchen with his suitcase. After setting it down, his first instinct was to grab himself a

small bottle of his favorite *grappa digestivo* from the cabinet where he knew it was kept, then head upstairs to his suite with it. Before sleep, all he wanted was to take a few sips to remind him he was back in the land of his roots.

But as he turned to pick up his suitcase, he bumped into another body and heard a cry.

"Mamma?" He automatically hugged her to him. "*Mi dispiace tanto.* I didn't think you'd be up this late. Did I hurt you?"

That's when the bottle slipped from his hand and cracked on the floor. But the strong scent of the 60 proof alcohol wasn't nearly as shocking as the feel of the woman in his arms.

She wasn't built anything like his wiry brunette mother or her housekeeper who came in several times a week. In fact she was taller than both of them. To add to his surprise, the flowery scent from her hair and skin intoxicated him. It took him a second to gather his wits.

"Don't move. There's broken glass. I'll turn on the light." He let her go and walked to the doorway to flip the switch. Cesare was shocked yet again.

If he didn't know better, he would think he'd released a gorgeous enchanted princess from her bottle. Her stunning figure was swathed in a lemon silk robe. Thank heaven she was wearing sandals. Between her medium-length black curls and eyes gray as the morning mist off the ocean, his gaze managed to swallow her whole before he realized she looked familiar to him. He knew he'd seen her before but couldn't place her.

She stared back as if disbelieving before taking a few steps away from the wet mess on the stone flooring. A hand went to her throat. "You're Cesare," she murmured, sounding astonished.

"I'm afraid you've got me at a disadvantage, *signorina*." Maybe he was in the middle of a fantastic dream, but so far he hadn't awakened. Quickly he walked over to the utility closet for a cloth and brush to pick up the glass and clean the floor.

"My name is Tuccia. I'm so sorry to have startled you."

Tuccia. An unusual name.

*Tuccia.* Short for... Princess Tuccianna of Sicilian nobililty?

Over the years there'd been photos of her in the newspapers from time to time, mostly stories about her escapades away from the royal *palazzo* where she got into trouble with friends and was seen partying in local clubs to the embarrassment of the royal household. But Cesare had never seen her up close.

The latest news in the Palermo press reported she was engaged to be married to some French *comte* who lived in Paris and was one of the wealthiest men in France.

No. It couldn't be, yet he realized it *was* she.

"I'm afraid I don't recognize it," he dissembled until he could work out why the daughter of the Marchese and Marchesa of the ancient Sicilian House of Trabia, was in his mother's villa.

"You probably wouldn't. It's not common."

She was trying to put Cesare off, but he intended to get to the bottom of this mystery. "Did Mamma hire you to be a new maid?"

She averted her eyes. "No. Signora Donati allowed me to stay with her for tonight." He frowned, not having known anything about this. Why hadn't his beloved mother told him what to expect when he arrived? "I—I thought I heard a noise, *signor*," she stammered, "but I didn't have time to turn on the light."

"No. We were both taken by surprise," he murmured, still reeling from the sensation of her incredible body clutched to his so she wouldn't fall.

Cesare had enjoyed various relationships with attractive women over the years, but he'd never gotten into anything serious. Yet the feel and sight of the beautiful young princess, whose face was like something out of Botticelli, had shaken him.

"I guess you know you have the most wonderful mother in the world," she gushed all of a sudden, breaking in on his private thoughts. He was amazed by her comment. It had sounded completely sincere.

He closed the utility door and turned to her, growing more curious by the second. "I do. How did you two meet?"

His question caused her to hesitate. "I think it would be better if you ask her. I'm truly sorry to have disturbed you and will say goodnight." She darted away, leaving him full of questions and standing there wide awake in the trail of her fragrance.

The princess, reputed to be a spoiled, headstrong handful, had elegance and manners. *Damn* if she didn't also have an unaffected charm that had worked its way beneath his skin.

He took a deep breath. Though Cesare didn't like waking his mother, he knew there'd be no sleep until he had answers. Before heading upstairs to her bed-room, he opened the cabinet for another bottle of *grappa*. All he found was a half-opened bottle of cooking sherry.

That's what he got for not turning on the light ear-lier. That and the memory of a moment in time he feared wasn't about to let him go.

With a pounding out-of-control heart, twenty-five-year-old Principessa Tuccianna Falcone Leonardi rushed to the guest room down the hall at the rear of the villa. She should never have made a trip to the kitchen, but needed something to drink. Lina had told her to help herself to anything, including the soda she kept on hand in the fridge.

Being crushed unexpectedly against a hard male body in the dark had come as such a huge surprise that her mind and body were still reeling. She could still feel the male power of him and smell the faint scent of the soap he'd used in the shower. The combination had completely disarmed her.

After he'd turned on the kitchen light, she'd had her first look at Lina's tall, incredibly attractive brown-haired son. Tuccia knew of him, but had no idea that Lina had given birth to the most striking man she'd ever seen in her life. Those deep blue eyes and his masculine potency had managed to make such an in-delible impression her heart still kept turning over on itself.

"I didn't know there was a man in Palermo who looked like that," she whispered to herself. Tuccia was positive there wasn't another one in all Europe who could match him.

More than ever she was revolted at the thought of marrying her forty-year-old French fiancé who had only stared at her with lust. The fabulously wealthy Comte Jean-Michel Ardois, who would soon inherit the title after his ailing father passed away, was always trying to touch her, and lately more and more inappropriately.

On occasion she'd seen him be quite ruthless with the people who worked for the Ardois family. He was a cold, calculating man whom she could never love or bring herself to marry.

Her betrothal at the age of sixteen had been a political necessity arranged by her parents, the Marchese and Marchesa di Trabia, whose funds needed constant bolstering. Since that time she'd felt doomed to an existence she'd dreaded with every fiber of her being.

After careful planning, she'd seized the moment to run away twenty-four hours before the ceremony was to take place. Taking flight from the boutique, she'd flown back to her home in Sicily. Thanks to her Zia Bertina, her mother's widowed elder sister, she'd been given the help she needed to escape on that jet.

Bertina lived in her own palazzo in Palermo where she entertained close friends and loved Tuccia like the child she'd never been able to have. Tuccia's *zia* was a romantic who'd always been in sympathy with her niece's tragic situation, and had prevailed on her cook, Lina Donati, to let her hide at her villa overnight. In the meantime she was still trying to arrange transport for Tuccia to stay with a distant cousin living in Podgorica in Montenegro until the worst of the scandal had passed.

But Tuccia had placed her in a terrible position.

Bertina had continued living in the palazzo after her husband died, but she needed monetary help on occasion. Tuccia's *zio*, Pietro Spadaro, hadn't been a wealthy man. If Tuccia's parents got angry enough at Bertina, they could stop giving her extra money. They might throw her out of the only home she'd known since her marriage.

Worse, if they knew Bertina had involved a cousin in another country, let alone asked such a desperate favor of her adored cook to help solve Tuccia's problems, who knew how ugly the situation could get. If Bertina were forced to lose the palazzo and any extra money, she wouldn't be able to pay Lina for being her cook. Lina could be out of a job for harboring her. All of it would be her fault.

She couldn't believe her bad luck in running into Lina's son. Naturally he was going to wonder why she was here and question his mother. What she needed to do was get dressed and pack her bag so she'd be ready to steal from the villa at dawn before anyone was up.

Tuccia knew a full-scale search by Jean-Michel and her parents had been underway for her since she had disappeared from the salon. At least with her gone from Lina's villa, Bertina wouldn't be implicated.

She had saved enough money to take a bus and travel to Catania where she could get a job through a friend who would help her. If she were careful, she could subsist for a while. She didn't dare access her bank account even though its pitiful balance had never been big enough to pay for as much as an airline ticket.

Tuccia had no idea how long she would have to remain hidden. But even if it meant being disowned and disinherited, it didn't matter because she'd rather be dead than have to marry Jean-Michel. She was sickened at the thought of him taking her to bed, let alone living with him for a lifetime.

# CHAPTER TWO

CESARE SAT AT the side of his mother's bed, still trying to comprehend what she'd just told him. "Apparently you and Princess Tuccianna have enjoyed a relationship you never told me about."

"Only since I started cooking for Bertina two years ago. Until tonight I'd been sworn to secrecy. She needs help desperately, Cesare."

He reached for her hand. "Don't you know what a terrible position this has put you in, Mamma? The authorities from two governments are looking everywhere for her. Her jilted fiancé could be dangerous. He has the kind of money and power that could crush you. If her parents found out you gave her shelter, your name could be ruined. You could lose your job with Bertina. They could make life miserable for you."

"It's Tuccia's life I'm worried about, not mine. You know how I feel about titles. It's a feudal system. No young woman should have to marry a man almost twice her age because of money and power. You can't imagine how frightened Bertina is for her niece. The *comte* will impose his will on her. She's very beautiful. And you know exactly what I'm talking about."

Cesare was afraid he did. He'd seen first-hand the

trouble that kind of will had created for Vincenzo and Vincenzo's cousin Dimi. The two had grown up together at the *castello* and had suffered through tragedy together because of overpowering parental dominance over both of them.

After Cesare had become close friends with the two royals he had learned their story, so he understood why the princess refused to be tied legally to a man who could do what he wanted to his young, helpless wife. Cesare was sickened by it himself, but his protective instincts had kicked in for his mother. He didn't want her to be a part of this and he got up from the bed.

"How long have you agreed to let her stay with you?"

"Until Bertina has worked out an escape plan to get her to a distant relative in Montenegro no one will trace."

He shook his head. "Of course they will! That's no plan," he bit out.

"I agree with you and I don't like any of it, either. But the princess is desperate. Bertina has told me that the father, Comte Ardois, was promiscuous and notoriously unfaithful over the years. She has it on good authority that his son Comte Jean-Michel is exactly the same way.

"He's had a mistress on the side for a long time. I can't bear that kind of life for her. Neither can she! Tuccia is like a lamb going to the slaughter. To me it's criminal!"

"What you're telling me sounds like a repeat of the stories Vincenzo told me about life at the *castello* growing up."

"So you do understand that Tuccia is a young sweet girl and needs to get far away from him while she still can."

"Yes, but not at your expense."

"Someone has to step up. If I lose my job because of this, I'll find another one. If that isn't possible, then I *will* let you take care of me. The point is, the *marchesa* and her husband have never been concerned about their daughter's feelings. They've spent their whole lives doing their royal duty and expect the same from Tuccia. The princess is alone in this. If Bertina hadn't chartered that jet for her so she could leave Paris, Tuccia would have been forced to walk down the aisle today and be married to a monster."

His hands went to his hips. "But now she has *you* involved."

"Because I want to be. I like Tuccia very much. If she were my daughter, I'd do whatever I could to save her from such a wretched life. You're the most brilliant, clever man I've ever known, *figlio mio*. If I asked for your help this one time, would you do it for your mamma?"

Her blue eyes beseeched him. She was serious! He could see it and feel it.

"What do you think I could do?"

"Fly her to Milan tomorrow on the Gagliardi ducal jet with Ciro. Help her find a place to stay in the city where no one will think to look for her. She won't be traced."

His eyes narrowed. "Is this the reason you let her stay here tonight? Because you knew I was flying in and planned to use me?"

"Yes," she answered with her usual refreshing honesty. "Have I ever asked you for a favor like this before? Time is of the essence."

"Mamma—" His head reared in exasperation.

She sat up straighter in the bed. "I don't see a problem. Tuccia's crisis takes priority. That girl needs to be far away from here by tomorrow. It won't hurt you to take her with you. Be sure she's wearing a disguise. Signor Fragala won't suspect who she is."

He stopped pacing. "He'll recognize her once we're on board."

"So you'll swear him to secrecy. If he can't be trusted, tell him you've changed your mind and won't let him have the coveted chef position after all. It's in *your* hands. Once you've settled her, you can take Ciro to the *castello* and get on with your business. Is that such a terrible thing to ask this one time?"

Cesare couldn't fathom that they were having this conversation at three in the morning. "There's no place she won't be recognized."

"Then take her to the *castello* with you. Smuggle her in a back entrance and hide her in one of the turret rooms for a few days. That will give her enough time to figure out a solid plan on her own. Besides being well-educated and well-traveled, she's a very intelligent girl and resourceful."

"And according to the papers, impossible," he added.

"If you knew the truth, you wouldn't judge her. Every time her name gets in the news, it's because she has tried to run away from her family. But she always gets caught and is brought back. Her parents cover it up by saying that she's an indulged, immature troublemaker. She's the loveliest girl I've ever known, and it's a tragedy how her life has been."

Such accolades for the princess shocked him. His mother wasn't about to relent on this. She was a fighter who had a heart of gold. That was how she'd made it through life.

"You'll help me to help her, won't you?"

Cesare loved and admired his mother more than any woman he'd ever known. After the hundreds of sacrifices she'd made for him and his sister growing up, how could he possibly turn her down?

Letting out a sigh he said, "Stop worrying. After Ciro arrives in the morning, I'll take her to Milan tomorrow with us." But not to the *castello*. He didn't want the guys to know what was going on.

"If you'll do that for me, I'll love you forever."

"I thought you already did," he teased.

Her eyes had filled with tears. "Oh, Cesare. My dear son. *Ti amo*." She started to get out of bed, but her phone rang. Her eyes darted to his in alarm. "Maybe something's wrong with your sister or my little grand-daughter—"

Cesare's body stiffened. A phone call in the middle of the night could mean anything. Probably it was Bertina calling his mother to tell her the police were on their way over to the villa looking for the princess.

She reached for the cell phone on her bedside table and checked the caller ID. "It says San Giovanni Hospital."

He stood stock-still while he waited to find out what was going on, but his mother did little talking. Once she hung up, she looked at him with haunted eyes.

"I'm afraid I have very bad news for you, Cesare."

"What do you mean?"

"Ciro was rushed to the hospital a few hours ago

with an infected lung and kidney. I thought he didn't seem well when I visited the restaurant a few days ago and assumed he had a cold.

"He must undergo an operation to drain off the fluid. The nurse said he had the presence of mind to ask the hospital to contact me before he lost consciousness."

*"Santo Cielo,"* Cesare murmured in disbelief. This whole night had turned into a bad dream. "The poor devil."

"It's terrible."

"Get dressed and we'll drive to the hospital in your car. Since he's my responsibility, I'll tell the hospital and take care of his medical bills."

"Bless you. I'm getting ready now, but I'll visit him alone and be your go-between until he has recovered. Right now you've got to take care of the princess. The sooner, the better. That phone call could have been Bertina alerting me that the police were on Tuccia's trail. There's no time to lose."

There was no time for sleep, either, not while this situation continued. He walked to his suite to shower and change clothes for the flight back to Milan. Afterward he went downstairs to the kitchen to fix himself coffee. He found the delicious sweet rolls filled with ricotta and chocolate his mother always made for him when he came and ate several.

During his early morning feast, his mother joined him before leaving for the hospital. After she went out to her car, he contacted the pilot to let him know they'd be returning to Milan shortly, then he arranged for a limo to come to the villa. Now all he needed was for the princess to make an appearance.

\* \* \*

It was six-thirty in the morning when Tuccia finished writing three letters at the desk in the guest bedroom. The first was her deepest apology to Jean-Michel, explaining why she couldn't marry him and had run away. They weren't in love with each other, and that was the only reason for two people to marry.

She put it in an envelope with his name and address on the front. When and where to mail it was the scary part and had to be considered carefully because her life depended on it.

Tuccia put the letter in her purse, then wrote two long thank-you letters to her *zia* and Lina. She signed them with love before leaving them on top of the dresser so Lina would be certain to see them. One of these days she would write to her parents, but that could wait.

After making the bed, she grabbed the small suitcase Bertina had loaned her and hurried through the villa to the kitchen for a piece of fruit. A ten-minute walk would take her to the shops where she could eat something more substantial and catch a bus.

"Where do you think you're going in that disguise?" a deep familiar male voice asked as she reached the foyer.

Her camouflage consisted of a scarf she'd tied around her head like a lot of local women did to cover their hair. She turned around to see the man she hadn't been able to erase from her thoughts, standing there in jeans and a jacket. He looked too marvelous to her this early in the morning.

"I wanted to slip out before your mother awakened

so I wouldn't disturb her. I left messages to thank her and my aunt."

"I'm sure she'll appreciate that, Principessa."

Of course he'd recognized her and had talked with Lina. Now he knew everything about her situation. She was so sorry he'd been dragged into her problem. "Your mother has been exceptionally kind to me. I'm embarrassed my *zia* asked for her assistance, and I'm ashamed I accepted it because it has placed her in danger."

"Mamma has a big heart. It sounds like Signora Spadaro does, too."

Tears glazed her eyes. "They're both strong, remarkable women, but they've done more than enough to help me. It's time I dealt with the mess I've created for myself."

She tried to open the door, but it wouldn't give. Tuccia looked over her shoulder. "Is there a trick to unlocking it?"

With a half smile that gave her heart a jolt, he activated the remote in his hand and the door swung open.

"Thank you." After a slight hesitation, she said, "It was a privilege to meet the famous son of Lina Donati. In case you didn't know it, she thinks the sun rises and sets with you."

Tuccia felt him follow her out the door into the balmy seventy-seven-degree air where a limousine had pulled in the drive. She put on her sunglasses. Apparently he was going somewhere. When she would have walked past it, he called to her.

"Mamma says you need to get out of Palermo immediately. If you'll climb in the limo, I have the means to make that happen."

His comment stopped her in her tracks. "You mustn't get involved in my problem. I'm already weighed down with guilt and couldn't handle any more."

He opened the rear door. "But I *am* involved. I don't believe I've ever helped a genuine princess in distress before and rather like the idea. Come on. You've been living dangerously since leaving Paris. Why stop now?"

His sense of humor caught her off guard and she chuckled in spite of the fear gripping her that this freedom couldn't last. Not wanting to hold things up, she climbed in. He set her suitcase on the bank of seats in front of them and sat next to her, pulling the door shut. His rock-hard limbs brushed against her jeans-clad legs. The contact sent a dart of awareness through her body.

She heard him tell the chauffeur to drive them to the airport. They drove through a breathtaking portion of Mondello to the main route leading out of the city. Tuccia had the sensation of being spirited away where nothing could hurt her.

It was a heavenly feeling she'd never experienced before. She'd sell her soul for it to last, but she knew this wonderful moment could only be enjoyed until they reached the airport.

"Where are we going?" she asked at last, alive to everything about this extraordinary man.

"To Milan."

"Where you work when you're not in New York."

"More importantly, it's where you'll be safe. I fear my mother has done far too much talking about me."

"That's because she loves you." Tuccia had heard about the spectacular *castello* restaurant he owned and ran with his business partners. His other business interests in New York City were legendary. "I can't imagine what it would be like to know that kind of love from my own parents."

"That's a lonely statement."

"Now *I'm* doing too much talking and sound so sorry for myself, I'm ashamed. But you have no idea what I'd give to erase the image the country has of me. I'm *not* the tempestuous, volatile woman everyone believes me to be. I just want to be free like other women to make the kind of life I want for myself."

"According to my mother, you've run away from a fate worse than death."

"Put that way it sounds ridiculous, doesn't it? Unfortunately it's true for me and I've dragged three innocent people into my personal disaster. I pray there won't be any repercussions for you," she half sobbed the words.

His hand grasped hers, sending a wave of warmth through her. "No one brought my mother and me kicking and screaming," he teased gently. "If I were in your shoes and betrothed to some odious *marchesa* twice my age, I can promise you I would flee to the other side of the universe where no one would ever find me."

Odious was the exact word to describe Jean-Michel.

The analogy was so ludicrous she found herself laughing. But it underlined the fact that Cesare Donati wasn't married. Tuccia couldn't help but wonder how many women must have flung themselves at him.

"That's better," he said before releasing her hand. Soon they arrived at the airport and were driven to the area where the private jets sat on the tarmac. The limo wound around and stopped next to one in silver and blue that stood out with a coat of arms depicting the Duc di Lombardi. A thrill of excitement passed through her to know she'd be flying to northern Italy with him. Just the two of them.

Once Cesare helped her out of the limo with her suitcase, the steward welcomed them aboard. He showed her to the elegant club compartment where she sat across from her protector as she thought of him. Pretty soon the Fasten Seat Belt light went on and she heard the scream of the engines as they taxied out to the runway.

After they'd taken off and achieved cruising speed, the light went off and the steward brought them breakfast trays. She found she was starving and ate everything, including a second cup of coffee to drink.

Cesare flashed her a searching glance. "How long has it been since you had a substantial meal?"

"My aunt kept trying to feed me after I arrived in Palermo, but I was so nervous I couldn't eat very much. Now I'm hungry."

"How did you manage your escape so perfectly when all of your other attempts have failed?"

"I can see my aunt has told your mother everything about my past." Tuccia heaved a sigh. "I've been planning this latest scheme since my first dress fitting two months ago. Yesterday morning I went to the dressmaker with my mother for the final wedding dress fitting.

"When Madame Dufy went to find the dressmaker and bring out my gown, I told my mother I needed to use the ladies' room and hurried down the hallway. As soon as no one was in sight, I shot out the back door of the salon. I knew there was a nearby *tête de taxi*. From there I was driven to the airport where Bertina had chartered a private jet for me ahead of time under a fake name. And here I am."

His gaze held hers. "That was a daring plan."

"I'm sure you think me selfish and cruel, but it was the only way to end the nightmare of my life. I've written a letter to Jean-Michel to apologize. It's all ready to be mailed except for a stamp."

"Where is it?"

"In my purse."

"May I see it?"

When she pulled it out, he walked over and took it from her. After examining the address, he put it in his pocket. "I'll make sure he gets it without the police being able to trace it."

"You must think me heartless and that I'm living up to all the falsehoods spread about me. Actually they're not all false. I do have a bad temper that erupts at times and I've gotten a lot of staff into trouble who were supposed to keep a close watch on me."

After a silence he said, "What I think doesn't matter." The Fasten Seat Belt light went on again. He strapped himself in. "We're descending to Milan. Very soon I'll take you to a place where you'll be hidden from the world and hopefully safe for another twenty-four hours. While you're figuring out what it is you would like to do with the rest of your life, I'll have to leave you, but I'll be back in a couple of days."

Her spirits plunged at that revelation. "Where are you going?"

"To Palermo."

"Again? I don't understand."

"I'm going to see the man I'd hired to be the *castello*'s new executive pastry chef."

Her brows met in a delicate frown. "Why didn't you visit with him before you brought me all this way first?"

The pilot set the jet down and it taxied to a stop. "Because he was rushed to the hospital during the night and couldn't come with me to start his new position. He was supposed to meet my partners today and get settled in."

"Oh, how terrible for him *and* you!"

"Since you needed to leave Palermo before the authorities caught up to you, I brought you instead."

The man continued to astound her. She shook her head. "I can't believe you would do that for me." Tuccia loved him already for his sacrifice.

His blue eyes darkened with an emotion she couldn't put her finger on. "Mamma said it was a matter of life and death. After learning how desperate you are to escape the life your parents and fiancé have orchestrated for you, I'm inclined to believe she was telling the truth."

His compassion filled her with feelings that threatened to overwhelm her. "Please—you don't have to send my letter to the *comte*. It's too much. I'll find a way to do it," she said in a throbbing voice he could probably feel.

"It's a simple thing that needs to be done so he'll call off his army. There's no one like you, and no question he wants you back. Needless to say, you're a royal prize he won't tolerate getting away from him."

Tuccia shivered because she felt he truly did understand the gravity of her desperate situation where Jean-Michel was involved.

A few minutes later another limousine drove them out of the city. They swept past farms and villas until they reached a small village at the base of a prominent hill. On the top she caught sight of a massive fortress. The ochre-toned structure with its towers and crenellated walls sprawled across the summit.

"That's the ancient Castello Di Lombardi," Cesare explained, "now a hotel *ristorante*."

The one he'd helped to make famous. Tuccia was eager to see it up close and thought they would drive up there. Instead he asked the driver to take them to a *pensione* in the village. Evidently he'd made arrangements for her ahead of time.

Just as he helped her out of the limo and told the driver to wait, the *padrona di casa* came out of another door. She greeted them and showed them inside the attractive apartment. After a few explanations she left. Cesare lowered Tuccia's suitcase to the floor and turned to her.

"You should be very comfortable here while I'm gone. I asked her to fill the cupboards and fridge with groceries to last several days. As you heard her say, if you need anything, just pick up the phone in the kitchen and she'll answer."

The last thing Tuccia wanted was for him to go, but she realized he was anxious to get back to Palermo and didn't dare keep him. What a terrible position he was in!

"I don't know how to thank you for all you've done for me. How can I make this up to you?"

He studied her features for a minute. "I've had two friends who helped me when I thought all was lost. It's nice to be on the giving end for a change."

She could feel her eyes smarting. "I don't deserve this."

"I remember telling them the same thing. A word of warning. Do you have a cell phone on you?"

"Yes."

"Don't use it for any reason and don't go walking in the village. The only person who knows you are here is the woman who let you in. She's a friend and will keep silent. When I return, we'll talk. Until then, try to relax, watch TV. *A presto*, Principessa."

"*Alla prossima*, Cesare." She followed him to the door and watched him drive away, causing her heart to act up until it actually hurt.

Once he was gone, Tuccia went back in the living room for her suitcase. Then she walked to the bedroom so full of emotions, she didn't know where to go with them. She didn't know another person in the world except her aunt who would make a sacrifice like this for her. Cesare Donati was the most incredible man she'd ever known.

While she was in the shower, her mind focused on the chef he'd hired for his fabulous *castello* restaurant. He had to be a spectacular cook. How sad he'd fallen ill at the very moment he was supposed to go to Milan with Cesare.

She wished she could help him in some way during the short interim while the chef was recovering. Cesare had been so good to her and she wanted to find a way to repay him. She'd much rather stay right here.

But of course the whole plan was to get her away from Jean-Michel and her parents.

*You're losing your mind, Tuccia.*

On his way back to the airport Cesare phoned his mother, wondering what kind of a mess she could be in if the police had already found out she'd been harboring Tuccia at the villa.

She picked up on the fourth ring. "Cesare—where are you?" she blurted before he could say anything.

"You'll be happy to know my mission has been accomplished. Are you alone?"

*"Si."*

"Good. Now I can tell you the princess has been installed in a safe place."

*"Grazie a Dio.* I can always count on you."

She didn't sound worried about the police yet. "I'm flying back to Palermo to be with you. If there are no complications, I should be there in about two hours. I'll come straight to the hospital. After we've talked to the doctor and done all we can do there, I'll take you out to eat and we'll have a long talk. How does that sound?"

"Wonderful, except that there's no point in your coming back unless you want me to help you find another pastry chef beyond Palermo. That could take months."

"What do you mean another chef? I don't understand. Ciro will get better with a treatment of antibiotics."

"I thought so, too, but *you're* not going to be happy when I tell you what I've just found out from the doctor. Ciro came close to dying during the night because he has developed a heart condition. The prognosis for a full recovery could be six months away."

*"Incredibile!"*

"I know how upset you must be to hear that news, Cesare. I'm so sorry. He's in the ICU and won't be able to talk to anyone for a few days. There'd be no point in your coming right now. You might as well turn around and stay at the *castello* until he's been given a private room and can have visitors. Then you can fly down and have a serious talk with him."

The situation had gone from bad to worse. "Thank you for watching over him. I'm indebted to you."

"Bless you for saving Tuccia's life. What will you do about the chef position now?"

Right now Cesare's concern over the princess had created the most stress for him. "That's not your problem. I'll just have to be the pastry chef myself and interview more applicants for the position. But let's agree that finding someone who knows how to make Sicilian desserts with an expertise close to his or yours will be an endeavor in futility."

"You make the best *cassatine* with almond paste in existence."

"I learned from you, but that was years ago."

"You never forget, but I'm desolate for you this has happened. What will Tuccia do? Did she talk to you about it during the flight?"

"Yes. She has a plan that might work." For a day maybe. "I'll think of something. Don't you worry about it. Have you told Bertina her niece is safe?"

"I drove to the palazzo to tell her in person and

give her Tuccia's letter before returning to the hospital. She was so relieved she broke down sobbing before burning it."

Good thinking on Bertina's part. "Have the police questioned her yet?"

"Yes. She told them she knew nothing."

"They'll be contacting anyone who is friends with her, especially her cook. You'll be receiving a visit soon. Don't talk to her on the phone."

"No worry. I'm at the hospital now and just finished reading Tuccia's sweet letter to me before burning it." He had a brilliant mother. "Thanks to your willingness to help the princess escape so fast, there's no evidence she was ever at the villa, and of course I know nothing." He chuckled in spite of his concern for her. "Stay in close touch with me."

"Haven't I always? Take care of yourself, Mamma."

"You, too. I'll talk to you later. *Dio di benedica*, Cesare."

After they hung up, he told the limo driver to take him to the main express mail outlet in Milan. Asking him to wait, he went in to have Tuccia's letter to the *comte* couriered overnight to Cesare's attorney. Rudy Goldman always spent this time of year at his retreat in Barbados. Inside the mailing envelope he put the following instructions.

*Rudy.*
*Put a stamp on this and send it airmail immediately.*
*Many thanks,*
*Cesare.*

His attorney was the soul of discretion and always did what he was told without question. When Cesare had addressed the mailing envelope, he paid the clerk who put it in the slot. Before long it would be on its way to Bridgetown. The *comte* needed to receive it ASAP. Cesare knew in his gut the other man would start a search for his fiancée.

She *was* a prize. No one knew that better than Cesare. His thoughts wandered. Not every man would be worthy of her love when she had an ancestry that had made her unique in the world. Certainly not Cesare, whose family tree might as well have half a trunk missing. What could a fatherless man bring to a marriage with a princess?

Depressed by his thoughts, he returned to the limo and told the driver to take him back to the *pensione*. It was the same apartment where Vincenzo's wife Gemma had once stayed when she'd come from Florence to the *castello* for an interview. The *padrona* could be trusted.

By the time the limo pulled up in front, Cesare had made up his mind to send Tuccia to the States in the morning. The police wouldn't find her there and he could put her out of his mind. She was on it too much already.

He got out to the pay the driver, then walked to the front door of her apartment and knocked loud enough for her to hear. "Tuccia? It's Cesare. May I come in?"

"You haven't left for Palermo yet?" she called out in surprise. "I'll be right there."

In less than a minute she opened the door in bare feet, dressed in the yellow silk robe she'd worn in the middle of the night. He could smell the peach shampoo she'd used to wash her hair. She had a brush in one hand and had been styling her naturally curly black hair.

The sight of such natural beauty would make any man go weak in the knees. Cesare was no exception. "I had a call from my mother and have been forced to change my plans."

"Uh-oh." Anxiety marred her features. He knew what she was thinking.

"Forgive me for making you stand there. Please come in."

Her faultless manners impressed him. "Thank you." He walked in the little living room off the kitchen.

She eyed him nervously. "Did the police interrogate her already? Is she in terrible trouble?" Tuccia put the hand not holding the brush to her heart. "Bertina should never have involved your mother and I shouldn't have listened to her."

"So far everything is all right. The police talked to your aunt who told them she knew nothing. I'm sure my mother will be next, but she'll have no information, either. They both received your letters."

"I'm so glad. Then why have you changed your plans? I don't understand. But before you tell me, let me get dressed. Please sit down. I'll only be a minute."

He chose the chair by the coffee table while she rushed to her bedroom. Cesare caught a fleeting glimpse of her long shapely legs beneath the flap of her robe before she disappeared. He was growing more enamored of her by the second.

How could it be that after all the years of working with attractive businesswomen, he found himself in trouble just being in her presence for a few hours total. Along with her attributes, her utter femininity blew him away. It was a good thing she'd be gone tomorrow so there'd be no temptation to spend any extra time with her.

# CHAPTER THREE

IN NO TIME Tuccia reappeared wearing a pair of white slacks and sandals toned with a café-au-lait-and-white print short-sleeved top. She sat on the end of the couch with one leg tucked under her. "Tell me what's wrong."

"As you know, the Sicilian pastry chef I'd planned to hire is in the hospital. But there's no telling when he'll be well enough to work again. Mamma found out he has developed an unexpected heart condition. I had high hopes for him. With his exciting creations, he would have brought a new clientele to our *ristorante*. Except for my mother's cooking, there's no one to equal him."

Tuccia sat forward with a troubled look on her lovely face. "My *zia* says she's the most superb cook in all Sicily. That means she has to know what she is talking about. What will you do?"

"Since I'm in charge of the *ristorante* at the *castello*, I'm the only one who has the authority to fix the problem. In an emergency, there are times when you have to do it yourself."

Her eyes widened. "You mean *you're* going to be the pastry chef?"

"It'll be nothing new to me while I find someone else. But right now I'm concerned about you. Have you decided what you want to do with your life?"

A slow smile broke out on her face. "That was a trick question, right?"

The woman was getting to him. "Not at all. Since you never intended to follow through on the betrothal, what had you imagined you would be doing when you finally made your escape?"

Her smile faded. She looked away. "To be honest I only thought about how to subsist until my parents stopped looking for me and go from there."

Cesare had assumed as much. "If I hadn't offered you safe passage on the jet this morning, what was your exact plan when you reached Catania?"

"I was going to find temporary work in a greenhouse through an old school friend until I'm forced to move on for fear of being spotted."

He hadn't expected to hear that. "Are you a gardener with a knowledge of horticulture that would make you an asset at the greenhouse?"

"Of course not."

"Yet you're willing to prevail on the friend you mentioned to get a job there?"

"Yes. She works at the university and could help me find a position for a while. But because you told me not to use my phone, I haven't talked to her yet and wouldn't be able to until I reached Catania."

"Do you have an affinity for flowers?"

Her head flew back. "Have you forgotten I'm a princess who has no knowledge of anything practical? But I'm strong and could cart plants around in a wheelbarrow if I have to."

"I wasn't trying to insult you."

"I know," she half moaned. "You're being so good to me. I'm sorry I snapped."

"I think you're handling your desperate situation with amazing grace."

She shook her head. "But it's one I created and I don't deserve your kindness."

"Why do you say that? Everyone deserves help from time to time."

He heard a deep sigh. "I guess because my parents rarely showed any kindness to me while I was growing up."

"Did they hurt you physically?"

"Oh, no. Nothing like that. But their stifling, rigid rules made my life unbearable."

"Nevertheless it doesn't mean you're not deserving of kindness," he reminded her. "Just so you know, your letter to Jean-Michel has been dealt with in a way that won't be traced to you. He should be getting it in a few days, so you can put that worry out of your mind."

Her eyes filled with tears. "You're a saint."

"Hardly." He leaned toward her with his hands on his thighs. "I've given your precarious position a lot of thought. Your idea to go to Catania would only be a stopgap for a few days. I still think it would be best if you leave Europe tomorrow. I'll arrange it."

She shook her head. "I couldn't let you do that. You've done more than enough for me and have your own problem to solve right here."

"First things first, Tuccia. You need to get far away. New York would be the perfect place to get lost. With my contacts, I could set you up in your own apartment and they would help you find a job that you would like to do. No one would suspect you're the princess who disappeared. You'd be safe. That is what you want, isn't it?"

"You know it is, but I've been thinking about the chef who's in the hospital and how desperate you must be feeling right now. You saved my life by bringing me to Milan. Instead of putting you in an impossible position, I'd like to do something of value for you in return," she said in an aching voice.

She had a way of running over every roadblock. He sat back and studied her for a moment, intrigued. "What do you mean?"

"Why not teach me to be a pastry chef so I can work at your *ristorante* until he's well and can fly here. I'd do anything to help you if I could."

It took all his self-control not to laugh. To his shock, he had the strongest suspicion she was being completely serious. "Are you saying you know how to cook?"

A small sound escaped her throat. "No. I'm embarrassed to tell you I've never cooked anything from start to finish in my life, although I spent a lot of time in the palazzo kitchen growing up. The cooks were kind to me and let me watch. I washed lettuce and sometimes they'd let me beat egg whites or stir the gravy. Once in a while they'd allow me to sift the flour into the cake bowl before it was baked."

"Does that mean you didn't learn to cook at boarding school?"

She laughed outright. "You have a strange idea of what goes on there."

"Actually I *do* know, and was only teasing." Despite the impossibility of what she'd said, the more they talked, the more he found himself enjoying her company. Too much in fact.

"I'm relieved to hear it, Cesare. To be honest, that boarding school in France happened so long ago I've forgotten. All I know is, I was waited on. When my parents enrolled me at the University of Paris, I had to live with them in an apartment in St. Germain des Pres. Would it reassure you to know that I told my maid I could make my own tea and instant coffee in the microwave?"

He laughed at her sense of humor and her sparse knowledge in the cooking department. A princess with a classic education from the finest schools and universities in Europe, but to make a pastry... "Tuccia—"

"Please hear me out, Cesare," she cut him off before he could say anything else. "According to your mother, you could head any Cordon Bleu cooking school in the world. You could teach me. It would be like getting a college education of a different kind."

His eyes searched hers. She wasn't kidding. Princess Tuccianna had been known for doing some daring, outlandish things, but this idea had shocked him to the core.

"As intelligent and resourceful as you are, you don't know what would be entailed."

She sat forward. "My parents' cooks didn't know how to cook in the beginning, did they? They had to learn from someone," she reasoned. "Why couldn't I do the same thing under your expert tutelage? I'd work fast and it would free you up to get on with running all your businesses. My anonymity would be assured hidden behind the *castello* walls. Within six months, the chef you hired would be back."

Cesare no longer felt like laughing. This beautiful young woman was bargaining for her life. He had to give her credit for possessing the kind of guts he hadn't seen in most people.

When he didn't say anything, she blurted, "I've been thinking about what you asked me."

"What was that?"

"About what I wanted to do with my life. If you were to teach me how to make pastry, I would have learned a marketable skill. When Signor Fragala returns, I'd be able to use all that knowledge I'd learned from you. With a reference from you—provided you gave me a good one if I deserved it—I could find a position in any country."

He could hear her mind working. It was going like a house on fire. To his astonishment he was listening to her because she was making a strange kind of sense.

"After a half year in hiding, I'm positive my family will have disowned me so it wouldn't matter where I chose to live and work. I'd be a normal woman with a good job."

"You'll never be a normal woman, Principessa." his voice grated. Nor would he want her to be. He liked her exactly the way she was. "Can you honestly sit there and tell me the thought of being disowned doesn't pain you?"

She lowered her head. "I guess I don't know how I'd feel about it until it happened. But what I *do* know is that I'm *never* going to bow to my parents' wishes again. Hopefully before long Jean-Michel will have comforted himself with another mistress while he hunts for a new titled princess to marry."

Cesare rubbed the back of his neck, unable to believe he was actually toying with the idea of teaching her the rudiments. In a perfect world, if she did follow through and did learn how to cook, it would give her the independence she'd never known. It would allow her to earn money and she'd be free to make her own choices, something that had been denied her from birth.

At some point in time she'd decide to get in touch with her parents, or not. He couldn't believe he was allowing his thoughts to go this far.

Quiet reigned before she said, "I know what you're thinking. I don't have any money right now to pay you to teach me. But if I were a good student and could work at the *castello*, you wouldn't have to pay me any money. Not ever! I'm already indebted to you for your sacrifice. It would be my gift to you for saving my life."

The last was said in a trembling voice. It was the wobble that did it to him.

"Are you a fast learner?" Cesare knew she was grateful. He didn't want her to go on begging for the chance to repay him. Her willingness to take a risk of these proportions made her a breed apart from anyone he'd ever known.

She stared at him with those heavenly gray eyes. "I guess that depends on the subject matter, but I graduated with honors in European history."

"Congratulations, Tuccia. That's no small feat. But to make a pastry chef out of you... I don't know."

"You're right. It's too much to ask and I'd probably be a disaster."

He didn't like the discouraged tone of her voice and it made up his mind for him. "Maybe not."

A gasp escaped her lips. "You mean you're willing to entertain the idea?"

Her excitement put a stranglehold on him. "Let's just say I'll put you on probation for a few days and see how it goes."

"You're not teasing me?" she cried.

"No. I wouldn't do that. Not about this."

He could tell she was fighting tears. "When would I start?"

"As soon as we've eaten dinner."

"So soon? Aren't you exhausted after everything you've been through in the last twenty-four hours?"

Her question stunned him because her first thought had been for him. He could have asked the same of her after being on the run.

"Not at all." In fact he'd never been so wired in his life.

"Does that mean we're going up to the *castello* right now?"

He stood up. "No. This *pensione* is going to be your home, your school room and your lab. You'll do everything hands-on right here. After a few days I'll decide if I can turn you into the next executive pastry chef at the Castello Supremo Hotel and Ristorante di Lombardi. Otherwise I'll put you on the plane for New York."

Tuccia let out an incredulous cry of joy and she jumped to her feet. She rushed over to him and put a hand on his arm. The contact sent a shock through him. His awareness of her made it hard to breathe.

"You mean it? You're not joking? But you just said you weren't joking. I'm sorry, but I just can't believe you're willing to give me a chance."

"Everyone deserves a chance." He looked her in the eye, trying to get a grip on his emotions. "What fake name were you going to use when you applied for the greenhouse job in Catania?"

His question made her blink, and she let go of him. "Come on," he prodded her. "You've obviously had one in mind for a long time."

"Not the same one my *zia* used to charter that plane for me. I guess… Nedda Bottaro."

"Nedda? The heroine in the opera *Pagliacci*?"

"Yes. I love opera and *Pagliacci* is one of my favorites."

"But Nedda meets such a cruel end."

"I know. She and Carmen suffered the same fate. I always cry."

Cesare heard pain in her voice. "Why use the last name Bottaro?"

"It means a wine cask maker. There'd be no connection to any of my family names."

He nodded. "Wise decision. If I deem you a promising pupil, we'll go with both when I introduce you to my partners. I'll tell them I stole you from the finest *ristorante* in Palermo."

She rubbed her hands against womanly hips in a nervous gesture. "How soon will that happen?"

"Not for a while. I'll have to teach you a lot first, and quickly, too. After dinner we'll start with something simple. I'll take a taxi to the grocery store and get the needed ingredients. While I'm at it, I'll buy you a new Pay as You Go phone to reach me if you need to and program it. By the time you go to bed, you'll be able to make the recipe I have in mind in your sleep."

She paced the floor, then wheeled around in front of him. "If I can pass your tests, that means I'll be making desserts for hundreds of people a week."

"That's right. Kings, sheikhs, presidents of countries."

Her radiating smile illuminated those hidden places in his soul that had never seen light. That thought appeared to delight her.

"You'll have assistants to help you."

"But I don't look anything like a chef."

No. She didn't look like anyone else in the whole wide world. "You will after we dress you properly. When I bring my partners to the kitchen to introduce you, no one will ever guess you're Princess Tuccianna."

Her cheeks had grown becomingly flushed. "I want to be good enough to meet your standards. You'll never know what this means to me."

He was beginning to. While she stood there, Cesare phoned for a taxi. After he hung up, he turned to her. "I'm starving and am going out to pick up a meal for us after I shop. When I get back, we'll get started."

She followed him to the door. "If I can't do the job you need done, does this mean you'll have to be the head pastry chef at your own hotel?"

He liked it that she was a little worried about him. "Yes. My partner's wife, Gemma, can no longer handle the job this late in her pregnancy. I'd promised I would produce her replacement by tomorrow, but with Signor Fragala in the hospital, the job has now fallen on my shoulders. I'll have to let them know in the morning. That doesn't give me time to find anyone else with his credentials. It could take me several months."

"And I don't have *any*," she half moaned the words.

In an unconscious gesture he put a hand on her shoulder and kneaded it gently. "I'm not my mother's son for nothing. You've convinced me you want this job more than anything. By the time I'm through with you, I'm hoping you'll be able to write your own ticket as a pastry chef."

After a long pause he said, "At this point I've been wondering. Is the difficult, uncontrollable, incorrigible Principessa di Trabia of Palermo, Sicily, worth her salt? It would be fun to find out the truth. I'll be back soon."

Tuccia rested against the closed door with her arms folded. His touch had crept through her body like a fine wine, weakening her physically. Yet his final comment before he'd gone out the door had caused a sudden surge of adrenaline to attack her.

*"Is the difficult, uncontrollable, incorrigible Principessa di Trabia of Palermo, Sicily, worth her salt?"*

Cesare had said that to get a rise out of her. Without question he'd accomplished his objective.

Frightened and excited by the whole situation she'd created for herself, Tuccia turned on the TV in the corner to distract her for a little while. She grazed the channels with the remote and came across two stations giving the four o'clock news. The second she saw a news clip of herself and Jean-Michel flash on the screen, she felt sick and sank down on the couch.

"Authorities in France and Italy are asking for anyone to come forward who knows anything about the whereabouts of Princess Tuccianna of Sicily, the daughter of the Marchese and Marchesa di Trabia. She's the fiancée of the acting Comte Jean-Michel Ardois of the House of Ardois and prominent CEO of Ardois Munitions. Princess Tuccianna disappeared yesterday morning in Paris and hasn't been seen since.

"The famous couple were to have been married today. Speculation that she was kidnapped by some foreign government faction for ransom has not been counted out.

"According to police, the Marchesa had been waiting in the lounge for her daughter to change after the final fitting of her wedding gown at the exclusive bridal shop on the Rue de L'Echelle. But she never came out. The police found her betrothal ring and are suspicious that some employees working at the shop helped aid in the kidnapping and are now being detained.

"Both families are desperate for news of the beautiful dark-haired twenty-five-year-old princess. So far any sightings of her have turned out to be false. She speaks French, Spanish, English, Italian, Sicilian and is known to be an excellent swimmer and sailor who—"

Tuccia turned off the TV and buried her face in her hands, swamped by guilt for the terrible thing she'd done. At least Jean-Michel would get her letter soon, but in the meantime innocent people were being questioned and detained. Hundreds of policemen in two countries were searching for her. She'd endangered her aunt and Cesare's mother. But she couldn't go back to that life. She just couldn't.

Jean-Michel wanted to marry a woman with a title, preferably a young one who'd give him children and not cause him trouble. Her parents wanted a son-in-law with a fortune that would never run out. No love was involved. Tuccia was a pawn and always had been. It was a fact of life that she'd been born to royalty.

It truly wasn't fair to Cesare, who'd been forced to come to her rescue this morning, flying her with him on the ducal jet no less. Knowing the huge risk of aiding a fugitive—that's what she was at this point—a lesser man might never have done such a favor, not even for his own mother.

To add to her crime, Tuccia had proposed an idea to save both their skins. But it was so audacious *and* dangerous if anyone were to find out who she was. For Cesare to be willing to go along with her idea made him a prince among men as far as she was concerned.

He had a reputation for being brilliant. She'd known that about Lina's son long before she'd ever met him. But she hadn't counted on him being so incredibly handsome, too. Working with him, she would fast lose her objectivity. How could she possibly concentrate on what she was doing while she was in his presence? If there was such a thing as love at first sight, she'd fallen victim to it.

By working with him, there was no doubt she'd be learning from a master. It would be an honor to be the student of a man famous on two continents for his business acumen as a restaurateur. He'd built an enviable empire of restaurants in New York.

Part of her wanted to show him she *was* worth her salt. But what if she failed? She'd passed lots of tests in her life, but none would be more important than this one now that she'd made the commitment.

While she was sorting through her tortured thoughts she heard a knock on the door. Tuccia rushed to let him in. He was loaded with three big sacks of food and carried them into the kitchen.

She shut the door behind him. "It looks like you bought out the store."

"Several stores to be exact." He washed his hands in the sink. "The risotto with veal looked good at the deli. I picked up some rustic wheat bread and a bottle of Chardonnay Piemonte to go with it."

"Wonderful. I'm hungry, too." She peeked in the sacks and found their dinner, which she put on the round kitchen table. Their gazes fused. "I take it the other two sacks contain enough pastry ingredients to feed a small army."

"You're partially right. The rest are provisions for you to take with you in case you change your mind before the evening is over."

Her spirits plunged. "What do you mean?"

"While I've been gone, you've had time to reconsider what we've talked about. After we've eaten, I'll be happy to take you to the train station if that's your wish. The standard service leaves at quarter to nine for Sicily. There'll be no amenities. You'll have to sit up in your seat all night. But you'll be like dozens of passengers with little money and melt into the crowd."

He pulled wine glasses from the cupboard and poured some for them, but what he'd just said to her had shocked her.

# CHAPTER FOUR

TUCCIA STOOD THERE with her hands on her hips. "You honestly expected that I would change my mind while you were gone? That I didn't mean any of the things I said?"

"It would be understandable," he said, sounding so reasonable she wanted to scream.

"Naturally you have every right to believe I'm not up to the task. No one would believe it."

"I have faith in you, but I want to give you the freedom to back out of this if you think you might have spoken too hastily."

As they sat down to eat, he handed her a copy of the *Il Giorno* newspaper to read. She came face-to-face with a two-month-old picture of her and Jean-Michel attending the opera in Paris. The headline read, *Sicilian Princess still missing*.

"You've done a good job of disappearing, Tuccia. So good I believe you have an excellent chance to reach Catania unobserved with your disguise. I had no right to suggest you go to New York. You're a grown woman and can make your decisions. It's time you were allowed to function without interference from anyone."

He ate a second helping of veal. The minutes were ticking away. Maybe he was wishing she would leave for Catania, then he'd never have to give her another thought in his life.

Her appalling selfishness sickened her. She couldn't help but wonder if he was disgusted with the overindulged princess who'd created an international incident. He'd have every right!

It was miraculous he'd let his mother talk him into bringing her to Milan, except that Tuccia's aunt was a force to contend with. Because his mother worked for Bertina, she probably didn't know how to say no to her.

Unable to handle her own ugly thoughts any longer, she got to her feet and clung to the back of the chair. He looked at her while he finished off the bread.

"Cesare?" she began.

"Yes?"

"When I was at your mother's last night, I was frightened out of my wits at what I'd done to escape my prison. Terrified would be a better word. That is until this morning, when you snatched me away from the jaws of death at great risk. I know that sounds dramatic, but that's how it felt to me and still does."

"I have no doubt of it."

She struggled to say the rest. "You've saved my life. If you're really willing to teach me how to make pastry, and you think I can learn, I'd like to try. I want to help you honor your commitment to your partners who are depending on you. I haven't changed my mind about any of it. But if the police don't find me first, I can only pray your friends won't discover I'm a fraud who has made a mess of everything for you."

The blue of his eyes darkened as they stared at her out of dark-fringed lashes. The male beauty of the man caused her to feel desire for him even to the palms of her hands.

"I believe you. No matter how you see yourself, Tuccia, in my opinion you're the bravest woman I ever met and I believe you can take the challenge head-on," he said in a husky tone. "What brought you to this decision?"

After the unexpected compliment, Tuccia had difficulty swallowing. "I couldn't let you get away with thinking I'm not worth my salt."

There was a gleam in his eyes. "I'm impressed by your willingness to put yourself in the hands of a stranger."

"That part is easy, Cesare. Because I've been friends with your mother, you haven't been a stranger to me, even if we didn't meet until last night." She was embarrassed because she could hear the throb in her voice. All it had taken was meeting him to be crazy about him.

He got to his feet and started clearing the table. "She likes you enough to have begged me to help you escape. That shows the strength of your friendship. It's good enough for me."

"I'm just sorry I'm the clay you have to work with to try and make a pastry cook out of me. But I swear I'll work my hardest for you."

"You've convinced me. Shall we get busy?"

"Yes. What will we make first?"

"The most clamored-for dessert in Sicily. I'm sure you've eaten virgin breasts before."

Tuccia should have been ready for that one, but it

was so unexpected heat scorched her cheeks. She went over to the sink to wash her hands. "You can't be a Sicilian without having eaten those cakes. But when I was little, the cook at the palazzo was offended by their name so she called them nun buns."

A chuckle escaped his lips. "They have several names. Mamma grew up in an orphanage run by the nuns," he continued. "They were known for being great cooks and made those special delicacies for which they're famous. She taught me everything she learned from them. Tonight we'll get started on the first of three different kinds."

"I didn't know there was more than one."

"You'd be surprised at the varieties."

She knew he was talking about the cakes, but her blush deepened anyway.

"Some of the ingredients have to be refrigerated before completing them, but we'll finish everything before you have to go bed. In a few days' time we'll present them to my partners as your specialty when I introduce you. A bite into them and they'll believe they'd been transported to heaven."

Laughter peeled out of her. "I hope you're right!"

His laughter filled the kitchen. "Why don't you sit down and we'll go over the recipe. It's known only to my mother and me." He walked over to one of the sacks and pulled out a notebook and pen. She shouldn't have been surprised all that knowledge was etched in his brain.

"Shall I write it down while you dictate?" she asked as he handed her the items.

"I think that would be best for you. To read your own writing rather than try to figure out mine will save you time in the long run. That notebook is going to be your bible. Don't ever lose it. Are you ready?"

"Yes," she said in a tentative voice.

Last night Tuccia had appeared to Cesare like a fantastic female apparition that had made him think maybe he was hallucinating. This evening she wasn't just a heavenly face and body. In the last eighteen hours she'd taken on substance and exhibited a keen intellect that had been growing on him by the minute.

In her desperation to remain hidden from the world for a while, she'd begged him to teach her. He knew she was frightened. This woman, who'd been raised to be a princess, was running on faith.

Right now she reminded him of a young child, submissive and obedient to her parent. Cesare was humbled by her determination to grab the lifeline he'd thrown her. He'd brought the newspaper with him to help remind her that anything—even learning how to cook pastry—was better than being forced to go back to her old life.

"The first item you'll be making is called *pasta frolla* for the shells. These are the ingredients: four cups of flour, one cup of granulated sugar, two sticks of sweet butter, one tablespoon of honey, five medium egg yolks, lightly beaten, and lemon zest. After you've kneaded it and put it in the fridge for an hour, you'll make the ricotta cream filling. That requires one cup of sugar, two pounds of ricotta, orange zest, cinnamon powder, one drop of vanilla, a quarter pound of candied citron and chocolate shavings to taste. Lemon glacé will be the final step that includes one and a half cups of granulated sugar, a quarter cup of lemon juice, and a sprinkle of raspberries. I realize this sounds like a lot, but it's straightforward. You'll like forming the shells. Are you with me so far?"

She looked up with a faint smile. "Yes. I can't wait to find out if I share your optimism."

Her response was encouraging. "Come on. We'll get started on the dough. While you find us a bowl in the cupboard, I'll put the first set of ingredients on the table."

He oversaw everything, but made her do all the work. She added the ingredients, making little mistakes, but soon she'd formed it into a ball.

"Okay. Now knead it."

"I know how to do that from watching the cook." But once she got started, the dough kept sticking to her fingers. "This is impossible!" she cried in frustration.

Cesare burst into laughter. "Wash your hands, and then dust them with flour before trying it again."

"But that will wash half the dough away."

"No problem."

"That's what you say," she mumbled, but did his bidding and started over with the kneading. "This is much better." She finally lifted her head and smiled. "Thank you."

"You're welcome. Now pat it into a disk and wrap it in wax paper. An hour in the fridge and it will be ready to shape into tart shells. While the dough is getting cold, you'll start making the filling."

Three hours and three tries later she'd produced a pan of tarts she was willing to let him taste. After she'd decorated them with the lemon glacé, she designed the tops in an artful way with raspberries and chocolate shavings.

With a hand he could tell was trembling, she put one on a dish and handed it to him. "Will you be the first to sample my *pièce de resistance*?"

Cesare knew what this moment meant to her and he bit into it. She'd followed the recipe to the letter. He found no fault with the taste or texture and was so proud of her effort after three tries that he wanted to sweep her in his arms. Instead he kissed her hot cheek.

"Congratulations, Tuccia. My partners will tell you these tarts are perfect." He swallowed the whole thing and had to be careful not to swallow her, too.

"Thank you. I know they're anything but. The shells are still uneven and in this batch I put a little too much cinnamon in the filling when I tasted it."

"The fact that you know what you can improve on makes you an excellent cook already. How does it feel to have made a masterpiece created by the nuns?"

She took a deep breath. "If these tarts meet your exacting criteria, it's because you were my teacher. To answer your specific question, after I got over being nervous with you standing there watching me, I had more fun than I would have expected."

"Good. I'm glad to hear it."

"It amazes me that I've eaten desserts of every kind all my life and never paid attention to the intricacies that go into the preparation. That's what frightens me. This was just one dessert. When I think of the dozen others I have to learn how to make, I feel totally inadequate."

"Keep in mind that all it takes is one step at a

time. I'll wrap up your pan of mounds and take them with me."

"Why?"

"I want my partners to try them." He heard her groan. "After the dishes are done, I'll say good-night."

While he called for a limo, he watched how hard she worked to clean up the flour on the table and floor, let alone her clothes. She'd proved she was worth her salt, but this had only been her first lesson. Another few days of this and the last thing she would tell him was that it was fun.

He had to give her full marks for putting the kitchen back together with little help from him. "You've done a great job, Tuccia. I'll be back in the morning and we'll talk about what's going to happen. I hope you get a good sleep."

She walked him to the front door. "I'll never be able to thank you enough for shielding me and giving me this chance."

"I'm equally grateful and impressed that you're willing to try something so different from the world you've come from to help me. Who knows? We may pull this off yet."

She flashed him a tired smile. "'May' being the operative word. *Bona notti*," she called to him.

On Cesare's way to the *castello*, her parting words resonated inside him. She'd said good-night to him in Sicilian, using the Palermo dialect. It reminded him of the language he used with his own family, making him feel more connected to the princess.

That was bad. He couldn't afford to have intimate thoughts about her, but that was a joke because he could still feel her body pressed against his in his mother's kitchen. That was a moment he couldn't forget if he wanted to, even if she'd just run away from her fiancé.

Cesare had offered to help her so she could gain her independence. He hadn't done it to take advantage of her. The last thing he intended was to come on to her. If he did that, he'd be every bit as bad as the lecherous *comte* Cesare's mother had described.

*You are just as bad, Donati.*

By the time the limo dropped him off around the back of the *castello*, he realized he had to tell his partners the truth about her. If they couldn't handle it—and he was pretty sure they couldn't—he would understand. So would Tuccia. Even though he hadn't been around her long, he knew she'd pretend it was all right.

It was five to ten when he stole through the passageway to the back stairs not used by the hotel clientele. Halfway to his room on the second floor in the private section, he ran into Takis coming down the stairs from the turret bedroom he and Lys used when they were in Milan. They had their own home in Crete and flew back and forth.

"Cesare—You're back! We didn't expect to see you until tomorrow. What have you got there?"

"You'd be surprised."

Takis frowned. "What's going on?"

"I had a slight change in plans. Where are you headed?"

"To the kitchen." Takis smiled. "Lys had a sudden craving for ice cream."

"So it's true about pregnant women."

"*Si.* One day it'll be your turn to find out."

A sudden vision of a pregnant Tuccia in her yellow silk robe flashed through Cesare's mind, disturbing him.

"*Eh, amico.* What's wrong?"

*Diavolo.* What wasn't? "Everything's fine."

"The hell it is." Takis could read him like a book.

"Your wife needs you. Is Vincenzo here or in Lake Como with Gemma?"

"In order for us to be together tomorrow and meet the new cook, they never left for home."

"*Perfetto.* See you two in the morning."

Not wanting to prolong this any longer, Cesare bounded up the rest of the stairs. When he reached his suite, he put the tray of tarts on the coffee table and went in the other room to take a shower.

Later, after throwing on a robe, he phoned his mother and found out the police had been by the villa asking questions about Tuccia.

"I said I didn't know what they were talking about. I'd been at the hospital all day and told them to check the nursing station at San Giovanni if they needed verification. That was enough for them and they left. I'm positive they won't be back."

"*Grazie al cielo.*"

"Bertina is overjoyed no one can find her niece."

It might interest his mother to know Cesare's relief was just as great. The more he thought about Tuccia's detestable royal engagement, the happier he was that he'd played a part in her escape. As for the rest... "I take it Ciro is still in the ICU."

"Oh, yes. The nurse told me she would call me

when they moved him to a private room so I could visit."

"That's good."

"Tell me how you are. How's Tuccia?"

"We're both fine." He'd told Takis the same thing. Fine covered a lot of territory, good and bad. "Don't worry about anything. Get some sleep, Mamma. That's what I'm going to do."

Not wanting to answer any more questions, he hung up wondering if he'd be able to get any while he was torn apart by thoughts of Tuccia and what would be the best thing for her. Now that he'd agreed to help her, he had to see this through one way or the other. But he couldn't seem to stop from touching her. Earlier tonight he'd kissed her.

Cesare was about to turn out the overhead light when there was a knock on the door. Instinct told him it was Takis. He crossed the room and opened it to discover both him and Vincenzo standing at the threshold.

"Shouldn't you two be with your wives?"

Vincenzo's silvery stare had a way of pinning you in place. "We think you need us more."

"I'd hoped to have this conversation in the morning."

Takis shook his head. "Let's talk now or none of us will get any sleep."

How true. But the fear that his partners might not be on board with his plan to train Tuccia had been bothering him. Deep inside lurked another fear that if she left Milan to do something else, she wouldn't tell him where she'd gone and he might never see her again.

"Come in." They walked in his sitting room and sat down. He paced for a minute before coming to a stop. "I don't want to keep you up all night, so here's the bottom line. The person I'd hired for our *ristorante* is in the hospital in Palermo as we speak."

In the next breath Cesare explained everything that had happened from the moment he'd arrived at his mother's villa until now. He told them about Ciro's sudden illness and Tuccia's plight.

"I took her to the *pensione* where Gemma stayed. She's safe there for the time being. During the flight I came up with a solution to both problems."

In the next breath he told them of his idea to turn her into the temporary new pastry cook for the *castello* until Ciro was well. He only left two things out; the fact that she'd been the one who'd begged *him* for the job, and his intense attraction to the *principessa.* Cesare had never burned for a woman like this in his life.

"Hearing about her disappearance is like a dose of déjà vu for me," Vincenzo commented.

Cesare nodded. "When Mamma admitted why she was hiding Tuccia, I could understand. It took me back to that morning in New York when you told me and Takis about your escape from your father at eighteen years of age. She's twenty-five, but still in much the same situation as you were back then."

"That was a horrific time. I can well imagine what Princess Tuccianna is going through right now."

"But she's my responsibility, not yours. Tonight on the way up here I decided I had to be out of my mind to think up such a ridiculous plan." She'd been so desperate, he hadn't been able to find the strength to turn her down. "On the jet she talked about another plan she had in mind to stay in hiding. I don't doubt it would work for a while.

"Once she's gone I'll be acting pastry chef while I search for the right person to replace Gemma. I can only hope Ciro might recover much sooner than the doctor estimated."

Without commenting, Takis eyed the covered pan on the coffee table. "Are you going to let us taste her first endeavor?"

"I was just going to ask the same thing," Vincenzo commented.

"There's no point. I'm not willing to drag you two into this mess."

"Why don't you let us decide."

"No, Takis." He shook his head. "All we would need is for the press to find out she's working within the walls of the *castello*. We'd be charged for obstructing a police investigation. I'd face an additional charge for flying her here. It would cause an international scandal that could ruin our business."

At this point Vincenzo had gotten to his feet. "Not showing up for her wedding would be a disappointment to her fiancé and parents, but it isn't a crime. As far as I can see, no crime has been committed by anyone. She turned to her aunt for assistance. That woman called on your mother who enlisted your help. The police don't know that."

"Vincenzo's right," Takis chimed in. "Besides, Tuccia is over twenty-one and is welcome here as a staff worker. If she wore a disguise and used a fake name, it's not our fault we didn't recognize her."

"Thanks, guys, but the police wouldn't see any of it that way."

"How are they going to find out?"

Cesare rubbed the back of his neck in frustration. "I don't know, but you can be sure there'll be a leak somewhere."

Takis looked up at Cesare. "Mind if we find out what a good teacher you are?"

"Go ahead. She's never cooked anything in her life, but she followed Mamma's sacred recipe for Sicilian nun buns to the letter." He uncovered the pan so they could take one.

Both men started eating and didn't stop until half of the decorated mounds were gone. Tuccia could have received no greater compliment.

Vincenzo lifted his head. "You swear you didn't cook these yourself?"

"I stood over her shoulder. That's all."

"She really made these on her own?" Takis looked astounded.

Cesare nodded. "It took her three tries. She even cleaned up the mess in the kitchen afterwards."

"Do you think this was a one-time accident, or is the princess the proverbial diamond in the rough?"

"I'd like to see her make half a dozen Sicilian desserts at the *pensione* before I could answer that question, Takis. Today it was fear that drove her. She'd do anything to stay hidden. But to master the art of fine pastry making and love to do it is a gift only a few people possess. Within a few days she could hate it.

"As for her working here as the pastry chef, it would mean dealing with the kitchen assistants. I have no idea how she would handle them under pressure. For all of those reasons I'm going to tell her this won't work."

"Not so fast," Vincenzo interjected. "Before you say or do anything, why don't I ask Gemma to visit her tomorrow? Let her lay out what a day in the kitchen would be like for Tuccia. She'd be able to ask my wife questions about the routine and the personalities she would have to deal with."

"But Vincenzo—Gemma learned from her mother and studied pastry making for ten years at the finest school in Florence. She would laugh in disbelief at such a ludicrous idea."

Vincenzo shook his head. "We've all heard the news about the princess who ran away. No one would be more understanding than my wife who saw first-hand what went on between my father and me years ago. Takis and I agree those nun buns the princess made were divine. I think it's worth going to the trouble to give her a chance. I know Gemma will feel the same way."

"You don't want her on her feet at this late date in her pregnancy. Neither do I."

"Cooking for hours every day is entirely different than having a serious talk with Tuccia."

Takis nodded. "He's got a point, Cesare."

"I don't know. I have a lot to think about. Tomorrow when I go down to the *pensione*, I'll probably discover she wants to leave. Whatever is decided, I'll let you know. I guess you realize I'm indebted to you two for being the best friends any man could ever have. Now go to bed. That's an order."

Both men stole the rest of the mounds from the pan before walking out the door.

Cesare tossed and turned all night, too eager to see her again to sleep. Early the next morning he got dressed and left the *castello* in his hard-top sports car parked around the rear. He took the empty pan with him.

When he reached the village, he stopped at a *trattoria* for takeout: breakfast for two. To his dismay he realized that he was so excited at the prospect of seeing her again he couldn't think about anything else. Though it had only been a few days, Tuccia had taken up space in his mind and heart.

He'd known desire for women and had enjoyed several short-term relationships, but they'd always stopped short of marriage because some crucial element had been missing. That was what he'd always told himself. But this was different because so far Tuccia appealed to him on every level and had already colored his world.

He reached the *pensione* at eight and got out of the car. After knocking on the door, he expected her to answer in tears and be anxious to get to the train station.

# CHAPTER FIVE

LAST NIGHT TUCCIA had wished Cesare had stayed. But if she'd asked him not to go, she would have given him the wrong idea. She had a problem because she knew she'd fallen in love with him and was more attracted to him with every passing minute. When the limo pulled away, she'd closed and locked the door, fearing she wouldn't get to sleep for a long time.

At four this morning, an exhausted Tuccia had turned off her watch alarm and got out of bed to do her homework. It was one thing to cook while Cesare had stood there directing her every step. The trick was to do it while he wasn't watching.

She knew there were enough ingredients for her to make one more batch of the tarts on her own. But with no big shallow pan, she'd had to improvise with two small round pans with higher sides she'd found in the cupboard. As a result, she still had half the batter to cook.

If she failed miserably, then she'd be the first to ask him to drive her to the train station. It would be the last thing he would ever have to do for her. Before she threw herself at him, she realized it would be better if she never saw him again.

Tuccia had thought her initial physical attraction to him would fade, but the opposite had happened. His underlying goodness as a human being had opened her eyes to the other qualities in his nature that had nothing to do with his striking male looks. Everything about him from his intellect to his humor stimulated her. So much, in fact, that she was breathless as she waited to see him again today.

The knock on the door came sooner than she had expected, sending her pulse racing as if she had a sickness. She put down the cup she'd been using to add the final lemon glaze to the tarts she'd made. There were still three to be coated and decorated.

After wiping her hands on a towel, she hurried to answer the door, knowing flour still dusted part of the same blouse she'd worn last evening. There was even some on her forearms.

When she opened it, their eyes met for a quiet moment. His were smiling, if there was such a thing. She got a fluttering in her chest as his gaze wandered over her.

"I bet you didn't know there's flour on the tip of your nose." Before she could blink, he removed it with his thumb. His touch sent an electricity-like spark through her body. "If I don't miss my guess, I would say you've already been hard at work this morning."

She was worried yet excited to show him. "Come in and find out."

Cesare walked through to the kitchen with another bag of food and the empty pan. He put them both on the counter and pulled a phone out of his pocket.

"This is for you. All programmed." He put it at the end of the counter.

Tuccia thanked him, but she had no idea where the batch of tarts he'd left with had ended up. She didn't think she wanted to know.

Without asking her permission, Cesare took a finished product from one of the small round pans. He examined it first. Then he bit into it. An anxious Tuccia waited while he took another bite and another, until it was all gone. *Uh-oh. Here it comes.*

"Why are you closing your eyes?" he asked in a quiet voice.

"I don't know. So I can handle the bad verdict better?"

"On your fourth try, you've achieved perfection. The cinnamon balance is just right. As for the shapes, my mother wouldn't know them from her own. If I didn't have a knowledge of your upbringing, I'd think you came out of the same nunnery." This time he brushed her mouth with his own.

She opened her eyes, trying to contain her joy. "Thank you, Cesare, but you don't have to overdo it."

He ignored her comment. "I'm even more impressed you found something else to cook them in. This apartment is ill-equipped for a chef. When Mamma told me you were resourceful, I don't believe that even she understood the scope of your abilities."

Tuccia scoffed. "She was only quoting my *zia* who thinks I can do no wrong. She and my *zio* wanted babies so much. What they got was me when my parents didn't know what to do with me. Bertina was the one bright light in my existence."

"As you still are in hers," he came back, seemingly deep in thought. "Otherwise she wouldn't have risked everything to help you." His blue gaze swerved to hers, sending more darts of awareness through her body. "That includes using my mother who happens to have the same favorable opinion of you."

"I'll never be able to thank her enough for what she's done. But right this minute I want the honest answer to one question. After talking to your partners, should I be getting ready to leave for Catania?"

He lounged his rock-hard body against the edge of the counter with his arms folded. "I'd like *your* honest answer to another question first. Why did you get up at the crack of dawn and go to all the effort of making another batch when you could have stayed asleep?"

She took a deep breath. "Because I needed to find out for myself if I was capable of following that recipe on my own."

"Which you've demonstrated beyond all doubt. Would it interest you to know my partners devoured the tarts you made?"

"No, they didn't," she said with an embarrassed chuckle.

"One bite told them everything they needed to know. They stuffed themselves and took the few uneaten mounds with them when they left my room."

"Now you're just trying to make me feel good because…because that's the kind of man you are," she said, her voice faltering.

"You don't have to compliment me back." Yes, she did. She owed him her life right now. "Let me prove it to you."

Tuccia watched him pull out his cell phone and make a call to Vincenzo, the present Duc di Lombardi. They talked for a few moments before he hung up.

"Vincenzo's wife, Gemma, will be arriving within

the hour. Shall we eat the breakfast I brought now? Then I'll clean up the kitchen while you get ready for our guest."

A slight gasp escaped her lips. "Why would she be coming here?"

He reached for the bag of food and set it on the table. "You've passed your first test by baking a dessert the *castello ristorante* would be proud to serve. But this is only the beginning if you decide to accept the daunting challenge facing you."

She averted her eyes. "You're right. It's so daunting, I'm terrified."

"Be frank with Gemma and see what happens."

"What's she like?"

"Only a few years older than you and one of the nicest, kindest women I've ever known."

"Besides being a master pastry chef."

He nodded. "A chef who's about to become a mother. She can't wait for their baby to arrive and is anxious to let someone else take on her former mantle."

"Which no doubt *you* will be doing before the day is out, Cesare. Please forgive me if I skip breakfast. That was very kind of you to bring it, but I'm afraid I can't eat anything right now."

She rushed to the bedroom to take a shower and change into jeans and a knit top. Tuccia had only packed a few understated clothes at Bertina's because she knew she would have to travel light on her trip to Catania and didn't dare stand out.

After being sheltered at Lina Donati's villa for one night, she could never have known she would end up here in Milan to face a situation undreamed of.

*Be frank with Gemma.*

Tuccia interpreted that to mean she must put the princess part of herself aside. For once she had to dig down to her core and decide if she thought she could pull this off.

This could all end in a second if she asked Cesare to call Vincenzo back and tell him not to bring his wife to the *pensione*. Within a few minutes Tuccia could be driven to the train.

That would leave Cesare to take on the exclusive role of executive pastry chef until he found someone else exceptional, or until Signor Fragala recovered.

But for Tuccia, it would mean never seeing him again. Her heart told her she couldn't handle that. He'd become too important to her.

Sucking in her breath, she reached for the brush to style her curls. Once she'd applied some light makeup and lipstick, she left the bedroom to face what was coming.

Cesare walked outside when he saw Vincenzo's Mercedes pull up in front. While his friend came around from the other side, Cesare helped a blonde, very pregnant Gemma out of the front seat and kissed her cheek. "Thanks for coming."

"It's my privilege. How *à propos* that the princess is staying here in the same apartment I did."

"I thought it the safest place to conceal her."

"You've found the perfect spot tucked out of the way. It takes me back to those first days when I left the *pensione* to meet you for the first time. I was shaking in my boots to be interviewed by the internationally famous restaurateur owner of the Castello Supremo Hotel and Ristorante di Lombardi."

"I would never have known it, Gemma. When you told me your mother's pastry would always be the best, I felt an immediate affinity to you since I felt the same way about my mother's Sicilian cooking. Your desserts were divine."

She kissed his cheek. "Little did I know I would come face to face with Vincenzo when I thought he'd disappeared from my life forever."

Her husband put his arm around her nonexistent waist. "None of us will forget that day. I too thought I'd lost the love of my life. *Grazie a Dio* we found each other."

While his friend chose that moment to kiss Gemma thoroughly, Cesare went back inside the apartment. Tuccia had come in the small living room looking so appealing he'd have liked to do the same thing to her. He was in serious trouble because he knew he couldn't hold back much longer in showing her how he felt.

"They're coming," he said, after answering the question in her misty gray eyes, which were more noticeable because of her black fringed lashes and black hair. She had the most remarkable coloring and light olive complexion. With her oval face and alluring mouth, she looked so irresistible he had to force himself to look away or he'd make her uncomfortable.

He heard the others file inside. "Princess Tuccianna, allow me to present two of my dearest and closest friends, Vincenzo Gagliardi, the Duc di Lombardi, and his wife Gemma."

"It's a real honor for me." Tuccia shook their hands.

"We're the ones honored, Princess," Vincenzo declared. Cesare could tell his friend was bowled over by her beauty, a feat that didn't happen often.

"Please, just call me Tuccia. Won't you sit down? I feel a fraud inviting you into this *pensione* Cesare not only found for me, but is paying for until I can reimburse him."

Cesare noted she was always grace itself. The spoiled princess as reported in the news wasn't the same person he'd pulled against his body a few nights ago for fear she would fall.

"Your desperate situation has called for drastic measures. I had a similar experience in my late teens and was anxious for any help I could get." Leave it to Vincenzo to make her feel comfortable.

"Nevertheless I've put all of you in a dangerous position simply by being here and want you to know I'm ready to leave after we've talked."

Gemma got up from the couch. Cesare noticed that she was a little slower these days. "Tuccia? Before there's any talk like that, why don't you and I go in the kitchen where we can be private and let the guys talk business in here."

Cesare nodded. "That's a good idea." He watched Tuccia follow Gemma into the kitchen. She might be nervous now, but before long she'd realize she couldn't be in better hands than Gemma's. His gaze swerved to his friend.

"How does your wife really feel about this?" he asked in a quiet voice.

"She ate one of the tarts I took back to our room. When she'd finished, she said, 'I know this was Cesare's recipe, but if Tuccia can make all his Sicilian desserts as exquisite as these, the *castello* is going to gain a new following.'"

"That's high praise, Vincenzo."

"Gemma is nothing if not truthful."

"If by any chance this works out, I'll insist Tuccia live here and make each dessert in the kitchen first. It will help her feel confident before she leaves for the *castello* every morning to manage her assistants. But I'm afraid that without the right disguise, someone will recognize her and the police will descend."

Vincenzo flashed him a subtle smile. "Meeting her explains a lot. She's a genuine knockout, Cesare. Gemma will be hard-pressed to come up with something that hides her beauty."

"Tell me about it."

"I don't think I have to, *amico*."

No. And the second Takis laid eyes on her, Cesare was in for it. "Was there anything on the morning news I should be concerned about yet?"

"Nothing. The police are at a standstill. Her parents have offered ten million euros for the person who finds her."

"Only ten for their precious daughter?" he bit out in disgust.

"No doubt the *comte*'s reward will be forthcoming before the day is out."

Cesare looked over his shoulder at Tuccia who was deep in conversation with Gemma. "I wonder how much he'd be willing to pay for her safe return. But it won't matter when he gets her letter explaining why she ran away." Cesare confided that he'd couriered it to his attorney in Barbados who would send it on.

"That was excellent thinking."

"She's been suffering terrible guilt."

"Understandable."

"But that part is done. When I arrived here this morning and saw that she'd already been up three hours making the recipe again, I knew for a fact that no amount of money would ever induce her to go back to him."

Vincenzo's brows lifted. "How did she do?"

"Hold on. I'll show you."

Cesare got up and walked into the kitchen. "*Scusa*, ladies." He plucked one of the round pans off the counter and took it into Vincenzo.

His friend reached for an iced tart and ate it in two bites before nodding in satisfaction. "After Gemma and I leave here, we'll drive into Milan and take the rest of these to my cousin and his wife to taste. Dimi will be in shock when we tell him what has happened."

"*Who* will be in shock, *mia cara?*" Gemma had just come back in the living room with Tuccia. Both men stood up.

"I thought we'd visit Dimi before we go back to the *castello* and let them sample Tuccia's nun buns. Did you get your business done?"

"We're off to a good start, aren't we, Tuccia?"

"Your wife has encouraged me to give it a try for which I'm very grateful." The relief on her face was tangible.

"*Meraviglioso!*" Vincenzo picked up the pan and helped his wife out the door to his car. Cesare knew how happy his friend was that someone else was going to be doing the work Gemma had done for so long.

He shut the door and turned to the woman who was transforming his life in ways he couldn't have imagined days ago. "I'm sure you have a great deal to discuss with me."

She nodded. "Thankfully Gemma is going to work two more days while I keep cooking desserts here at the apartment. Then it'll be my first day in the *castello* kitchen. She'll acquaint me with everything and stay long enough to introduce me to the staff before I'm on my own."

"You won't be alone. I'll be there in the background until you get your bearings. But tell me what it is that concerns Gemma the most?"

"A disguise for me, especially for my hair."

Her crowning glory was a dead giveaway. "Why don't you freshen up. Then we'll drive to the uniform shop in Milan used by the kitchen help. We'll find something that works. You'll have to wear your scarf and sunglasses."

"It'll be wonderful to get out for a little while." He could imagine. "I'll hurry."

After she disappeared, he reached in the fridge for a soda. Their shopping spree would include a stop to the grocery store. Once that was done they'd pick up some takeout and bring it back to the apartment for a meal. Toward evening they'd get busy working on a couple of new desserts. He loved being alone with her.

Tuccia hurried out to his sports car. Once again she had that sensation of being spirited away where nothing could hurt her. But this time she wanted Cesare to be more than her protector. Though he'd kissed her several times, she wanted… She wanted the impossible.

He drove them into Milan with expertise and parked

in front of a shop labeled Uniforme di Oggi. "Remember to keep your head mostly down."

"I will."

She couldn't get over the huge selection of chef apparel at the back. While she was taking it all in, Cesare seemed to know exactly what he wanted.

"Here. Try this on."

Cesare handed her a short-sleeved white lab coat that fell above the knee. After she put it on, he shook his head. "It needs to be larger to cover a T-shirt and chef's pants." He handed her a coat two sizes bigger. She tried it on.

"That will do fine. We'll take six of them. Now for six sets of pants and T-shirts that fit. Everything white."

Once she'd pulled the clothes off the racks and handed them to the clerk, they walked over to the counter to look at the chef hats and beanies of all kinds. Again, Cesare already had something in mind and reached for the traditional white floppy hat.

He handed it to Tuccia. "Go in the changing room and try it on where no one will see you. If it's not the right fit, call outside the door to me and I'll get the right one." They walked down the little hall. "Don't get any ideas about slipping out the back way, or you'll be on your own, Principessa." He said it with a slow smile that sent a river of warmth through her body.

Once inside, she removed her scarf and tried on the hat. It was too big. She told him as much. He returned in a minute with a smaller version. This one was just right. It would keep her hair snug inside and prevent any strands from slipping.

She put the scarf and glasses back on before emerging. "This one is the right size."

"Good. We'll take six of them."

He walked her over to the counter and before long they left the shop for his car with her new clothes. Talk about fun. Being with Cesare like this was turning out to be the happiest day of her life. To know the two of them would be working together for months and months was her idea of heaven. She didn't care how hard she had to work.

He drove her around to another store featuring eye glasses. "Stay in the car. I'll be right back."

With his brown hair and tall male physique, he made every man walking along the street look pathetic in comparison. When he came out of the store a few minutes later and flashed her a smile, she couldn't breathe. He handed her a bag with several sets of eye glasses for her to choose from.

"I have an idea," he announced. They'd already left the city for the village. "I'll pick up a meal and ask Takis to join us. My other partner needs to meet you. When he walks in the apartment, I want you to be wearing a complete chef's outfit. Of course he knows what you look like. If you can pass his inspection, then we'll know we have a chance that your identity will remain a secret."

"It *has* to," she whispered.

For a second time in several days Cesare reached for her hand and squeezed it. "This is going to work, Tuccia." She got the feeling he wanted this to work as much as she did. Soon they reached the grocery store and he let go of her. "I'll try not to be too long." He turned on the radio. "In case you want to listen."

While he was gone taking his warmth with him, she moved the tuner and heard the top-of-the-hour news. Her disappearance was still the lead story and a reward was being offered for help in finding her.

How odd that she felt so removed from the princess they were describing. In just a few days she felt like she'd turned into someone else. People were walking around the village and here she was, right in the middle of them with no one the wiser.

Cesare's energy was something to behold. He came back to the car loaded with more groceries and their dinner. She smiled at him. "That was fast. I'm sorry I couldn't be of help." She would adore shopping for groceries with him. Anything where they could be together.

He started the car. "One day all this will be behind you. Let's go home. I gave Takis a call. He'll be here at five which doesn't give you much time to work on your disguise."

"I have an idea about what to do with my hair. If I pull on a nylon stocking first, it will help keep it in place."

"That ought to work. Do we need to buy you some nylons?"

"No. I have a pair with me. Do you think it will be all right if I wear my leather sandals?"

"If they're comfortable, I don't see why not."

When they reached the *pensione*, she got out and helped carry in the bags. "I'll put the clothes in my bedroom."

"Don't come out until you've morphed into a chef. I admit I can't wait to see what you look like."

Neither could Tuccia. After a quick shower she put

on a pair of white semi-baggy drawstring pants. Next came the short-sleeved crew neck T-shirt. Now for the tricky part. She took off the scarf and rummaged in the dresser drawer for a stocking.

She fit it around her head so no hair could escape and pinned it to the crown. After grabbing a chef's hat and sack of eye glasses, she dashed in the bathroom. First she pulled out a pair of the clear lenses with neutral brown frames. Very professional looking. They fit over her ears just fine. Then she put on the hat, slanting the floppy part. The whole thing actually worked. She didn't recognize herself.

Tuccia normally wore a melon colored lipstick. She decided that wouldn't do and wiped off all traces. Pleased with the effect, she went back in the bedroom and pulled on the lab coat. It had pockets and seven buttons down the front opening, leaving the top of the T-shirt exposed. Her figure was non-existent, but that was the whole point.

Still dressed in her sandals, she felt ready for the fashion show. With pounding heart she tiptoed in the living room and found Cesare putting the groceries away. He'd laid the table for their dinner.

"*Signor?* May I have your attention, *per favore?*"

He wheeled around with a sack of flour in his hand. But when he saw her, it dropped to the counter, reminding her of the night in his mother's kitchen. She burst into laughter at the shock on his painfully handsome face.

She moved into the kitchen. "Perhaps you don't recognize me. I'm the new executive pastry chef at the Castello Supremo Hotel Ristorante in Milan, Italy. I can see by your expression that I've achieved a certain amount of success in that department, *signor*."

Loving this, Tuccia turned around like a model on a runway. "If you'll take a closer look, you'll see the detail of the stitching on the pockets of this stunning creation." His eyes played everywhere, as if trying to figure out where she'd gone.

"Pay attention to the large puffy hat, the latest in chic chef wear. This designer was chosen by the world famous five-star restaurateur Cesare Donati. He features nothing but the best in his kitchens, whether here or in New York. It's the greatest privilege I've ever known to be working for him."

His hand rubbed his chest as if he were in a trance. "I saw you go into the bedroom a little while ago," he began in a deep voice. "But I still can't believe it's you underneath all that white."

"Then you think I'll do?"

A knock on the door prevented him from responding. "Come on in, Takis."

Tuccia watched his dark-blond partner walk inside and shut it. Here was another incredibly attractive man who she'd been told had come from the island of Crete. His hazel eyes narrowed on her before he turned to Cesare. "I thought you said that Princess Tuccianna would be here."

"Did you hear that?" Cesare asked her.

"Yes. If the *signori* will excuse me, I'll tell her your guest has arrived for dinner."

She darted back to the bedroom so excited, she had trouble taking off all of her disguise. In a few minutes she returned to the living room with her hair brushed and lipstick on her mouth, wearing the same clothes she'd worn to town with Cesare.

His eyes pierced hers. "Princess Tuccianna, may I present my friend and partner, Takis Manolis."

"I've heard a great deal about you, Signor Manolis. It's a real pleasure to meet you."

He looked taken back. "It *was* you dressed as a chef." A grin broke out on his face. "After knowing what you look like, I would never have guessed. I'm honored to meet you." He shook her hand warmly.

"Even though I'm a wanted fugitive who's putting all of you in jeopardy?"

"Last night Cesare filled us in on the details. After I ate half of those nun buns you made, I told him I believe you'll make an excellent chef. And now that I've seen you in your uniform, I'm convinced no one will recognize you."

"I agree the transformation was miraculous," Cesare murmured. She couldn't wait to hear more about it once they were alone. "Let's eat, shall we? I'm afraid all the shopping we did has worn me out and I'm ravenous."

They sat at the kitchen table where Cesare treated them to scallops, beef *tagliati*, parmesan aubergine and pasta *con le sarde*. Tuccia could hardly believe she was sitting here with these two amazing men, chatting and enjoying the take-out food as if she didn't have a worry in the world. She'd entered into another realm of existence and never wanted to be anywhere else.

"Gemma told me her meeting with you went very well."

"She's a lovely person who answered a lot of questions for me."

"I'll tell you something honestly. She's convinced your Sicilian pastries will create a new sensation with our clientele."

Tuccia put her wine glass down. "You mean Cesare's."

"In time they'll become yours, too."

Takis had a charm almost as lethal as Cesare's. "One dessert does not make a chef, but I'm going to do my very best not to let you down. This evening Cesare will be assigning me a new recipe to cook."

"That's right." Cesare smiled at her. *"Cassateddi."*

She took a deep breath. "Those half-moon-shaped pastries were a favorite of mine growing up, but I never dreamed I'd learn how to make them."

"I loved them, too. So will Takis and Vincenzo. But they're only the beginning. Tomorrow you'll be making *testa di turco*, followed by *sfingi di San Giuseppe, casstelle di Sant'Agata* and Sicilian chocolate torte."

Cesare had just done an excellent job of frightening her to death.

"I think you're overwhelming her, *amico.*"

She leaned toward Takis. "His mother told me he drove her crazy growing up. No matter what she cooked, she'd find some of it missing the second she turned around," Tuccia confided.

Immediately Takis burst into rich male laughter. But Cesare didn't join in.

Too soon their visitor announced that he had to leave and said good-night. She was sorry to see him go because she'd gotten a little carried away with her out-of-school tale where Cesare was concerned. She'd been having too good a time and feared she'd crossed an unmarked boundary in their relationship.

While Cesare walked him out to his car, she hurriedly cleaned up the kitchen. When he came inside, she was already seated at the table with her bible, ready to write down the recipe for what she hoped would turn out to be a worthy *chef d'oeuvre.*

He washed and dried his hands, then he sat down, eyeing her with an intensity that made her squirm. "Tuccia," he began, "I—"

"I know what you're going to say," she broke in on him. "I apologize for saying something so personal in front of your friend. It was wrong of me to overstep like that. I promise it won't happen again."

His brows met in a frown. "I wasn't going to say anything of the sort. Before Takis drove off, he told me you were as sensational as your nun buns and we should keep you at all costs. Takis would never say anything like that unless he meant it."

She looked down because emotion had caused her eyes to smart.

"Before you interrupted me, I was going to tell you the disguise is perfect. I have no doubt you'll be a new trendsetter for the kitchen assistants. They'll take one look at you and want to be just like you, but they'll fail because there's only one Princess Tuccianna."

Tuccia was afraid her cheeks were on fire. She wanted him to forget she was a princess. She wanted him to see her as a woman he could love heart and soul. Looking up she said, "That's absurd, but thank you. Don't you think we should get started on the *cassateddi*? I'll need half the night to make it several times."

Those blue eyes narrowed on her features. "I thought *I* was the slave driver around here."

"Would you rather leave and come back tomorrow morning? I'd understand if you have another engagement."

"I have no plans to meet another woman."

Maybe not tonight. But it didn't mean there wasn't someone who loved him and was waiting anxiously to be with him. She couldn't bear the thought and was ridiculously jealous of any woman he'd been with.

"You're wrong, you know, Tuccia."

"What do you mean?"

"I can read your mind. There's no room in my life for any woman until the *castello*'s new pastry chef can create masterpieces without my help."

Just like that he'd drawn a sharp line in the sand. Meaning she shouldn't get any ideas about him for herself?

She sucked in her breath. "Since I'd hate to see you deprived of that kind of pleasure too long because of me, I'll work day and night to achieve that goal." She tapped the notebook with her pen. "I'm ready when you are."

# CHAPTER SIX

Two hours later Tuccia was in tears. She'd turned out two batches of half-moon shells filled with cream, but they'd been failures. Cesare had tried to eat one and it had fallen apart because she hadn't shaped it right. He had to eat it in pieces. She had to smother a moan watching him.

"The taste of this is superb."

"That doesn't count when its misshape falls apart before reaching your mouth. I tried to execute your directions to the letter, but I couldn't seem to get it right." She dried her eyes with a towel, but they kept falling. "This will never do. I'm going to make the recipe again."

He reached for the towel and wiped her cheeks. "We don't want your tears falling into your next attempt." His comment made her laugh and he kissed both her cheeks before she got started again on a third batch.

His pride in her work ethic kept growing while she took pains to crimp the edges just right. Another hour passed before he tested a sample of her latest work. "I find no fault in this presentation or the taste."

"Thank you," she murmured, but he could tell she still wasn't happy.

Cesare had no doubt that when he left the apartment, she'd make up another batch. Her fighting spirit was a trait he admired more than she would ever know. He stood against the doorjamb and watched while she put the third tray of shells inside the fridge.

"Did Gemma tell you about Maurice Troudeau, our executive chef?"

A corner of her delectable mouth lifted. "She said the key with him was to praise his work often and ask for help once in a while, even if you don't need it. I used that technique on Auguste Senlis, the most difficult history professor at the Sorbonne, and it worked."

Of course it did, but he wasn't smitten because of her smarts. No man anywhere who came into her sphere could remain unaffected. Takis and Vincenzo were a case in point.

"If I have a concern, it's because your French is too perfect. You're a princess on the run who speaks it fluently. Unfortunately you can't afford to speak it with him at all. When I introduce you, you'll be known as Nedda Bottaro from Sicily who speaks Sicilian with a Palermo dialect. Your knowledge of English is too minimal to count on. That's it."

"I understand."

He was sure she did. "Have you thought of a back-story? The staff will ask and you'll have to be ready."

"Yes. I was born in the back room of a bordello in Trapani and never knew my father. My mother didn't, either."

Cesare was having trouble holding back his laughter.

"When I was old enough to be of use, she gave me to the woman next door who was a cook and needed a helper. I never went to school. After my mother died of an infection, I ran away to Palermo and did all kinds of jobs until I prevailed on a baker to let me work for him. I liked that work best and stayed there until I was discovered by you!" Her gray eyes stared straight into his. "What do you think?"

At this minute he didn't dare tell her what he thought or felt. He was in love with her. "I have one suggestion. At least say that you went to school once in a while. Your intelligence shines through in everything you say and do."

"So does yours. Thank you for tonight's cooking lesson. I'll see you in the morning."

If she had any idea he would rather stay with her all night and every night, she'd fly out the door. "Tuccia? Before I leave, let's go in the living room and talk for a minute about something serious. You've been cooped up here for several days, no doubt missing a few friends to talk to."

Cesare went in the other room first so she'd follow. They both sat down. He took a chair and she the couch. "I know you've run away from your parents, but deep down this has to be torturous for you."

She curled up against the side. "If I told you the truth, I'm afraid you might think me a person with no natural affection."

He steadied himself. "Explain that."

"I know you're supposed to love your parents. I suppose I do in a philosophical way, but it's Zia Bertina I've always turned to. She was the mother I needed. My own was cold and my father was always a stranger to me. When I think of them, I get an empty feeling inside. With a mother like yours, I know you can't comprehend it."

Cesare shifted in the chair. "You're right." He had no words.

"I don't tell you this so you'll feel sorry for me, but only to explain that I've lived with this situation for twenty-five years. Your concern for my feelings has touched me very much, but you needn't worry yourself on my account because I have to stay secluded. As long as I have my *zia* who has loved me all my life, I'm happy."

He sucked in his breath. "But it's still not too late for you to leave Milan and do what you want, whether in Catania or elsewhere. You should be able to embark on a new life, work at something that interests you and make new friends."

"Find a lover *I've* chosen?" she added in a voice that made her sound much older.

He closed his eyes for a moment. "Why not?"

"I never wanted the fiancé I can't stand, let alone some lover, followed by another and then another that goes on and on like a revolving door. We royals are known for it. To be honest I can't think of anything worse."

Neither could Cesare.

"Right now there's just one thing on my mind. To prove that I can make a success of something truly important, not only to me, but to you and your partners. Your *ristorante* is without a pastry chef. If I could pull this off, nothing would make me happier."

Her earnestness crept through him, causing his throat to swell. "I believe you mean that."

She nodded. "I've surprised myself. Do you know what a shock it is to discover that I *like* such painstaking work? Who would have thought I'd find it a challenge to crimp the edges of those half moons so they were just right? But if you think there's still too much danger, or that it's really not going to work, then please tell me now and I'll leave whenever you say."

Humbled by an inner purity in her, Cesare got up from the chair. When he'd suggested they come in the living room for a little talk, he never expected to feel his heart torn apart by the confessions of a girl whose parents hadn't been able to show her how precious she was.

The backstory she'd concocted for the staff could only have come from a princess who'd been born with every advantage under the sun except love.

"Rest assured we need you right here, Tuccia." He leaned over to kiss her lips briefly, unable to help himself. But if she'd wanted to respond, he didn't give her the chance and stood up. "Stay where you are. You look too comfortable to move. I'll let myself out and see you in the morning with breakfast and more groceries."

After a detour to the kitchen for one of the pans of *cassateddi* to share with his friends, he left for the *castello* a different man than the one he'd been four hours ago.

On the drive home, Cesare pulled out his cell to call his mother. He was glad to hear that his sister was there visiting with her husband and baby. They all chatted for a few minutes until Isabella got off the line.

"Now we can talk about important matters, Cesare. I have to tell you Bertina is out of her mind with worry."

"Let her know I just came from being with Tuccia. She sends her love and wants to assure her *zia* all is well. She would phone, but knows the police have tapped the lines."

"I'm sure of it. Tuccia is really all right?"

"Would I tell you otherwise?"

"No, *figlio mio*. I trust you with my life."

"That's nice to hear. Does Bertina have any more news about the search?"

"The police are baffled. Their bungling has enraged her sister and brother-in-law. Bertina's sources tell her that Jean-Michel is so overcome he has remained incommunicado to the media. There's been no ransom note and they fear for her welfare."

"I have something to tell you, Mamma." In the next breath he told her about the letter being sent to Jean-Michel. "Once he receives it, everything will change."

"It can't get to him soon enough!"

"I agree." In the meantime Tuccia would hear the worst when she turned on her TV. "I hope Bertina is putting on the show of her life to prove how grief-stricken she is."

"If I didn't know the truth, I'd be convinced she's in the depths of despair. I've decided she could have been a great actress."

Superb acting appeared to run in the royal family. Tuccia's fashion show earlier this evening had stunned him close to speechless.

"One more thing you should know, Cesare. Bertina says Tuccia's parents are truly distraught over the situation and she can tell this experience has caused them to realize it's their fault that she's run away. They are beside themselves with worry and she senses a softening."

"That's wonderful news, Mamma." When he could, he'd relay that message to Tuccia. "Tell me about Ciro."

"If there are no more complications, he'll be taken to a private room tomorrow."

"We'll hope for the best. I have to hang up now, but I'll call you soon. *Bona notti*, Mamma."

It was ten after one in the afternoon and Tuccia still hadn't finished cooking this latest recipe. She let out a moan. "These *sfingi di San Giuseppe* balls are all wobbly. I can't make them even."

Cesare chuckled. Nothing seemed to bother him. The man had arrived early that morning in jeans and a silky claret-colored open-necked sport shirt looking devilishly gorgeous. There ought to be a law against it.

She hadn't slept all night remembering the taste of his mouth on hers. He wouldn't have kissed her if he didn't have feelings for her. It was the reason she'd been a mess after he'd left the apartment the night before. Since then she'd been reliving that moment and wanted to repeat the experience. But this time she wouldn't let him go.

"They're supposed to look like that."

"No, they're not! What am I doing wrong?"

"Nothing. When they're fried, their centers will hollow out so you can fill them."

She shot him a glance. "You promise?"

"I swear it. Have you put out the toweling?"

"It's right here on the counter next to the stove."

"Have you checked the temperature of the olive oil?"

"Yes. The thermometer says it's ready."

"Then get started. Remember not to let the ball plop, but don't be afraid of it."

Tuccia began the laborious process of cooking and draining. They smelled good and everything was going fine until the last one. It fell off the spoon too fast and some drops of oil splashed on her wrist. She cried out in surprise.

Cesare was there so fast he had her hand under the cold water before she could think. "Keep it there for a few minutes," he said while he removed the oil and turned off the burner.

"I tried to be careful, but I was clumsy."

"I defy anyone cooking with oil for the first time to escape with no burns."

While the water was still running he examined the three small welts on her skin. "These will hurt, but I have a remedy my mother used that works well."

She couldn't feel the pain, not while their bodies were so close and he was touching her. "Thank you," she said in a tremulous voice before lifting her head.

His eyes searched hers before his free hand caressed the side of her face. "I'm sorry you got burned," he whispered.

Tuccia felt his breath on her lips. Her heart felt like it was going to pump right out of her chest. Driven by her love for him, she pressed her mouth to his, daring to let him know she wanted more. "It's nothing," she whispered, then quickly turned to put her hand under the water once more.

He moved away from her. "I'll run to the *farmacia* and be right back." Cesare was out the door before she could think. It was just as well. If he'd stayed close to her a second longer, she would have made a complete fool of herself and thrown her arms around his neck.

She'd never known the white-hot heat of desire for a man until now. To experience its power for herself was life-changing. The few guys at college she'd flirted with in class had meant nothing more than a little experimentation that couldn't go anywhere.

Though she'd always planned to run away before she had to marry Jean-Michel, she never expected to find loving fulfillment with one man. Tuccia hadn't believed such a thing was possible. First she had to *find* the right man, and he had to find *her*.

But when she heard the door open and Cesare walked back in the apartment with a small sack in his hand, she knew beyond a shadow of a doubt she was looking at the right man. The *only* man for her. She felt it in the marrow of her bones.

Tuccia turned off the water and waited. He walked over to the counter and pulled from a shelf the bottle of honey she'd used in one of the recipes. Next, he opened the sack and drew out some gauze pads and a small box of plasters.

Without looking at her he covered the gauze with honey and said, "Put out your arm and we'll get rid of that pain."

Tuccia did his bidding. Within a minute he'd covered the three welts with the gooey gauze pads and secured them with a plaster. She marveled at his dexterity. "I had no idea honey could be used like this."

"It has dozens of restorative elements."

"Thank you, Cesare. I'm very lucky to have a boss who's a doctor, too."

He smiled a smile that sent her pulse off the charts. "You should be feeling relief soon."

"That's good because I need to poke a hole in those balls and fill them with the ricotta cream I've made."

Cesare darted her a glance. "All of it will keep. Before you do any more cooking, I thought we'd pick up lunch and have a picnic. It will give those burns a chance to settle down."

"A picnic? I'd love it! When I think about it, I haven't been on one of those since I was a little girl. My *zia* would take me to the park and we'd feed the birds. I'll grab the things I need and meet you at the car."

She dashed into the bedroom for her scarf. When she'd put it on, she slid her sunglasses in place and hurried out of the apartment. Cesare, the striking, quintessential Sicilian male, was there to help her in and they drove off.

For once in her life, what was happening to her wasn't a dream her mind had concocted while she'd been asleep. She was wide awake. This was real. Her feelings were real and she wanted to shout to the world that she was madly in love with him.

He stopped at a local deli for takeout and they headed toward Milan. Before long he turned onto the grounds of the Giardino Della Guastalla. "These gardens are five hundred years old," he explained. "I know the perfect spot where we can be alone. Maybe we'll be able to feed a few birds the remnants of our lunch. Do you mind sitting on the grass?"

"To be out in nature is exactly what this warm day calls for."

He parked and they walked to a lush spot beneath a giant oak tree. The freedom to be out here alone with Cesare made her giddy. After removing her sunglasses, she lay down in the grass on her stomach and rested her head against her arms.

"Careful of those burns," he said, sitting down next to her.

She squinted up at him. "Honestly? I forgot I was hurting. Your honey has worked miracles."

"I'm glad." Cesare opened up the cartons. She turned on her side and leaned on one elbow while they ate shrimps and pasta salad with little forks. He opened a bottle of red wine and poured it into cups. She drank some and munched on a French bread roll.

"I feel sinful lying here."

Blue eyes full of amusement roved over her. "Because you're with me instead of your former fiancé?"

"No." She smiled. "Because I'm with someone I care about to the exclusion of anyone else," she said before it was too late to stop her thoughts from becoming verbal.

He drank the rest of his wine. "Surely there've been some men you've liked who have tried to have a secret relationship with you?"

"I was always under surveillance, Cesare." She looked at him through veiled eyes. "As you know, there are different levels of liking without much emotional involvement. I liked some of the guys in my classes, but didn't have the freedom to do anything about it. But to actually care for someone means having the time to explore feelings that touch on the deeper elements of the human heart."

Realizing she'd said too much, Tuccia sat up and wound her arms around her upraised knees. "I'm afraid I've embarrassed you when I didn't mean to."

Cesare leaned closer. "Why would I be embarrassed to be paid a compliment like that?"

She put her sunglasses back on. "You always know the right thing to say, so I'll never see what's really going on inside you. But I'm thankful for this moment out of time to enjoy the company of a man revered by his mother and his friends. No men from my world can claim that distinction."

"Do you mind if I ask you a question about Jean-Michel?"

"Of course not."

"When your marriage was arranged, had you already met him?"

"No. My parents gave one of their many parties at our palazzo and insisted I attend. I was only sixteen and had refused to go because I couldn't bear to be around grownups. But this time my father came to my room carrying a long dress. He said he would wait while I put it on. It was humiliating to be walked from my apartment to the grand ballroom like I was a baby.

"He led me through their usual set of guests to my mother. She was standing next to a man twice my age I didn't recognize and didn't like on sight. He was shorter than my father and overdressed, reminding me of a peacock. I shrank from his dark eyes where the lids remain at half mast like some French men's.

"My father introduced me to Jean-Michel Ardois, the son of Comte Ardois of Paris. He wasn't Sicilian, another huge strike against him. The man kissed my hand and slid a ring with a crest on my finger. While I stood there in shock, my father announced our engagement."

Tuccia smiled at the man who'd become the center of her universe. "Aren't you sorry you asked?"

His expression had sobered. "I want to know everything about you. Where's the betrothal ring now?"

"I'm sure it has been returned to Jean-Michel. I left it on the floor of the ladies' room at the salon."

He studied her features. "How often did you have to spend time with him?"

"Twice a year I endured a visit from him at my parents' palazzo until my father enrolled me at the University of Paris. He said I would have to learn French in order to be the *comte*'s wife. Once my parents took an apartment there, I had to go to the ballet or the opera with him every few months. Several times we went horseback riding on the Ardois estate. Our desultory conversations were worse than waiting for a train that never seems to come."

Cesare drank more wine. "You're not only articulate, you paint haunting pictures. Tell me more."

It was wonderful being able to open her thoughts and heart to him. "The first time we went out alone, I made up my mind I would run away before the marriage on my twenty-fifth birthday. If I could have disappeared the night of the betrothal, I would have. But I was never left alone until that morning at the salon for my dress fitting,"

"Literally never?" He sounded incredulous.

"Never. My parents accused me of being a willful child and didn't trust me. Someone was always watching me, even when I stayed with Zia Bertina."

A strange sound came out of him. "Did he ever try to take advantage of you?"

"Yes. I was so disgusted I slapped his face hard and pushed him off me. It left a red mark that probably branded him for several hours."

"Did he try to accost you every time you were together?"

She could tell Cesare's dislike for Jean-Michel was growing more intense. "No. I don't think he dared for fear I'd do something worse. Instead he bided his time until he had legal power over me. *Grazie a Dio* that never happened."

On that note she got to her feet and put the cartons back in the bag with the rest of the wine. To her surprise he stood up and put his arms around her from behind. "I thank God it didn't happen to you, either." He kissed her neck.

Tuccia could have died of happiness right there, but a group of people were walking by. Cesare had seen them, too, because he let go of her.

"We—we need to get going so I can finish the *sfingi* and start the *testa di turco*," she stammered. Before he could say anything else she added, "My arm is so much better I can hardly believe it, so you don't have to worry that I can't work anymore today, Dr. Donati."

His quiet laughter hid whatever he was really thinking. Together they walked to the car. He gave her arm a squeeze before helping her get in. She'd wanted him to crush her against him and tell her he was in love with her, too.

Unfortunately this interlude was over, but it was yet another one with him she'd always treasure. The memories were stacking up and her love for him was exploding.

# CHAPTER SEVEN

WHEN THE LAST batch of *testa di turcos* were finished and decorated, Cesare proclaimed them perfect and announced he was leaving. One more day tomorrow to guide Tuccia through two more recipes and then this private time with her was over.

He would no longer have a legitimate reason to come to the *pensione*. From that point on their business would have to be conducted at the *castello* kitchen. A limo could take her back and forth. After today he realized he couldn't afford to be in such close quarters with her. Her burns had given him a reason to touch her, something he should never have done.

To see her lying there in the grass while he wanted to get down there with her and kiss them into oblivion had almost killed him. Another time like that and he'd have to act on his desire. If those people hadn't walked by while he was kissing her neck, he would have pulled her back down and shown her how he felt.

But he'd picked up enough on hearing her talk about her life with her parents to realize how lonely, how empty her life had been. Being forced to think about marriage at the age of sixteen *was* criminal, as his mother had said. Cesare refused to be the man who came along at the most vulnerable time in her life and took away her chance to be emotionally free.

Today at the park he *knew* she wanted him. But she deserved marriage. That was the only way Cesare would make love to her. She would have to be his legal wife, but the situation with Jean-Michel wasn't yet resolved. And deep down inside, he didn't feel worthy of her.

"Cesare?" His head jerked around. "I guess you didn't hear me. Who is the person who prints the menus for the guests? How far ahead do I have to get the names of the desserts to that person?"

"Don't worry about that yet. Gemma's pastries will be served until next Monday." He was impressed she'd been thinking that far ahead.

Tuccia bit her lip. "What about the ingredients that come to the kitchen from town? Am I in charge of ordering them, or do I coordinate with Maurice? There's so much I don't know."

"How could you have learned everything in a few days?" Her ability to consider all the ramifications of her new job astounded him. "I'll be there to answer your questions.

"Right now we're concentrating on your feeling good about the half-dozen desserts you're mastering. That way you'll have confidence talking to your assistants and giving them instructions on how to prepare what you've planned. I promise things will fall into place. Now I have to leave."

She walked him to the door. "I can't tell you how nice it was to eat at the park this afternoon. If you're tired of my thanking you, then you'll just have to get used to it."

"That works both ways. You're helping me so I don't have to go back to doing a chef's job I gave up a long time ago. We're even."

Tuccia shook her head. "No, we're not." She clung to the open door. "How long were you a chef?"

"From the moment I arrived in New York. The pay put me through part of college. I took out a loan to buy a small restaurant that was going under and called it Mamma's. People love Sicilian food and pretty soon I'd made enough money to buy another restaurant."

She let out a sigh. "And history was made. It explains why you're such an expert teacher. Your mother must have been so proud of you to leave Sicily and put your stamp on the world. *I'm* proud of you, Cesare. Does your father have any idea what an outstanding son he has?"

No one had ever asked him that. Her sweetness was getting to him. He rubbed the back of his neck. "I don't even know if he's alive. When he left my mother, she never saw or heard from him again."

"What a tragedy for him. Your father missed out on the whole point of life. I'd love to meet him and tell him what a fantastic son he has."

Cesare cleared his throat. "I thought the same thing about your parents when you told me about your emptiness."

A shadow crossed over her stunning features. "Forget me."

That would be impossible.

*Donati. If you stay here talking to her any longer, you're a fool.*

"I spoke with my mother earlier. She said your parents are genuinely upset over your disappearance. I was glad to hear it. Bertina sees a fissure in the ice where they are concerned. I just thought you should know."

Her eyes clouded over. "That's pretty hard to believe."

"I don't think she would have said anything if she didn't think it were true." He kissed her temple. "See you in the morning. I'll make breakfast when I get here. Same time?"

She nodded, causing her black curls to shimmer. He longed to plunge his fingers into that silky mass and devour her.

Without lingering any longer, he walked out to the car and drove away without looking back. Needing a distraction, he turned on the radio and found a twenty-four-hour news station. But he didn't hear anything about her case until he'd pulled into the parking area of his favorite sports bar in the village.

That's when he learned that Interpol was now involved to coordinate police cooperation throughout Europe in order to find the princess.

After shutting off the engine, he went inside and ordered, a pale lager from a Lombardi brewery both he and Takis enjoyed. While he waited for the waiter to bring some appetizers, he phoned Vincenzo. His friend wouldn't be taking Gemma to their home in Lake Como until next week. Cesare needed some advice and no one had a better head.

He reached Vincenzo's voice mail and asked him to call him when he could. Once he'd finished his lager, he headed for the *castello* and let himself in his private office off the lobby. While he did some work on the computer that had been piling up, his friend returned the call and Cesare talked to him about Tuccia's disappearance.

"Tonight I heard that Interpol is now involved. It's getting ugly. Tuccia has sent Jean-Michel a letter of apology. He should be getting it soon. But part of me wants to urge her to get in touch with him right away and settle this thing quietly with him and her parents. The press could then be informed that she's safe and they've called off their marriage."

A long silence ensued. "In a perfect world, Cesare. But I was born in her *imperfect* one. She's done something uncommonly courageous. It's just my opinion, but I think she needs to see it through on her own inspiration, come what may. That's what *I* did with no regrets."

It was the "come what may" part that made Cesare shudder. He couldn't ignore what she'd told him at the park about her caged life, but he valued Vincenzo's judgment. "Thanks for listening. I appreciate it."

"We've been through a lot together, *amico*. Are you going to be all right?"

"I'll have to be, won't I."

He hung up. There'd be little sleep for him tonight. Instead of going up to his room, he began printing off copies of the recipes she'd been following under his supervision. When the time came, she would have to hand them to her assistants.

Dozens of other tasks needed to be taken care of. Why not now while adrenaline surged through his veins over the cruelty Tuccia had endured this far in her life. She'd been robbed of a normal existence. If he didn't have responsibilities, he'd disappear with her to some hidden spot on the other side of the globe and love her without worrying about anything else.

This morning Tuccia had got up at five-thirty to finish her surprise for Cesare and make some rolls. She'd started their breakfast before she'd gone to bed and hoped he'd love it. He'd done so much for her that she wanted to do this small thing to repay him. Today would be their last for working together alone.

In the past when she'd gone out on the royal yacht with her parents and their friends in the summer, one of the aspects she looked forward to was the Sicilian breakfast served on board. Curious to know how *granita* was made, she'd prevailed on the cook to show her.

When the mixture of sugar, water and almond paste was melted, then frozen, stirred, mashed, frozen, stirred, mashed and frozen many times until it came out looking like snow, it was served in a goblet. Eaten with a yeast brioche, it tasted like heaven. The cook also made fruit *granitas* topped with whipping cream, but she'd preferred the almond and dipped her roll in it.

From the window over the sink she saw Cesare arrive. It was ten to eight. He was early! Every time he came to the apartment, excitement exploded inside her. Thank goodness she'd set the table ahead of time and had made coffee. She'd even designed a menu for him, describing what he would be eating. She folded and propped it where his plate would go.

Though she wanted to fling the door open and run into his arms, she steeled herself to wait until he knocked before answering the door. The second he walked in wearing a dark blue polo shirt and white trousers, he paused. His gaze zeroed in on her.

"Something smells wonderful."

Somebody *looked* wonderful.

"I'm glad. Welcome to Tuccia's, Signor Donati!" She made a sweep with the arm that had fresh honey gauze pads taped over her burns. They wouldn't be necessary after today. "If you'll come in and find a seat, I'll be your server."

She watched him walk in the kitchen and sit down to examine the menu. His head reared. He stared at her with a stunned expression. *"Granita di mandorle?"*

*"Si, signor."*

Delighted with his reaction, she rushed to pour their coffee. She'd already put sugar on the table because he liked a lot of it. Then she pulled two filled snifters out of the small freezer compartment. After putting them on a plate with a warm roll, she set them on the table and sat down.

Tuccia had already tasted it and knew it was good. Not as good as the cook on the yacht had made it, but she was proud of it. Out of the corner of her eye she watched Cesare take his first few bites, wishing he were her husband so they could do this every morning.

Pretty soon he was dipping his roll into the concoction the way she always did. Halfway through his meal, he ran out of roll and reached for her hand across the table.

"You told me you didn't know how to cook anything except to make instant coffee and tea in the microwave."

"I forgot about this. I love it so much I begged the cook on my parents' yacht to teach me how."

He released her fingers. "It's superb...just the right taste and consistency. You must have been up all night."

"I wanted to treat *you* for a change. It was worth it."

He seemed taken back. "My mother's version isn't as good as this one. We're going to be serving your rendition for one of our nightly desserts starting next week."

She moaned. "It's so much work!"

His deep laughter filled the kitchen. "That's what the assistants are for. I have a gut feeling our fame for fine Sicilian cuisine is going to spread and we'll be inundated with too many would-be guests to accommodate."

He got up from the table and brought back a plate with more rolls. Having finished off the flavored ice, he devoured the rest of them in no time at all. "These are delicious by the way. You're such a fast learner it's breathtaking. I'm convinced you could do anything at all if you put your mind to it."

"I think you're flattering me into giving you another serving of *granita*. I made enough if you want more now."

"I'll definitely want some later." He sat back in the chair. "Tell me. Would you rather lie down for the rest of the morning and catch up on some much-needed sleep? Later on this afternoon I'll come back and we'll work on the chocolate torte. Once you've made it, we won't have to worry about your cooking anything new for a few days."

"I'd rather do it now if you don't mind. Then I'll be able to relax enough to face tomorrow."

"So be it. Let's get started. I'll clear the table while you find your bible."

"It's on the shelf." She got up to reach for it and saw Cesare put the menu in his trouser pocket. If that meant what she hoped it meant, all the hard work and loss of sleep had been worth it.

Later, while she was icing her next five-layer creation, Cesare's cell phone rang. She kept working while he walked in the living room. He didn't come back to the kitchen for at least fifteen minutes. She couldn't read his expression.

"Is everything all right?"

He lounged against the wall with his hands in his pockets. "Ciro took a turn for the worse during the night and has ended back up in the ICU."

"His heart?"

"Yes."

"How sad." She waited to hear more. "What else is wrong? I know it's something serious."

"I'd rather not have to tell you this, but you have the right to know."

"What is it?" Her voice shook.

"My mother had just arrived at Bertina's palazzo to prepare meals this morning when the police showed up without notice and took her to police headquarters for further questioning."

Tuccia put a hand to her mouth.

"Mamma returned to the villa to phone me. The police know that Bertina is the person you've always turned to and that she was the one who chartered the jet for you. Naturally they believe she knows where you are hiding."

"Of course."

"Just remember your aunt is a strong woman who loves you very much. She says your parents have softened a great deal and went to the station with her to lend their support."

"You're kidding—"

"No. I really do think they are suffering over what they did to you. Mamma and I agree she'll be able to handle an interrogation. The police don't have evidence of any kind. Bertina doesn't know where you are, only that you're safe. The police won't be able to hold her."

"The situation is growing unbearable. I could end all the pain for Bertina by just going home."

In the next breath Cesare walked over and put his hands on her shoulders. He looked into her eyes. "That's not going to be necessary. Once Jean-Michel gets your letter, he'll tell the police and the princess hunt will be over. But if you feel strongly about this, I'll fly you to Palermo today to see your aunt."

"I know you would, but I couldn't let you down now."

"Forget about me."

"You're too wonderful to be real." She buried her face in her hands. "I wish I knew what to do. I don't want my *zia* to suffer, but I've made a commitment to you. Hearing the bad news about Ciro only makes things worse."

Cesare pulled her against him and wrapped his arms around her. "I have an idea that will make the most sense. Let's wait another day until I hear from my mother. Hopefully your fiancé will have gotten your letter. Nothing may be as bad as you're imagining."

His tenderness was too much. Tuccia broke down sobbing quietly against his chest, unable to stop. "Forgive me for soaking your shirt. I'm a disaster and you shouldn't have to put up with me for another second."

"What if I want to."

When she tried to pull away, he lowered his head and started kissing her wet face until his mouth covered hers. It all happened so naturally that her lips opened. In another second she experienced the full intensity of a kiss that thrilled her to the very depths of her being.

"Cesare—" she cried, so completely besotted she started kissing him back with a passion she didn't know herself capable of. For this fabulous man to be loving her like this brought a rush of joy to her heart she could hardly contain.

"Forgive me if I've been needing this," he whispered in a shaken voice. "You have no idea how you've affected me. Tuccia—" He drew her so close there was no air between them. "Tell me to stop."

"I can't. I want you to go on kissing me and never stop." Once again they were devouring each other. The more she clung to him, the more she realized she'd never be able to appease this growing hunger for him. He'd come into her life and changed it forever.

She wanted him with her whole heart and soul, but if he was only kissing her in order to comfort her, then she had to do something to turn this around. All he needed now was to have to worry about being stuck with a fugitive who was desperate for love and attention and had begged him to let her remain here and work for him.

It was up to her to see this for what it was and not get carried away. Deep down she was fearful he saw her in that light. How could he not? She broke their kiss and wheeled out of his arms. It took all her strength to turn and face him head-on, knowing her cheeks were flushed and her lips swollen.

Tuccia had to prove that he could count on her. "I—I'm afraid we both got carried away," she stammered. "You're a very attractive man. I'm shocked you're not married yet. Any woman could lose her head with you. I'm no exception. I've thought about what you said. It would be best to give the situation another twenty-four hours before I make any kind of decision that could impact both of us."

"I was hoping you'd say that."

She could believe it. The man was depending on her to keep her head at this point. Needing to stay busy, she cut a piece of torte and handed it to him on a plate with a fork. "Try this and tell me what you think."

*Please just do it, Cesare.*

He did her bidding, eating half of it before putting the plate on the table. "You pass with flying colors, Tuccia."

"It was your recipe." Relief swamped her. "You don't think I need to make it again right now to improve it?"

"No." His eyes had narrowed on her mouth. Her heart felt like it was running away with her. "The torte is exquisite."

"Then do you mind if I lie down for a little while?"

One brow lifted. "I was about to suggest it. You need sleep. I'll come by at five with a meal and we'll talk over what's going to happen tomorrow."

"Thank you for understanding." She took a quick breath. "Thank you for everything."

"Try not to worry too much, Tuccia."

"That would be impossible."

He looked like he was going to say something, then thought the better of it. The moment he walked out of the apartment, she locked the door, then ran to the bedroom and flung herself on the bed in agony. After fleeing from a man she'd despised, she'd run straight into a man she adored.

Tuccia wondered if she dared tell him exactly what she felt, that she loved him and wanted to be his wife. Maybe that was what she would do the next time they were together. No more holding back.

At ten to five, Cesare, showered, shaved, and wearing a tan summer suit, walked in the *castello* kitchen. He nodded to Maurice before packing a bag of *fettuccini Alfredo* with chicken to go. Nothing else was needed. Tuccia had cooked rolls and cake that morning. There was still a half bottle of Chardonnay waiting to be enjoyed with another snifter of her fabulous *granita*.

Princess Tuccianna was so full of surprises he decided there wasn't anything she couldn't do. One taste of her mouth and he knew he wanted to go on tasting it for the rest of his life. When she'd surrendered herself to him, he'd experienced ecstasy like nothing he'd ever known and had come close to having a heart attack.

He'd sensed he was in deep water the first night he'd caught her in his arms in his mother's kitchen. But since then his feelings for her had escalated to such a degree his life had been irrevocably changed.

She was in his heart, in his blood, but that wasn't enough. Cesare wanted her in his life day and night. He wanted her in his bed. He wanted babies with her.

He wanted everything that he'd feared would never happen because he hadn't believed love would come to him.

Yet now that he'd found this extraordinary woman, he feared it was too soon to tie her down with his own needs. For years her parents had exerted too much pressure on her to conform to their demands, and she'd run away.

After the ecstasy of their kiss, Cesare wanted to marry her and never let her go. But Cesare sensed that would be the wrong thing to do. She needed time to develop her sense of self first.

The greatest gift he could give her would be to hold back and allow her to become the incredible person he knew her to be. As long as she worked for him, he could keep her close to him until the time came when he had to tell her how he felt.

On his way out of the kitchen he walked over to Gemma who was setting up for the evening crowd. It was a good thing tonight would be her last night as pastry cook. Her baby would be coming before long. She needed rest.

"Tuccia and I will be here at nine in the morning."

"I'll be watching for you. Is she nervous?"

"She doesn't show it."

Gemma smiled at him. "What about you, Cesare?"

"I know she's going to be fine."

"With you helping her, she couldn't possibly go wrong."

If Gemma had seen him kissing Tuccia earlier as if his life depended on it—which it did—she would probably have told him to slow down. He kissed Gemma's cheek and left the *castello* for his car.

On the way down to the village he turned on the five o'clock news. Following the latest world events he learned there'd been a break in the case involving Princess Tuccianna's disappearance. But the police weren't revealing the details yet. That had to mean the letter had reached Jean-Michel.

Pleased by the new development, he turned it off and pulled up in front of the *pensione*. Tuccia must have seen him arrive because she opened the door for him, appearing to have gotten some rest.

This evening she wore the same print blouse and pants from a few nights ago. Her wardrobe didn't consist of more than three or four changes of clothes. The apartment's washer and dryer had been a necessity, but he intended to rectify the situation and take her shopping.

She eyed the bag he carried. "More goodies?"

"Maurice's version of *fettuccini*."

"I can't wait to try it. Then I can compliment him on it tomorrow. Come in." Tuccia closed the door and followed him into the kitchen. She'd cleaned it spotless and had set the table. The TV was on in the living room. "I've been listening to the news."

"So have I," he stated and reached for some plates to serve their dinner. "We both know what that new development in your case means. By now Jean-Michel will have called off the search. Within the next few hours he'll make some kind of statement to the press. In the meantime I'm sure your aunt is going to be fine, otherwise I would have heard from my mother by now."

"I pray you're right."

"Even so, the letter provides proof that you're alive.

Therefore your family will have to hire private detectives to look for you if they are still intent on finding you. According to Bertina, they're hoping you'll come home because they love you. So I'd say tonight is a time for celebration!"

He reached for the Chardonnay and poured it into glasses before putting them on the table. "Where are your delicious rolls?"

"There were four left. I put them in the microwave and will warm them up."

When they finally sat down at the table, he raised his wine glass. "Before we eat, I'd like to make a toast." Her gray eyes sparkled as she lifted hers. "To the princess who overnight has turned into a pastry cook *par excellence*."

"I'm going to try." They touched glasses and sipped their wine. "Now I'd like to make one." She raised her glass again, staring straight into his eyes. "To her teacher, a man who is without equal."

Cesare wished it were true.

Everything she said and did had such impact he didn't know where to go with his feelings without betraying them. But he'd made himself a promise to keep things professional for a while longer. She, too, was behaving as if their soul-destroying kiss that morning had changed nothing.

*But they both knew that it had.*

All he could do was clink her glass and drink more wine.

"Hmm," she said after tasting the *fettuccini*. "This is exceptional. I can see why Maurice was hired."

"We've been very happy with him." Cesare ate another of her rolls. "It's a balmy night out. After we finish dinner, would you like to go for a drive while we talk about tomorrow?"

"You must be reading my mind. I was afraid to ask."

She'd probably be shocked if she knew what was going through his. He'd rather take her in the other room and dance with her. Unfortunately if he did that, they would end up in the bedroom and not come back out for days. So much for him following his own advice to put those thoughts out of his mind.

He took a deep breath. "I thought I'd show you around the *castello* estate to get you acquainted. You'll enjoy seeing the swans on the lake."

"Ooh. How beautiful."

"It's quite a sight on a moonlit night, though the moon won't be out for several hours. When we return, I'll finish off the *granita* and another slice of torte."

After they finished eating and had cleared the table, they walked outside and took off in the car. Tuccia turned to him in her seat. "I've wanted to see the fortress up close. It has such a rich history. I can hardly believe that Vincenzo's family home has been turned into a hotel and restaurant."

"Vincenzo's father and uncle squandered everything and the estate was seized by the government to be sold to the highest bidder. Vincenzo asked me and Takis if we wanted to pool our assets and buy it with him."

"When was this?"

"The three of us were in New York at the time. He had the idea to turn it into the business proposition it is today. That way he could preserve his family legacy and do something honorable for the region. I thought it a fantastic idea. So did Takis."

"Bravo for Vincenzo," she exclaimed. "I can understand that happening in a family as power-hungry as his. It's the only reason my parents made sure early in my life that they would have a son-in-law with a fortune. That would be their insurance to keep them living their lavish lifestyle to the end of their days."

Her words caused Cesare's stomach muscles to clench. He drove them to the summit and took the road that wound behind the *castello*.

"This place is massive."

"You're right."

Two sets of guests from the hotel were out walking. He drove the car past them until they reached the lake much further away. She rolled down her window. "It's so lovely and peaceful, but I don't see any swans."

"They're probably hiding in the rushes, but they'll come out." Cesare turned off the engine and turned toward her. "Tomorrow will be here before you know it. Gemma is ready to ease many of your concerns. But I'd like to know what is worrying you most and relieve you if I can."

Tuccia shook her head. "Do you know what I wish? That I could have been a normal person you'd hired at one of your restaurants in New York. Think how much I could have learned from you."

He had news for her. If she'd come into his life back then, they'd be married by now. He wouldn't have hesitated asking her. "Instead you're learning to be a pastry chef here."

"But it isn't fair to you," her voice cracked.

*"Tuccia..."*

"It's true. You're playing a dangerous game in order to protect me, Cesare. I honestly don't know what Jean-Michel would do if he caught up to you."

Cesare smiled. "I'm afraid you should be worried what I'd do to him if I had the opportunity."

"You don't mean that."

"Try me. What can he do except rage?"

"I suppose you're right."

"All I know is, your mother should never have asked you to help me."

He slid his arm along the back of the seat. "Aside from the fact that I met you at her house in the middle of the night, she didn't have anything to do with my decision to fly you here."

She stirred in the seat. "How can you say that?"

"Because I've had to live with Vincenzo and Gemma's story for many years. The night my mother told me about *your* situation, the horror of their history came back to haunt me. For you to be forced to undergo a betrothal at your age was not only feudal, it was criminal."

"Zia Bertina said the same thing many times. That's why she agreed to help me escape. I'll love her forever for what she did for me."

"The emotional damage to you was as bad as anything physical," Cesare spoke his mind. "When Mamma asked if I would help you leave Palermo, I didn't have to think about it and was determined to help you any way I could. That hasn't changed for me. Does that answer your question?"

Once more she hid her face in her hands, but she nodded.

He ruffled one of her curls with his fingers. "You

said you wished you were a normal girl I'd hired to work in one of my restaurants in New York. In truth it's exactly what I've done, but this restaurant happens to be in Milan. Shall we put all the angst of the past aside and concentrate on tomorrow? You're my new pastry chef who's going to be running the show."

She finally lifted her head. "I intend to make you proud. Maybe you should take me back to the apartment. I rested a little today, but I didn't sleep. If I go to bed now, I'll be in much better shape by morning. Another time I'll come out here and watch for the swans."

Tuccia's resilience was something to behold.

"There'll be many opportunities." Cesare started the engine and he drove them back to the *pensione.* When they arrived, he walked her to the door.

*Don't touch her, Donati.*

If he made that mistake, he would never leave her apartment. "I'll be by for you at eight. We'll have a working breakfast with Gemma."

"I'll be ready. Thank you for the dinner and the tour, Cesare. *Dormi bene.*"

"*E tu.*"

Giving in to unassuaged longings, he pulled her in his arms, kissing her long and hard.

He walked back to his car aware of a new fear attacking him. How would he handle it if he asked her to marry him and she turned him down?

# CHAPTER EIGHT

CESARE WOULD BE by for her in a few minutes. Tuccia stood in front of the bathroom mirror in full chef regalia. She peered through her glasses. No lipstick. Not a hair in sight. No perfume, either. Gemma had told her not to wear any, but she could use a non-scented lotion.

"This is your big day. If you're recognized by someone on the kitchen staff, then it's all over. Until then you're going to do whatever it takes to prove worthy of Cesare's faith in you."

Last night he'd pulled her in his arms and kissed her as she'd hoped. Now she was longing for the day when that happened again. Tuccia had felt his touch in every fiber of her being. She'd ached for him until she was afraid she'd never get to sleep. To her relief a miracle did happen, but only because she'd been up most of the night before.

She walked through the apartment to gather her purse and bible. This place had become her home. Hers and Cesare's. She'd never known such happiness. While she stood looking out the window, she saw his car pull up. Would her heart always palpitate with a frenzy when he came near?

Not wanting to keep him waiting, she walked out-side and climbed in before he could help her. His eyes were alive as they wandered from her floppy hat and down her body clothed in white to the sensible walk-ing shoes she'd drawn out of her suitcase. She could tell he was thinking about what she really looked like under her disguise and it sent her pulse racing.

"*Bon jornu,* Signor Donati," she said in Sicilian.

"Chef Bottaro. I've been searching a long time for you." The way he'd said it in such a husky tone gave her hope that he was letting her know he loved her. With a smile, he started the car and they took off. "There are many things I want to discuss with you, not the least of which is how you're feeling this morning."

"Like I've climbed to the top of Mount Pellegrino. There's no going back and I'm looking down at a roil-ing ocean, terrified to make my first jump."

Something flickered in the depths of his eyes, in-triguing her. "You sound like you've done that sort of thing before."

She nodded. "When I was a lot younger and hadn't been put on as tight a leash."

His mouth tightened. "I used to climb that cliff regularly before I left for New York."

"All those ships going out to sea," she mused. "Lucky you that you could leave and fulfill your des-tiny."

They'd reached the summit, but this time he took another road leading around the back of the *castello* where she saw a sign that said "Staff Parking Only." He pulled to a stop and shut off the engine. Turning to her, he clasped her hand and entwined his fingers with hers.

"In case you didn't realize it yet, today you're about to fulfill yours." He leaned closer. "This is for luck, even if you don't need it." To her surprise he gave her a long hungry kiss on the lips that sent a surge of warmth through her body.

She started to kiss him back, but he eased away too soon, leaving her bereft. Then he levered himself from the driver's seat. After coming around to help her out, Cesare used a remote to let them in the rear entrance and walked her down a hall with several offices. He knocked on the last door. "Gemma?"

"Oh, good. You're here!" She opened it. But the second she saw Tuccia, she let out a small gasp. "Am I having a hallucination, or is it really you?"

Cesare gave Gemma a hug. "Allow me to introduce Nedda Bottaro, the new Sicilian executive pastry chef who's going to set a trend."

"I'll say you are." Gemma in turn gave Tuccia a hug. "I would never have known you," she whispered. "You look more sensational than Maurice, who's always immaculately turned out in the latest *haute couture* style for the well-dressed chef. When he sees you, he'll be speechless."

"Is that good or bad?"

"Definitely good after he finds his voice. Come in the office which is now going to be yours and have some breakfast I had brought in. Then we'll all go to the kitchen and I'll introduce you to everyone."

They sat down to eat and talk. Later, as Gemma was showing her what she kept in the desk drawers, Vincenzo unexpectedly appeared at the door. "Excuse me for interrupting, *cara*, but I knew you would all want to see this morning's headlines. The police have called off the search for you, Tuccia."

She almost fainted from the news. So Cesare had been right. The letter had reached Jean-Michel.

Vincenzo thrust the newspaper in her hands, but in her dazed state, she turned to Cesare. "You're the reason this has happened so fast. I'm almost afraid to believe it. Will you please read what it says?"

"If that's what you want." He put down his coffee cup. "*Sicilian Princess No Longer Missing* is the headline. Le Comte Jean-Michel Ardois of Paris has released the following information to the press: 'Princess Tuccianna Falcone Leonardi, daughter of the Marchese and Machesa di Trabia of Sicily, has sent him a letter offering her deepest apologies for having disappeared the day before their marriage and causing grief to him and his family. In her letter to the *comte*, she says that throughout their betrothal, it became clear that they weren't suited for each other. She thought about it for a long time and was convinced that they both needed to find someone else in order to be fulfilled. At the last minute she decided she had to run away to spare both of them a lifetime of unhappiness because the only reason two people marry should be for love.'"

Tuccia heard a nuance in Cesare's voice that told her he was touched by her words.

"She lives in hope he'll forgive her and that one day soon he'll find a wonderful woman deserving of his love. The princess wishes him the very best in the future and hopes that in time she too will find happiness for herself."

He broke off talking. The room had gone quiet.

At this point Cesare's gaze flicked to hers. Emotion had darkened his eyes to a deep blue color. If he but knew it, Tuccia had already found her happiness. The most wonderful man on earth stood just a few feet away from her.

Vincenzo took the newspaper from him and finished reading the article, but he too sounded emotionally affected as he read the rest. "'Her parents, the Marchese and Marchesa di Trabia, have told the press they won't give up searching for their beloved daughter. She's their only child and they're praying she's safe and will want to come home soon.'"

Tuccia lowered her head. "It's hard to believe my parents would say those words. Up to now they've thought of me as the willful, unrepentant daughter who deserves to be punished. But if Cesare's mother is to be believed, my *zia* says they are sorry for what has happened. I hardly know what to think."

"Let's be thankful you've accomplished the most important thing," Cesare murmured, sounding more subdued than she'd ever heard him. "The *comte* isn't going to come looking for you now."

She lifted her head. "You're right. It would be too humiliating for him. I really do wish him well. But it's not so easy to forgive my parents."

Vincenzo wore a sober expression. "I relate to your feelings completely, Tuccianna. That's why you'll continue to work here in that disguise and we'll do everything possible to protect you until you know it's safe."

She got up from the chair. "Thank you so much," she whispered. Tuccia needed time to comprehend all this news.

Vincenzo smiled. "I defy anyone to know it's you hiding under all that white."

"When I look in the mirror, I surprise myself," she quipped. "Thanks again to all of you for helping me. I owe you a debt of gratitude I'll never be able to repay in this life."

She looked at Gemma. "If you don't mind, I'm so keyed up with this being my first day I'd like to meet the kitchen staff and get this part of it over with."

Gemma chuckled. "It'll be my pleasure. Let's go."

Tuccia stepped past Cesare. The four of them left the office and walked down another hall to the huge, state-of-the-art kitchen filled with a dozen assistants in aprons and beanies.

Her heart almost failed her to think she was going to be the pastry chef here. At the far end she saw a man in a tall chef's hat who was busy talking to Takis. Everyone was here. Her big day had arrived.

*Help.*

"Come on," Gemma urged. "I'll introduce you to the head man first."

Tuccia followed her.

"Maurice Troudeau? I'd like you to meet my replacement, Nedda Bottaro."

The middle-aged French chef gave Tuccia a blank stare. Obviously he didn't know what to make of her.

She took the initiative. In her heaviest Sicilian accent she said, "It's my honor to meet you, Signor. Thanks to Signor Donati, last evening I was treated to your *fettuccini Alfredo*, which I confess is the best I have ever eaten. I'm sure the herb you put in it is a secret I would never ask you to reveal.

"But I can tell you it's just one of the reasons your

reputation has spread all the way to the tip of Sicily where I come from. They think they make the best *fettuccini Alfredo*. Not true." She swiped the backs of her fingers under her chin in a typical gesture of her Palermitan heritage to make her point.

The Frenchman eyed Gemma. "So you brought us a real *Siciliana*."

"To our delight, Cesare found her."

Tuccia spoke up. "It's a great honor for me. I know I'm going to need your help if you're willing, Signor Troudeau."

His gaze swerved back to her. "You can call me Maurice."

She was excited to have made that tiny breakthrough. "*Grazie*, Maurice. Please forgive the interruption when I know you are so busy. I, too, must get myself organized."

Opening her arms, she put her palms out in front, a Sicilian gesture to indicate there was much to do. When she turned, she almost walked into Cesare.

He'd seen her gestures and his blue eyes twinkled as if to say she was doing everything right.

By now Gemma had asked the pastry assistants to assemble around them. One by one Tuccia was introduced to the six of them. Three men and three women from Spain, Crete, France and Italy. After she'd chatted with each of them for a few minutes about their backgrounds and experience, she got down to the crux of what she'd planned to say ahead of time.

"Call me Nedda. We're going to be making Sicilian desserts from my part of the world. Such a change from the delectable Florentine desserts created by Signora Gagliardi. Everything will be different at first, but she says you are all experts so I'm happy to be working with you. Some day I'll tell you my story, but not this morning.

"Don't be afraid to ask me any questions you want. Signor Donati says we should work together like one happy family. I agree. Of course there will be little squabbles from time to time, but that it is to be expected. *Si?*"

*"Si!"* they said in a collective voice.

"He's going to give you the recipes we'll be making for the next few weeks. I'd like you to study them. *Pignolata, cassata, biancomangiare, cannoli*—so many you'll be counting them in your sleep like the proverbial sheep." Except that she hadn't made them yet and had a lot of homework to do first. Cesare had printed them out for her.

Everyone laughed.

"Tomorrow we will begin." She nodded to Cesare. "Go ahead, *signor*, while I get acquainted with this kitchen. I don't like working in such a large space and will probably want to move some things around."

Vincenzo and Takis talked with Cesare for a few minutes, then left.

While Gemma gave Tuccia a two-hour tour of her new world, she felt Cesare's gaze on her the entire time. Eventually the three of them ended back up in the office.

A tired-looking Gemma smiled at her. "I never saw anything so amazing in my life as the way you made the kitchen your own. When you rattled off all those desserts, you sounded as if you'd been making them all your life." Ha!

"I've eaten them all my life, if that counts," Tuccia interjected with a smile.

"Maurice is so dazzled by the Siciliana I don't think he'll ever be the same again."

"Neither will the assistants," Cesare stated. "Everyone was mesmerized beyond their ability to talk, including me. What do you say I drive you back to the *pensione*, and we'll let Gemma have her freedom."

"Of course," Tuccia exclaimed. "I can't thank you enough, but I know you need to rest."

"I'll admit I can't wait to go upstairs and lie down. But I also have to admit I'm envious of the experience you're about to have, Tuccia. With Cesare's help you really are going to turn into an outstanding chef. I just hope you won't have to leave us prematurely."

"That's the last thing I want."

"Amen," Cesare murmured. "Shall we go?"

After thanking Gemma and giving her a hug, they walked out to the car and left for the village. Tuccia felt Cesare's gaze on her. "You're very quiet all of a sudden. You must be as hungry as I am. It's after three."

"That's not it. I was thinking about the latest news. Jean-Michel will probably demand recompense from my parents for his pain. And how do I know if my parents really are sorry?"

"Time will tell. But that isn't all you need to be worried about." He'd pulled up in front of the deli.

Her head jerked around. "What do you mean?"

"You're going to have to watch out for Mario and Manoussos, the two assistants who aren't married yet. Both seem to be besotted by you."

"That's ridiculous."

"I overhead them talking in the pantry about who was going to bed the *squisita* Siciliana first."

She scoffed. "You made that up."

"I wish I had. Little do they know they'll never be able to get you alone, not when I bring you to the *castello* every morning, and take you home every night."

Tuccia loved the possessive ring she'd detected in his voice.

"Even though there are strict rules about the staff having relationships, they'll try everything in their power to persuade you to go out for lunch with them. After one success, they won't stop."

"Cesare—I don't pl—"

"I know what I'm talking about," he cut her off, "because the types in my restaurants in New York are no different when it comes to a beautiful woman. Don't say you weren't warned." He reached for the door handle. "I'll be right back."

He actually sounded upset, but that was because he felt totally responsible for her safety at this point. That meant physically and other ways, too. They'd shared a moment of intense passion, but to her chagrin she knew Cesare would never take advantage of her. Furthermore he wouldn't allow anyone else to, either.

If he only knew what was in her heart, he wouldn't give a thought to what he'd overheard. But it thrilled her to think that on his watch, he might not like the idea that she could get interested in a man she found attractive.

Manoussos, the assistant from Crete, had a rather dashing appeal in his own way. Kind of like a younger Takis. While her mind was still mulling over their conversation, Cesare came back to the car with their food and drove them to the apartment.

"Excuse me while I change out of these clothes. I'll be right back."

It was wonderful to discard the hat and stocking. Now her head could breathe. After removing her uniform and shoes, she put on jeans and a top. Once she'd run the brush through her curls, she hurried back to the kitchen. Cesare had already laid out their meal and poured the red wine they'd opened the other day.

"I can see you've bought enough *polenta* and *cotoletta alla Milanese* for half a dozen people."

"I'm partial to both."

She would have to remember that considering he was a connoisseur of fine food. After a few bites she agreed the ribs were delicious. "But I'm afraid that for me the grilled *polenta* is an acquired taste."

"Long ago it was considered the food of the poor, but I loved it when I first moved to Milan."

"My friend in Catania loves it, too. She said it reminds her of the porridge she ate when she was studying in England. I miss talking to her. She wouldn't believe it if she knew what I've been doing."

He drank the rest of his wine and sat back in the chair. "Today has marked a drastic change in your life. After nine years, you're no longer engaged to be married, releasing you from your prison. Even better, you're employed with a vitally important job and benefits."

"All because of you," she blurted.

"You don't need to keep thanking me, Tuccia." He'd turned serious all of a sudden. She hardly knew what to think. "This job is going to run your life for a while.

To make it a little easier, you're going to have to take breaks in order to handle the stress. It's time we talk about a schedule for you."

"All right."

"Basically you come to work at eight-thirty and can leave by three o'clock Monday through Friday. You'll alternate being on duty Saturday or Sunday evening twice a month from six to nine. Not to cook, but to make certain things are running smoothly."

She thought about it for a minute. "If there are problems, then I need to improvise. Is that what you're saying?"

"Should there be any issues, I'll be there to help."

"I see. But who spells you off?"

He raked a hand through his hair. "We're not talking about me."

She shouldn't have asked. Cesare was in a strange mood.

"Gemma and I worked out a schedule where she had two weekends off a month and Maurice the other two. I believe it's still the best way to arrange your time. When you're off, Maurice will handle any difficulties that come up."

"That sounds more than fair. Does it mean that you'll be taking those same weekends off?"

"Yes. That's how it has worked in the past so I can fly to New York and get my business done there."

The knowledge that he'd be gone at the same time she had two days to fill on her own private agenda was more than disappointing news. It was awful. Tuccia was so used to being with him she couldn't imagine him being so far away. To think that a week ago they hadn't even met. Now…

"Do you know how to drive, Tuccia?"

His question surprised her. "Yes. My *zia* taught me how. But I don't have a license because my parents never allowed me to have a car. Why do you ask?"

Frown lines formed around his eyes. "Always assuming you'll wear your disguise, I was going to let you use my car when I'm not in Milan. Under the circumstances, I'll make an arrangement with the limousine service so a driver will be on call for you at any time, day or night, when I'm not available. You need freedom to do the things you want and have to do."

No one in the whole world was more thoughtful than Cesare. *No one.* But in his odd frame of mind, she chose not to tell him that he didn't have to do that for her.

"Thank you. I'm very grateful for your generosity. But what would you think if we altered the daily routine a little?"

"In what way?"

"If you picked me up in the mornings, we could talk about the day ahead of me. But at three o'clock I could go home in the limo with another recipe you wanted me to make. I could get the groceries needed and do my errands. Then I'd make the dessert. When it was done, you could come by to test it. It will free up your time. What do you think?"

"It's your decision."

"I see."

If she dared, she'd ask if she could fly to New York with him. She'd traveled all over Europe under supervision, but she'd never been in New York before. Tuccia would love to see the original Mamma's, and where he'd lived before he'd put the *castello ris-torante* on the map.

"Just so you know, your first weekend off will be in two weeks, starting when three o'clock rolls around on Friday afternoon. Do you have other questions for me right now?"

Too many, especially one about how she would fill her time while he was away, but anything she wanted to ask him wasn't about her schedule and she feared he didn't want to hear it.

"No. Between you and Gemma, I'm feeling much more confident about everything."

"You were brilliant today."

"The credit goes to my teacher."

A strange silence followed before he suddenly got up from the table. "I'm afraid I have to go, but I'll be by for you at eight in the morning."

"Could you do one more favor first and buy the ingredients I need to make the pastries I've never prepared? I'll start practicing on a couple of the recipes before I go to bed."

He smiled. "I'll be right back." Twenty minutes later he returned with the items needed.

"Thank you so much, Cesare. Now don't let me keep you any longer."

He was probably so sick of teaching her how to cook his recipes he couldn't wait for some breathing space. It was only five in the afternoon and there wasn't a thing she could do about it. He'd done his duty, now he was out of there.

"Thank you for lunch," she said after following him to the door with her heart dragging on the tiles.

He gave her a heartbreaking smile, but didn't try to hold her or kiss her. "I promise, no more *polenta*."

"It was good for me to try it. I'm a cook now and need to be open to new taste experiences from the expert himself."

"You're becoming a very fine pastry cook," he corrected her.

"*Arrivederci*, Cesare."

He nodded before getting in his car and took off like a rocket.

Trying to pull herself together, she walked back in the kitchen to clean everything up. While she worked, Cesare's words rang in her ears.

*Today has marked a drastic change in your life.*

No kidding. Her teacher had done his job.

She remembered something else he'd told her days ago.

*There's no room in my life for any woman until the castello's new pastry chef can create masterpieces without my help.*

That day had come. Though they were Cesare's masterpieces, he'd decided it was time to push his needy fledgling out of the nest.

*You're on your own, Tuccia. You'd better get used to it fast.*

# CHAPTER NINE

Tuccia couldn't believe how fast the next week flew by. It didn't take her long to get into a rhythm. So far the camaraderie with her assistants was building. They were remarkably trained and skilled, hoping to become a chef at a great restaurant one day themselves.

The two guys who constantly flirted with her made the day fun, but she could never take either one of them seriously despite Cesare's reminders to be careful not to lead them on. She loved it that he was always around in the background, watching everything without being obvious about it.

Tuccia still felt a fraud at having been promoted to executive pastry chef status in a week. But the others had no idea how it had happened. With Cesare her mentor, she'd been hyper-glided into the coveted position, one that was saving her life.

Maurice liked to tease her about her Sicilian ways. Things were coming along. In truth she liked having an important reason to get up in the morning and go to work. She liked cooking! With every new dessert, she needed less help to figure it out and perfect it.

On Thursday, just before quitting time, Cesare

came in while she was testing the results of her assistants' creations in the ricotta cheesecake department. Each cook had put his or her initials on a piece of tape on the side of the pan. "This particular cake is lacking two essential ingredients that were included in the recipes I passed out." She knew who had made it. "Why don't we ask Signor Donati to tell you what they are?"

Manoussos no longer looked happy as she cut Cesare a piece and walked over to give it to him with a fork. Their gazes met in silent amusement. He started to eat. Tuccia was loving every second of this. Cesare finally put the empty plate down on the counter.

"Signorina Bottaro is right. I don't detect the strong flavor of chocolate or amaretto."

"You see," she exclaimed. "The secret of this cheesecake is to crumble amaretto cookies into the crust, and add two extra tablespoons of chocolate. Leave out either of these ingredients and it will taste like all the mediocre cheesecakes you've ever eaten."

"It was my mistake," Manoussos spoke up. "I was playing a little joke to see if you could tell. But I didn't realize Signor Donati would be doing the testing. I'm very sorry."

"I'm glad you did it and I forgive you," Tuccia said with a smile. "Now perhaps you'll take me seriously and understand the *castello ristorante* doesn't do mediocre!" She stared at all of them. "That's it for today. See you bright and early in the morning."

Cesare broke into laughter after they'd walked out to his car. "He's still upset that he can't get anywhere with you. I have it in my heart to feel sorry for him because he'll never get the chance."

That made two people who were upset because Tuccia wasn't getting anywhere with Cesare and she was in pain over it.

She loved him to the bottom of her soul. They could be together all night every night if that was what he wanted. But maybe she needed to face the cold hard fact that he didn't feel the same way about her. She didn't want to believe it, not when she was so deeply in love with him.

During the second week of her being in charge of her crew in the *castello* kitchen, Cesare had come by the apartment after work to test the chocolate *setevelli torta*, a nine-layer cake he'd taught her how to make. When he tested the end result, he told her it tasted like the food of the gods.

She smiled and thanked him. "Such praise makes a girl's head swell." In horrible pain because he wasn't being more demonstrative in an intimate way, she had to do something to end it. "Since I'm thrilled I've passed your exacting test, please feel free to leave and enjoy the rest of your evening."

For once he looked taken back. Was it shock, or could it possibly be disappointment that she'd brushed him off so fast and he didn't like it? She got excited to think it might be the latter.

"Why do I get the feeling you want me to go?"

"It's not that. If you must know, I've made plans for tonight and I don't want to put them off. The limo will be here soon."

"To do what?" he asked in a controlled voice.

*Oh, Cesare—tell me what's going on inside you.*

"To do some important clothes shopping in Milan."

"You could have asked me at any time. I would have taken you."

"I know you would, but I'm no longer like the in-flight helpless woman who developed an embarrassing crush on her protector during those first few days." There! She'd said it to disabuse him of any notion that he needed to worry about her any longer.

From the look of his tautened mouth, she'd found her mark. It encouraged her to go on and finish making her point. "That fairy tale has ended now that you've given me the tools to help myself. Since the police are no longer looking for me, I want to get out on my own."

"Tuccia—it's probably not a good idea for you to walk alone at the shops this time of evening. It'll be dark soon. A beautiful woman is a target for unsavory types."

"But it's what I've been wanting to do, and any woman is a target for a pickpocket. I can defend myself and I'll take my chances. To be a normal person without a bodyguard following me around sounds like heaven."

His jaw hardened. "Is that what I've become to you?"

She folded her arms, tamping down her elation that he was upset. "I'm going to forget you asked me that question. It's not worthy of you. I was referring to the security my parents hired to keep me watched day and night. Cesare—I need my freedom. Is it so inconceivable that I would want you to have yours and get on with your life the way it was before we met?"

The lids of his eyes had lowered so she couldn't read their expression.

"In fact as long as we're having this conversation, I want you to know that the salary you've put in the bank account for me will remain untouched until I've paid back every cent I owe you. Wait—" she said when he started to protest.

"I don't want to be beholden to you or anyone. Because of your incredible generosity, I've been given an option that opens many doors to my future when I no longer work here."

"You're planning on leaving us soon?" His voice sounded almost wintry.

His reaction was more than she could have asked for. If by some miracle he'd fallen in love with her, too, then she had to do something to get him to break down and tell her how he felt.

"I would never do that to you. But yesterday you told me you heard from your mother and received wonderful news. Ciro is starting to make progress. It's possible he'll be well enough to work again in a couple of months rather than six. You have to be so relieved if he's able to come back much sooner than expected."

Ignoring her comment he said, "Do you wish you could get out of our agreement sooner?" He wasn't letting this go. She prayed it was a good sign.

"No." She shook her head. "Every day I'm here I learn something new and valuable. There isn't a cook in Europe who wouldn't sell his or her soul to be the executive pastry chef in a restaurant as renowned as yours. Don't you think I know that? Until Ciro is ready to come to work, I'll do everything I can to justify your faith in me."

He stood at the door, ready to leave. "Would you rather I didn't pick you up in the mornings?"

She hadn't expected that question, but she'd done it to herself and had to live with it. "I love being picked up. Who wouldn't? But I'm sure it isn't always convenient for you. All you have to do is phone me if something comes up and I'll send for the limo." Tuccia moved closer to him. "Do you want to know what my greatest concern is?"

"I don't have to guess," he muttered. "You're talking about your aunt."

"Actually I'm not as worried now. But I'm thinking about you and the risk you took to talk your partners into helping me in the first place."

"I didn't have to go that far," he bit out. "When they heard about your situation and ate that batch of tarts you made, they wanted to protect you."

"Nevertheless I wish I could do something important for you to pay you back."

"You are," he said in a gravelly voice. "Talk among the staff is growing that your desserts have already resulted in rave reviews from our latest guests. In fact several of the top food magazines, including *Buon Appetito*, already want an interview with the new pastry chef."

"That's nice to hear, but I can't take any credit for it. The people they need to talk to are you and your mother."

He cocked his head. "Would it interest you to know that the top dessert so far is your *granita*? Maurice says it's perfection."

Tuccia adored Cesare for saying that. She loved him so terribly she was going to blurt it out if he didn't leave in the next few seconds. "Then the credit for that goes to the chef on my parents' yacht."

"Not everyone can follow a recipe the way you've done and improve it. Why won't you take credit for what you're doing?"

She averted her eyes.

A sound of exasperation came out of him. "I can see I'm not going to get the answer I'm looking for from you."

*Nor I from you, my darling.*

"Enjoy your evening out, but be careful. Unless there's an emergency, I'll be by at eight in the morning." He opened the door.

"Cesare?" She was dying inside.

He turned around so fast it startled her. "*Si?*"

"Would you mind answering a question for me?"

"Have I ever?"

Oh, dear, but she was determined to ask him anyway. "I was just wondering if you would consider taking me to New York with you on my first weekend off. To see it with you would mean everything to me."

"I'm afraid that would be out of the question. I have too much business and couldn't show you around."

His rejection was swift and true, cutting her to the very marrow of her bones. Tuccia would never make that mistake again. "I just thought I'd ask. I hope you have a lovely night without any worries for a change."

"That'll be the day," he ground out, "but I appreciate the thought."

It was the hardest thing she'd ever done to keep a smile on her face and pretend he hadn't destroyed her with those words. But somehow she managed to maintain her poise until he drove off.

Now that he was gone, she knew what she had to do. After he'd left and she could no longer hear the engine, Tuccia called for a taxi rather than the limo service Cesare had arranged for her to use. She didn't want her whereabouts this evening to be traced.

When it drew up to the apartment, she walked outside and exchanged greetings with the *padrona* before she got in. Once she shut the door, she asked the driver to take her to the airport and drop her off at the main terminal.

Then she sat back and contemplated what she had to do. If Cesare had been willing to take her to New York, everything would have been different. But with that dream gone, she needed to follow through on a plan growing in the back of her mind.

Before long the limo pulled up to the drop-off area. She paid the driver and got out, waving him on. Then she walked through the crowds to the ticketing counter and booked a round trip ticket from Milan to Palermo. Bless her *zia* for slipping her a little money in case of an emergency. Bertina must have been psychic!

She would leave next Friday after work, the beginning of her first weekend off, and return Sunday evening. The police weren't looking for her so she didn't worry about being spotted. If by chance any detectives her parents had hired did see her name on a passenger list and alert her parents, she'd have to deal with it then.

As soon as she'd booked both two-hour flights and had paid cash, she got another taxi and headed right back to the *pensione*. Relieved that she'd finally done something about an impossible situation, she prepared for bed and climbed under the covers.

Her plan was to take a taxi to Bertina's palazzo. Tuccia couldn't bear to put her *zia* through any more grief. They needed to talk face-to-face about everything. She needed the woman who'd been like a mother to her growing up, before she faced her parents.

Without doing that, she could never embrace the newfound independence Cesare had tried to give her at great risk to him. Whatever happened, it was time to take total charge of her life.

On the next Friday afternoon at three o'clock sharp, Cesare said good-night to Tuccia and watched her leave the *castello* in the limousine. He decided to give her an hour after she got back to her apartment before he made a surprise appearance at her door. She believed he was leaving for New York. That was what he'd wanted her to think.

Surely she knew why he'd told her she couldn't come with him when she'd asked him. She had to know he was madly in love with her.

For the last week he'd been functioning on automatic pilot and knew it couldn't go on until he got Tuccia alone. His plan was to whisk her away in his car to Lago di Garda. Italy's largest lake was situated two hours away from Milan by car. He'd booked a romantic hideaway near the picturesque town of Salo where they wouldn't be disturbed.

In three weeks she'd become his whole world and he wouldn't rest until they'd talked everything out and he'd told her what was in his heart.

He let Vincenzo know he was leaving. After he cleared the decks with Maurice, his work was finished here. Cesare showered and packed a bag. With everything done, he took off in his car for the *pensione*.

When he walked to her door and knocked, he felt an adrenaline rush impossible to contain. "Tuccia? It's Cesare." He waited and listened, but didn't hear anything. "Tuccia?" He knocked hard. "I have to talk to you."

Nothing.

Had she already gone somewhere in the limo?

He got back in his car and called the limo service. The dispatcher told him she'd rung for a car to pick her up at the *castello* at three o'clock, but she hadn't requested another limo. Cesare thanked him and hung up, not liking the vibe he was getting.

His next thought was that she must have gone for a walk in the village. Rather than try looking for her, he called her cell phone, but she didn't answer. If she was inside the apartment, he couldn't imagine her not picking up when she saw the caller ID.

Growing more anxious, he phoned the *padrona* and asked if she'd seen Tuccia. The older woman said the last time she saw her was yesterday when she came home still wearing her chef's outfit.

"Will you do me a favor and let yourself inside to find out if she's too ill to answer the door?"

"*Naturalmente.* I will call you right back."

Cesare watched her leave her apartment and enter Tuccia's. Suddenly she reappeared at the entrance and waved for him to come in. At this point he broke out in a cold sweat fearing what he would find.

He jumped out of the car and rushed inside, dreading to think what he might find. But instead of Tuccia passed out on the floor or ill in her bed, the *padrona* handed him a sheet of paper. He could see it was lined and had come from Tuccia's bible.

"I found this on the table, *signor*. She left this for you. I will go now."

*"Grazie,"* he murmured, feeling gutted.

After the door closed, he read what she'd written.

*In case someone from the* castello *tries to reach me and can't, I've gone to my* zia *in Palermo for the weekend.*

His eyes closed tightly. He squeezed the note into a ball. Pain almost debilitated him. She had to have taken a plane because a train or bus would never have gotten her there in time. Cesare knew how terrible she felt for her aunt, but he hadn't expected Tuccia to fly into the hornet's nest this soon.

Blackness had descended on him. After locking her front door, he took off for the airport in his car. The first thing he did en route was phone the pilot and alert him he needed to fly to Palermo ASAP. Next he called his mother, but she didn't answer and it went to her voice mail.

He left the message that he'd be in Palermo tonight and needed to talk to her the second he got there. Cesare had come to the low ebb of his life. He couldn't lose Tuccia.

When the taxi drove up to the gates of the palazzo at quarter to ten that night, Tuccia paid the driver and jumped out. She ran into Paolo. Her aunt's grounds-keeper looked shocked when he recognized her, and he let her through.

She put a finger to her lips. "Shh. I want to surprise my *zia*. How is she, Paolo?"

"Very, very sad and missing you. Praise the angels you have come back."

Tuccia kissed his ruddy cheek and darted up the long flower-lined walkway to the main entrance. She tugged on the door pull and waited for Adona to answer. The housekeeper never went to bed until late.

After a minute she could hear someone talking on the inside and then the door opened.

The second Adona saw her, she put her hands to her mouth in shock. "Ah! Ah! Principessa!" she cried and called out to Bertina. Her booming voice must have reached the second floor because suddenly there was Tuccia's *zia* hurrying down the staircase in her robe with her dark hair undone, to find out what was going on.

Tuccia put down her suitcase and ran toward her. They met at the bottom step. She flung her arms around the woman who'd made her life worth living.

*"Mia cara ragazza."* Bertina kissed her over and over again while the tears ran down her cheeks. "I've been afraid I might never see you again. My prayers have been answered."

"So have mine," Tuccia cried, kissing her cheeks once more. "I've missed you more than you will ever know. Let's go up to your room so you can get back in bed and we'll talk in comfort."

"Do you need anything? Something to eat? Drink?"

"No. I just got off the plane and had a meal in flight. The only thing I need is to have a long, long talk with you about so many things."

With their arms hooked, they climbed the staircase where she'd rushed up and down so many times growing up. She could have found Bertina's boudoir wearing a blindfold. The room smelled like her lemon perfume, bringing back so many memories.

"Come on. I want you to get back in bed. You've had a great shock. I'll sit right here beside you and we'll catch up. Shall I ask Adona to bring you some tea?"

"No, no. I don't want to bother her."

Tuccia helped her off with her robe and puffed the pillows. Then her *zia* leaned back and pulled up the covers. "I just want to look at my beautiful daughter for a little while. You *are* my daughter, even if my sister gave birth to you."

"You already know how I feel about you." She kissed her forehead. "Ever since I ran away, I've worried about you until I've been ill over it."

"I've been all right. Over the last few days I've had several long talks with your mother who is suffering over what has happened. We're not sisters for nothing, and I know she has a sorrow in her heart until she can make peace with you."

"Then it's true what you told Lina?"

"Of course. She and your father, though he doesn't show it, were frightened when they thought you'd been kidnapped. It was one of those life-changing experiences for them. I don't believe they're the same people from before."

"So you believe what was printed in the newspaper?"

"Yes. They miss you and want you to come home. I'm convinced of it."

Tuccia stared into her eyes. "I want to believe it."

"I think that if you call them and have a talk, you'll find they're full of regrets, especially for the cruel betrothal forced on you, and they want a fresh start. You don't have to do it, of course."

"No. I want to do it, Zia. That's why I'm here."

She clapped her hands. "My prayers have been answered."

"Mine, too. If it hadn't been for Cesare's mother keeping him informed so he could tell me how you are, I would have lost my mind."

"Lina has become my close friend and has been a great blessing in my life."

Tuccia held her hand. "You have no idea *how* great, Zia."

Bertina heard the inflection in her voice. "Tell me what you mean."

"Do you know where I've been for the last three weeks?"

"No. I only know her son flew you to Milan so you could get away."

"There's so much to tell you I don't know where to start."

"At the beginning!" Bertina squeezed Tuccia's hand hard, causing her to chuckle. "Do you know that even though you've had to live through such a terrible ordeal, you seem happy. I don't think it's just because you're free of that deplorable engagement. I detect a glow about you."

"You do?"

"Yes. Your eyes are alive, like you've come out of a deep sleep. What's going on?"

"Did Lina tell you that the chef her son had hired

for the *castello ristorante* had gone to the hospital the same night she let me stay at her villa?"

"Oh, yes. We've both been to visit him at the hospital." Tuccia didn't know that.

"But she hasn't told you anything else?"

"Only that he found a place for you to stay in Milan."

"At a *pensione* in a village at the base of the *castello*."

"So you didn't have to leave Milan. It sounds like he was very good to you."

She took a big breath. "I'm afraid good doesn't begin to cover what he has done for me. What I'm about to tell you is going to come as a huge shock."

Bertina looked at her in that amazing way she had of reading between the lines. Tuccia had never been able to keep secrets from her, not that she'd wanted to. "Why do I get the feeling that the devilishly handsome Cesare Donati is more involved in all this than I had imagined?"

She bit her lip. "I'm in love with him, Zia! Wildly, passionately in love."

Her brows lifted. "Have you been living with him?"

"Not in the way you mean. I *wish* he'd asked me to live with him."

"Tuccianna—"

"That may sound terrible to you, but it's how I feel. We've been together every day and I've never known such joy in my life."

Bertina nodded. "Is he in love with you, too?"

She looked down. "I don't know. I think he is—I pray he is."

"You mean he hasn't told you?"

"No."

"Nor you him?"

"I couldn't! Our relationship hasn't been like that. One night he started kissing me and I thought I would die from happiness, but since then he hasn't tried to make love to me. I'm still trying to figure out why. I think he loves me, but—"

"You only think?" the older woman laughed.

"Unless I don't understand men and have been reading everything wrong."

"Why don't you start again, slowly, and give me a minute-by-minute explanation of what you've been up to that has turned you into a different person? Don't withhold any details. Together we just might figure everything out."

"I want to do that, but first I need to talk to my parents."

"Why don't I call them and tell them to come over here now."

"You think they'll come this late?"

Bertina shook her head. "If you only knew how much they've missed you, you wouldn't have to ask that question."

While Tuccia sat there trembling, she listened to the brief conversation. When her *zia* hung up, she said, "They're coming this instant. Why don't you freshen up and meet them at the door?"

"Will you come down with me?"

"No, my darling girl. This is a conversation you need to have with them alone. It's been twenty-five years in coming."

After going the bedroom she always used here, Tuccia hurried downstairs and waited until she heard the bell pull outside the door. When she opened it and saw her parents standing there, she was stunned by the rush of emotions that bombarded her.

"Tuccianna—" her mother cried and ran to embrace her. "You've come back. I was so afraid we would never see you again." They hugged for a long time.

After they broke apart, she looked at her father. "Papa?"

*"Figlia mia."* Tears poured down his cheeks. For the first time she could remember, he reached out and hugged her so hard she could barely breathe, but she didn't care. "Forgive us," he cried and broke down sobbing.

"Let's all go in the salon," she said, putting her arms through both of theirs. Once in the other room they sat down on the couch. She pulled up a chair so she could be close and look at them. Gone were the severe expressions of two people who'd been so rigid.

"I'm the one who's sorry for doing something so terrible, for frightening you and embarrassing you and Jean-Michel. But I couldn't marry him. I just couldn't!"

Her mother nodded. "I knew that the moment you'd disappeared from the bridal shop. I don't think I'll ever get over the shame of forcing you into an engagement that ruined your life for years. Bertina made us see how wrong we've been."

"We didn't mean to hurt you, Tuccianna," her father murmured in the saddest voice she'd ever heard. "While you've been gone, we've learned some things about Jean-Michel that let us know he would never have made you a good husband. You don't ever have to worry about him again. We've been so blind. How can we make this up to you?"

"By accepting me for who I am, and accepting the most wonderful man on earth whom I hope to marry."

"You've met someone?" her mother cried.

"Yes. Cesare Donati. I'm terribly in love with him. He came to my rescue the day I ran away. We've been together ever since. Let me tell you about him. About us."

For the next little while she related her experiences, leaving nothing out. "I'm now the executive pastry chef at the *castello* in Milan. I can't wait for you to meet him. You already know his wonderful mother."

"We do?"

"Yes, Mamma. She's Zia Bertina's cook."

Her father's eyes widened. "Lina Donati?"

She nodded. "Bertina asked her to hide me at her villa that first night, and I bumped into Cesare. It was love at first sight for me. But I don't know what's going to happen now." Tuccia knew he'd tried to be so careful with her to honor her because that was the way he was made. But she needed to know why he wouldn't take her to New York. They had to talk.

"We want you to be happy, Tuccia," her father declared.

"That's all we want." Her mother had broken down in tears again. "Will you let us be a part of your lives?"

Overjoyed to hear that question, she flew off the chair and embraced both of them.

# CHAPTER TEN

THIS TIME WHEN Cesare arrived at the villa near midnight, his mother was up to greet him. They hugged before he followed her into the kitchen. She'd made his favorite *tarelli* lemon biscuits and her own version of espresso.

"I was at the hospital when I got your message and hurried home. You'll be pleased to know Ciro is making amazing strides. I think he might be released from the hospital sooner than anyone expected."

Cesare let out a deep sigh. "That news couldn't come at a better time." He had plans for him and Tuccia.

"It's clear you have something serious to say to me, Cesare. Tell me what has happened for you to show up like this late at night in such a frantic state."

They sat around the kitchen table while he drank his coffee. "I'm afraid you're going to be shocked when I tell you. I'm in love with Tuccia Leonardi."

She leaned forward on the table and eyed him seriously. "I've been wondering when you would finally tell me about what you did with her. What's wrong?"

"She left Milan without telling me. I'm terrified I might have lost her. If the worst has happened, I don't know how I'm going to live without her. Mamma, how did you handle it when Papa left you? I can't comprehend it."

His mother reached for his hand. "Where did that question come from?"

"I guess from the time I heard you crying in the bedroom when I was six. You were looking at his picture."

She squeezed his fingers before letting him go. "You thought I was crying about him. I wish I'd known. I could have saved you years of grief."

"What do you mean?"

"My tears over him had been shed long before he ever left. He didn't want marriage or responsibility. When I realized how unhappy we both were living together, I asked him to leave."

Cesare frowned. "You asked him?"

"Yes."

"So he didn't just walk out?"

"No. But I knew he wanted to and so I gave him his freedom. The day you saw me in tears, I was crying because he never did come back to see you and Isabella. You deserved a wonderful father and I could only be your mother. But I thank God every day he was your father because I have the two most wonderful children on earth. Now tell me why you think you've lost her?"

"Tuccia's my life, but when I went to her apartment earlier today, she'd gone. There was a note that said she'd flown here to see Bertina."

"Does she know how you feel about her?"

"Not in so many words."

"Because she's a princess?"

"I don't know. Maybe I've felt I wasn't good enough for her."

"Nonsense! My brilliant son. You're as blind as a bat where the *principessa* is concerned. Now let's really talk."

He sucked in his breath. "There's a lot you don't know. Without telling me, Tuccia flew here on her own."

His mother eyed him curiously. "How come you know so much about what the princess does? What have you been keeping from me?"

"A lot."

She smiled in that irritating way that said she'd already figured everything out. "You fell in love with her when you whisked her away to Milan without Ciro on board."

"I'm afraid I did more than that." He had her complete attention now.

"What man with blood in his veins wouldn't have done the same thing? Bertina and I have often said it's sinful how beautiful she is. Her parents did a cruel thing forcing that betrothal on her, but it has protected her. Until *I* interfered," she added. "So what did you do?"

"I made her the pastry chef at the *castello* in order to hide her."

A laugh escaped. "You mean a kitchen helper."

"No. She's the chef who has replaced Ciro and has been for two weeks."

"With your partners' approval?"

"Yes."

"Did she even know how to cook?"

"Not when she started."

"I presume you've been teaching her everything you know."

He nodded. "Except for an exceptional *gratina* she'd learned how to make years ago by watching the cook on her parents' yacht."

"I told you she was resourceful. I take it you've forgiven me for asking you to help her get away."

Cesare sat back in the chair. "I want to marry her, Mamma."

"At last you've found a woman who's your equal."

"But—"

"But nothing! Do you imagine for one single second she would have begged you to teach her if she weren't halfway in love with you by the time you arrived in Milan? She's known her own mind for years. When she met the man meant for her, she did whatever she could to get you to fall in love with her."

That was what he'd wanted to believe. "She's beyond wonderful."

"I know, and I can't tell you how delighted I am."

"In that case, I need a big favor from you. Will you call Bertina right now? Tell her I found out Tuccia is with her. Ask them to come for breakfast first thing in the morning. Tell her this has to do with Tuccia's parents and it's absolutely vital. But don't let her know I'm here. I'll do the rest."

He waited while she reached for the phone and made the call. "Bertina?" she said, putting it on speaker. "Forgive me for disturbing you this late, but this is an emergency. I've had word that Tuccia is with you."

"Oh, Lina—she arrived earlier tonight. I'm so happy I think I'm dreaming!"

"I can only imagine your joy at seeing her again. But before anything else happens, you must bring her to my villa first thing in the morning."

"Why? What's wrong?"

"There's something of great significance going on you don't know about. We have to talk, Bertina. I wouldn't ask this of you if I weren't frightened for both of you."

"After all you did for me, of course we'll be there."

Cesare's mother smiled at him in in relief. "Good. I'm looking forward to seeing Tuccia again."

"There's so much I have to tell you. We'll come early."

The second she hung up, Cesare shot out of the chair and walked around to hug her.

At eight in the morning, Tuccia and her aunt left the palazzo in a limo. Once again she found herself being driven through the streets to Mondello, one of the poshest areas of the city.

Before Tuccia had gone to bed in the suite she always used, Bertina had phoned to tell her about the conversation with Cesare's mother. She'd insisted she had some news they needed to hear.

Her heart thumped with sickening speed. The only way anyone knew she'd flown to Palermo tonight was through Cesare. But that meant he'd had to go to her apartment and find the note she'd left. Since he didn't have a key, he would have been forced to ask the *padrona* for help if he thought something was wrong. Why had he bothered?

She'd thought he'd flown to New York after they'd said goodbye. Evidently he'd dropped by the *pensione* before leaving for the airport. There'd been a phone call from him while she'd been on her way to the airport in the taxi, but she'd turned her phone off. Though she could have answered it—had wanted to respond—she was trying to keep her distance.

Had he phoned his mother because he was worried her parents would try to prevent her from returning to Milan? Surely he knew she would never allow that to happen. Tuccia had made a contract with him, one she would never break. How could he think she wouldn't return on Sunday night to fulfill her obligations?

But maybe he still saw her as a young woman who'd been so sheltered she'd be unable to stand on her own once she faced her parents. That was crazy. All she wanted in life was to be his wife. Nothing else could ever satisfy her.

"We're here, Tuccianna."

"I'm nervous, Zia. What do you imagine Lina needs to tell us that's so important?"

"I don't know, but I trust her with my life."

Just the way Tuccia trusted her son.

They got out of the limo and walked to the villa entrance. When the door opened, Tuccia expected to see Lina. Instead she let out a gasp and came close to a faint. *"Cesare—"*

His blue gaze traveled over her, missing nothing. "Won't you both come in? It's good to see you, Bertina." He kissed her on both cheeks. "Mamma is waiting for you in the kitchen where she has breakfast ready. Tuccia and I will join you in a few minutes, but first we have some unfinished business to talk over."

Bertina had been to the villa many times before

and walked down the hallway to the kitchen without needing directions.

Tuccia stayed where she was, glued to the spot. "What are you doing here? I thought you'd flown to New York."

"That's what I wanted you to think while I worked out a plan to take you away to a place where we could be private. But when I got to the apartment, you'd gone.

Like a fool I've given you too much time and space, but that's over. Come on. We need to be alone."

To her joy he reached for her hand and walked her up the stairs. She followed him down a hallway to what had to be his suite. After he shut the door, he lounged against it and grasped her upper arms.

"Let's get something straight right now. I only flew after you for one reason. It's the only reason I took you to Milan in the beginning. Since running into a princess in a yellow robe three weeks ago, it's the reason why I've been turned inside out and upside down. I'm in love with you, Tuccia, but you already know that. The question is, are you in love with me?"

*"Oh, Cesare—"* She couldn't believe what she was hearing. "How can you even ask me that? I'd fallen in love with you by the time the ducal jet landed at Milan airport. You're all I think or live for. I need you more than you will ever know."

They both moaned as he pulled her against him and he started kissing her the way he'd done at the apartment. Tuccia lost track of time as she tried to show him how much he meant to her. His mouth was doing such incredible things to her she burned with desire for him. To her joy she no longer had to hold back. He loved her!

Somehow they ended up on his bed where they began to devour each other. After three weeks of starvation, she realized she had absolutely no self-control, but she didn't care. This incredible man loved her and was making her feel immortal.

Yet Cesare was the one to call a halt before they got too carried away. He slowly relinquished her mouth and looked down at her. His eyes burned with love for her. "We're not alone in this villa and there are two people waiting for us to join them."

"I know."

"Before we go down, I have something else to say. I want to marry you as soon as possible."

"I want that, too."

"We'll make it work and live at the apartment until Ciro can come to the *castello*."

"I love the apartment. To me it's been like our little home. I'd be happy living with you there forever."

"I've felt the same way. Though I haven't dared touch you and you know why, cooking and eating together have been the highlights of my life."

"Mine, too."

"I need to meet your parents and tell them our intentions while we're here in Palermo."

"They already know my intentions."

"So you've seen them already?"

"Yes. I was with them tonight at Bertina's. It's true that they've become different people. We hugged and kissed and they can't wait to meet the man I told them I planned to marry. I'm free to live my own life and

I love you for helping me find the courage to face them."

He kissed her mouth. "I love you so much I can't live without you."

"I've been waiting to hear you say that!" she cried for joy.

"You're an amazing, loving woman. If it's all right with you, we'll go see them together so I can ask for your hand."

"They're old-fashioned and will love it."

He held her tighter. "If I have you, I have everything."

"I love you, Cesare. Way too much." She kissed each masculine feature of his striking face before kissing his mouth over and over again.

"There's something else we have to talk about. I'm anxious to plan our wedding. It needs to take place as soon as possible, or I won't be able to stand it," he whispered.

"It's all I've thought about since I met you."

"By some miracle I've found the woman for me."

"I feel the same way about you and can't belong to you soon enough."

"Two weeks from this weekend is your next time off. Our marriage can take place then. I would like Gemma and Vincenzo to be there, but I doubt they'll be able to. Still, I'm not waiting any longer to make you my wife.

"Depending on your parents' wishes, we'll have it performed in my church here, or in yours. We'll return to Milan Sunday night and take a honeymoon later after Ciro is back at the *castello*."

She ran her hands through his hair. "We'll have to

make as many arrangements as we can while we're here, but I don't want a big wedding. Just a few family friends."

"I love the way you think because I'd prefer a quiet wedding too, Tuccia." He gave her a long hungry kiss. "Now much as I don't want to leave this room, I think we'd better go downstairs to the kitchen. My mother and Bertina are dying to know what has been going on."

"I'm pretty sure they know exactly." She kissed his hard jaw, loving the taste and feel of him.

"It'll be fun to make their day."

She laughed. "I know it will."

They had trouble letting each other go. When she got up from the bed, she felt positively dizzy. "I need to fix myself first." She opened her purse and got out her styling brush.

Cesare took it from her and started running it through her curls. "I've been wanting to do this forever. But don't put on any lipstick yet. I need another kiss from you before I can go anywhere."

She threw her arms around his neck and kissed him so passionately that they wove in place. "I've ached to do this since we went to the park. I almost pulled you down and begged you to make love to me. Every time you said good-night to me and walked out without holding me in your arms, I could hardly bear it."

"In two weeks we won't ever have to suffer again. We'll be together day and night."

"By night I'll be Signora Donati. By day I'll be Nedda Bottaro."

He shook his head. "Once we've said our vows, you'll be my wife in the kitchen, too, and you'll wear whatever clothes you feel like wearing. Manoussos will be in pain when he finds out the truth."

They left the room and started down the stairs. "No he won't. You're being silly."

"Trust me. I'm a man and I know these things."

She turned to him when they reached the foyer. "Oh—I know you're a man. The most wonderful man who ever lived. Kiss me again, Cesare."

Ten days later, while Tuccia was checking the last of the desserts for the evening meal, Cesare reappeared after being gone most of her work day. Every time she sensed his presence, her heart almost burst out of her chest.

It was almost three o'clock. She'd never known him to be away from the kitchen this long. He walked over to her with a gleam in his eyes. "I'd squeeze your waist if I could find it," he teased.

Tuccia chuckled. She'd been so happy since their return from Palermo, she felt like she'd been floating. Her parents were both so impressed with Cesare that they'd given the two of them their blessing and hadn't found fault with anything. Not now that she'd come home to them.

The wedding at her family's church would be going ahead on Saturday. That day couldn't come soon enough for Tuccia.

"Guess who's in labor and has been in the hospital since eight this morning?"

"Gemma? Oh, I'm so excited for her! How's Vincenzo?"

"A complete wreck. The doctor told him it could take a long time because it's her first baby. I stayed with him as long as I could. Now Dimi and his wife are there. Takis and Lys are on their way from Crete on the jet. I'll drive you home to change and then we'll go over to the hospital."

Before long she said good-night to everyone. Cesare gathered some sandwiches in a bag and hustled her out of the kitchen to the car. When they reached the apartment, she got out of her uniform and changed into a skirt and blouse in record time.

"You look fabulous. Three more days before our world changes." He gave her a long, hungry kiss, then they left for the hospital in Milan. Everyone had gathered round in the hospital lounge. They talked about the coming wedding. It was going to be a very small morning ceremony of twenty people with a brunch afterward at the palazzo of Tuccia's parents.

Afterward she and Cesare planned to fly to Milan and spend Saturday night and Sunday at Lago di Garda before returning to their apartment. That was the place where he'd planned to take her the evening he'd come by the apartment and had found her gone. So much had happened since that night.

While they were chatting, a nurse walked toward them. "Signor Gagliardi says for you to come. If you'll follow me."

Cesare grasped her hand and they walked through the swinging doors to the second room down the hall. When they entered the room, Tuccia's breath caught. There was Gemma holding a baby in her arms with a cap of black hair. She was beaming. An exhausted-looking Vincenzo sat next to her. Both were examining their new arrival.

The proud father looked up at them. "Come all the

way in and meet our baby. We've decided to call him Nico. He's seven pounds six ounces and measures twenty-two inches long. Though he came two weeks early, the pediatrician says he's perfect."

*"Felicitazioni!"* sounded their cry. "A new Duc di Lombardi has graced our world."

Soon they left the hospital. She kissed Cesare's cheek. "That's a perfect family."

He reached for her hand. "That's what we're going to have, Tuccia."

"I know we're not even married yet, but already I want your baby."

"There's one promise I'll make to you. I'll do my best to get you pregnant."

"I'll do my best to get pregnant," Tuccia gave a happy sigh. "Everything has worked out because of you, Cesare."

His hand slid to her thigh. "I don't think you have any idea how much I love you."

Her heart was too full to talk. All she could do was cover his hand with her own.

"Takis seems to be handling his wife's pregnancy well," he said, "but he can be inscrutable at times. I would imagine that deep down he's holding his breath until she delivers."

After they reached the apartment and he took her inside, he pulled her down on the couch so they half lay together. "I've made a decision about something and wanted to talk it over with you."

"What is it?" But being this close, she couldn't resist kissing him again and again.

"I'm going to sell all my business interests in New York and invest the profits. I don't want to have to fly there anymore and leave you. Our life is here. We always have a place to stay at the *castello*, and at the villa when we visit my mother. But I'd like to think about a home of our own in Palermo."

"I'm so glad you said that. It's what I want. Our own place. It doesn't have to be big. Just large enough to hold two or three children. I want us to have a normal life."

"I want the same thing. You know Takis has worked things out so he can be here part of the time. The rest of the time he spends with Lys at their home in Crete. And Vincenzo lives in a villa on Lake Como with Gemma. There's no reason we can't do the same thing and fly back and forth when it's necessary."

"I think you've just made me the happiest bride-to-be in the whole world. Please don't go home tonight. Stay with me."

He hugged her tighter. "I'd like to take you in the bedroom, lock the door and throw away the key forever. Don't tempt me. Just three more days to wait, *amore mio*. We're almost there."

# CHAPTER ELEVEN

CESARE STOOD AT the front of the church in Palermo with Dimi and Takis. They all wore dark blue dress suits and ties with a white rose in the lapels. He'd put the rings in his pocket. Even though Vincenzo couldn't make it, this made four times that they'd celebrated each other's weddings.

Six weeks ago, if anyone had told him he'd be married to the love of his life this morning, he would have laughed in disbelief. He kept looking at the back of the church, waiting for Tuccia to enter on the arm of her father.

The *marchesa* and her sister Bertina sat together by Cesare's mother. Behind them sat Isabella and her husband, Tomaso. They'd left the baby with Tomaso's mother. Filippa, Dimi's wife, and Lys sat by each other. The few other guests were the close friends of Tuccia's parents.

She'd insisted on keeping their wedding as low key as possible. Her life growing up had been filled with too many bad memories. She'd begged for simplicity and a non-princess wedding. Cesare had seen to her wishes.

As he wondered if something had gone wrong, he

saw the priest out of the corner of his eye. Behind him walked Tuccia on her father's arm. She looked a vision in a full-length white silk wedding dress. The lace mantilla covering her gorgeous black curls was a sight he'd never forget. She held a bouquet of white roses from her aunt's garden.

The priest had agreed to perform their short ceremony in Sicilian.

"Cesare Donati, please take Princess Tuccianna Falcone Leonardi by the hand and repeat after me."

Their eyes met before he grasped it. The love and trust in those gray orbs melted him on the spot. Thus began the age-old ritual that took on indescribable meaning to him as he kept looking at the woman who'd agreed to marry him. There was no person more precious to him.

They exchanged vows and rings.

"I now pronounce you man and wife. In the name of the Father, the Son and the Holy Spirit."

The priest didn't have to tell him to kiss his bride. Cesare gathered her in his arms and embraced her. Her hunger for him matched his. They were on fire for each other. If he could run away with her now, he would, but they had one more celebration to get through.

Holding her hand tightly, he walked her down the aisle to the foyer where everyone hugged and congratulated them. Afterward they went outside to get in the limos that drove them to her parents' palazzo for their wedding brunch on the east patio.

While they ate, Tuccia's father made an announcement. "Unbeknownst to Tuccianna and her new husband, I've made arrangements for them to have a small honeymoon aboard our yacht, so they won't be flying back to Milan for a few days."

Cesare's heart leaped. They wouldn't have to endure a flight. At least not for a couple of days.

At that juncture Takis rose to his feet. "No man should have to worry about getting back to work right away. Maurice knows about your marriage and has agreed to run the kitchen until the Siciliana gets back. He told me to tell you he's looking forward to seeing the new Signora Donati without your uniform and that floppy chef's hat."

Everyone laughed, but Tuccia's face went crimson. Cesare loved it.

"How soon can we leave?" he whispered near her ear.

"As soon as I change. I'll be right back."

She gave him a wife's kiss to torture him and hurried through the rooms to the upstairs. Once she'd gotten out of her wedding dress, she put on a pale pink summer suit and strappy high heels. Grabbing the case she'd packed earlier, she hurried back down. More hugs and kisses ensued.

But his impatience was too great. He put his arm around her shoulders, waved goodbye to everyone and they rushed outside to get in the limo. What an amazing experience to be headed for the dock in Mondello and go aboard the royal yacht.

Cesare had seen it out in the harbor many times along with the other yachts after he'd hiked the bluff. When he'd been younger all his thoughts had been intent on leaving for New York to make his way in the world. Little did he dream that his great adventure would bring him right back home, right to this yacht where his new wife had learned to make *granita*.

The deck steward showed them to the master bedroom below deck. Once he left them alone Cesare picked Tuccia up in his arms and twirled her around. "Finally I have you all to myself the way I've dreamed."

"I've had the same dreams. Love me, Cesare." Her voice shook.

"As if you need to ask me." He carried her to the bed and followed her down. They started to kiss, one after another until there was no beginning and no end. "I'm so hungry for you, I'm afraid I'll eat you alive."

"I'm afraid you won't," she cried, feverish with longing.

"*Amata.* You're so beautiful I can hardly breathe. My adorable, precious, beloved wife."

Those words were still part of her euphoria when she woke up during the night. They'd made love for hours, only to fall asleep, then start the whole heavenly process over again when they came awake.

She'd tried to imagine what it would be like to really love a man. But nothing could have prepared her for the kind of love showered on her by her new husband. There were no words to describe the ecstasy that had her clinging to him throughout the night.

At one point her rapture was so great she wept.

"What is it?" he cried.

"I was just thinking. What if I hadn't run away? What if your mother hadn't let me stay overnight? I might have missed *you*." She moaned.

He buried his face in her neck. "Don't even think about it."

"I can't help it. I'm too happy, Cesare. No woman could ever be as happy as I am."

"You're supposed to be when you've found the right person to love. *Ti amo*, Tuccia. This is only the beginning."

*Two years later, the Castello di Lombardi*

Tuccia followed little Cesare around on the grass behind the *castello* near the ruins of the fourteenth-century church. Their little brown-haired son had just turned a year old, but was still unsteady on his feet. Filippa and Dimi's little dark-haired boy, Dizo, was just two months older, but handled himself with amazing agility. Her gaze followed two year-old Nico around. He was Vincenzo's clone.

Cesare came up behind her and put his arms around her waist, nuzzling her neck. "It's hilarious out here with all the children running around on the grass. Look how Nico runs after Zoe. She's the image of her mother."

"Lys is a beauty, and I can tell Zoe is going to be a heartbreaker, too, when she grows up," Tuccia said, eyeing the two-year-old with a smile.

"I think she has already stolen Nico's heart."

Tuccia turned around and gave her husband a long, passionate kiss. "Wouldn't it be amazing if they grew up loving each other?"

"You mean like Gemma and Vincenzo? It wouldn't surprise me."

"I love having a birthday picnic for all of them. Maurice and Ciro have really outdone themselves for this celebration."

"He doesn't make pastry as good as yours, my love."

"Of course he does, Cesare. Doesn't Gemma have the best ideas? This is so fun! Uh-oh. Cesare fell down."

He kissed her cheek. "I'll go get him."

Tuccia joined the women sitting on the blanket while she watched her gorgeous husband run after their son. As far as she was concerned, this was heaven.

The men were tending the children to give the women a break. All the women except Tuccia were pregnant again. Gemma was seven months along with a girl this time.

"Is Vincenzo as freaked out as this time around?" Lys wanted to know.

"He's not nearly as bad as he was the first time."

"Thank heaven," Filippa exclaimed. They all laughed.

Gemma raised herself up on one elbow. "Do you know what's really strange? To be out here on the same grass where I played as a little girl with Vincenzo and Dimi. Sometimes they had sword fights."

"Who won?" Filippa wanted to know.

"They were both pretty fierce and equally matched. One time when it was Vincenzo's birthday, my mother made a little cake for him and I brought it out to him."

Tuccia smiled. "Did you always love him?"

"Always."

"And soon you were making cakes."

"And then I met Filippa at cooking school."

Tuccia stretched out. "I can't believe how lucky I was to meet Cesare. I fell so hard for him I actually learned how to make his mother's pastry in order to be near him."

"Are you taking my name in vain again?" a deep familiar voice sounded behind her. The girls chuckled.

She rolled over and looked up at him holding their son. "Afraid so. We were just saying how lucky we are to be married to such remarkable men."

Cesare's smile melted her on the spot. "Funny. The guys and I were just having the same conversation about the superb women in our lives. It all happened one morning in Vincenzo's New York apartment when he asked if Takis and I wanted to go into business with him and Dimi across the water." He stared into her eyes. "And here we are. Life truly is more fantastic and wonderful than fiction."

"I agree, Cesare." *I love you*, Tuccia mouthed the words before getting to her feet. "Come on. Let's go back to the hotel room and put little Cesare down for a nap. I want some alone time with my husband."

They hurried inside the *castello* to the private wing on the second floor. After putting their sleepy boy down, they went in their bedroom. Tuccia started to take off her clothes, unable to wait until she held Cesare in her arms.

He removed his faster and within seconds he pulled her down on the bed. *"Bellissima?"* he whispered against her lips. "Do you still love me as much as you did when we got married?"

She heard a hint of anxiety his voice.

"My darling husband, how can you even ask me that?" Except that she *did* know why. His mother had confided in her about his father. "Listen to me." She leaned over him, cupping his face in her hands.

"You're stuck with me forever. I'm never going anywhere. You're my whole life! It began the moment you crushed me in your arms. I've never told you this before, but I'm telling you now. That magical night, I felt like you'd imprinted yourself on my heart and soul. When you turned on the lights, there stood the most gorgeous man my eyes had ever beheld."

Cesare kissed her until they were both out of breath. "It was a magical night. You looked like an enchanted princess escaping her bottle."

"That's how it felt, and there you were. I love you, Cesare. Never doubt it for an instant."

"Never again, *amorada*. Never again."

\* \* \* \* \*

*If you missed the first two books, check out the rest of* THE BILLIONAIRES' CLUB *trilogy!*

*RETURN OF HER ITALIAN DUKE*
*BOUND TO HER GREEK BILLIONAIRE*

*And if you enjoyed this story, check out these other great reads from Rebecca Winters*

*THE BILLIONAIRE'S PRIZE*
*THE BILLIONAIRE WHO SAW HER BEAUTY*
*THE BILLIONAIRE BABY SWAP*
*HIS PRINCESS OF CONVENIENCE*

*All available now!*

## "Looks like you've been cleared to go," he told her as the other woman stepped away.

Anne felt butterflies fluttering in the pit of her stomach. Why did she feel as if she was about to go out on a first date? She wasn't, for heaven's sake. This wasn't even a date at all. She was just getting a cup of coffee with someone who had once meant a great deal to her.

*Someone you had a baby with*, the voice in her head reminded her.

With effort, Anne forced a ghost of a smile to her lips as she said, "Just let me get my purse and then I'm ready."

After taking out her purse from one of the bottom drawers, Anne rose to her feet. She glanced at the phone, willing it to ring.

It didn't.

She had temporarily run out of possible excuses.

"Okay," she told Danny as she came around to the front of the reception desk, "let's get that cup of coffee."

Taking her elbow to help guide her out of the clinic, Dan murmured, "I thought you'd never ask."

The butterflies went into high gear.

\* \* \*

**Montana Mavericks:**
The Great Family Roundup—
Real cowboys and real love in Rust Creek Falls!

# THE MAVERICK'S RETURN

## BY
## MARIE FERRARELLA

First Published in Great Britain 2017
By Mills & Boon, an imprint of HarperCollins*Publishers*
1 London Bridge Street, London, SE1 9GF

© 2017 Harlequin Books S.A.

Special thanks and acknowledgement are given to Marie Ferrarella for her contribution to the Montana Mavericks: The Great Family Roundup series.

ISBN: 978-0-263-92335-3

23-1017

Our policy is to use papers that are natural, renewable and recyclable products and made from wood grown in sustainable forests. The logging and manufacturing processes conform to the legal environmental regulations of the country of origin.

Printed and bound in Spain
by CPI, Barcelona

To
Marcia Book Adirim,
Whose multilevel mind
Always leaves me in complete
Awe

## Prologue

Daniel Stockton wearily walked into the log cabin he lived in at the Comanchero Ranch. For the last ten years, he'd been in charge of booking vacations for city dwellers who yearned to sample the cowboy life for a week or two and pretend they lived back in the days of the old Wild West. The dude ranch, one of Colorado's most popular, was currently in the height of its busy season. Attendance was at an all-time high and would probably remain so until somewhere around the end of next month.

As he concentrated on putting one foot in front of the other on the way to his secondhand sofa, Dan felt as if all those years had been packed into this last week and a half.

He sighed and collapsed on the worn, cracked sofa in the center of his small living area.

His stomach rumbled, asking to be appeased, but for now, Dan felt as if he couldn't move more than the first two fingers of his right hand. The hand that was currently wrapped around the remote control for the TV that had been in the cabin when he'd initially moved in. The cabin was too quiet and he just wanted some background noise to distract him.

Even now, after all these years, he didn't like being alone with his thoughts.

Aiming the remote at the twenty-four-inch TV screen, he pressed the power button, content to watch whatever program came on. He just wanted some company he didn't have to explain anything to. The tourists who came to the ranch always seemed to be filled to the brim with questions.

Most of the time, that didn't bother him, but there was this one family this last week that had a kid with them—Harlan—who just wouldn't stop asking questions no matter what. The kid, all of eleven or twelve, was obviously trying to trip him up.

Dan felt as if his head was throbbing and, quite possibly, on the verge of exploding.

The pay at the Comanchero Ranch was fairly decent and he did get to spend most of his life on horseback, which he loved, but there were times—like this last week—when the loneliness caught up to him, wrapping its tentacles around him so hard he could scarcely breathe. That was when he found his patience to be thin and in relatively short supply. And when that happened, his tolerance went out the window.

This afternoon he'd come dangerously close to telling Harlan's parents that they needed to take their son in hand and teach him some much-needed manners. But he'd managed to hold his tongue long enough to get those "dudes" back to the ranch house where they were staying.

However, it had been close. Closer than he really liked.

"Get a grip, Dan. This isn't a bad job. And you sure as hell can't afford to lose it," he told himself as he got up again.

His stomach was growling way too much. It was time to rummage through his refrigerator and find something that could pass for food.

As he walked to the small refrigerator, his back was to the TV when he heard it.

The voice from his past.

Dan froze, listening. Convinced that he was imagining things.

It couldn't be, he told himself. It was the loneliness getting to him, wearing away his edge, nothing more.

He forced himself to proceed to the kitchen and open the refrigerator. Instead of getting something to eat, he took out a bottle of root beer, twisted off the cap and closed the refrigerator door.

He'd just put the bottle to his lips when he heard it again.

The voice from his past.

"This is Travis Dalton and you're watching *The Great Roundup*. We're coming to you live from Rust Creek Falls, Montana, and I'm here talking to Jamie Stockton, the valiant dad of year-old triplets. Jamie, until just recently, had to juggle being both father *and* mother to these fine, hearty little human beings. Tell us how that felt, Jamie."

"I don't mind admitting that I was pretty over-whelmed at first," the young man the narrator had addressed as Jamie answered.

The root beer slipped from Dan's hand, meeting the floor at an obtuse angle. Mercifully, it avoided shattering. Instead, a small shower of foam emerged from the bottle, christening his boots and the bottom of his jeans.

Dan didn't notice.

His eyes were glued to the TV, staring at the screen.

Staring at Jamie Stockton.

His younger brother.

The wave of loneliness Dan had been harboring turned into a twelve-foot sweeping tidal wave, all but drowning him in memories.

Memories he had been struggling so hard to bury and ignore for the last twelve years.

Listening to the voice of the young man telling his story caused those years to instantly melt away as if they had never happened.

Except that they had.

## Chapter One

Daniel shifted from foot to foot, standing before the closed ranch house door.

His brother's door.

He had absolutely no idea what to expect. What if, when his brother Jamie opened the door and saw who was knocking, he slammed it in his face?

Of course, there was a small chance, one that he was silently rooting for, that Jamie would mercifully allow him to plead his case.

The way he felt, however, the odds were probably against that happening.

It had taken Dan more than a whole month of intense soul searching to finally get up the nerve to take this giant step, to leave Colorado and travel all this distance back to Rust Creek Falls, Montana.

Back to his hometown and his roots.

Back to the place where it had all fallen apart twelve years ago.

Ironically, the very things that were drawing him back to Rust Creek Falls were the same things that had caused him to stay away so long in the first place.

The same things that made him hesitate reconnecting this last whole month.

Dan had raised his hand to knock on the door a total of three times now. And all three times his courage had failed him, causing him to drop his hand back down again to his side.

*Come on. You didn't come all this way back to Montana just to chicken out at the last minute. This isn't you.*

Except that, maybe, it was. Why else had he not tried to get back in contact with *any* of his siblings for over a decade?

The first two years of his self-imposed exile he'd been with his two older brothers, Luke and Bailey. But then they had gone their own separate ways, too, leaving him to fend for himself.

The simple truth of it was he was tired of being alone. Tired of having no one who shared at least part of the same memories from his childhood and adolescence.

Tired of not having any family.

It would have been different if he'd never had any siblings. He had very nearly made his peace with that. After all, he really had no idea where any of his brothers or sisters were anymore.

But then he'd heard Jamie's voice on that broadcast last month and everything had changed.

Suddenly, he felt as if he was part of something again. He knew that at least Jamie was still back in Rust Creek Falls. All he had to do was reach out, reestablish that familial connection with his younger brother and just like that, he would have a family again.

It had sounded so easy when he had first thought of it. But now he wasn't so sure.

*At least find out if he'll talk to you.*

Taking a deep breath, Dan raised his hand again and this time, his knuckles finally made contact with the door, creating a rhythmic sound as he knocked.

He could feel his heart pounding as he stood there, waiting.

It was late afternoon, almost early evening. What if there was no one at home? What if Jamie and his triplets were away on vacation? After all, that could be a possibility, Dan thought.

Or what if Jamie *was* home, opened the door and then told him to go to hell?

Dan's breath caught in his throat, all but turning solid.

What if—?

Suddenly, there was no more time for speculation or waffling. No more time for hypothetical what-ifs. The door opened and an older, adult version of the boy he had left behind twelve years ago, the young man he'd seen more than a month ago on his TV, was standing in the doorway, looking at him.

For a moment, the expression on Jamie Stockton's face was blank. It was the kind of expression a person wore when they opened their door to someone they didn't recognize.

But then, in the next moment, a multitude of emotions washed over Jamie's face in quick succession, one after the other.

Like a man caught in a dream, Jamie stared at him. And then, finally, he asked hoarsely, "Daniel?"

Dan's lips quirked in a quick, nervous smile. "Yeah. It's me," he confirmed, still feeling incredibly uneasy and uncertain about this reunion that he had instigated.

And then Dan cleared his throat and forced himself to push on and say something further. "I would have called ahead first, but I didn't know how you would react to seeing me and I didn't want to take a chance on you turning—"

Dan didn't get a chance to finish his sentence. Whatever else he was going to say about his concerns regarding their first meeting in twelve years evaporated when Jamie pulled him into his arms and enfolded him in a giant bear hug.

"Oh my God, Danny. It really is you!" Jamie cried, holding on to him tightly, as if he was afraid that if he opened his arms, his older brother would suddenly just vanish.

When after a couple of minutes Jamie gave no sign of releasing him, Dan finally had to say, "Um, Jamie, I think you're crushing my ribs."

"Oh, right. Sorry." Jamie let his arms drop. He took a step back and looked at Dan. Disbelief highlighted his face as his eyes raked over every square inch of his older brother. "It's just that I never thought I'd see you again. Come in, come in," he urged, gesturing into his house even as he ushered Dan in and closed the door behind him.

"Is everything okay? Are you here for a visit? Are you staying?" And then Jamie stopped asking questions. He took a deep breath, as if trying to get hold of himself. "Sorry, I don't mean to overwhelm you. It's just that there are so many things I want to know."

Before Dan could say a single word in response, Jamie broke out in another huge smile. "Damn, but it's good to see you!" he cried, pulling Dan into another heartfelt, although slightly less rib-crushing, bear hug.

This time, he released Dan without being prompted. A long sigh escaped him as he took a step back again.

"You've lost weight," Jamie finally noted.

"I wasn't exactly fat to begin with," Dan reminded his brother with a self-conscious laugh.

"No, you weren't. But I don't recall your face looking this gaunt before— Damn, it's so great to see you," Jamie exclaimed again. "I thought… Well, for a while, I thought—" Jamie waved his hand. "Never mind what I thought. You're alive and you're here and that's all that counts." He blinked back tears that threatened to spill out. "Sit down. Make yourself comfortable," he urged, gesturing toward the leather sofa in his living room.

Relieved, Dan sat down beside his brother. "This is quite a welcome," he told Jamie, then confessed the fear that had almost made him turn around and go home before Jamie even knew he was there. "I was afraid you'd be angry with me."

"You mean for leaving?"

Dan nodded, looking uncomfortable as well as embarrassed. "Yes."

"I was," Jamie admitted. "I was really angry for a while. Angry and bitter that you and Luke and Bailey had just picked up and left us. Left me," he emphasized because that was what had been at the heart of his initial anger. "But then I realized that it wasn't your fault. After Mom and Dad died in that car crash, Grandma and Grandpa didn't exactly make it easy for the three of you to stick around."

As his brother spoke, memories of his grandparents assailed Daniel. Reliving those harsh days, even now, was painful. But he needn't explain them to Jamie, he realized, when his brother continued.

"I didn't find out the truth till much later. That they'd made it quite clear that they might have to take in Bella and me—since they managed to get the other girls adopted—but the three of you who were eighteen or older could fend for yourselves somewhere else. They all but told you, Luke and Bailey to leave town, so you really had no choice but to go."

Daniel could remember the day so clearly, though it had happened twelve years ago.

"But I didn't know at the time that they had said that to you," Jamie said. "All I knew was that my parents were dead and my big brothers had abandoned me just when I felt that I needed them the most." Jamie shook his head, trying to block the painful feeling those memories aroused. "I was really angry at you for a long time."

Dan made no effort to attempt to deflect the blame.

However, the way Jamie had welcomed him was not the greeting of a man who still held a grudge.

"But you're not anymore?" Dan asked, wanting to be perfectly clear just where they stood in relation to one another.

"No, I'm not," Jamie readily confirmed.

Relief swamped him. Dan knew he should just accept that and be happy. He was aware that he was pushing his luck, but he had to know. "What changed your mind?"

Jamie laughed. "Simple. I found out that life's too short to carry around all this anger and bitterness. And the triplets came into my life. Nothing like being responsible for three tiny, helpless souls to make you get over yourself—fast," Jamie emphasized. "Once I stopped being so angry about everything, I left myself open for the good stuff, like love," he told Dan with a wide grin. "And that's when I fell in love with Fallon O'Reilly. After that, my whole world changed for the better—and now I couldn't be happier."

As if suddenly hearing himself, Jamie stopped right in the middle of his narrative, embarrassed. "Hell, I'm sorry."

"About what?" Dan asked, confused.

"Well, I'm doing all the talking here."

Dan shook his head. "That's okay. I think it's great. I haven't heard your voice in so long," he told Jamie. "Just keep talking."

But Jamie was not about to get sidetracked again. He had questions for his older brother.

"No, first tell me what made you suddenly turn up on my doorstep now, after twelve long years." Fresh fears suddenly surfaced in his mind. "Did something happen?" he wanted to know. "Has something suddenly changed? You're not dying, are you?" he asked, alarmed.

"No, I'm not dying," Dan assured his brother. "What happened was that I was in my cabin—"

Jamie cut in, surprised. "You have a cabin?"

"Yes," Dan answered. He didn't want to get into all that right now. That was for later. "Long story," he said, waving it away.

Jamie was starved for any and all information concerning Dan, not to mention the rest of his family, except for his sister Bella, who was still in Rust Creek Falls, and other sister Dana, who had recently been found.

"Go ahead, I'm all ears," Jamie told him.

Dan wanted to tell him about this part first, because it was what led to his coming back to Rust Creek Falls and to his seeking out Jamie. "I'll tell you about that once I finish answering your first question."

"Sorry, I didn't mean to interrupt," Jamie said, then coaxed, "Go ahead, I'm listening."

"All right, then." Taking a breath, Dan began again. "I'd just put in an extra-hard day. Walking into my cabin, I turned on the TV for some company—"

"So you live alone?"

*Alone.*

Each time Dan heard it, the word burned more and more of a hole in his gut. "Yeah, I do."

"You never married?" Jamie asked.

Dan shook his head. "Nope."

How could he marry? His heart was not his to give to anyone. It was already spoken for—even if the woman who it belonged to had no use for it.

When he hesitated, Jamie apologized.

"Sorry, didn't mean to pry," he told Dan. "Go on. You walked in, turned on the TV for company and then what?"

When he heard Jamie summarize the events he'd just told him, the words had this incredibly lonely ring to them. He knew he'd felt the same thing time and again, but he'd talked himself into living with it. He'd made himself believe that his life wasn't as soul-draining as it really was. But now he knew the truth. That he was exceedingly lonely—and that he had made the right decision in coming home.

At least for now.

"And then I heard this voice," Dan said, continuing with his narrative, "this voice that was filled with pride and love, talking about his triplets."

"Wait," Jamie said, stopping his brother. "You heard me on TV? You caught that program that Travis Dalton taped in town? You actually saw *The Great Roundup*?"

Dan smiled at the eager disbelief he heard in his brother's voice. "I did."

"But that segment was on more than a month ago."

Dan merely nodded and said, "I know."

"You've been here in Rust Creek Falls all this time?"

"No, I just got here," Dan corrected. He wanted his brother to understand that it had been his cold feet that had kept him from coming. "You're my first stop. Possibly my only stop because I don't know where everyone else is, or even if they're still in Montana."

But Jamie was still having a hard time making sense out of what he was hearing. The brother he remembered, the one he had idolized, had never been someone to drag his feet.

"I don't understand. If the show was on over a month ago, what took you so long to get here?"

Dan wasn't about to lie or make up excuses. "It took me a month to get up the nerve to come and see you. I wasn't sure if you'd even let me come in your front door, or if you'd take one look at me, slam the door in my face and tell me to go to hell."

Jamie stared at him, an incredulous smile widening on his lips.

"You were afraid *I'd* reject you?" he asked.

Dan nodded. "Something like that."

The idea was so outlandish it almost made Jamie laugh out loud. "You were afraid of your little brother?" he asked, unable to believe that Danny could be afraid of anyone, least of all *him*.

Dan made no attempt at excuses, or to brazen the situation out. He was long past that sort of thing as far as he was concerned.

"Yes," Dan admitted, "I was. Because, as far as you were concerned, Luke, Bailey and I had run out on you and the girls. Left you at the mercy of a couple of cranky grandparents, neither of whom was ever going to be up for grandparent of the year. Left you and never tried to get in contact with you," Dan concluded with a sigh.

For a moment, the stark, honest answer left Jamie

speechless. And then he said, "Well, at least you're not trying to sugarcoat any of it, I'll give you that."

"I can't sugarcoat it," Dan admitted. "I want you to know that I wanted to see you and the girls, wanted to get in contact with you." He put a hand on his brother's shoulder, anchoring him with the sincere look in his eyes. "Not a day went by in those years when I didn't think about you."

Jamie believed him. But he still had questions. "So if you felt that way, why didn't you get in contact with any of us?"

"I didn't want to disrupt your lives any more than they'd already been disrupted," Dan told him with sincerity.

"You wouldn't have disrupted them, you idiot," Jamie cried. "You would have only made them better."

Dan sighed again. "Yeah, well…" His voice trailed off. At the time, he'd been convinced he was doing the right thing.

And then, of course, there had been the guilt. That had all but paralyzed him. It had definitely kept him from returning.

Jamie took pity on him. "Water under the bridge," he told Dan. "Just water under the bridge. What really matters is that you're here now," he said, sounding genuinely happy. "Makes my suffering through the taping of that program worth all the agony," he added with a warm laugh. "Oh damn, where are my manners? Can I offer you something to eat or drink?"

"No, I'm fine," Dan told him. "Just seeing you again after all this time is all I need."

"Speaking of need," Jamie said, "I need you to fill me in."

"On what?"

"On what you've been doing these last twelve years," Jamie said.

Dan blew out a long breath. He knew he owed Jamie that much. Still, going over that ground would bring up memories he wanted left buried and undisturbed.

He looked at Jamie, wondering where to start. "That, my brother, is a tall order."

## *Chapter Two*

"Well," Jamie said in response to the unreadable expression on his brother's face, "think of it as the price you have to pay if you want to get to meet your nephews and niece."

The triplets, Dan thought. He'd almost forgotten about them.

"Okay," he replied gamely, "if you're really serious."

Jamie managed to keep a straight face for approximately fifteen seconds, and then he finally broke down and laughed.

"I'm just curious about what you've been doing, but if you don't want to talk about it," he said more soberly, "that's okay."

Dan appreciated that his brother wasn't pressuring him for information. The very fact that Jamie wasn't encouraged him to share.

"It's not that I don't want to talk about it, Jamie. I just don't want to put you to sleep." The smile on his face was a tad sheepish. "The last twelve years have been pretty boring."

The sadness Jamie saw in his brother's eyes told him that those years weren't boring so much as they might have left a scar on Dan's soul. Jamie found himself aching for his brother.

"Tell me when you're ready," Jamie said. "No pressure."

Dan was about to say something in response, but just then, a slender, willowy redhead with lively blue eyes and an infectious smile walked into the room, coming from the back of the house. She looked straight at him.

"I thought I heard you talking to someone," she said to Jamie.

Both Jamie and his brother rose to their feet in unison.

"Danny," Jamie said, putting his hand out to the woman who had just crossed over to them, "I'd like you to meet the light of my life, my wife, Fallon." Affectionately wrapping his arm around her waist, Jamie continued the introduction. "Fallon, this is my older brother Danny."

Jamie expected a nod of acknowledgment from the pretty young woman. A smile at best. But he quickly discovered that Fallon was just like her husband. Rather than greeting him with a few pleasantries, she left the shelter of her husband's arm and went straight to him.

The young woman embraced him, giving him a warm hug that swirled straight into his heart.

"Danny! It's so wonderful to finally meet you," she cried enthusiastically. "Jamie's told me so much about you!"

Stunned, still caught up in Fallon's embrace, Dan looked over her shoulder at his brother. He'd thought that by now, Jamie would have thought of him as a distant memory—if that.

"Really?" he asked.

"Yes," Fallon replied. Releasing her brother-in-law, she stepped back next to her husband. "Can't get to know the man without getting to know his family. Though I must admit it took a bit of work at first. Jamie wasn't much of a talker in the beginning," she confided. "I think he kind of felt overwhelmed, and under the circumstances, who could blame him?" she said, looking at Jamie fondly. "But once I got him going, he told me all about you and Luke and Bailey, as well as your sisters. Bella and Dana, of course, I got to know myself. You've all had a rough life," she readily acknowledged, "but it can only get better from here on in."

Before Dan could ask about either Bella or Dana, Jamie told him, "Bella's still in Rust Creek Falls. She's married now. And Dana came for a while late last year. Turns out she's living in Portland, Oregon with a nice family who had adopted her. No word on Liza yet, but we're still looking." He smiled broadly at Danny. "Bella and Dana will both be thrilled to know that you're actually alive."

The revelation stunned Dan. He stared at his brother. "You didn't think I was alive?" he asked Jamie incredulously.

"Well, I didn't hear from you for twelve years. The thought had crossed my mind," Jamie said. "Anyway, it was Fallon who encouraged me to start looking, not just for you but for all the lost sheep of our family," he said. He paused to press a kiss to his wife's temple. "I don't mind telling you that this woman saved my life."

Fallon put her hand on her husband's chest. "Now, don't get all melodramatic on your brother, Jamie," Fallon chided.

"No melodrama," Jamie responded. "Just the plain truth. I was in a really bad way after Paula died," he told Dan.

"Paula?" Dan asked. It occurred to him that he knew next to nothing about what Jamie had gone through in the last twelve years, just what he had gotten from the TV program.

A pang twisted his gut. He should have been here. Somehow, even though his grandparents had all but thrown him and his older brothers out, he should have found a way to be there for Jamie and his sisters. A way to get over his all-but-soul-crushing guilt, a way to keep them all together as a family.

"His first wife," Fallon interjected.

The fact that Jamie had been married to someone else first didn't seem to bother her, Dan observed. She seemed to take it all in stride. Jamie had really lucked out with Fallon, Dan thought. He was genuinely happy for his brother. At least one of them had found happiness, despite the fact that the odds had felt as if they were against all of them.

"The triplets were born prematurely," Jamie explained, continuing to fill his brother in. "Paula died shortly after that from complications caused by the C-section. For a long while, I felt it was all my fault."

Confused, Dan wondered how that could possibly be his brother's fault.

"Paula didn't want kids. I did." A semi-sad smile played on his lips. "I guess I missed the sounds of a big family."

Fallon took over her husband's narrative. It was clear that she didn't want him to dwell on what she felt were his unfounded feelings of guilt.

"The whole town pitched in to help Jamie out when Paula passed on. A bunch of us took turns volunteering to take care of the triplets so that he could regain his foothold."

"I wouldn't have made it without you," Jamie told her.

"Without us," Fallon corrected. "Like I said," she told Dan, "the whole town pitched in."

Deftly, Fallon changed the subject, asking Dan, "So, have you come back to Rust Creek Falls to stay?"

"Not to sound as pushy as this redhead," Jamie interjected, "but have you?"

Dan was still trying to make his mind up about that. "I'm not sure yet."

Fallon didn't hesitate. "Well, you're staying with us while Jamie helps you to make up your mind," she told Dan. Her tone, warm and friendly, left no room for argument.

Still, Dan felt he had to at least offer a protest. "I can't impose."

"Family never imposes," Jamie insisted. "End of discussion. You're staying," he said with finality. Then he got back to his initial question. "So where have you been all this time?"

That was simple enough to answer. "The last ten years I've been in Colorado."

"Colorado?" Jamie repeated. "I can't picture you in Colorado."

Dan understood where Jamie was coming from on that. Colorado brought up images of big cities and he was a country boy at heart.

"I've been booking dude ranch vacations for city dwellers who fancy themselves cowboys," Dan told his brother and Fallon. "It's not a bad living," he was quick to add. "And I get to spend most of my time on horseback."

"Now, *that* I can picture," Jamie told him. "You said you've been in Colorado for the last ten years, but you've been gone from Rust Creek Falls for twelve. Where did you go before then?"

"Cheyenne," Dan answered. "I worked as a ranch hand there—along with Luke and Bailey. But they didn't much care for it," he confessed with a sad smile. "They got restless and then, one night, they just took off." He paused, trying to deal with an unexpected wave of sadness that washed over him. Suppressing a sigh, he told Jamie, "I haven't seen them since."

Fallon leaned forward and put her hand up on her brother-in-law's shoulder. "We'll find them," she promised.

"Isn't she amazing?" Jamie asked him. There was

pride in his eyes. "She just keeps spreading optimism wherever she goes, no matter what."

A light pink hue rose to Fallon's cheeks as she point-edly ignored her husband's compliment. Rerouting the conversation again, she asked Dan, "Would you like to meet our kids?"

He could think of nothing that he would like better. "I'd love to," Dan responded.

"Then come this way. You can come too, Jamie," she added playfully, as if it was an afterthought. "Now, brace yourself," she told Dan. "These are not your typi-cal year-and-a-half-old babies. They could use Jared, Henry and Kate in caffeine commercials," she confided.

"By the way, Kate's the one with a bow on her head," Jamie told him as they walked to the bedroom that the triplets occupied when they were downstairs.

He explained that the official nursery was upstairs, but because they wanted the triplets near them as much as possible, they'd created a second room for the babies downstairs where they could take their naps.

"She had such short hair," Jamie explained, "every-one thought I had three sons. After a while, I got tired of telling them that Kate was a girl, so I put a bow on her to set them straight."

"Now her hair is finally growing in," Fallon told him as she led the way into the back room. "Which is a good thing, because she keeps pulling that bow off."

Dan couldn't hold back the smile when he stepped into the room and saw the triplets. The two boys were both on their feet, their chubby little fingers grabbing the side of their playpen and shaking it. Dan had a feeling that the playpen's life expectancy was in serious jeopardy of being severely shortened.

The third triplet was seated on her well-padded bottom, serenely playing with a floppy-eared stuffed bunny, seemingly totally oblivious to the commotion her brothers were creating.

Beaming with unabashed pride, Jamie introduced his triplets.

"Dan, I'd like you to meet Henry and Jared," he said, indicating the two standing boys. "And this little sweet-heart is Kate. Kids," Jamie said to his triplets, "this is your uncle Danny. Can you say 'Hi' to him?" he prompted.

An uneven chorus of something that could be thought to pass for "Hi!" rose up following Jamie's request.

"They talk?" Dan asked, his voice a mixture of sur-prise and envy. He knew next to nothing when it came to children and even less than that when it came to ba-bies.

"Talk?" Jamie echoed, then said with a laugh, "They don't stop talking. Not even in their sleep. Of course, most of the time it sounds like gibberish and I can't un-derstand what they're saying, but they seem to be able to communicate with each other just fine."

"That's because twins and triplets have a language all their own," Fallon told her husband.

Dan dropped to his knees beside the playpen to get closer to the three little people who had been instru-mental in getting him to finally come home. Something stirred within him as he watched them for a moment.

"Hi, kids."

Again he received an uneven chorus echoing the greeting. Kate pulled herself up to her feet and made her way over to him. She offered him a sunny smile and just like that, she took him prisoner.

Dan ran his hand along her silky hair. "She's going to be a charmer," he told Jamie.

"What do you mean 'going to be'?" Jamie asked. "She already is one."

"You're right," Dan laughed, unable to take his eyes off the little girl. "My mistake."

Dan spent the next hour getting to know his brother's children as well as his brother's wife. It was the best hour he could remember spending in the last twelve years.

But then it was time to put the triplets down for a nap.

"I'm afraid you're going to have to leave the room now," Fallon told him, apologizing. "I'll never get them down for their naps if you're in eyesight."

"I understand," Dan said. He was already at the bedroom door, although he did pause for one last backward glance.

"They're something else, aren't they?" Jamie said with pride.

"They're beautiful kids," Dan agreed. And then he thought of the circumstances that Jamie had been forced to go through shortly after the triplets' birth. "You must have had a really hard time coping right after Paula's death," Dan said with immense sympathy. Again, he fervently wished he could have been there for Jamie.

"It was hard," Jamie admitted. "But Fallon wasn't

kidding. It felt like the whole town pitched in to help. Otherwise, quite honestly, I don't know what would have happened or what I would have done. When you have just two hands and three kids, the numbers aren't exactly in your favor," he told his brother, his words underscored with a good-natured laugh.

Dan had been under the impression that Fallon had really meant a few people at best. But there was no reason for Jamie to exaggerate. That hadn't been in the nature of the boy he'd known.

"The *whole* town?" Dan asked in amazement, just to be sure.

"Yeah, the whole town." Jamie paused for a moment before adding, "Anne helped, too."

The mere mention of her name was like a fissure in the dam. The crack split open, spewing forth a deluge of memories upon Daniel.

"Have you been by to see Anne since you got back?" Jamie asked, breaking into his thoughts.

Not a day had gone by in the last twelve years that Dan hadn't wanted to see Anne Lattimore. That he hadn't wanted to pack up his meager belongings and find Annie. But he had staunchly never given in to that desire.

Mainly because he was convinced that she was far better off without him.

And even now, as he stood in his brother's house, battling the urge to ride up and see the woman he had loved practically from the first moment he'd drawn breath, a part of him still felt that she would be better off if he just left well enough alone.

"No," Dan answered quietly, "I haven't. When I came into town, I didn't stop anywhere else. I came straight to your place."

"I appreciate that, I really do," Jamie told him. "But if you ask me, I think that you really should go see her."

Jamie was tempted to say more, but he stopped himself. He pressed his lips together, as if physically blocking the words that had risen to his tongue.

"Maybe later," Dan demurred.

"There's already been too much 'later,' Danny. Twelve years of 'later.' You need to go see her. Now. Before any more time is lost. You can't get that time back. And the more you drag your feet, the more time you lose," Jamie insisted.

"When did you get this philosophical bent?" Dan asked, amused.

"Right about the time that I realized that I'd been in love with Fallon for a long time and needed to make her aware of it. Now, no more talk. It's still early. Go!" He opened the front door and all but pushed his brother out. "And when you've seen Anne and talked to her," he told Dan, "you can come back here—to your home."

## Chapter Three

She missed him.

After all this time, she still missed him. Not every minute of every day the way she once had. Sometimes, Anne Lattimore could go a whole week without feeling that awful, painful hollowness boring a gaping hole into the pit of her stomach and working its way out to her soul. And then, suddenly, without giving her any warning, the feeling would be back, descending on her with its full weight, making her ache.

Making her remember.

And then she would have to struggle to fight her way back out of the oppressive pit. Back into the light of day. Back into her life as a single mother and a full-time receptionist at Dr. Brooks Smith's Veterinary Clinic.

Heaven knew there was enough in her life to keep her

busy and most of the time, she was. Very busy. It was only during those evenings when Hank, her ex, would pick up Janie to have her stay overnight with him and the house was extra quiet that her mind would unearth images of Danny Stockton. That was when she would feel tormented.

Tormented, because even now she couldn't make peace with the fact that he had left town without saying anything.

Left *her* without saying anything.

After everything they had meant to one another…

No, Anne upbraided herself, she had only *thought* that they had meant so much to one another. Obviously, she hadn't meant to Danny nearly as much as he had meant to her.

She knew all the facts by now, having ferreted them out over the years. She knew that Danny's grandparents had refused to be responsible for him and his older brothers. Knew that they had all but *told* him and his brothers to leave. But if she had meant something to him, if Danny had loved her the way she loved him, he would have found a way to stay.

And if he couldn't abide staying in Rust Creek Falls, if he wanted to go somewhere else, she would have gone anywhere in the world with him. All he would have had to do was say that he wanted her to come with him and she would have left in a heartbeat. Left town, left her family, left her dreams of going to college. Left it all for Danny.

All he would have had to do was ask.

But he didn't ask.

Instead, he just disappeared without a trace, like some magician's big trick.

Even so, her pride badly wounded, she'd still tried to find him. But no one knew where Danny and his two brothers had gone. It was like they had vanished into thin air. Eventually, she gave up trying to find him, decided to go on with her life and went off to college.

And then Hank Harlow had happened in her life. It wasn't long after they met that Hank, clearly smitten, asked her to marry him. Ten years her senior, Hank wouldn't allow the age difference to get in the way. He told her that all he wanted to do was to make her happy.

Anne turned him down as gently as possible.

But Hank wouldn't be deterred. He kept after her, always the well-mannered gentleman, but at the same time, completely determined.

Eventually, he wore her down.

Or more to the point, Anne's circumstances had worn her down. She found out that she was pregnant.

Alarmed and yet thrilled about the baby, she tried to find Dan again. She wasn't any more successful this time around than she had been with her first attempt.

Growing progressively more afraid and feeling completely alone, despite the fact that she did have family back in Rust Creek Falls, she'd accepted Hank's proposal.

But she couldn't marry him until she had told him everything. Summoning all her courage, she'd confessed to Hank that she thought he was a very good man, but that she couldn't love him the way that he loved her. She'd also told him that she was pregnant.

Hank had listened to her very quietly. When she was finished, he told Anne that none of it made any difference to him. He'd still wanted to marry her. Very much.

Moreover, because it was important to her, he'd wanted her to finish college and get her degree. He'd told her that he was financially comfortable, which meant they could hire someone to look after the baby once he or she was born and she could attend her classes.

They were married shortly after that and Hank was true to his word, hiring a nanny when Janie was born. He wouldn't let anything interfere with Anne finishing college. When she graduated, they came back to Rust Creek Falls. Hank bought a ranch and she found a job as a receptionist at the vet clinic.

For five years, everything seemed to be going well. Hank was good to her and he doted on Janie. He was definitely a good husband and a wonderful father, no one could dispute that, least of all her.

But eventually, Hank came to terms that he was never going to win her over, never get her to love him the way that he had hoped. Because she was in love and would always be in love with Daniel Stockton.

Their divorce was amicable and while Hank agreed to give her custody of Janie, he reserved the right to see the little girl and to have her over at his ranch whenever he wanted.

His only stipulation for the divorce was that their secret would remain a secret. As far as Janie and everyone else in Rust Creek Falls knew, he was Janie's father. Anne agreed and Hank continued to cherish the role of father.

As for the divorce, though it was sudden, no one really questioned it. Their friends and family all just assumed that she had been too young to get married and that, most important of all, she had married Hank while still on the rebound from Danny.

Anne never told anyone otherwise, thinking it was best for Janie if everyone just went on believing that. That way, they wouldn't go digging any further.

And her secret would remain just that, a secret. There was no reason for it to be otherwise.

Anne sighed as she pushed the memories aside. Instead, she rummaged through her pantry for dinner ingredients, not really sure what it was that she was looking for.

"What's the matter, Mom?" Janie asked.

Anne blinked, realizing that she'd allowed herself to really drift off. She hadn't even heard her daughter come into the kitchen. Facing her now, she quickly offered Janie a smile.

"What makes you ask that? There's nothing the matter, honey," she told her daughter a bit too quickly.

"Yes, there is," Janie insisted. "You've got that funny look on your face, that look you get when something's wrong."

At eleven, Janie looked younger because of her size. She was a shade under four foot ten and weighed seventy-five pounds, making the blue-eyed blonde smaller than average. Despite that, Janie acted older. Sometimes, Anne had the feeling that her daughter was the adult and she was still that young girl who had fallen head over heels for Danny Stockton.

But this was *not* the time to indulge herself or wallow in old memories that belonged locked away in the past.

She knew that Janie was waiting for her to say something. She said the first thing that came to her mind. "I'm just trying to figure out what to make for dinner," she told her daughter. It wasn't exactly the most creative excuse, but for now, it was all she had. "Any suggestions?"

"How about hamburgers?" Janie asked brightly.

Anne shook her head. "Hamburgers are for when I don't really have time to make dinner. The whole point of my coming home early is that I could make you something special."

Far more intuitive than most girls her age, Janie was immediately alert. She looked at her mother suspiciously. "Are you going away, Mom?"

Caught completely off guard, her daughter's question surprised her. Why would Janie think something like that? "No—"

"Am *I* going away?" Janie wanted to know.

Not for the first time, she couldn't help thinking that her daughter was exceptionally bright. Janie could always pick up on her moods and seemed to instinctively know if something was bothering her—sometimes even before *she* knew it.

"No, of course not," Anne denied, making certain that she sounded calm. "Can't a mom come home early and make something special for her best daughter?"

Janie gave her a look as she said, "I'm your only daughter."

"There's that, too," Anne said with a fond laugh as

she gave her daughter a one-armed hug. "My best and *only* daughter."

"I like hamburgers, Mom," Janie reminded her pointedly.

Anne surrendered, secretly relieved that she was getting out of this so easily. Janie would normally grill her a lot longer.

"Okay, hamburgers it is," she told her daughter. "But later on, when you're staring down at your plate and you decide that you would have wanted to have something a little fancier, just remember, the hamburgers were your idea."

"I'll remember," Janie promised.

Anne opened the refrigerator to make sure she had the necessary main ingredient for this particular "feast." She did.

"Okay," she said to Janie, closing the refrigerator door again. "Now go do your homework."

"I can do it after dinner," Janie protested, suddenly acting her age again.

"Yes, I know. I also know it's better to get your homework out of the way first so that you don't have it hanging over your head all evening. Remember, your father's coming to pick you up for a sleepover tonight."

Janie sighed dramatically, accepting defeat. "Okay, okay, if you don't want my bright, shining face looking up at you adoringly while you cook, I will go and do my homework."

*Eleven, going on thirty*, Anne thought with a smile. "Thank you," she said. "I'll see your bright, shining face looking at me from across the dining room table at dinner—*after* you finish your homework."

Janie walked away, shaking her head. "You know, you should have been a teacher, not a receptionist," the little girl complained.

"Oh no," Anne answered, pretending to shudder at the very thought of being a teacher. "Corralling one student is all I can handle. I'd never survive a whole classroom full of them," Anne assured her daughter. "Now go, make me proud."

A giant, deep-down-from-her-toes sigh was her daughter's only response.

Anne's laugh was followed by a soft sigh as another memory corkscrewed through her. Janie was just like Danny had been at that age. Bright, sunny, eager to twist things until he got his way. And he always managed to do it without annoying anyone.

Sometimes, when she looked at Janie, she could really see Danny. See his face, see his mannerisms.

Anne could feel a tightening in the pit of her stomach again.

She supposed that was what had gotten her started today. Remembering what it had been like when she and Danny had been together.

*Well, you just stop it right now!* she ordered herself fiercely. She didn't have time for this. There was no point in thinking about someone who hadn't been in her life for twelve years.

Anne glanced at her watch. It was still early. Dinner was not for another hour and a half. Since Janie wanted hamburgers, dinner would take no more than fifteen minutes to prepare. That left her with enough time to do something she could actually regard as being fun.

That didn't happen very often.

So infrequently, as a matter of fact, that she couldn't think of anything right off the bat.

Stumped, she was tempted to call her daughter back into the room. They could watch a program together, one of those cartoons that Janie used to love so much when she was a little girl. Granted Janie was almost an adult—or so her daughter liked to think—but Anne knew that Janie secretly still loved watching animated films, especially the ones that were well made and had heart.

Heaven only knew how much longer that would last, Anne mused, going into the family room and looking at the television guide. It wouldn't be all that long before Janie would feel obligated to turn her back on everything and anything that was connected to the little girl she had once been.

It was a rite of passage, Anne thought sadly.

She was just about to turn on the TV and call her daughter into the family room when she heard the doorbell.

Someone was at her door.

Anne looked at her watch. Ordinarily, she would be still at the animal clinic at this time. Her friends all knew that, which meant that this wasn't a social call. And it was way too early for Hank.

Maybe one of her neighbors had seen that her car was in the driveway and was bringing over their beloved dog or cat for some free medical advice. For some reason, some of her neighbors thought that just because she worked at the vet clinic, she knew everything that the vets did.

Only one way to find out who was at her door, she thought with a resigned sigh.

She went to the door, preparing to dispatch the neighbor and their pet as quickly as possible.

Opening the door, Anne said, "What seems to be the problem?" before she actually looked at the person who was standing on her doorstep.

The word *problem* came out as more of a squeak than an actual word.

Her heart was suddenly pounding in her ears. Anne blinked, just in case she actually *was* seeing things.

The person on her doorstep didn't vanish, didn't change.

She had imagined this very scene so many times in the last dozen years, she couldn't even begin to count them. Now that it actually seemed to be taking place, she felt as if her entire body had been dipped in glue, then held fast against some invisible canvas. She was unable to move.

Unable to even breathe.

All she could do was stare at him in complete disbelief.

Slowly, she fought back from the emotional paralysis that held her in its grip, struggling to say something, a sentence, a word.

A sound.

"Hello, Anne."

His deep voice rumbled, the sound echoing within

her very chest, interfering with the beat of her heart, or what might have passed for a beat right now if it wasn't as paralyzed as the rest of her.

Finally, with the inside of her mouth drier than the desert and swiftly turning into sand, Anne forced herself to say something.

Or rather, to say a word. A name.

*His* name.

"Danny?" she asked hoarsely, her throat all but closing up.

She saw a smile, that same faint, funny little smile she had loved so well, curve his lips just before he confirmed what she was asking.

"Yes, Anne, it's me."

The moment he said that, she felt them. Felt the tears that she had been harboring within her for the last twelve years, tears she'd forbade herself to ever shed, even once. She had been able to maintain almost superhuman control over herself, afraid that if she ever allowed herself to cry, to shed so much as a single tear, then there would be no way to stop the flow.

Twelve years' worth of tears.

Anne bit her lower lip, desperately trying to prevent them from falling. Struggling to keep from losing the battle she felt she was doomed to lose.

And then she heard him hesitantly say her name again, the name he used to call her, when the world was so full of possibilities and their love was brand-new.

"Annie?"

*Chapter Four*

In the minutes before he'd knocked on Jamie's door, anticipating the end of a twelve-year separation, Dan had experienced a strong bout of nerves. But he realized now that that had been a piece of cake in comparison to what he'd went through just before he finally rang Annie's doorbell.

For one thing, he hadn't been sure who would be on the other side of that door, Annie or her husband.

Jamie hadn't told him about Annie's marriage when he'd urged him to go see her, but he'd known about Annie's marriage to Hank for a long time now.

He wasn't quite as technologically backward as everyone obviously seemed to think. During one of his bouts of homesickness, he had availed himself of the computer in the ranch town's library and poked around on social media, searching for information about someone he knew.

About Anne.

He himself wasn't on any websites, but that didn't keep him from looking for information about Anne.

And he'd found it.

He found several photos of Annie, her husband and her little girl posted. He remembered the first time he saw the photo of Annie and Hank. It felt as if someone had taken a jagged knife to his chest and savagely carved out his heart. It was also the last time he looked at that site. It hurt too much.

But then he told himself that he had no right to feel that way. He'd left her life; there was no reason to believe she would spend her days pining away for him. He'd left town—and Annie—because he felt he was unworthy of her, felt that he didn't deserve someone as good and pure as her.

That meant that she was free to go on with her life, to marry anyone she chose.

And he was happy for her, happy that she had found someone to love, someone to take care of her. Someone who had obviously started a family with her. He had no right to feel as wounded as he did.

Nonetheless, wounded was how he felt.

And after all these years, there was no denying that he still loved her.

Dan had thought twice about just turning up on her doorstep.

And then he'd thought some more.

However, his need to see Annie again, to just *look* at

her outweighed his fear that she would see right through him and guess how he still felt about her.

But that was his problem, not Annie's, and for her sake, he intended to keep his guard up and maintain a tight rein on all those feelings. Above all, he didn't want to risk making her feel uncomfortable in his presence, not for anything in the world.

Annie stared at the man on her doorstep. A thousand questions instantly sprang up in her head, crowding out one another. A thousand questions that she wanted to put to him. But giving voice to any of them would only tear at the scabs that covered wounds which had taken so very long to heal.

And then there was the little girl who was only two rooms away.

*Danny's* little girl.

It was one thing when she couldn't find Danny to tell him that he was a father, but it was entirely another thing when all that separated Danny from finding out that he was a father was her sudden, very strong on-slaught of cold feet.

It went beyond cold feet. Telling him wouldn't just upend Danny's world. Finding out that Danny was Janie's father instead of Hank would cause total chaos in her world, as well.

And then there was Hank to think of.

He'd been good to her. Good when he didn't have to be. She couldn't allow him to be on the receiving end of such a blow. For all intents and purposes, Hank had been Janie's father from the moment the little girl had been born. She hadn't forced the role on Hank; he'd taken it on gladly.

Hank loved their daughter and Janie *was* their daughter. He had raised Janie with her for five years. And then, even after they had gotten a divorce, he hadn't divorced himself from Janie, hadn't taken himself out of her life. He considered himself to be Janie's father even after Anne had told Hank who Janie's real father was. She couldn't just pull the rug out from under him now, not without giving him fair warning.

A *lot* of fair warning.

And yet, here he was, Danny Stockton, like some ghost out of the past, standing on her doorstep. If Janie came into the room, all he would need was to take one look at the little girl and he'd know she was his.

She could feel her stomach tying itself up into a knot.

"What are you doing here?" Anne heard herself finally asking, feeling as if she was trapped in some sort of a surreal dream.

All this time and she hadn't changed a bit, Dan thought, trying not to stare at her. If anything, Annie was even more beautiful than he remembered.

"I was in the neighborhood and thought I'd drop by," Danny answered glibly. "No?" he asked, seeing the look on her face. He shrugged, feeling awkward, something he'd never felt around her before. "Well, it was worth a shot. The truth is, I saw a clip on TV a month ago. Jamie and his triplets were in it. After the program was over, I couldn't stop seeing their faces. I knew I had to come back to Rust Creek Falls to see them."

*You had to come back to see them. But not me.* "Oh, I see," Anne murmured, her voice stilted.

"And you," Dan added awkwardly, realizing his oversight. "I wanted to see you." He blew out a ragged breath and then asked, "Can I come in?"

For a moment, it looked as if she was going to say no. But then she stepped back and gestured for him to enter the house.

"Mom?" Janie called out. She ventured into the living room and looked uncertainly at the stranger talking to her mother.

For the second time in as many minutes, Anne felt her heart lodge itself in her throat as she all but stopped breathing.

Could Danny see it? Could he see that Janie was his daughter?

She slanted a hesitant look in his direction. Danny was smiling broadly at the little girl.

"Hi. You must be Janie," he said. There was clearly awe in his eyes.

The picture of confidence and self-assurance, Janie raised her chin. "I am. Who are you?" she wanted to know.

"Janie," Anne chided her daughter for responding so bluntly.

"No, that's okay," Danny was quick to tell her. "She's being direct. That's a very positive quality to have." He turned his attention to the little girl. "I'm Daniel Stockton," he told her. "I used to live in Rust Creek Falls."

"And you were friends with my mom?" Janie asked, curious.

Anne felt a sharp pang in her heart, afraid of saying anything. Afraid of giving herself away.

He looked at Anne for a moment before he answered. "Yes," he replied quietly. "I was friends with your mom."

"And my dad?" Janie wanted to know, probing further.

"No," Dan answered truthfully. "I'm afraid that I never met your dad."

Growing progressively more apprehensive, Anne didn't want this exchange to go any further. Not until she set a few ground rules to make sure that nothing was exposed ahead of time.

Until then, she needed to keep Janie and Danny away from one another.

"Did you finish your homework, young lady?" she asked her daughter.

"No, not yet," Janie began. "But—"

Anne cut her off. "Then I suggest you go back and finish it. That's what we agreed to, remember?" she reminded her daughter.

Janie made a face. "I don't remember agreeing," she protested. "You just told me to do it."

"Same thing, puddin'," Anne told her daughter affectionately. "Now go," she said, pointing toward the rear of the house where Janie's room was located, "and don't come back until you've finished doing it."

"Yes, ma'am," Janie sighed with a pout. Turning, she dragged her feet as she went to her room.

"She looks like you."

So worried that he'd see himself in their daughter,

Anne didn't hear him at first. And then his words replayed themselves in her head. She turned around to face Danny, a little stunned.

"What?"

"I said she looks like you." There was no missing the fondness in his voice. Or the wistfulness. "A miniature carbon copy of what you looked like at that age. She's what, about nine, right?"

Nine would make her safe, Anne thought. If Danny thought that Janie was nine, then he'd definitely believe that the little girl was Hank's daughter and that would be that. Fear of discovery would be taken off the table once and for all.

But saying yes would be lying, Anne thought and somehow, she just couldn't bring herself to lie to Danny after all these years.

The word stuck in her throat like a fishbone that had been accidentally swallowed.

Rather than say yes or no, Anne focused on something else he had just said. "You really think she looks like me?"

"Absolutely," he assured her. "Right down to her stubborn streak."

"What does a stubborn streak look like?" Anne asked wryly.

Dan smiled at her, fighting a very strong desire to touch her. Not in the intimate way he used to—after all, she was another man's wife now—but just to put his hand on her shoulder, to connect with her for the smallest of moments.

"I'm looking at it right now," he told Annie. And then

his smile faded as he grew serious. "When you opened the door just now, you asked me what I was doing here."

Anne inclined her head, slightly embarrassed. "Not exactly the politest way to greet someone after twelve years," she admitted, then went on to say, "but in my defense, you did catch me by surprise."

Lord, but she looked good, he couldn't help thinking, all but devouring her with his eyes. "You know, I didn't exactly tell you the truth when I said I was in the neighborhood."

"I had my suspicions," she replied with a soft laugh. Rust Creek Falls was in no one's neighborhood. "So why are you here?" she asked.

Dan cleared his voice before saying, "I came to apologize for leaving you the way I did."

Stunned by his admission, Anne looked at the man she had once thought of as the love of her life. It took her more than a moment to find her tongue.

"You know, over the last dozen years, I must have imagined this scene a hundred different ways. The only thing all those scenes had in common, besides your apology, was that I always felt relieved when I heard you apologize. I felt somehow vindicated.

"But I'm not vindicated, not relieved," she told him with feeling. "I'm just…sad, I guess. Sad about all the years in between that were lost. Why did you leave like that?"

Dan shook his head. That was something he didn't want to get into. It was a secret he would most likely take to his grave rather than burden someone else with.

"I didn't have a choice," was all he allowed himself to say.

Anne frowned ever so slightly. That excuse just didn't hold any water for her. "Everyone always has a choice," she told him.

"*I* didn't," he replied.

There had to be more, something he wasn't telling her. "But—"

Dan changed the subject. "I also wanted to tell you that I'm happy for you."

For a moment, still trying to understand what Danny wasn't telling her, she was caught off guard. His last words completely confused her.

"What did you say?"

"I said I'm happy for you," Danny repeated. "Happy that you've moved on. That you found someone you cared about and got married. That you went on to have a beautiful daughter."

*She's your beautiful daughter*, she thought, an unexpected wave of anger filling her.

Anne continued staring at him. "You're happy for me," she repeated in disbelief, like someone who didn't quite understand the gist of the words she was saying.

Dan nodded, forcing a smile to his lips. "Yes, I am."

Did he even have a clue how much it stung to hear him say that to her? How much it actually physically tore her apart?

*Why didn't you come back to me? Why didn't you show up on my doorstep years ago and tell me that you couldn't bear to live without me? Why did you just van-*

*ish out of my life without a trace, leaving me to face being pregnant all by myself?*

But she couldn't say any of that, couldn't risk him knowing the truth, at least not yet. Perhaps not ever. There were other people to consider.

So, instead, she asked, "Where were you all these years?"

Anne struggled to keep the accusation out of her voice, doing her best to sound like just an old friend trying to catch up with another old friend instead of a spurned lover who'd given her heart away and had it torn in two more than a decade ago.

Dan looked at her, wondering how to reply to her question. There wasn't that much to tell her, really. For all intents and purposes, his life had ended the day he had left town with his brothers.

"Wyoming first," he finally said. "Then Colorado."

She could almost picture him going to Wyoming if she tried. But not Colorado.

"Colorado?" Anne echoed. "What did you do there?" she asked.

"Actually, I'm still there," he told her. "I look a temporary leave of absence to come out here," he said, then went on to answer her question. "I'm a sales manager for an exclusive dude ranch."

"A dude ranch?" It seemed like such an unlikely place for him to land, Anne thought. "What does a sales manager do at a dude ranch?"

He laughed dryly. "Mainly I put together vacation packages for burned-out city slickers who think that riding around on a horse for a couple of weeks, pretending to be Roy Rogers, is guaranteed to make a whole new man out of them."

The mocking tone of his voice had her wondering other things. "Are you happy?" she wanted to know.

He shrugged and smiled. "It's a living."

"That's not what I asked," she told him, wondering if he was purposely trying to be evasive. Was he unhappy? Had he been as unhappy as she had?

"The pay's good and the dude ranch reminds me of the Sunshine Farm," he told her, referring to the ranch where he and his siblings had lived while growing up—before his parents were killed.

"Are you going back?" she asked him. "To the dude ranch," she specified when she realized that she hadn't been clear.

He hadn't worked that out in his head yet. He still had his job waiting for him and part of him had every intention of returning to Colorado. But seeing Jamie and his family—seeing her—had caused all sorts of doubts to spring up in his head.

"Well, I—" he began hesitantly, not wanting to lie, but not wanting to mislead her, either.

Just then, the doorbell rang, curtailing any further conversation between them.

Anne wanted to ignore it, wanted him to finish answering her question as to whether or not he would be leaving her again. Suddenly, she felt on the verge of telling Danny about Janie even though she knew it would be like dropping a bombshell on him.

But it also might be just the incentive he needed to convince him to stay in Rust Creek Falls.

The doorbell rang again.

Dan looked at her quizzically. "Aren't you going to answer that?" he asked her.

When the doorbell rang a third time, she fixed a smile on her face, said, "Sure," and then went to answer the door.

Before she reached it, she heard the sound of her daughter running into the room. For such a slight little girl, she had very heavy feet and the ability to make her presence known, Anne thought.

"In case that's Dad, I've got my bag all packed and ready," Janie announced cheerfully.

"That's good, dear. You wouldn't want to keep your father waiting," Anne told her daughter as she opened the door.

Hank Harlow walked in.

## Chapter Five

The first person Hank Harlow saw when Anne opened the door to admit him in was not his ex-wife, nor was it the little girl who'd had him completely wrapped around her little finger from the moment she was born. It was the tall, lanky cowboy in the room. The one standing near Anne.

The man who had been his competition, sight unseen, all these years.

His dark eyes darted back to Anne, an unspoken question in his pointed look.

Anne knew what her ex-husband was silently asking her and very slowly, she shook her head just enough to let him know that she hadn't said anything to either Dan or to the little girl Hank considered his daughter.

The next second Janie had launched herself into

Hank's arms, eager for their evening together to get started.

"Hi, Dad!"

"Hi yourself, Short Stuff," Hank responded affectionately, hugging the little girl who had her arms tightly wrapped around his waist.

These were the moments to savor, Hank thought. Even if he wasn't looking at a very real threat to his fragile world right here in his ex-wife's living room, it wouldn't be all that long before Janie became a teenager. Teenagers weren't all that keen on public displays of affection when it came to their dads.

He was going to miss this.

"I packed early," Janie told him proudly as she finally dropped her hands to her sides.

Hank saw the stuffed backpack she'd dropped on the floor as she'd run to hug him. "That's my girl," he said with approval, ruffling her hair.

His words carried a slight territorial ring to them, Dan noted. Obviously, the man thought he was here to try to break up his family, but he would never do anything like that. He'd had his chance twelve years ago and he'd missed it, Dan thought.

Stepping forward, he put his hand out to the man who had his arm still protective around Janie's shoulders. "Hi, I'm Dan Stockton," he said, introducing himself.

"Yes, I know," Hank replied frostily. After a beat, he took Dan's hand and barely shook it before let it drop. "I'm Hank Harlow." He slanted a quick, meaningful glance in Anne's direction as he added, "Janie's dad."

"C'mon, Dad, let's go," Janie urged, tugging on Hank's hand as she turned in the direction of the front door.

"Don't forget to take your schoolbooks with you," Anne reminded her daughter.

Janie pointed toward the bulging backpack. "They're in there, Mom," she assured her mother. "I just packed them."

"Homework, too?" Anne stressed.

Janie signed dramatically as if it irritated her to be treated like a child. "Homework, too."

Anne smiled at her. "Then I guess you're all set," she concluded. "We'll have those hamburgers another night."

"I'll bring her to school in the morning," Hank made a point of telling her.

Anne nodded. Crossing to the duo at the door, she kissed the top of her daughter's head. "Behave yourself," she said affectionately.

"She always behaves herself," Hank said. "Short Stuff's perfect."

Janie beamed as she looked up at him. She tugged on his hand again, more urgently this time.

"Let's go!" she pleaded insistently.

"Have a good time," Anne called after her daughter.

Janie waved at her as she ran to the car.

She watched as Hank opened the passenger door for Janie. Once the girl was strapped in, he shut the door and rounded the hood to the driver's side. He paused to give her one last warning look before getting into his truck himself.

Anne could tell from her ex-husband's expression that she clearly didn't want her saying anything to Dan about Janie being his daughter. She knew how Hank felt about Janie, knew he feared that if the truth came out, he might lose Janie's love.

She sincerely doubted that would happen, but she could understand his concern.

Watching Hank, she bit her lower lip, utterly torn between the truth and her sense of loyalty.

She continued watching until Hank started up the truck and then pulled away from her house.

With a sigh, she closed the front door and then turned around to face Dan. Her heart hammering, she was acutely aware of the fact that they were now completely alone in the house.

For a moment, she wasn't sure just what to say to him, how to even begin a conversation.

The question Dan asked her the next moment didn't help, either. "When did you get divorced?"

Her mouth felt like dry cotton. How did he know? *How could he not know? Hank was picking Janie up for an overnight stay. Only divorced parents do that sort of thing, idiot*, she upbraided herself.

"You didn't know?" Anne asked, doing her best to sound nonchalant.

"I didn't even know you were married until I started prowling through social media, looking to see if I could find any photos or information on you. I came across pictures of you and Janie—and him," Dan told her, remembering how much it had hurt, seeing her with Hank, so much so that he never went back. But he wasn't about to tell her that. "But, funny thing, there aren't pictures posted that can capture a divorce."

She didn't want to have this conversation, afraid that she might accidentally let something slip before she was ready—assuming she would ever be ready.

Taking a breath, she deliberately ignored his question regarding her divorce and switched gears to act like a hostess.

"Can I offer you something to drink? Coffee, a soft drink, water?" she asked, doing her best to keep her voice light.

Dan understood what she was telling him. That this topic was off-limits. He could respect that. Divorces could wound a person far more effectively than a bullet. He had his untouchable subjects and she had hers, he thought, so he backed off.

"No, I'm fine," Dan assured her.

"Something to eat, then?" she offered. "I've got some leftover fried chicken in the refrigerator—I made it," she told him, then made a point of adding, "I've learned to cook better now."

"There was nothing wrong with the way you cooked," Dan said kindly.

She laughed a little, some of the tension between them temporarily backing off. "That was because you were in love with me back then."

*I'm still in love with you*, he silently told her. Out loud, Dan contradicted her. "Bad cooking has a way of cutting through that," he assured her. Knowing a little shot of honesty was called for here, he added, "You weren't going to make Martha Stewart pack up her pots and pans, but you weren't bad."

"So then, can I get you something to eat? I could

make hamburgers," she offered, already crossing to the refrigerator, eager to do something with her hands. Preparing a light dinner would take care of that.

His stomach felt so tied up in knots, Dan knew if he consumed something, he ran the serious risk of having it come back up.

Maybe it was time to leave, he told himself.

"No, really, I'm fine. I didn't come here to eat," he told Anne. "I really did just come to apologize. And now that I have, I should get going." Needing a way to gracefully pave his way out, he grabbed at the first thing that occurred to him. "I promised Jamie I'd be back by a certain time. If I'm not there when I said I would be, I don't want him thinking I've taken off for another twelve years."

"That's very thoughtful of you," Anne told him stiffly.

About to leave, he took Anne's hand for a moment, only to have her pull it back as if she'd just been touched by a hot poker. And then he saw her flush, her cheeks turning a shade of pink he would have found infinitely appealing if it wasn't for the fact that she had just acted as if she couldn't stand being touched by him.

This was going to take time and patience, he told himself—if he wound up staying, he added, and that hadn't been decided yet.

"I really am sorry, Annie," he told her quietly. And then he crossed to the door and opened it.

"Wait!"

Dan slowly turned around, waiting, a silent query in his eyes.

"You can't— I mean, when—" She sounded tongue-tied, till she finally said, "Will I see you again?"

"If I decide to go back to Colorado, I'll stop by to let you know and say goodbye," he promised.

And with that, he turned away from her and left.

He heard Anne flip the lock on the door. It had a prophetic, final sound to it.

Trying to shake off the thought, he hurried to his truck.

"So, how did it go?"

Jamie's question met him the moment Dan walked through the door his brother held open.

"Have you been standing there this entire time?" Dan wanted to know, walking across the threshold.

"Not standing," Jamie corrected, and then he admitted, "Pacing, maybe."

"This whole time?" Dan asked again. Was his brother that uncertain that he would return?

"No," Jamie answered defensively—and then he relented. "Just for the last hour. So how did it go?" he repeated.

Dan walked into the living room. He expected to find his newfound nephews and niece in the room, or, at the very least, his new sister-in-law.

But the room was empty.

Dan sank down on the sofa and looked at his brother, waiting for him to sit down beside him. He'd heard the nervousness in Jamie's voice. It didn't take a rocket scientist to guess the reason behind it. Did Jamie expect him to be angry?

It was best to get this out of the way sooner than later, he thought. "You didn't tell me Annie had gotten married."

He saw the apprehension in Jamie's eyes as his brother answered, "I was afraid you wouldn't go see her if you knew about that."

And it was obviously important to Jamie that he saw Anne, Dan thought, still somewhat mystified. "Why did you want me to go see her?"

"Because you wanted to," Jamie answered simply. And then he added with emphasis, "And I think that you needed to."

"Is that why you didn't tell me about the little girl, too?" Dan guessed, doing his best to try to piece everything together.

Jamie blew out a breath. "Yes," he admitted. "I'm sorry I kept that from you, but—"

Dan raised his hand, not letting him finish. "And the divorce?" he asked, focusing on the final point. "Why didn't you tell me that she was divorced?"

"Because if I told you that, I would have had to tell you that she'd gotten married first and I didn't want to get into any of that. Besides, I wanted Anne to tell you about her divorce herself." An almost sheepish smile curved the corners of his mouth. "I figured you'd get the good news after you weathered the bad. Bottom line is that Annie's a free woman. The rest of it is just history."

"History that produced a little girl," Dan pointed out.

Jamie didn't know how his brother felt about that part, but he was not about to get into an argument with

Dan. Not after Dan had only just now come back into his life after more than a decade's hiatus.

He deliberately focused on the positive aspect.

"Janie's a real cutie, isn't she?" Jamie asked.

For a long moment, Dan remained silent. And then he slowly smiled and said, "She's Annie's daughter. How could she not be?"

"I know, right?" Jamie asked. Getting up, he crossed over to the small liquor cabinet in the corner. He poured two shots of Wild Turkey and brought them both over to the sofa, placing one on the coffee table in front of Dan. "What did Annie say when she opened the door and saw you standing there?"

"Her exact words were 'What are you doing here?'" he told Jamie.

Jamie laughed, shaking his head. "That's Annie, direct as ever." He nodded at the untouched shot glass. "Would you like something else instead?" he asked. "My liquor cabinet's not well stocked, but I've got a few different things you can chose from," Jamie told him, getting up again.

But Dan shook his head. "That's okay, don't trouble yourself. I don't drink."

Jamie looked at him in surprise. He'd never actually seen Dan drink. However, one of the last nights they were still a real family, he remembered that Dan, Luke and Bailey had snuck out to a bar to go drinking.

"You don't drink?" he repeated. "Seriously?" he asked his brother.

"Seriously," Dan replied.

"Not ever?"

"No," Dan answered stoically.

Jamie put down the shot glass he was just about to raise to his own lips. He wasn't going to have a drink if Dan wasn't.

"Since when?" he asked.

Dan wasn't all that eager to talk about it, but then, he knew he couldn't keep running from this forever. Because he had things to hide, he fed Jamie the barest information.

"Since the night Mom and Dad died," Dan told him simply.

"Because they were killed by that drunk driver," Jamie guessed.

That wasn't the reason, but Dan let it go at that. Because if he didn't, if he told Jamie that wasn't the real reason, he would have to explain further and let Jamie in on the terrible secret he'd been carrying around with him for the last twelve years.

It was enough that he was burdened with that secret. He wasn't about to tell Jamie and have him share the burden. Jamie didn't deserve to have to put up with that.

So instead, he nodded his head and said, "Yeah, something like that. But you don't have to abstain just because I'm not drinking," he told Jamie, nodding at the drink that his brother had set down.

"They were my parents, too," Jamie needlessly reminded him.

*Yeah, and I'm the reason they're not here right now. I'm the reason you and Bella had to put up with being raised—if you can call it that—by Grandma and Grandpa while the other girls were adopted and farmed out. I'm the reason Luke and Bailey had to leave home and why our whole family wound up being shattered and split up.*

Though he had kept his silence all these years, it still felt as if the secret was cutting him up with small, jagged knives.

"Hey, what's the matter?" Jamie asked. "You look like you've just seen a ghost." Compassion filled him as he put his hand on his brother's shoulder. "Danny, talk to me. Are you okay?"

"Just a little emotionally wrung out, I guess," Danny told him. "I just need some rest. I'll be fine by morning," he promised.

Jamie looked at the clock on the mantel. "It's a little early for bed," he noted. "Don't you want to have some dinner first? Fallon's putting together this Prodigal Brother Returns Feast, guaranteed to knock your socks off. Are you sure you want to miss that?" Jamie asked him.

Dan really wanted some time to himself to process everything that had happened today. But at the same time, he didn't want to insult his new sister-in-law or hurt her feelings by taking a pass on dinner. Especially after she had gone to all this trouble for him. That wouldn't be right.

"No, I surely don't want to miss that," he told Jamie. "It's not every day that I have a feast in my honor."

"So you'll have dinner with us?" Jamie asked, looking at him hopefully.

"Hey, I wouldn't miss it for the world," Dan assured him.

The expression that came over Jamie's face was the epitome of happiness as well as relief.

## Chapter Six

Dan couldn't remember the last meal he'd had with family, and he didn't want this one to end. But it was getting late and he was exhausted.

Pushing aside his now cold coffee, he was about to call it a night when his brother finally brought up the subject that had been on Dan's mind all throughout the meal.

"You know," Jamie said, leaning in to him, "when Hank divorced Anne, she came to see me, as well as Bella, asking if either one of us had finally heard from you and knew where you were." He sighed, shaking his head. "Of course, we couldn't help her because we had no idea where you—"

"Wait," Dan cried incredulously, interrupting his brother. "Hank divorced her?"

"Yes." Jamie looked at him quizzically. "You said that you knew they had gotten divorced. Why do you look so surprised?"

"Well, yes, I knew they were divorced, but I thought that Annie was the one who had divorced Hank," Dan answered.

He frowned, confused as he tried to figure the situation out. How could Hank, after getting someone like Anne to marry him, throw all that away and actually divorce her? That just didn't make any sense to him. In Hank's place, no reason in the world would have made him do that.

He put the question to Jamie. "Why would Hank divorce her?"

"Well, I don't know any of the particulars," Jamie confessed, "but if I had to make a guess, off the top of my head I'd say that Hank finally came to terms with the fact that Annie was still in love with you and always would be. He didn't want to continue in second place."

Dan thought back to the awkwardness of his first meeting with Anne after all this time, and the way she had pulled back when he'd tried to take her hand. He made a small, dismissive guttural sound.

"I think you might have been kicked in the head by one of those horses you like to baby."

Jamie shrugged. "Make jokes all you want, but I have a very strong feeling that I'm right about this," he told Dan.

"I wouldn't try to argue him out of that if I were you," Fallon advised as she rose to clear away the dishes from the table. "Jamie might look mild-mannered, but once he gets something into his head, there's no budging him."

"All right, then I won't try," Dan told his sister-in-law agreeably. "Even though he *is* dead wrong. Here, let me help you with that," he offered, reaching for the plates Fallon had just stacked.

"Don't you dare," she warned Dan, a smile belying the sharp tone she'd taken. She swatted Dan's hand away from the dishes. "In case you've forgotten, you're a guest here."

"I'm crashing at your place and taking full advantage of your kindness. That means I owe you—big time— and should do something to earn my keep," Dan pointed out.

Fallon sighed, surrendering the plates to him. "Looks like Jamie isn't the only stubborn Stockton here." Her smile grew wider as Dan cleared the table. "I think I could get used to this."

Just then, one of the triplets decided to make themselves known. "Uh-oh. Sounds like duty calls," she told the two brothers, glancing toward the source of the cries. "I'd better see what's going on before all three of them wake up."

"It was a wonderful dinner, Fallon," Dan called after her. "Thank you."

"Jamie, make sure you tell your brother he can stay with us as long as he likes," Fallon tossed over her shoulder as she walked upstairs to check on which of the triplets wanted to be fed or changed.

"You know, Jamie, you've got it made," Dan told his brother enviously as the latter followed him, carrying another large batch of plates and utensils to the kitchen sink.

"I do, but I didn't always," Jamie responded. "I thought my life was over when Paula died, leaving me with three infants to raise. I felt like the bottom had completely dropped out of my world," he confided.

He looked at Dan, deliberately making his point. "But I hung on, determined to be there for my kids, to make them as happy as I possibly could. I wasn't prepared to find love again, but somehow, it found *me*." He gave his brother an encouraging smile. "And you'll get there, too, Danny. Just hang in there and don't give up."

Danny shrugged the advice away. "I missed my chance and I know it," he replied, totally convinced of what he was saying.

Danny might have been convinced, but Jamie didn't see it that way.

"You're still breathing, aren't you?" Jamie asked, rinsing off the plates before stacking them on the counter on the way to the dishwasher.

"Yeah, but—" Danny began to protest.

Jamie talked right over him, not wanting to hear any excuses. "And so's Annie."

Danny sighed. "It's not that simple, Jamie," he insisted.

"It's not that complicated, either, Danny. Like they say, where there's life, there's hope."

For a moment Danny was silent, then he brightened as he turned to Jamie.

"Tell you what, brother," he said. "Instead of putting these dishes into the dishwasher, why don't we just han-

dle this the old-fashioned way? You wash and I'll dry.
This way, you can surprise Fallon when she comes back
out into the kitchen to start the dishwasher."

Jamie knew what Danny was trying to do, but he'd
said what he'd wanted to say and for now he let the subject drop. The Danny he had grown up with had been
quick to smile and quick to lend a helping hand, but
reaching out to his onetime love was something Danny
would have to mull over before he finally decided to
make a move.

All Jamie could do was plant the seed in Danny's
head and fervently hope that with enough time, it would
germinate.

"Fallon'd like that," Jamie said, agreeing to the suggestion.

"Well then, let's get to it," Danny responded, turning up the water.

Jamie's comment to him about the situation with
Annie not being as complicated as he felt it was kept
replaying itself in his head until he finally fell asleep
that night. And they were the first words that sprang
into his head the following morning.

Thoughts of Annie were temporarily put on hold,
though when shortly after breakfast Dan heard the front
door burst open, someone demanding, "Where is he?"
and before he knew what was happening, he found himself enveloped in a huge embrace from behind.

"You're here. You're really here!" an excited female voice exclaimed. When he managed to shift in
his seat—and the embrace—he discovered that he was
being hugged by his sister Bella.

Sitting opposite him, Jamie grinned. "Told you she'd be happy to see you."

"Talk to me," Bella cried, making herself comfortable in the chair next to his. "Tell me everything!"

Which was how Dan wound up spending the rest of the day, talking to his sister and catching up on her life. A life which he was happy to learn had ultimately fared better than his had.

Dana, taking a quick trip from Portland, came to see him the day after that, and although there was less squealing, it almost an instant replay of the day before.

Both days were filled with the stuff that emotional, happy reunions were made of.

But all those stirred-up emotions caused thoughts of Annie to creep back into his brain, haunting him during the late evening even though he tried his best to ignore them.

Dan sought refuge in work. He volunteered and worked beside Jamie on the range, doing his best to forget about Annie.

At breakfast the fourth day Jamie leaned over the table toward him and said, "You know, I've got an awful lot to take care of on the ranch today—"

The admission was like music to Dan's ears. Keeping busy was the best way he knew of to keep from thinking and torturing himself with would-be scenarios that all began with "what if."

"Just tell me what you need done and I'll do it," Dan was quick to offer.

Jamie got up from the table and went to the writing

desk that was nestled in the alcove between the kitchen and the small dining room.

"This will be a real time-saver for me," Jamie told him.

Dan was still seated at the table, finishing the last of his second cup of extra-dark coffee. He heard a drawer being opened and then closed again. Half a beat later, Jamie walked back into the kitchen holding an envelope in his hand. The name of the veterinary clinic in town was written across the front: Dr. Brooks Smith's Veterinary Clinic.

"I need to make a payment on my vet bill," he told Dan, holding out the envelope. "Would you mind very much bringing it into town for me?"

"Wouldn't I be more useful helping you out here, on the ranch?" Dan questioned.

"Trust me, this'll take a big load off my mind. You know how I feel about owing someone," he reminded his brother.

A smile played on his lips as fragments of distant childhood memories returned. "Vaguely," Danny said, tongue in cheek.

"Well, I've only gotten worse." He pressed the envelope into Danny's hand. "Do you mind?"

It really seemed important to him, Dan thought, so he took the envelope and slipped it into his shirt pocket.

"Of course not. Consider it done." Habit had him checking his pocket for the keys to his Jeep as he rose from the table. "I'll be back as soon as I can," he promised.

"Take your time," Jamie told him. "The work's not going anywhere."

Dan took his jacket off the hook by the front door. Putting it on, he gave his brother a quick wave and left the house.

"You're terrible," Fallon told her husband the moment Dan closed the door.

Jamie gave his wife a wide-eyed look. "What makes you say that?"

Fallon rolled her eyes. "Don't play innocent with me. You could have just as easily put that check in the mail."

Jamie pretended to find the suggestion lacking. "I've always found the personal touch to be the better way to go," he told his wife.

"Ha! You just want Danny to walk into the vet clinic so that he can see Annie when he hands your check to her."

"Well, that's definitely the personal touch, isn't it?" he asked her, daring his wife to possibly suggest otherwise.

"There's no arguing with that," Fallon agreed. "But I'm not sure if Danny's going to appreciate being manipulated."

"He will," Jamie said confidently. "Once he comes to his senses," he added. He looked at Fallon, wanting his wife to side with him. "Someone's got to make the first move."

"Don't you think it should be one of the two people involved in this?" Fallon asked.

"It should," Jamie readily agreed. "But when that doesn't look like it's about to happen, sometimes a little divine intervention is necessary."

"Divine intervention?" Fallon repeated, laughter in her eyes. "Meaning you?"

"Hey, if the description fits…" His voice trailed off as a whimsical expression played hide-and-seek on his face.

Fallon shook her head. But he knew there was no way she could be exasperated with him. Not when he was obviously attempting to do a good thing for his brother.

"I love you, Jamie Stockton," she said.

His eyes softened as he looked at her. "I know," he told her. "And I love you, too."

Just then, not one, not two but all three very loud, plaintive voices blended, creating an indignant, highly unhappy chorus.

"Sounds like our children are calling," Fallon said as she got up from the table.

"Calling?" he echoed. "I'd say that it sounds more like they're bellowing," Jamie told her. "C'mon," he urged his wife. "I'll help. There's supposed to be safety in numbers."

"Safety?" she laughed. "Not hardly. In case you hadn't noticed, it's two to three. That means that those little critters still outnumber us."

"We can brazen it out," he told her as if they were actually planning strategy to use against their babies. "Remember, when we enter the room, don't make any eye contact. They can detect fear a mile away. It'll only go downhill from there if they do."

Fallon shook her head. "You should write a book on raising triplets," she teased.

"Maybe I will," Jamie responded, pretending to mull the idea over. "All I need to do is to learn how to type."

"That would mean that you would have to change and I don't want you to change even a single thing about yourself," Fallon told him with a great deal of affection in her tone. "I love you just the way you are."

"Good to know," Jamie said as he kissed her. It was all the fortification he needed to deal with their brood.

Rust Creek Falls had done some growing since he had left it, Dan thought as he drove into the heart of town. The place had more stores than when he'd lived there, but the ones that he did recognize reminded him of the same sleepy little town that it had been.

The town vet had been part of that expansion, going from what had been essentially a one-man show to a clinic. The word *clinic* suggested at least more than one vet, Dan mused. And that was a good thing, as he suspected that the ranches in the area had done their own growing. More cattle and horses meant that more of them needed looking after.

There was a time when a rancher would do his best for his livestock and then just allow nature to take over, tipping the scales one way or another. Now ranchers relied on vets to keep the scales tipped in their favor, but there were fees for that, he mused, thinking of the envelope he had tucked into his pocket.

He was surprised that Jamie had asked him to run the payment into town for him rather than just putting it in the mail, but then he gathered that mail service hadn't kept up with growth quite the way other things had. Besides, he didn't mind being useful. It was one thing to be earning a paycheck, and another thing to feel useful to someone who counted.

He preferred the latter.

Dan scanned both sides of the street as he slowly made his way through the town, taking note of a couple of new restaurants that had opened up. There was a new bar, too, but that held no interest for him, nudging at memories he didn't want stirred. He kept his eyes peeled for the vet clinic.

He finally spotted it after traveling more than halfway through Rust Creek Falls. In one of the older buildings in town, the clinic didn't create much of an impression at first sight, but then, it didn't have to, he thought. All it had to do was keep good veterinarians in its employ.

There was parking for the clinic across the way and he chose a spot closest to the building. Getting out of the Jeep, he didn't bother locking it. If anyone was going to steal a vehicle, Dan figured that they wouldn't bother with one that had as many miles on it as his did.

He made his way to the clinic's front door and went right in. The receptionist's desk was front and center, visible the second he stepped inside the building.

There was no one ahead of him so he stepped right up to the desk. The greeting he was about to offer died on his lips as the receptionist turned her chair around to face him.

*Annie.*

## Chapter Seven

Annie was speechless.

It took her more than a moment to collect herself. Her accelerating pulse, however, was a whole other story. But at least Danny had no way of knowing that it was currently going faster than a NASCAR racer, she thought, and all because of him.

When she finally regained the ability to form words, she bluntly asked him, "How did you know I work here?" She was grateful that at least her voice hadn't cracked at the last second.

"I didn't," Dan answered.

*But obviously Jamie did*, he realized. Now his brother's unusual request to run into town and make a payment in person made sense.

His younger brother had a lot of explaining to do once Dan got back to the ranch.

Anne assessed his response. Taking a breath, she peered at him over the desk. "If you didn't know I'd be here, then what are you doing here?" As far as she could tell, he didn't have an animal in tow.

"Jamie sent me," Dan answered. Then, almost as an afterthought, he added, "He asked me to drop off his monthly installment on his vet bill."

"Monthly installment?" she repeated, looking at him in confusion.

"That's what he said," Danny told her, handing over the envelope that his brother asked him to deliver.

Annie set the envelope down next to her computer. He watched as her finely shaped eyebrows drew together in perplexed consternation while her fingers flew across the keyboard.

"Something wrong?" he asked Annie, already sensing that something had to be off.

Unwilling to get specific just yet, she merely told Dan, "Just checking."

But she'd aroused his curiosity. There had to be a reason for that doubtful expression on her face. "Checking what?"

She didn't bother looking up. Instead, she evasively said, "If I made a mistake."

"A mistake," he echoed, waiting for some more information. When Annie said nothing further, his curiosity doubled in proportion. "In the accounting in general," Dan pressed, "or—?"

Annie slanted a glance at him. This felt awkward

all around. Why couldn't he just back off like a normal person?

Because he wasn't a "normal" person, she reminded herself. He was Danny and everything that entailed. He didn't just go along with things; he had to have them spelled out.

"I'm afraid I'm going to have to go with 'or,'" she told him.

He laughed dryly as he watched her type on the keyboard.

"I guess a lot of things have changed in the last twelve years," he remarked. "When did you learn to talk in code like that?"

The phone rang at that moment, preventing her from answering him. One eye still on the computer screen, she picked up the receiver.

"Brooks Smith's Veterinary Clinic," she answered as she put her finger up, indicating to Dan that their conversation was temporarily on hold. "How may I help you?"

For the next minute or so Annie questioned and advised the person on the other end of the call.

She sounded so self-assured, Dan thought. When he'd left Rust Creek Falls with his brothers, he'd left behind a sweet, loving, shy teenage girl who'd just touched the edges of self-discovery. He was looking at a woman now, a woman who had obviously known love, and pain, and during all that, managed to raise a daughter who reflected well on her.

"If you're willing to wait until four," Annie was saying to whoever was on the other end of the call, "I can have Brooks come out to your place to take a look at your mare." She listened to the person's response. "Good, I'll let the doctor know. He'll be at the ranch around four o'clock."

Hanging up, she turned her attention back to him.

"Now can you tell me what you were talking about?" he asked Annie.

Her eyes darted back to the computer screen. "Well, it's just that—"

The door behind him opened and they were interrupted again. Dan heard someone coming in. From the sound of it, the person wasn't alone. Danny didn't have to turn around to know that. He'd suddenly found himself to be a person of interest for an overly energetic bloodhound who all but inhaled him.

"Heel, Bowser," a gruff voice behind him ordered. The bloodhound behaved as if no command had been issued, sniffing that much harder and all but climbing up on the side of Dan's leg. "I said heel, damn it!" the man behind Dan said, irritated. "I'm sorry about this," he apologized when Dan turned around.

"Mr. Mayfield," Anne addressed the bloodhound's owner as she got up from behind her desk and came around to the front. "Why don't we check Bowser's weight and then you can take him into the second room to wait for the doctor?" she suggested, making her way to an oversize scale in the corner just beyond the front door.

But the bloodhound hadn't quite gotten over his fascination with Danny. "Why don't I walk over to the scale?" he suggested to the dog's owner. "It might make things easier for everyone."

"I'm sorry," Mr. Mayfield apologized. "Bowser's usually better behaved than this."

The man gladly took Dan up on his suggestion, holding tightly onto the bloodhound's leash as Bowser followed Dan right to the scale.

Confronted with the scale, the bloodhound only put three of his four paws down on the scale. It took three tries and all three of them to get all four of the dog's paws onto the scale at the same time in order to get an accurate reading.

Closest to the readout, Dan looked down at the numbers and announced, "One hundred and twenty-nine pounds."

"You can take Bowser to room two," Anne declared. Mr. Mayfield set off down the hall and she returned to her chair behind the desk. She looked a little frazzled and her hair was falling into her eyes.

Seeing her like that conjured up images out of their past. Images Dan had tried very hard to banish over the years.

Damn, he was never going to get over her, he thought, resigning himself to his fate.

"Why don't we grab some coffee later when you get your lunch break?" Dan suggested to her. "You seem a little busy now."

The phone was ringing again. "You think?" she asked, reaching for the receiver as she pushed her hair out of her eyes.

"What time's lunch?" he asked. He didn't want to

turn up early and have Annie think that he was hovering.

She only had enough time to answer, "Twelve thirty," before she picked up the receiver. "Brooks Smith's Veterinary Clinic, how may I help you?"

The corners of Danny's mouth curved as he walked out of the clinic. At this point, he knew that Jamie had deliberately manipulated him, using the so-called outstanding vet bill as an excuse to get him together with Annie again. He had no more place in her life now than he had earlier this week when he'd gone to see her, but he had to admit that it was nice getting to see her a second time.

He had no idea how much longer he was going to be in Rust Creek Falls—technically, he'd taken only a month's leave of absence from his job to come out here, but he could always leave earlier.

He could also stay longer, he told himself.

It all depended on how things wound up arranging themselves, he thought. But that was something he intended to keep to himself, at least for now.

While he waited for twelve thirty to come, Dan decided to explore the town of Rust Creek Falls so he could feel like a native of the area again and not like some clueless tourist finding his way around.

He found himself gravitating to a diner rather than a restaurant. The diner had caught his attention because of its sign out front. It boasted having "the best cup of coffee for thirty miles around" so he decided to put the claim to the test.

Dan didn't know about "best" but the coffee was at least decent enough to merit a second order.

He nursed the second cup while sitting in a small booth next to a window. It was a deliberate choice. The vantage point allowed him to observe the citizens' comings and goings without really being observed himself.

At this point, he wasn't quite ready to reconnect with anyone he might have known back when he lived here. The truth of it was, he wasn't quite up to answering questions that might come his way, either about what he was currently doing or about what had prompted his brothers and him to leave. That was something he wanted to tackle gradually—after he sorted a few things out with Annie.

Starting with her explanation as to why she'd acted so strangely when he'd said he was here with Jamie's monthly payment.

Sipping his coffee, he scanned the entire dinner. There was an old-fashioned clock on the wall just behind the counter. He caught himself staring at it periodically for the next two and a half hours.

It seemed to him that the minute hand dragged itself from one number to the next with all the speed of a turtle whose feet had been dipped in molasses.

He put up with it as long as he could, then finally paid for his coffee, plus a tip, leaving ten dollars on the table and walking out.

Danny debated killing some more time by walking around Rust Creek Falls, but he still didn't want to run into anyone that he might possibly know, so instead, he got into his car.

Driving around downtown, even at a snail's pace, didn't take any time at all. Before he knew it, Danny found himself back in the parking lot across from the vet clinic.

He killed another half hour just sitting in his Jeep. But this was Montana and it was definitely nippy in October. He didn't want to just run his engine, using up gas needlessly. Besides, running an engine and going nowhere seemed almost too much like a metaphor for his life.

When it got too cold for him, he got out of his vehicle and went back to the clinic.

The moment he entered, the difference in temperature hit him immediately. There were far more warm bodies in the reception area now than there had been earlier.

Annie looked swamped.

There were people standing at her desk, looking less than patient, and she had just put the receiver down into its cradle, ending another call.

Even with all this activity going on simultaneously, she immediately looked toward the door the second he walked in.

Was she waiting for him? he wondered.

Nodding at her, Dan took a seat and made himself as comfortable as he could, given the current circumstances. He was prepared to wait as long has he had to. At this point, he felt as if he had earned that cup of coffee with Annie.

"You're early," Annie said to him when she finally

had dealt with the three people at her desk and had answered the two more calls that had come in.

"I didn't want to take a chance on missing you before you went to lunch," he told her.

His words drew several interested looks from the people sitting in the waiting area.

Anne looked at the people in the crowded waiting room. "It might be a little later than twelve thirty," she told him.

He shrugged almost philosophically. "I waited this long, what's another half hour or so?"

Annie pressed her lips together, suppressing the words that rose to her lips in response to his comment. This wasn't the time or place to say anything off-the-cuff. She knew that if she did, within less than a heartbeat, she would find herself the unwilling subject of a barrage of gossip.

Rust Creek Falls was a small town and there weren't all that many things going on to spark people's imaginations or to cut through the all-but-numbing boredom that was known to arise periodically.

In the background, Debi, one of the clinic's technicians, had obviously overheard the exchange between Danny and her because the older woman stepped forward now and approached her.

"If you'd like to go out now and get lunch a little earlier," the technician told her, "that's all right. I'll take over the desk while you're gone."

Anne bit her lower lip and looked at the other woman hesitantly. "Don't you have to assist Brooks, Debi?"

The blonde shook her head. "Ellen's doing that. And

Kim is with Dr. Wellington, so you'd better take advantage of this very temporary lull before I change my mind or one of the doctors decide they need more than one tech at their side for a procedure," Debi told her.

"But what about you?" Anne wanted to know. "When will you take your lunch?"

"Nathan is coming by later so I'll wait for him. He says he 'wants to talk,'" the woman confided. "I'd really rather stay busy until he gets here."

From his vantage point, Dan had managed to overhear Anne's part of the exchange and lip-read the rest of it. The moment the older technician told Anne to take her lunch early, he was on his feet, crossing to the reception desk.

"Looks like you've been cleared to go," he told her as the other woman stepped away.

Anne felt butterflies fluttering in the pit of her stomach. Why did she feel as if she was about to go out on a first date? She wasn't, for heaven sakes. This wasn't even a date at all. She was just getting a cup of coffee with someone who had once meant a great deal to her.

*Someone you had a baby with*, the voice in her head reminded her.

With effort, Anne forced a ghost of a smile to her lips as she said, "Just let me get my purse and then I'll be ready."

Taking out her purse from one of the bottom drawers, Anne rose to her feet. She glanced at the phone, willing it to ring.

It didn't.

She had temporarily run out of possible excuses.

"Okay," she told Danny as she came around to the front of the reception desk, "let's get that cup of coffee."

Taking her elbow to help guide her out of the clinic, Dan murmured, "I thought you'd never ask."

The butterflies went into high gear.

*Chapter Eight*

"Where would you like to go?" Dan asked her as they crossed the parking lot to his Jeep.

"Back to the clinic." The words came out before she could think to stop them.

He paused, intense blue eyes meeting blue eyes.

"Really?" Dan asked.

It wasn't his intention to force her to go anywhere with him. Although if he were given a choice, he would have opted to spend a little more time with her. Who knew when the opportunity to do that would arise again—if ever? Because if he *did* decide to go back to Colorado, he knew that he might never get the chance to see Annie again.

"No, not really," Annie admitted, relenting. "I guess I'm just nervous."

That took him aback. "Nervous?" Dan asked incredulously. Grabbing the passenger door, he held it open for her. "Around me?"

That didn't seem to make any sense to him. He could see Annie being angry at him for leaving and even more angry that he hadn't tried to get in touch with her in all this time. But nervous? Why would he make her nervous? They'd hit it off from the very first day all those years ago. They'd been friends from the very beginning and that friendship had eventually blossomed into love. A case of nerves had never been part of that equation.

"This is me. Danny," he reminded her. "You don't have anything to be nervous about around me."

A lot he knew, Anne thought. Just being near him like this made everything inside of her quiver like a bowlful of Jell-O perched on the side of an active volcano.

One would think, she told herself, trying not to press her hand to her abdomen, that after all this time and everything that had happened, she would have gotten over him.

But she hadn't.

All it had taken was seeing him again, watching him walk back into her life, and all the strides she thought she had made toward overcoming her feelings for Danny just curled up like leaves that had dried out in the summer sun and blew away.

"If you say so," Anne murmured under her breath, sitting down in the passenger seat and putting on her seat belt.

About to start the Jeep, Dan left his hand on the key

in the ignition and studied her face. "Why would you be nervous around me?"

She'd said too much, Anne thought. But his question needed an answer so she grasped at the first thing that occurred to her.

"Maybe because I don't know you. The Danny Stockton I knew would have never just disappeared without a word and left me hanging, facing each day wondering if *this* was the day you'd come back to me. But you didn't and after a while, I stopped hoping, I stopped waiting. It got to the point that I thought I just imagined all of it, except for…"

Her voice trailed off when she realized she'd almost said *except for Janie*.

But he had obviously heard her. "Except for what?" Dan prodded.

Anne waved away the mistake she'd very nearly made. "Never mind, it doesn't matter," she told him.

"Annie, if you'd really rather I just take you back to the clinic, I will," Dan offered, although not happily. Still, he could understand how she felt and he couldn't really fault her for it. He didn't want to be the cause of any more unhappiness.

Annie looked at him, her expression unreadable. "Do you want me to go back?"

How could she even *think* that? "Hell, no," he answered with feeling. "I know I can't begin to make up for what happened, for just disappearing the way I did. All I can tell you is that I had a good reason and you're just going to have to trust me. And if you can find it in your heart to forgive me," he told her in all sincerity, "I'd really love to spend a little time with you."

He knew he had no right to even ask that, but just being here with her like this made his soul sing.

"*Little* is certainly the word for it," she answered. "I've only got an hour for lunch."

An hour was more than he would have hoped for. "It's a start," Dan told her, relieved that she had decided to have lunch with him. "So, where do you want to go to eat?" he asked again.

An amused smile played on her lips. "Maybe you haven't noticed, but Rust Creek Falls is not exactly brimming with restaurants." She thought for a moment. "Daisy's Donut Shop serves coffee and the pastries are really good."

That didn't make for much of a lunch, but if that was what she wanted, that was where he'd take her. "Any place you want to go is fine with me," Dan told her. "Or we could order something to go," he suggested.

She thought the idea was to sit and talk over the meal. "You don't want to be seen with me?" Anne asked.

Where would she get an idea like that? He was just trying to be accommodating. Maybe he was trying too hard, he thought.

"I was just thinking that you might not want to be seen with *me*," he told her. Granted, she was divorced, but that wouldn't stop tongues from wagging in Rust Creek Falls. "I was afraid that you might be worried that it could start some gossip."

Annie shrugged. Gossip had never bothered her.

"I'm single, you're single—" She stopped, wondering if she was perhaps taking too much for granted. "You *are* single, right?"

"Very," he answered. There'd never been another woman who had made him feel the way he did about her. He didn't see the point in just marrying someone for the sake of being married.

But Anne wasn't totally convinced about his status. "There's no one back in Colorado waiting for you? A 'Miss Dude Ranch' maybe?"

"Not in Colorado or anywhere else, either," Danny assured her.

Danny had always been the handsomest guy that she had ever laid eyes on. She knew what women were like—he'd be a trophy for anyone who landed him.

"So you've been a monk all this time?" she asked with just the slightest touch of sarcasm in her voice.

His face was completely straight as he told her, "Pretty much."

She gave him one last chance to come clean. "With those muscles and those brilliant blue eyes?" She knew that they had been her undoing and thought that they would easily do the same for another woman.

Danny's eyes looked into hers. "Yup."

Annie still had her doubts, but for now, she went along with his answer. She tried to hang on to the fact that Danny had never lied to her.

"Okay, then there's nothing to gossip about," she concluded. "Just two single people having coffee."

Taking that to be the end of the discussion, he drove to Daisy's Donut Shop.

* * *

The donut shop was crowded when they got there. It turned out to be standing room only by the admittedly small counter.

"Looks like we're going to have to get that coffee to go anyway," Dan told her. She nodded and for a moment, he could have sworn that Annie actually looked a little disappointed. He found that encouraging. "We could go to Wings To Go instead," he suggested.

They might be able to grab a little table there, Danny thought.

The look on Annie's face reflected confusion. "I thought you wanted coffee."

"What I wanted," he told her truthfully, "was just to spend a little time with you. The coffee was actually just an excuse."

"All right, then. We're having wings," Annie agreed.

He was getting to her, she thought, but as long as they were out in public, she had nothing to worry about.

Wings To Go was a cozy little restaurant that, in Dan's estimation, showed a lot of potential. He could see investors making a lot of money here if they expanded the place. Right now it was packed, so he ordered two plates of wings and two soft drinks to go, one for each of them, along with a ton of napkins, and took them back to his Jeep.

"I guess this is kind of like a picnic," he told her. Danny pushed back his seat so that he had enough room to spread out several napkins and balance his box of wings on his lap.

"Remember the one we had on your family's ranch?" Annie asked, instantly stirring up a whole bunch of memories.

"I remember that the stars were out by the time we finished eating," Dan recalled.

More than that, he remembered every detail of that night. It had been the closest thing to perfect he had ever experienced.

*That was the night we made a baby*, Anne thought.

When his eyes met hers, she knew that Danny was remembering the same thing. Not the baby part, because he had no way of knowing she'd gotten pregnant. Instead he was remembering that had been the night when they'd made love for the first—and the last—time. A week after that, his parents were in that awful car accident. And then, right after the funeral, he was gone.

The mention of the picnic not only brought a flood of memories back for Danny, but it also made him feel utterly drawn to her.

There they were, in his Jeep, two orders of buffalo wings spread out between them and all he could think of was taking her into his arms and kissing her.

That would be all she'd need, he upbraided himself, to have him force unwanted attention on her. Desperate to change the subject, he searched for something else to say and remembered the look on her face when he'd explained why he had walked into the clinic.

Like a drowning man grasping at straws, he asked Annie, "Um, why did you look so confused when I told you that Jamie wanted me to bring in his monthly payment to the clinic?"

Stunned, Annie blinked. The subject had changed so fast, she'd almost gotten whiplash. For a second there, Danny had had that look in his eyes, that same look he'd had that night at the picnic.

She'd thought he was going to kiss her.

*Idiot!* she chided herself. She couldn't allow him to kiss her. That would be starting something that *couldn't* be started.

At least one of them had some sense.

She forced herself to think back to this morning. "Um, because Jamie doesn't have an outstanding balance with the vet. Your brother makes a point of paying each time the vet comes out to the ranch."

That was the impression he'd gotten when she'd appeared so confused and surprised this morning. "So what was in the envelope when you finally opened it?" he wanted to know.

"Oh, there was a check in there," she told him. "It was for a small amount. And he included a note. He said it was an advance against the vet's next visit."

"I guess he was trying to come up with an excuse to get me to see you again," Dan said, feeling somewhat self-conscious.

He didn't like being manipulated, but at the same time, he understood why Jamie had done it. His brother's heart was in the right place. Having found happiness, Jamie no doubt wanted the same for him.

*Not going to happen, Jamie.*

"Yes, I kind of figured that part out," Annie told him with a self-deprecating laugh.

"And I would like to see you again," Dan told her.

Finished eating, she wiped her fingers on one of the many napkins Danny had thought to bring with the take-out orders. "You mean for lunch?"

Danny shrugged, not wanting to restrict himself with anything so specific. "For lunch. For a walk. Or maybe we could go horseback riding the way we used to," he reminded her. Danny saw the uncertain expression slip over her face. Maybe that was too much, he thought as he backtracked. "Or just to talk."

"About what?"

"We don't need to have a topic outlined ahead of time," he reminded her. "We can talk about whatever comes up." And then he went another route. "Or we don't need to talk at all. We can just enjoy each other's company." Finished with his lunch, he packed the wrappers back up into the box and folded it over to contain the denuded bones and used napkins. "Tell you what. I'll come by Daisy's Donut Shop tomorrow at twelve thirty. If you want to join me, that'll be great. If you decide that you don't want to, or you have second thoughts, I'll understand." His eyes met hers. "No pressure," he promised softly.

Danny's magnetic blue eyes had always had a way of getting to her. She could recall getting happily lost in them for hours.

"Twelve thirty," Annie repeated. And then she glanced down at her watch. "Oh damn," she said, clearly distressed. Before he could ask her what was wrong, she told him. "I'm late. I'm supposed to be back in the office. I went to lunch early, remember?"

He did now. Time had stood still for him as he'd reveled in her company, but she was right. The hour she'd had was gone.

"I'll tell your boss it was my fault," he volunteered as he started the Jeep and pulled away. "I made you late."

She appreciated what he was offering to do, but it wasn't necessary.

"No, that's all right. I'm a grown woman, Danny. Nobody 'makes' me anything. I've been working for the doctor for a while now. I'll just tell him that I lost track of time and I'll promise to make it up by coming in early tomorrow. Brooks is a good guy. He'll understand."

Danny was skeptical. "Are you sure? I don't mind talking to him and taking the blame."

"No," she said firmly. There was no way she wanted to have someone make excuses for her, least of all Danny.

He was silent for a moment. "I didn't mean to make you late."

Having him feel guilty about something so minor was not the way to go if their relationship had any hopes of being repaired. There were far bigger issues that still needed to be resolved, not the least of which was whether or not to tell Danny the truth about Janie's parentage.

She also sensed that there was something he wasn't telling her, and until he could trust her enough to level with her, their relationship was going to be in a suspended state.

"You didn't know what time I was supposed to get back. It's up to me to keep track of the time," she informed him.

He laughed softly. "I guess motherhood really changed you."

He meant it as a compliment, but he had a feeling from her answer that Annie didn't quite take it that way.

"Twelve years changed me," she corrected. "I was a teenager when you left Rust Creek Falls. I'm not a teenager anymore."

He came to a stop right in front of the clinic rather than in the parking lot across the way. His eyes washed over her, as if seeing her for the first time since he'd arrived back.

"No," he replied, "you're not."

There was notable appreciation in Danny's voice that was not lost on her. She felt a warmth climbing up along her throat, leaving its mark on her cheeks.

Annie felt it best not to say anything in response to his comment. Instead, she got out of the Jeep.

"Thanks for lunch," she said just before she ran through the clinic's front door.

Without being able to explain exactly why, Dan felt as if he'd been on the receiving end of a one-two punch. Blowing out a breath, he pulled away and drove back to Jamie's ranch.

Dan looked at his watch.

It was thirty seconds later than it had been when he'd looked at his watch the last time. Twelve thirty had come and gone and one o'clock was looming on the horizon, just ninety seconds away.

He was sitting in Daisy's Donut Shop.

Alone.

Annie hadn't come.

He thought—again—of calling the vet clinic to speak to her. He'd already thought of doing that twice before and each time, he'd wound up talking himself out of it. He didn't want to make Annie feel like he was bothering her at work or even worse, that he was stalking her.

Most likely, she had gotten swamped at the clinic again the way she had yesterday. Or maybe one of the vet techs had called in sick and there was no one to man the reception desk when she went to lunch.

Or, for that matter, maybe she had just changed her mind and decided that seeing him again—especially seeing him two days in a row—was a bad idea. Undoubtedly Annie was just going to work through her lunch and completely forget about seeing him today.

Or possibly ever.

If that was the case, Annie was definitely within her rights, he thought. For that matter, she might even view this as payback for what she felt he had done to her by taking off the way he had right after his parents' funeral.

Thinking back to that day, he recalled that she'd held his hand all through it, squeezing it the way people did when they were trying to infuse their own strength into someone else, hoping to help them get through something particularly devastating.

Annie had really tried to help him get through that difficult time, doing the best she could—and he had still left her.

Danny sighed. Annie wasn't coming, he realized, resigning himself to the fact.

Very slowly, he got up, easing himself away from the tiny table for two. His appetite gone, he left the coffee and donuts he'd bought in anticipation of her company and headed for the door.

Just as he was about to push open the door in order to go out, the door was suddenly moved out of range. Hand outstretched, he found himself tripping forward.

## Chapter Nine

Danny managed to catch himself a second before he made bodily contact with the customer who was entering the donut shop at that exact moment.

Annie swallowed a gasp. Instinct took over and rather than stepping back out of harm's way, her hands flew out to him, anticipating his fall.

Her heart was pounding wildly in her chest as she asked him, "Are you okay?"

Dan caught himself grinning like a kid who'd stumbled across Christmas presents in the closet in October.

"You came," he exclaimed. "I'm terrific."

Anne stepped inside the coffee shop to get out of people's way.

"You were leaving, weren't you?" It wasn't a question; it was an assumption. She flushed just a tad. Her heart slowly began to settle down. "I'm sorry I'm so late, but things went a little crazy at the clinic."

Dan nodded understandingly. "I figured as much," he told her. Now that Annie was here, he didn't want her to waste any time with needless apologies. "I ordered for us. I'm afraid the coffee's probably cold, but the pastries are still fresh."

Annie smiled. "No problem. I love cold coffee."

She said it so that Danny wouldn't feel bad, but the truth of it was she really did like coffee no matter what state it was in.

Placing his hand against the small of her back, he steered Annie toward the little table he'd just occupied for the last forty-five minutes.

As he approached, he saw that one of the people from behind the counter was beginning to clear away the coffees and pastries.

"No, hey, wait," he called out to the woman, "I wasn't done with that."

The waitress immediately deposited the dishes of pastries back onto the table. "Oh, I'm sorry, I thought I saw you leaving."

"No, I was just going to get a little air." He pretended to inhale. "You've got great air here in Montana. Crisp and clean."

The waitress looked at him as if he'd taken leave of his senses.

"It's cold," was all she would say about it. Putting the closed containers of coffee back on the table, the woman withdrew.

As she did, she gave Annie a warning look. "I'd watch myself around him if I were you."

"I fully intend to," Annie answered with a smile, looking at Danny and not the waitress. "Do you want to take those somewhere and eat?" she asked him, thinking that he would probably like to get out of the little shop.

"No, she's right. Montana's cold. You don't want to spend your lunch hour sitting in a Jeep, shivering." He pulled out her chair for her, then took his own after taking off his jacket and draping it on the back of the chair. "So," he started, amicably, giving her his full attention, "what happened?"

"What happened?" she echoed, not quite sure what he was asking her about.

"To make you late," he prodded.

Annie waved his question away. It was just the usual work stuff, compounded. She had no desire to bore him to death.

"Oh, you don't want to hear about my morning."

"Sure I do," he told her with feeling. "It's got to be more interesting than standing outside in the cold, fixing twenty feet of fencing."

"Well," she allowed, "I guess it was warmer at any rate."

He smiled at Annie, watching the way the rays of sun played off her hair, turning the blond strands into gold. "Sounds more interesting already."

Annie's expression was somewhat dubious as she looked at him. "All right," she agreed, "but remember, you asked for this."

"You won't hear one single word of complaint," he promised, making an elaborate show of crossing his heart with the hand that wasn't holding a cream-filled chocolate donut.

Annie laughed and the sound was like music to his ears.

The next fifty minutes passed much too quickly. Annie did most of the talking and it was as if they had regained some of their former relationship, at least a little of the ease that they had once felt around one another.

And then, just as she finished the last of her pastry, he told her, "You'd better be getting back." Annie looked at him, puzzled. "Your lunch break is almost over," he explained.

"You're keeping track?" she asked, surprised. She hadn't seen him look down at his watch.

He nodded. "I didn't want you to be late two days in a row," he told her, rising and coming around behind her chair. He held it as he helped her out of it.

Bemused, Annie asked, "You actually timed this?"

He couldn't tell if she was amused or offended by his action. All he could do was restate his reason. "Like I said, I didn't want you to be late getting back again because of me."

As they walked out of the shop, Danny held the door open for her. She smiled at him as she crossed the threshold.

"What?" he asked. He needed to know why she was

smiling so he could do whatever it was again. "Do I have some cream filling on my face?"

Annie shook her head. "No."

"Then why are you looking at me that way?" he wanted to know.

"It's nice to know that there's a little of the old Danny still left inside you."

There were times when he really doubted that, even though he had done his best not to let what had happened—what he had *caused* to happen—bury him in despair. "What makes you say that?"

"Because someone else would not have gone through the trouble of keeping track of the time, or worrying about me being late getting back to work." There was a fond look in her eyes as she said, "But the old Danny would have. And you did."

They were by her car now and Dan realized this was the last moment he was going to spend with her for at least a while. A feeling of sadness corkscrewed through him.

"Terminal nice guy, that's me," Danny responded with just a touch of sarcasm.

She saw that the sadness in his eyes that had been missing for a little while as they'd talked in the donut shop was back. She wanted to erase it even though she told herself it shouldn't matter to her one way or another.

"Nothing wrong with being a nice guy," she told him softly.

He made no comment. Instead, he told her, "This was nice. Maybe we can do it again sometime."

She noticed that he didn't say anything definite the

way he had yesterday. Was he afraid of committing himself to something specific?

"I'd like that," Annie told him. "But right now, I have to go."

"Right."

Dan stepped back, although in reality, he wasn't blocking her from her car. Annie's vehicle was right behind her, a ten-year-old pickup truck whose paint was fading in several places. The step back he'd taken was more symbolic than actually necessary. He didn't want to seem as if he was trying to detain her for even an extra minute.

"I'll see you, Annie," he said as she got into her truck.

"I hope so," she answered just before she started up her vehicle and pulled away.

Danny lost no time in getting into his Jeep. He'd told Jamie he'd be back in plenty of time to help him fix the north gate. He intended to keep his word.

*I hope so.*

The words echoed in his head all the way back to Jamie's. It accompanied the smile that was on his face.

"So things are going well?" Jamie asked, eyeing Dan over the gate that they were trying to put back up after they'd mended it.

Jamie had waited to ask his question for what he thought was a decent amount of time after Danny had gotten back from town. He was proud of himself for not immediately jumping on his brother to pump Danny for information.

"Yeah, I just about got this gate straight," Danny answered, grunting for effect.

"I'm not talking about the stupid gate," Jamie said in exasperation.

Waiting until he had hammered the three nails he'd been holding in his teeth to the two sides of the gate, Dan looked at his brother with mock innocence and asked, "Then what are you talking about?"

Jamie scowled. "You know damn well what I'm talking about, Danny. Those trips of yours into town."

"Oh yeah. I'm really beginning to find my way around town again."

Jamie thought he'd been patient long enough.

"I'm holding a hammer, Danny," he told him, grasping the tool harder, "and I know how to use it."

Danny gave him a look as he held up his hammer. "That makes two of us, brother," he answered.

"So she shut you out?" Jamie asked, assuming the only thing he could since Danny wasn't saying that things had gone at least moderately well. "Hey, Danny, I'm sorry. Maybe it just wasn't meant to—"

"You want to work or you want to gossip?" Danny wanted to know.

"What I want is to work and to have a conversation with my brother while I'm working," Jamie answered.

Danny sighed. He supposed he owed Jamie this much. "It's going well enough. There, you satisfied?" he asked, looking at Jamie pointedly.

Jamie was light years away from being satisfied. "What do you mean by 'well enough'?"

Danny sighed again. "You're worse than Old Mrs.

McKinley, you know that?" The woman their mother
had known years ago had loved to gossip and to ferret
out information about people. Some people had felt that
it was her whole life.

Jamie looked annoyed by the comparison. "You're
my brother. Forgive me for caring," he retorted.

Danny pressed his lips together, debating what to
do. He knew he was being secretive about something
that was most likely general public knowledge, at least
to anyone who lived in town.

"I'm sorry. It's just that I'm afraid if I say anything
at all about it, then it will no longer be the truth."

Jamie saw through the flimsy excuse. "You mean
you're afraid of jinxing it."

The game was up. Danny felt he might as well relent.
"Something like that."

"Since when did you get so superstitious?" Jamie
wanted to know.

"I didn't realize I was until just now," Danny admitted. "And to answer your question, it's been going well
enough." He paused, searching for something more to
give Jamie. There really wasn't anything. "Baby steps,"
he finally told his brother. "The whole thing is progress-
ing with baby steps."

Jamie nodded. "Sounds hopeful."

"Yeah, maybe," Danny allowed. He didn't want to
say anything more about it at the moment. To him, the
whole thing was very fragile in nature and he didn't
want to count on it too much one way or another. "Now
if you want to finish this gate before the triplets are

ready to start high school, I suggest you talk less and work more."

Jamie laughed. Now *that* sounded like the old Danny. "Welcome back, brother."

Danny merely grunted as he hammered.

"Is that guy your old boyfriend?" Janie asked that evening as she was helping her mother clear the table after they'd had dinner.

The question had come out of nowhere and caught Anne totally off guard. Gathering up the utensils from the table, she forced herself to make eye contact with her daughter.

"Who are you talking about?" she asked, although she knew full well there could only be one person that Janie was referring to.

Janie gave her an impatient look that preteen daughters had been giving their mothers since the very beginning of time.

"That guy that came to see you last week before Dad came to pick me up."

Rather than give Janie an answer, she deflected with a question of her own. "Just what makes you ask something like that?"

Janie pursed her lips together as if the answer was self-evident. "You had a funny look on your face when you were talking to him."

"I was just surprised to see him," Anne said, thinking fast. "He hasn't been in Rust Creek Falls for a long time."

"Then he wasn't your old boyfriend?" Janie asked, clearly wanting an answer one way or another.

Anne turned to load the dishwasher. She didn't want to lie to her daughter, but she really didn't want to get into this at the present time. "Why do you want to know?"

Janie gave her an annoyed look. "Because I want you and Dad to get back together and you can't do that if your old boyfriend is hanging around, getting you all dreamy-eyed and stuff," she said in disgust.

"Honey, your dad and I aren't going to get back together," Anne said, repeating what she'd already told her daughter more than once. "But we still both love you very much. As for Danny, I knew him a long time ago. Before I met your father," she added. "Do you like him?"

Janie shrugged. "He's okay I guess. For an old guy."

Ouch, that stung, Anne thought. "He's the same age as I am," she pointed out to her daughter.

"Yeah, but you're old, too," Janie said as she brought over the plates to the kitchen counter. "Not frumpy old," she quickly corrected. "But old."

Anne smiled. She couldn't ever remember being as young as Janie. Had she said things like this at the time? She certainly hoped not.

Very tactfully, she told Janie, "Sometimes 'old' people like to see old friends."

"Dad's old," Janie pointed out, brightening. "You can see *him*."

"I do see him," Anne replied. "When he comes by

to pick you up and on the following day, when he drops you off."

Janie's scowl deepened. "I mean *more*, Mom," she stressed. "Like you used to see him. All the time."

Anne sighed. She knew this mode. Janie was just going to keep on harping on the subject until she either broke Anne down, or she lost her temper. Anne didn't want to do either.

She fell back on her old standby. "Have you finished your homework for tomorrow?"

"Not yet, but—"

"Then go finish it," Anne told her, cutting through any more rhetoric.

"But this is *important*, Mom," Janie insisted, becoming irritated.

Finished loading the dishwasher, Anne measured out the detergent, put it into the proper compartment and started the cycle.

"So's your homework," she declared. "If you don't do it, you'll get left back and that'll throw everything off. How will it look when you're running for president and your opponent finds out you were left back in fifth grade?"

Janie sighed dramatically. It was audible over the noise of the dishwasher. "I'm not going to run for president, Mom."

"You need to pass fifth grade no matter what you intend on doing in life," she told her daughter matter-of-factly.

"Okay, I'll do it, I'll do it," Janie declared, putting her hands over her ears to shut out any further pep talk from her mother. "I'll do my homework so I don't flunk out of fifth grade."

"That's my girl," Anne said with a smile. She went back to cleaning up the kitchen.

"This isn't over, you know," Janie promised as she left the kitchen.

Anne shut her eyes as she leaned her head against the wall, struggling very hard to collect herself.

*Yes, I know*, she said silently.

It wasn't going to be over until she made a full confession—to both Janie and to Danny.

## *Chapter Ten*

There was no word from Danny the next day. Annie tried to pretend that she didn't care one way or another. That she was relieved not to have to deal with having Danny coming around. But the truth was that not hearing from him had her concerned and wondering if something had gone wrong.

Again.

Had he decided to go back to that dude ranch in Colorado, the one he said he worked on? Or had he decided, after seeing her twice, that he was making a huge mistake starting things up again? That he was actually opening up a can of worms that was best left unopened and buried somewhere back in the distant past?

It was the not knowing that was putting her on edge,

so much so that she found people were talking to her twice because she'd drifted off.

It was happening, she realized. She was letting Danny get to her, just as she had let his disappearance get to her twelve years ago.

*C'mon, Anne, you're better than this. You're not a teenager anymore. You're a grown woman and a mother with responsibilities. Your world isn't supposed to revolve around whether or not Danny Stockton turns up on your doorstep.*

She forced herself to focus on her work and remained at the reception desk, working straight through her lunch break.

But no matter what she told herself, all that day it felt like every fiber of her being kept waiting for Danny to turn up, first at the clinic and then later, at her home.

He didn't.

By the middle of the second day, she'd almost convinced herself that Dan Stockton had gone from her life just as abruptly as he had turned up.

Now she just had to make her peace with it. She told herself she could—but it was far from easy. So far that when Hank came by her house later that afternoon to pick Janie up for an overnight stay, he asked her, "Something wrong, Anne?"

"Nothing more than usual," she answered evasively. "They were shorthanded at the clinic today, and between the house calls the vets had to make to the different ranches and the pets people brought in themselves, things have been pretty hectic all week."

She noticed Hank peered closely at her face and fig-

ured she was in trouble. She'd never been one to maintain a poker face. "That the only thing bothering you?"
he wanted to know.

She tossed her head as she looked up, doing her best
to bluff her way through this. "Why? What else would
there be?"

She could both feel and see Hank studying her. It was
all she could do not to shift uncomfortably.

"Maybe an old flame turning up without any warning," he suggested.

Rather than deny anything, she decided to brazen it
out and hopefully make Hank back off. "That's not really any of your concern, Hank."

But Hank obviously saw it another way. "Yes, it is.
Daniel Stockton ran out on you when you needed him
most," he insisted angrily.

"Stop!"

She didn't want Hank saying anything about Danny
that Janie could accidentally overhear. She wasn't ready
to tell her daughter about the circumstances of her birth
and she certainly didn't want the girl to find out by hearing Hank talking about it.

"That's all in the past," she informed him sternly.
"And as far as I'm concerned, that's exactly where it
belongs."

But the expression on his face told her that Hank was
far from convinced. "Are you sure, Anne?"

She moved closer to him, but not out of any desire
to rekindle something between them. There had never
been anything between them except for respect and

gratitude on her part. But she didn't want what she was about to say to Hank to be overheard.

"As far as Janie knows, you're her father and she's always going to think of you that way." She lowered her voice even more as she added, "You've got nothing to worry about."

He looked relieved to hear her say that. "I love that little girl, Anne," he told her, emotion brimming in his voice.

"I know, Hank, and she loves you. That's never going to change."

He looked over Anne's shoulder as Janie came into the room, backpack in tow. His whole countenance changed, lightening up right before her.

"Well, speak of the devil," he declared in a louder, more jovial voice.

"I'm not the devil, Dad," Janie protested as she came over to join him.

"Well, sometimes you act like a little devil," Hank teased affectionately.

They had a good relationship, Anne observed. She couldn't remember Hank ever raising his voice or saying a cross word to Janie. She found herself almost wishing that Hank really *was* Janie's father. Things would have been a lot simpler that way.

"I'm all ready to go, Dad," Janie announced, impatient to leave.

Hank took her backpack from her and pretended that he found it extremely heavy. Suppressing a grunt, he said, "I can see that."

"Be good and listen to your dad," Anne instructed her daughter.

Janie rolled her eyes. "Yes, Mom." Turning to Hank, she confided, "She thinks I'm a baby."

"You'll always be my baby," Anne interjected, deliberately giving the girl a big hug.

Janie groaned and squirmed, acting as if she was being subjected to corporal punishment. The second Anne released her, Janie deliberately moved out of her mother's reach.

Pretending not to notice and giving no indication that it hurt, Anne walked Hank and her daughter to the door.

"Have fun, you two," she told them.

"Oh, we will," Hank promised, saying the words more to Janie than to her. "Tell your mother goodbye," he told the girl.

"Bye," Janie said without bothering to look back in her mother's direction. She was too eager to begin whatever adventure her father had planned for them.

As was her habit, Anne watched them go. Watched how her daughter skipped beside Hank, the picture of uncomplicated happiness—and the total antithesis of the way she usually behaved when it was just the two of them, without Hank.

Janie's change in behavior had been recent, no more than about three, four months old. It was around that time that Janie had gotten it into her head to play Cupid and bring Hank and her together. Anne had explained to her daughter a number of times, in as many ways as she could think of, that sometimes parents just couldn't stay together and that it was far better for all parties involved if parents weren't forced to live together. But that never seemed to stick in Janie's mind for more than a few minutes at a time. It certainly wasn't anything that Janie took to heart.

Anne saw Hank say something to Janie as she got into his car and the child laughed in response.

Anne sighed as she closed the door. She wished that Janie could be that happy around her.

It hadn't always been like this, she recalled. When it had been the three of them together, Janie had always turned to her first. But ever since the divorce, Hank had slowly become her daughter's go-to person.

Anne frowned. She supposed she was being a little jealous of Hank. That was something she was going to have to work on. It wasn't right to feel like that about someone who was so good to—

Her thought pulled up short when she heard the doorbell.

Anne laughed softly to herself. Janie had probably remembered she hadn't packed one of her video games.

Opening the door, she asked, "Forget something?"

"Yeah. My manners."

It wasn't her daughter but Danny standing on her doorstep, just as he had the first time he'd turned up in Rust Creek Falls several days ago.

Damn, was her heart ever going to stop leaping up this way at the very sight of him? Anne wondered, annoyed with herself.

Forcing a smile to her lips, she said, "I hear there's a current shortage of that." Then she stepped back from the doorway to let him come in.

Dan crossed the threshold, but went no further into the room. He looked just a touch apprehensive. "Am I interrupting anything?" he asked hesitantly.

"Only my solitude," she answered truthfully. "Janie just left for a sleepover at Hank's and I was about to go over some bills I've been letting pile up."

"So in other words, no?" he asked, an engaging smile on his lips. He looked very happy with her answer.

Anne inclined her head. "In other words, no," she repeated. "Would you like to come in?" she asked, assuming that was why he was here.

"Actually, I was wondering if you'd like to come out," he told her.

She suddenly realized that the carefree girl who would take off at a moment's notice at the slightest suggestion from Danny was gone. Instead, she heard herself asking, "Come out where?"

"I was going to ask if you and Janie would like to go horseback riding with me, but since you just said that she's not here, I'm asking if *you'd* like to go for a ride with me."

"Now?" she asked, looking outside over his shoulder. "Isn't it going to be dark soon?"

"I was thinking of going out for only a short ride," he explained. "But if you'd rather not, we can do it some other time."

Temptation won after what turned out to be an extremely short internal debate.

"Sure, why not?" Anne agreed. "As long as it's a short ride," she qualified. "Give me a minute."

Getting her jacket and keys, Anne stepped out onto

her porch and looked around. She didn't see what she was looking for.

"Where are you keeping the horses?" she asked in amusement, fully expecting him to tell her that he'd only been teasing her.

Instead, Danny said, "C'mon and I'll take you to them."

Her curiosity definitely aroused, Anne climbed into his Jeep.

Dan drove only a short distance until he arrived at a stable located not that far out of town. Anne hadn't even known of its existence.

The scope of her world had shrunk a great deal since she'd come back to Rust Creek Falls after college, she thought.

"I thought you might like to go for a horseback ride," Dan told her, "just like we used to when we were young."

There were five stalls inside the stable. Three were empty. The other two had horses that were already saddled. She thought that was rather unusual, but made no comment about it.

"Which one's mine?" Anne asked. She was instinctively drawn to the smaller mount.

Dan nodded toward the horse that was closer to her. "The mare."

It was a Palomino and she thought the horse was absolutely gorgeous. But something wasn't right. "There are only two saddled horses," she noted, turning to face Dan. "I thought you said that you were inviting Janie, too."

"I had a feeling you'd say no to that if she was home.

Besides, I took a chance that her father might have picked her up for the evening," he confessed. "Turns out I was right." Taking both horses out of their stalls, he led them outside the stable. "Ready?"

"Ready," she answered.

Dan handed her the reins to her horse and Anne happily swung into the mare's saddle. She hadn't ridden in years. Not since she and Hank had been divorced. Once they had gone their separate ways, her access to horses and even to a ranch became a thing of the past. Although Janie still got to ride whenever she stayed over at Hank's ranch.

Hank had bought her a pony for her fifth birthday, just shortly before the decision to get a divorce had been made. The pony, Anne suspected, was Hank's way to ensure that Janie would want to come over and spend time with him.

As if he needed to bribe Janie, Anne thought. The girl worshipped the ground he walked on.

Less than five minutes into the ride and it was as if she had never been off a horse. Anne was exhilarated and revitalized.

Urging her mount into first a brisk walk, then a canter and finally a full gallop, she laughed with glee as the seductive feeling of freedom she always experienced on horseback surged through her veins.

Dan was quietly relieved that she wasn't asking any questions about where the horses had come from. He didn't want her to know he'd arranged for Jamie to bring them over in his trailer to what was essentially an abandoned stable, and to get them saddled.

The look on Anne's face made all this worth it, Dan thought.

He let her set the pace and kept up, happy just to see her like this, with the wind in her hair and nipping at her cheeks, turning them an enticing shade of pink.

The ride was over all too soon. Daylight was beginning to fade. It would be dark before long. Dan called out, "We'd better head back."

Like a gleeful child, Anne wanted to ask for five more minutes. But at the last moment, she stopped herself. He was right. She couldn't just ride off into the night the way she used to.

For one thing, they weren't on Dan's family ranch and she didn't know her way around. For another, she wasn't the girl she'd once been. Freedom in this case belonged to the very young. She'd had her taste of it, but now it was time to go back home.

They brought the horses back to the stable and returned them to their stalls.

"Shouldn't we take their saddles off?" she asked. She didn't see anyone in the stable to take care of the animals.

"That's taken care of," he told her, not going into details. "Come on, I'll bring you back to your place."

Perplexed, Anne got into his Jeep, then waited until he had pulled the vehicle away and was heading to her house before she told him, "Thank you. That was really fun. I've forgotten what it was like to have fun," she confessed.

"You should always be able to have fun," he told her with sincerity.

She looked at his profile, wondering if he actually meant what he'd just said. And if he did, then why had he ever left her?

Oh, she understood the basic reason that had supposedly compelled him as well as his older brothers to leave town. She knew all about his grandparents and their unwillingness to take in any of the Stockton siblings, much less the three older boys who were legally old enough to be out on their own.

But if Dan meant what he'd just said, *really* meant it, and if he'd really loved her the way he'd told her that wonderful night they'd spent beneath the stars, then why had he left her? Why hadn't he found some way for them to remain together?

That question had been eating away at her for twelve years.

"Why'd you leave me, Danny?" she asked quietly.

"I told you why. You already know the answer to that."

"No, I don't. Not really," she said, then placed her hand over her heart. "Not in here."

He pulled up in front of her house. "You want me to go?" he asked.

"No, I want you to come inside and talk to me. Really talk to me," she told him. She felt that he needed to give her an explanation, a *real* explanation, just as much as she needed to hear one.

Turning off the ignition, he began to get out of the vehicle, but then he wavered. "Maybe I'd better not," he began.

But Annie had anticipated Danny's possible change

of heart and she felt that she had gone too far out on that limb to allow him to make his way back to where it was safe.

To where he could act as if their last night together— their only night together—hadn't happened. Because it definitely had. Janie was living proof that it had.

She took hold of Danny's hand and tugged on it, drawing him to her doorstep.

"Maybe you should," she coaxed. "Remember," she told him as she unlocked her door and held it open, "confession is good for the soul."

"That only works if you still have a soul," he qualified.

"Everybody has a soul, Danny." Anne closed the front door behind them and then locked it.

"No," Dan contradicted. "Everyone starts out with a soul. That doesn't mean that they still have it as time goes by."

Anne had no idea what he was talking about. All she knew was that something was apparently haunting Danny and she was convinced that he needed to get it off his chest in order to get better.

# *Chapter Eleven*

He needed to talk to her.

It was obvious that he had demons, despite his outward facade.

"Would you like a drink?" she offered. Whenever Hank had been tense about something in the past, he always said that a little scotch and soda could always make him feel calmer.

The mere mention of a drink brought that awful night back to Dan in vivid, chilling terms. He could almost feel the hairs on the back of his neck standing up.

"Danny, what's wrong?" Anne asked, reacting to the way the color had drained from his face. "You just turned pale."

It was a mistake coming inside, he told himself. He needed to get away.

"Maybe I'm coming down with something. I should go." He turned toward the door. "I don't want to risk you catching anything from me."

But Annie caught his hand in hers. He found her grip to be surprisingly strong.

"You're not coming down with something," she told him knowingly. "Danny, trust me. Please," she implored. "You have to tell me what's eating away at you, what kept you away from me all these years."

He fell back on his old standby. It was, after all, true. "I left because my grandparents didn't want me. You know that."

Anne's gut told her that wasn't true. "You didn't leave because of your grandparents. You left because something was wrong. I sensed it at your parents' funeral. Just talk to me," she pleaded. "You can't keep running from whatever this is for the rest of your life."

There was no reason to burden her with this. It was his cross to carry, not hers.

"There's no point in talking about it. I didn't deserve you then, and I don't deserve you now." It was crazy for him to have thought things could be different from what they were. "I should have never come back to Rust Creek Falls."

"Don't tell me what I deserve or don't deserve," she told him angrily. "I'm the only one who can be the judge of that. And in order to be the judge, I need to know what's at the bottom of all this." Her eyes held his as she begged, "Talk to me, Danny. You owe me that much. If I ever meant anything at all to you, you owe me that."

Danny sighed as he stared up at the ceiling, searching for the right words to tell her about this awful segment of his life.

There were no "right" ones, he realized. There were only the ones that described what had happened and what he did that brought about the horrific chain of events. Words that he had kept locked up inside of him for more than a decade. Words he'd never shared with anyone, not even his brothers.

Words that weighed so heavily on him that right now he felt close to the breaking point.

"Please," Anne whispered, squeezing his hand, her eyes silently pleading with him to tell her what had taken him away from her and what was still ripping him apart this way.

Telling himself she was right, that he had to try to tell Annie about it, Dan took a breath and began talking.

"The night of the accident, I went out with Luke and Bailey. They said they wanted to celebrate—I don't even remember what it was that they wanted to celebrate," he said. That memory had gotten lost. "But I didn't realize they were talking about drinking until we walked into a bar.

"Even so," he continued, "I thought they were just going to have one or two drinks. But that turned into more and before I knew it, they were both drunk. Only Luke was old enough to legally drink," he confided, "but Bailey had a fake ID. I asked them to stop, but they told me I was a mama's boy and I needed to 'man up.'"

"Did you drink?" Anne asked.

"No. They taunted me a little, but I knew it was just the alcohol talking. Pretty soon, they were too drunk to drive home and I knew that if *I* tried to drive them home, they'd both gang up on me and never let me take the wheel."

He pressed his lips together, hating what he was about to say because it just reinforced his feelings of guilt. If he hadn't done what he did next, his parents would still be alive and everything that had happened in the last twelve years—all the pain, all the hurt, all the estrangement—none of it would have ever happened.

Everything was *his* fault.

Dan's mouth felt like cotton and he could swear that his tongue felt like it was sticking to the roof of his mouth.

"What did you do?" Anne asked gently, prodding him to talk.

Dan took a deep breath, as if that would somehow shield him.

It didn't.

An almost surreal feeling came over him as he spoke. "I called my parents. I told them what was going on and where we were." He sighed, the guilt all but choking him. "I ratted my brothers out."

She wouldn't allow him to see it that way, to blame himself. "You *had* to tell your parents. From what you're telling me, neither one of them was in any condition to drive home. They could have killed themselves and you, or they could have killed somebody else."

She could see by the look in his eyes that what she was saying wasn't helping him cope with the tragedy. But at least he was getting it all out.

"What happened next?" she urged.

Dan closed his eyes for a moment. Though he tried to distance himself from the event, he was reliving every moment of it.

"Dad sounded pretty angry when I told him what was going on. He told me not to let Luke and Bailey out of my sight. Then he said that he and Mom were coming to get us." He let out a long, shaky breath. The words all but stuck in his throat. "They never got there."

He looked up, expecting to see condemnation in Annie's eyes. But there was only sympathy.

She didn't understand, he realized. "Don't you see? If I hadn't called my parents, they would have never been on the road, never been in the wrong place at the wrong time. Never been hit by that drunk driver."

Dan looked away from her, so guilt-ridden he could hardly breathe. "I killed my parents," he told her in a hoarse whisper.

"No, you didn't," Anne insisted fiercely. "All you're guilty of was trying to look out for your brothers."

He'd been over and over this in his mind a hundred times in the last dozen years. "Maybe if I had looked out for my brothers and hadn't let them drink, or maybe if I never called my parents and instead made Luke and Bailey stay put until they were sober again and could drive home, my parents would still be alive. Or what if I hadn't gone out with my brothers? Then I wouldn't have known they were drinking and I wouldn't have had to call my parents to come get us."

"Then Luke and Bailey might have been killed trying to get home," Annie pointed out.

"Maybe not," he countered. "But my parents would have still been alive."

She felt his desperation. "Danny, you're going to drive yourself crazy with all these conjectures." Her eyes searched his face and saw how tortured he was. "You *have* driven yourself crazy with all these what-ifs. Don't you see? You've got to stop torturing yourself like this."

"But I'm the one responsible for their accident," he insisted.

"No, you are *not*. You didn't make that drunk driver plow into them. Maybe if someone had called *his* parents or someone else to come get him, then *he* wouldn't have been driving and he wouldn't have killed anyone. All you were ever guilty of was trying to think like a responsible person."

Anne moved closer to him on the sofa, wrapping her hand around his. "Oh, Danny, I wish you would have told me about this right from the beginning. I could have been there for you, supported you. We could have faced this terrible thing together. And then you could have saved yourself all this useless pain and anguish that you've been going through all these years."

*And spared both of us more than a decade of loneliness*, she added silently.

"I never told anyone," Dan said, his voice barely above a whisper. "Because then they'd know that it was my fault that my family was destroyed."

"You didn't destroy them," Anne stressed. She had to make him see that. "And there was more than one family at stake," she added quietly, thinking of Janie and the life the three of them could have had together.

Danny met her gaze and he saw that there were tears in her eyes. He assumed that she was referring to them and the family they could have created if he'd remained in Rust Creek Falls.

"I'm sorry, Annie. Sorry for everything. Sorry I left you," he whispered.

The compassion he saw in her eyes drew him in. Before he could summon all the reasons he shouldn't be doing this, he did.

He kissed her.

Because after a whole decade with nothing but memories to sustain him, there was nothing he wanted to do more at this very moment than to kiss her.

To show her how much he still cared about her.

He was afraid that if he did, she would pull away from him.

When she didn't, when she returned his kiss, he automatically deepened it. Framing her face with his hands, he was suddenly propelled back in time. Back to that last night they'd shared.

A myriad of urges and desires began to swirl through him like a twister picking up steam.

He'd missed her. Oh Lord, how he had missed her.

Missed this feeling.

Missed feeling alive.

He felt his blood surging through his veins, doing double time.

Old desires reared their heads, begging that he make up for lost time.

But as much as he wanted it, as much as he wanted *her*, he knew that he couldn't push, couldn't rush. Despite the temptation he felt through every inch of his body, this had to be entirely Annie's call and he would follow whatever signals she gave him.

Annie felt as if she was on fire.

Kissing Danny was even more wonderful than she remembered. It was as if she'd been sleeping all this time and, like the prince in *Sleeping Beauty*, he had woken her up, brought her out of her hibernation.

Every inch of her was tingling with desire. It was incredible that after all this time, she could vividly recall what it felt like to make love with him that one time. Every fiber of her being literally ached to do it again.

The thought sliced through her, frightening her so much that she found herself actually trembling. Not from desire, but from fear.

Summoning as much strength as she could, she pushed Dan away. "I can't!" she cried.

To his surprise, Dan realized that she was shaking. Annie *was* afraid of him. He'd never wanted that, never wanted her to be frightened of him. Did she actually think that he was going to force himself on her? Did she really believe that he had changed that much? That he would just grab what he wanted, ignoring decency?

"Annie, I never meant to—"

"Please leave." If she heard Dan out, she knew she'd succumb to him. To herself. And she couldn't afford to do that.

Dan wanted to talk to her, to explain that she had

nothing to fear from him. To tell her what it meant to him to finally be able to open up to her the way he had.

But it was clear that somehow, he had managed to shake her up. Clear that somehow, signals had gotten crossed. Though he didn't understand *why* she felt this way, he definitely didn't mean for her to feel threatened by him.

He kept that to himself. Kept all his apologies to himself until he could find a way to deliver them without appearing threatening to her.

Murmuring, "I'm sorry," he let himself out the front door and left.

What the hell had just happened back there? he asked himself. He thought he had read all of Annie's signals correctly, but apparently he was no better at picking up signs now than he had been as a teenager. However, Annie was his best friend; she always had been. He didn't want to risk losing her now that he had finally gotten up the nerve to return to Rust Creek Falls and confront all his demons.

But maybe he already had lost her. Maybe Annie would be better off if he just went back to Colorado.

It looked like he had a great deal to think about, Danny told himself as he drove back to his brother's place.

Jamie. What was he going to tell his brother when Jamie asked how the evening had gone? Jamie had been the one who had insisted on having his best horses there for them so that Dan could take Annie for a ride the way he used to.

It was obvious that Jamie was determined to play

Cupid for him. Too bad that right now, Cupid's arrows seemed to all be blunt-tipped.

What had she almost done? Annie thought, pulling her feet up under her on the sofa. If she hadn't pulled back when she had, she would have wound up making love with Danny—just like that.

Even after all this time, she would have made love with Danny in a heartbeat.

Hadn't she learned *anything*?

Even now, after he had gone, her heart was still pounding wildly.

She was afraid.

Very afraid. Because all it had taken was one kiss from Danny and she was ready to melt right there on the spot.

Anne blew out a breath, pulling herself together.

No matter how much she wanted to, she couldn't allow herself to lead with her heart. Not again. She absolutely refused to be that vulnerable a second time. Once had been more than enough.

Once had resulted in Janie coming into the world.

*Janie.*

Oh Lord, she still had to tell Dan about Janie. That he was Janie's father.

How was she going to do that without hurting Hank? And for all she knew, Danny might be angry with her for not telling him as soon as he had come back into her life. Never mind that she had tried as hard as she could to find him. Never mind that he was the one who had run out on her, not the other way around.

And there was Janie to think of. If she made this revelation, Annie's whole world could just come crashing down on her once she found out that her father wasn't Hank, but Dan.

So much to consider, she thought. And none of it clear.

## Chapter Twelve

Keeping his distance from her was absolutely killing him.

He had promised himself after that last encounter between them that he would wait for Annie to make the next move no matter how long it took her.

Of course, if he was being honest with himself, Dan only expected that to take a day. Maybe two. But one day had come and gone, as had the second, and then the third, and still no resolution, no visit.

No Annie.

Maybe he'd been too optimistic about all this. Maybe she wasn't going to make that "next move." Maybe Annie was actually grateful for this respite and intended to stretch it out as long as she could.

Possibly indefinitely.

Or maybe she was determined to wait him out until he finally decided to throw in the towel and went back to Colorado.

The more Dan thought about it, the more likely that last scenario seemed. He became afraid that it was over between them, really over.

Several times when he was at the tail end of his day, Dan had picked up the phone, thinking to call Annie and ask if he could come see her. He'd managed to talk himself out of it each time.

But the desire to see her was never far away. And it was getting progressively stronger.

After a week passed and still no call from Annie, Dan told himself that he had to face the inevitable: it was really over. He'd been a fool for thinking that they actually stood a chance of getting back together. And that, he knew, was on him, no one else.

He was still trying to decide whether it might be better for everyone all around if he just went back to Colorado early. The debate raged in his head one early morning as he prepared to meet Jamie out on the range. It felt like work on the ranch never seemed to be completed.

Leaving the house, he almost barreled right into Annie. Almost knocking her over, he quickly caught her in his arms, keeping her from hitting the ground. He was aware of his body fairly sizzling from the sudden, unexpected contact.

*Let go of her!* he silently ordered.

Still, it took him a moment to come around and re-

lease Annie. Clearing his throat, he said, "I'm sorry, I
didn't know you were coming over."

He thought he heard her laugh softly. "That makes
two of us," she confessed.

He wasn't sure he understood her meaning. All he
knew was that, sudden or not, it was wonderful to hold
her, even for a moment. Wonderful to see her.

Dan realized that there was silence between them.
"I'm sorry, it's a little early in the morning for riddles."
He stepped back, as if to check her over. "Are you all
right? I didn't hurt you, did I?"

"You mean now? No." That had been a slip and she
shouldn't have said that to him, she thought, upbraiding
herself. "No," she repeated, adding, "you kept me from
hitting the ground."

She was obviously here for a reason, he thought.
Most likely to tell him something. Something he had
a feeling he wasn't going to like hearing, based on the
serious look on her face.

His survival instinct warned him that this wasn't
going to be good. She was going to make it official, he
thought. She was going to tell him not to come around
anymore.

Damn, he should have left the house earlier.

Taking a breath, Annie plunged in, beginning slowly.
"Danny—"

The least he could do was bail her out, he told himself. He wasn't going to let her suffer through this.

"Annie, you don't have to let me down easy," he
told her. He saw her eyes widen. Probably because he'd
guessed her reason for being here, he thought. "I know

I was a fool for thinking I could just waltz back into town and pick up where we left off twelve years ago. I was a fool for thinking we still had a chance."

"I'm sorry, did I miss the part where you waltzed?" she asked.

He felt too tense, too sad, to laugh although he sensed she was doing her best to try to lighten the moment. But that really wasn't possible from his viewpoint.

"It's just an expression," he murmured.

"I know." Growing serious, Annie tried again. "We need to talk."

"And there's another expression," he noted sadly. "Probably one of the most dreaded expressions in the English language," he estimated. "But in this case, we don't really 'need to talk.' Don't worry, I won't be bothering you again."

Annie stared at him. Where was Danny getting this from?

"That's not what I came to say—and you're not bothering me," she added. "How could you be when I have been hoping for the last twelve years that you'd come back? What bothered me was that you left, not that you came back."

He was really confused now. "The other night, when I kissed you, you didn't act as if you were glad that I came back," he pointed out. "You acted as if you were afraid of me."

Annie shook her head. He was getting it all wrong. "No, I was afraid of being vulnerable."

Dan took that as an accusation. "I wouldn't have

taken advantage of you," he told her. "You know me better than that."

"That's not what I mean by vulnerable."

Obviously he was tripping himself up. "Maybe I should just shut up and let you talk," he told her. "That way you can say what you've come to say."

Now that she had his full attention, fear undulated through her. Annie pressed her lips together, trying to gather her thoughts as well as her courage. It was one thing to tell herself she was going to tell Danny the truth—it was another thing entirely to actually find the words to do it.

Because once she said the words, she couldn't unsay them.

But Danny deserved to know. He had unburdened himself the other night and told her what had made him leave town and had kept him away for so long. The least she could do was tell him *her* secret. It was only fair.

"Can I help you get started?" he offered when he saw how much difficulty she was having beginning to impart whatever it was that she had come to say.

To his surprise, Annie laughed at his offer. It was a nervous laugh, but it was a laugh all the same.

"I think that's how the whole thing began," she told Danny, recalling that moonlit night when they had made love.

"No offense, Annie, but you're still not making any sense. *What* whole thing?" he wanted to know.

She took a deep breath. "Do you remember that last night we spent together?" she asked him.

Dan nodded. "The night before the accident." The night before his world turned to ashes.

"In more ways than one," Annie interjected, murmuring the words to herself.

Dan stared at her, utterly confused. "I don't understand. What are you telling me?"

"That night you made love to me?" she said, starting again. "Well, the evening had a slight by-product."

His eyebrows narrowed as he looked at her intently. All sorts of half-formed thoughts began running through his head.

"What kind of slight by-product?" he asked in a deadly quiet voice.

There was no way to say it but to say it, Anne told herself. She took a deep breath and let the words out. "You met her the first day you came over."

"Janie?" he asked in a disbelieving voice that was scarcely above a stunned whisper.

"Janie," Annie confirmed.

Danny stared at her, shell-shocked as he tried to understand the full import of what she was saying. "She's...?"

"Yours," Anne spelled out for good measure. "That night on the hilltop, my first time with you—with *anyone*," Anne stressed more for herself than for him, "we created a baby."

It felt as if his mind was stuck in first gear, unable to process, unable to go forward. "Janie's my daughter?"

"Yes."

His mouth had dropped open and it took effort to

close it. He asked Anne the first question that flashed across his mind.

"Why didn't you tell me that I was a father?"

She almost laughed at that, but it really wasn't funny. He had no idea what she'd gone through when she'd realized that she was pregnant.

"I tried, Danny. Heaven knows, I tried. I asked everyone in town if they'd heard from you, including Bella and Jamie. But nobody had. It was as if you had fallen off the face of the earth right after the funeral."

"And Hank?" he asked Annie suddenly. "Does Hank know?"

"That Janie's yours? Yes, Hank knows," Anne told him, a sad smile curving the corners of her mouth. "But he married me anyway. He thought he could make me happy." But it hadn't worked out that way, she thought. Because she'd only ever loved one man. The man who stood before her.

Dan got up and began to pace around the room, too agitated to be able to remain seated.

Danny looked at her in disbelief. "My Lord, I'm a father," he said, dragging his hand through his hair as if that could help imbed the idea in his brain, make it take root. "I should have seen it. When I looked at her, I should have seen that she was mine."

She realized that he was blaming himself for the oversight. "People say she looks like me," Annie told him. "You said so yourself. And don't forget, in your defense, you thought she was Hank's."

"And you didn't tell me any differently," he accused, cycling through disbelief, disappointment and anger.

Trying to work his way through all those emotions to a safer, happier place because, after all, discovering that he had a child was supposed to be a happy event.

She knew that Danny didn't mean that the way it sounded. "That's not exactly a conversation opener, Danny. 'Hi, where have you been the last twelve years? And oh yes, by the way, you're a father.'"

He shook his head, his sanity coming back to him as his agitation began to ebb.

"You're right. Sorry. You're right," he repeated, doing his best to get a grip on himself. Brightening, he sounded almost eager as he asked, "What's she like?"

"You met her," she reminded him.

"Just for a second," he protested. Opinions couldn't be formed in a second. Neither could impressions. "Is she smart in school? Is she a handful? Does she have friends? Is she close to Hank?"

"One question at a time." Annie laughed, relieved to see that he was ultimately taking the news well. "Yes, yes, yes and—" She paused for a moment before saying, "Yes."

She knew Danny didn't want to hear the last answer, but she couldn't lie to him. Not after all this time. He deserved to hear the truth about everything concerning his daughter, even truths that weren't welcomed.

"I want to see her," Danny told her, excitement gathering in his voice.

He wanted to look at Janie as his daughter, not just Annie's.

"It's a school day. She's in class right now," Annie told him.

He wasn't thinking clearly. "Right. Okay, when she comes home," he amended. "I want to see her when she comes home."

She loved that he was happy about the news. But she hadn't told him everything and he had to hear it before they went any further. "I understand, but there's a problem, Danny."

He looked at Annie, his euphoria abruptly on hold. "I don't understand," he confessed. "What kind of a problem?"

This just wasn't getting any easier, Anne thought. She felt as if she was trying to slog her way through a five-foot-high snowdrift and she kept losing her footing.

"Janie doesn't know that you're her father," she said, watching his face carefully for any telltale signs of anger. "She thinks Hank is."

Dan had to admit it wasn't welcomed news, but it wasn't entirely unexpected, either. After all, when he'd met the girl, she hadn't given him any indication that she thought he was her father.

Nodding, he said, "I've got a lot of years to make up for."

"Yes, I know, but—"

He knew what Annie was going to say and he reassured her. "You're right, you're right. I've got to think about what's right for Janie. I want to tell her, but I don't want to turn her whole world upside down. She might even hate me for doing that and that's not what I want. I want to build a relationship with her. I want her to get to like me." He stopped abruptly and looked at Annie as it hit him again. "Wow, a daughter. I have a daughter." He became as eager as a kid at Christmas. "Do you have pictures of her? I mean when she was a baby and then a toddler?"

Annie smiled. She found his attitude rather sweet. "Yes, I have pictures."

"I want to see them," he told her. "Every one of them."

She laughed. This was, ultimately, what she had dreamed about, that he would welcome the news.

"That can be arranged. I have them in several albums. Would you like to see them now? I took the day off from work, thinking that maybe, if I told you about Janie and you didn't tell me to go to hell once you heard, that you might need to talk."

He looked at her, stunned by what she'd said in such an off-handed manner. "Why on earth would I tell you to go to hell?" he asked, totally puzzled.

Trying to be realistic, she'd played this scenario a hundred different ways in her head over the years. "Well, not everyone greets the idea of finding out they're a father in a positive light."

He knew that, but that wasn't him. The idea of having a family with Annie had once been a cherished dream of his. "I just really wish that there'd been a way for you to have let me know you were pregnant."

"So do I, Danny," she said, meaning that from the bottom of her heart. "So do I."

And then, rethinking the first time he saw Janie, he shook his head again. "I still don't see how I didn't see it the moment I saw Janie."

"Janie's small for her age. You probably thought she

was younger than she is. Besides, there'd be no reason for you to suspect she's yours."

"When's Janie's birthday?" he wanted to know. When Annie told him, he grinned broadly. "She and I share the same month."

"Yes, I know." And then added, "And the same mouth."

That caught him off guard. He looked at Annie quizzically. "We do?"

"Uh-huh." She remembered looking at that small mouth for hours when Janie was a baby, wondering if she would grow up to look like Danny. "Look at it the next time you see her. Just don't stare," she cautioned.

"I won't stare," he promised. "But I do intend to see a great deal of her. I was serious about building a relationship with her."

Anne could feel her nervousness resurfacing. "Remember, we can't tell her you're her father until I think she's ready to hear that."

"Don't worry," he promised. "I won't tell her anything. I just want to get to know her and to get her to like me. That's just putting down groundwork, nothing more," he told her. "That's okay, isn't it?"

Annie nodded. "Yes, that's okay. I really appreciate you being patient about this."

He smiled. "I waited years to find out I was a father. I can wait a little longer to actually act like one."

Annie grew serious again. "I do have to warn you about something," she told him.

Dan told himself not to anticipate the worst. "What is it?"

"If she doesn't seem to respond to you, it's not you," she told him. "Janie's been a little down lately. Her best friend moved to France with her mother and her new dad recently and she can't seem to find a place for herself."

Dan appreciated the heads up. "Duly noted," he said. "My one immediate goal is to befriend her and to find a way to make sure she likes me. After that, we'll go from there. Deal?"

Anne smiled at him, more relieved than she could possibly say. "Deal."

## Chapter Thirteen

When she heard the knock on the door the first time, Janie just looked toward it with mild disinterest, expecting her mother to answer it even though she was in the kitchen, making dinner. As for her, she was busy watching one of her favorite programs, a show about a group of preteen girls who had superpowers.

But the second knock sounded more insistent. Muttering under her breath, Janie grudgingly paused the action on the TV and went to answer the door. Since her mother obviously hadn't heard the knock, answering the door was her superheroine good deed for the day.

Standing on her toes, she looked through the peephole to see who was on the other side. Reluctantly—because she knew her mother would want her to—Janie unlocked the door and pulled it open.

"Oh, it's you," she said by way of a bored greeting when she let Dan in. "Mom, your old boyfriend's here again," Janie shouted over her shoulder, then turned to face the less-than-welcome visitor again. "Mom's in the kitchen," she told him matter-of-factly. She pointed in the general direction as she closed the door, expecting him to go straight to the kitchen.

A thousand emotions were racing through Dan as he crossed the threshold, looking at Janie.

This was his daughter. His daughter. The thought almost paralyzed him. He made no move toward the kitchen.

After a beat, he found his tongue. "I didn't come to see your mother," he told her.

Janie was already walking away. Reaching the sofa, she took her seat again and hit the pause button on the remote control, unfreezing the action.

Following Janie, he walked into the living room behind her. His heart was pounding hard although he exercised extreme control over himself not to say or do anything to give himself away. "I came to see you," he told the girl even though she hadn't asked. He nodded at the TV. "What are you watching?"

*"Ellie and Her Friends,"* she answered. And then she looked at him suspiciously. "Why?"

"I was just curious what you like to watch," he told her. It occurred to him that he had faced friendlier bucking broncos during his very brief rodeo days.

"No," Janie retorted impatiently, "why did you come to see me?" Her brilliant blue eyes were all but drilling holes into him.

"Because I'd like to get to know you," he answered. "I thought maybe we could be friends."

"So you can get my mom to like you again?" Janie demanded.

Janie was obviously not your typical eleven-year-old, he thought. No one was ever going to pull anything over on her. Which was a good thing, he thought, but not right at the moment.

"You think I'm underhanded?" he asked, then quickly explained, "That means sneaky."

Janie looked insulted. "I know what underhanded means. I'm not dumb."

Dan backtracked as quickly as he could, knowing that for better or for worse, today was going to be crucial in setting up the groundwork for a relationship between Janie and him.

"I'm sorry, I didn't mean to imply that you were," he told her.

"And," Janie continued with an imperious toss of her head, "I think all adults are sneaky. Except for my dad," she quickly amended. Her eyes bored into him, all but nailing him to the floor. "He thinks people should be honest with each other."

"Your dad's right," Dan agreed pleasantly. He knew this was a competition between Hank and himself, but he couldn't act like it. "People should be honest with each other. Is it all right if I sit down?" he asked, indicating the sofa.

Janie's small shoulders rose and fell in an indifferent shrug. "If you want to," she sniffed. She regarded him critically for a moment when he sat down on the sofa.

"If you think people should be honest with each other, tell me the truth. Why do you want to get to know me?"

He knew this had to come out just right, otherwise the girl would go completely silent on him. "Because you're important to your mother and your mother is important to me."

A knowing, triumphant expression slipped over her small oval face. "You want her to be your girlfriend again."

"I want her to be my friend again," Dan deliberately corrected.

*Baby steps*, he told himself. *Baby steps.*

Janie looked as if she didn't believe him. "And if she says no, she doesn't want to be your 'friend,' you'll go away and forget all about me, so don't pretend you want to be *my* friend," she told him, annoyed.

"I'm not pretending," Dan insisted. "I do want to be your friend." *More than you could possibly guess*, he added silently.

Janie shifted on the sofa to look at him, her hands fisted at her waist. "Even if Mom won't be yours?"

"Even if your mom won't be mine," he assured his daughter.

"Huh!" Janie uttered the word as if it were a grunt and said nothing for more than a minute as she went back to watching her program. Then, still keeping her eyes on the TV, she pointed to the dark-haired character who was currently talking. "That's Ellie," she told him. "She's the one who got her superpowers first. There was this magic meadow with this really strange silver rock…"

Dan tried not to grin. Instead, he solemnly listened as his daughter told him the origin of the group's superpowers, acting as if he was listening to her reveal the mystery of the Holy Grail. He hung on every one of her words because they were *her* words and she was imparting them to him.

As he listened, he couldn't get over the fact that he was listening to his daughter.

*His* daughter.

The very thought left him in complete awe. He felt as if he was seated beside an honest-to-goodness miracle. A miracle that had been created by Annie and him.

The very thought left him speechless—and incredibly grateful.

Janie abruptly stopped talking. She was staring at him. "You've got a funny look on your face," she told him. It was technically more of an accusation than a stated fact.

Dan quickly tried to explain away the look she was referring to. "I'm just really interested."

"Oh yeah?" It was obvious that she didn't believe him for a moment. "If that's true, then tell me what I just said. Tell me how the group all got their superpowers."

"Okay."

And then Dan proceeded to do just that, going back to the very first thing Janie had said and then continuing on to the very end. He left none of the five "superheroines" out. Finished, he smiled at his daughter.

The fact kept hitting him in waves. Just when he thought he was used to it, it hit again.

*His* daughter.

"Did I forget anything or leave something out?" he asked her, fairly certain that he hadn't.

The suspicion vacated those blue eyes of hers, replaced by wide-eyed wonder.

"No," she said, her voice tinged with disbelief. "No, you didn't. You were really listening."

"Sure. I told you I wanted to learn about the program you were watching. I'd like to learn more if you'd like to tell me," he encouraged.

Dan was rewarded with a guileless smile. A smile that reminded him so much of Annie. It was clear that Janie was warming up to him, he thought happily, at least a little.

"Okay," she told him. "About Amanda—" And she was off and running.

Anne heard the entire exchange between Danny and Janie from the kitchen. It was really hard for her to stay out of the way like this. More than anything, she really wanted to go into the living room and watch her daughter interacting with Danny.

But she had given Danny her word that she would let him talk to Janie alone, at least this first time. To be honest, part of her had worried that Janie would clam up or sound off like a typical preteen even though she had raised the child to be respectful and polite.

After all, preteens were unpredictable.

She was happy to see that this was going far better than she had ever hoped.

Maybe Janie would learn to like Danny, she thought hopefully. If her daughter did, then maybe, just maybe, in time, they could tell her the truth: that Danny was her real father.

But not today. Definitely not today, Anne thought as she continued to prepare the chicken parmesan that was Janie's favorite dinner.

But someday, she thought, hugging the idea to her.

Maybe someday, if things went really, really well, they could finally get to be a real family, the way she'd dreamed so many times that they would be.

Anne finally ventured out of the kitchen an hour and a half later when she'd finished preparing dinner.

"Dinner's ready, Janie," she announced, stopping just short of the sofa.

Dan had progressed past Janie's favorite TV program and now he appeared to be in the middle of playing a video game with her. He was making moves like someone who had played video games all of his life. She knew for a fact that he hadn't.

Anne had to admit she was more than a little impressed by the display.

"You play video games?" she asked Dan.

"He almost beat me," Janie told her. To Anne's huge relief, there was no hostility in her daughter's voice. There was even a smattering of respect. "Not bad for a newbie."

Anne didn't bother trying to hide the smile that rose to her lips. "In case you don't know, she just gave you a huge compliment," she told Danny.

Dan inclined his head and smiled at the girl beside him. "Thank you."

"It's nothing," Janie told him carelessly.

"Well, you're having dinner so I'd better go," Dan said, retiring his game controller before rising to his feet. He nodded at his companion for the last hour and a half. "Janie, it's been a pleasure. Thanks for letting me spend the afternoon with you."

For a second, Anne thought that her daughter wasn't going to say anything in response. But then Janie spoke up in a nonchalant voice. "You can stay for dinner if you want." The girl's eyes shifted toward Anne. "That's okay, right, Mom?"

She wasn't going to cry, Anne told herself. She wasn't. But it wasn't easy.

Exercising extreme control over her emotions, Anne replied, "Yes, that's okay—if Mr. Stockton doesn't have any other plans for dinner."

Danny smiled broadly. "I can't think of a thing I'd rather do," he told Janie with a wink.

"But after dinner," Anne interjected, looking at her daughter as she repeated the familiar refrain, "you have to finish all your homework."

"I can do that after Danny leaves—I mean Mr. Stockton," Janie corrected herself when her mother gave her a reproving look.

"That's not how it works, Janie," Anne told her as all three of them went into the kitchen and she added a third place setting to the table. "You know how important it is for you to do your homework."

"Don't worry, I'll get it done," Janie insisted. "You know I'm smart."

"Maybe a little too smart for your own good," Anne countered.

Rather than argue with her mother, Janie turned her eyes toward her new friend.

Janie was looking for him to intercede, Dan realized. He didn't want to lose ground with the girl, but he didn't want to tread on territory that was clearly Annie's. After all, she was the one who had done all the heavy lifting, been there through everything from diapers to braces and everything in between.

"I don't really think there's such a thing as being too smart," he finally said, hoping that was diplomatic enough to appease both females. "But just to keep the peace, maybe you should do as your mom says. After all, she spent all that time making this really great meal for you."

Annie had told him that chicken parmesan was Janie's favorite so he felt he was on safe ground bringing the meal up to Janie.

Janie sighed, relenting. "Okay, I'll do my homework after dinner."

"That's my girl," Annie said fondly. She wanted to hug Janie, but she held herself in check, knowing Janie might be embarrassed if she was on the receiving end of any public displays of affection.

Janie rolled her eyes, "Yeah, yeah, let's eat!" she declared.

"Music to my ears," Dan said as he sat down at the table.

*And mine*, Anne thought, glancing first at her daughter, then at Danny.

\* \* \*

Dan was being carefully optimistic, but there was no other way to view this.

His campaign to win his daughter over was going very, very well.

He'd been dropping by Annie and Janie's home in the afternoon for a week now and each time, he and Janie spent at least some time together.

In addition to playing the video games she loved and watching her favorite programs with her, Dan introduced his daughter to a few old-fashioned board games, ones he used to play when he had been Janie's age.

"These are ancient," Janie hooted when he had produced the first board game out of the backpack he had brought with him.

"I prefer to think of them as having withstood the test of time," he told Janie. He emptied out the backpack, taking out five board games in all. "It takes precision and skill to play these."

Janie looked at the boxed games disdainfully. "Not interested," she told him.

He was beginning to pick up subtle clues on how to deal with his daughter. "Not interested or afraid you're not good enough?" he challenged.

Janie tossed her head as she braced her shoulders. The girl was indeed her mother's daughter, Dan thought affectionately. Like Annie, Janie was unable to walk away from a challenge.

So they played the board games he brought and eventually they progressed to checkers, and then, finally, to chess.

When he first set up the board, Annie, who had taken to being around somewhere in the background for this interplay between Danny and their daughter, frowned. Intelligent or not, she thought that chess was far too difficult a game for someone Annie's age.

"Do you really think this is a good idea?" she asked Dan.

"Sure." A little taken aback by her protest, Dan continued to set up the pieces. "Why not?"

"Because it's *chess*," Annie stressed. "It requires a great deal of concentration. It's a game for adults, not eleven-year-olds."

Janie did not take her mother's intercession kindly.

"I'm not a baby, Mom," her daughter said, bristling at being dismissed so out of hand. "I can do it." Her eyes turned toward Dan, this time challenging *him*. "Teach me," she all but commanded.

A satisfied smile spread across his lips. "I fully intend to," Dan told the girl. Finished setting up the pieces, he put the empty box aside. "My dad taught me how to play when I was about your age," he told her. He'd really been twelve, but Annie didn't need to know that. "He loved the game but no one wanted to play with him, not even my mom. So he taught me how to play so he would always have someone to play against."

Danny expected her to ask why no one wanted to play his father. Instead, she had a different question to ask him.

"Were you good?" Janie wanted to know, scanning the way the pieces were laid out on the board.

Dan smiled nostalgically. "Good enough to beat him once or twice."

"Oh." By the expression on Janie's face it was obvious that wouldn't have been enough for her. "Too bad."

"No, that's good," he corrected Janie, "because my dad was a really top-notch player. Winning against him was really a big deal. The first time it happened, I was walking on air."

Even the skeptic, Janie suggested, "Maybe he let you win."

The girl was sharp, he thought. "I thought of that," he admitted. "But my dad said that letting me win wasn't teaching me anything. He always said that the wins you earn are the ones that really stay with you. Okay," he said, turning the board toward her, "are you ready to learn?"

He could swear her eyes were sparkling as she said, "Ready!"

"Then here we go," he said as he began to teach his daughter the basic moves of the game, just the way his father had taught him.

## Chapter Fourteen

"Just what were you thinking?" Hank demanded gruffly.

Annie bristled at his question. At least he'd waited until Janie had gone to her room to unpack from her sleepover at his ranch before he confronted her.

Startled by Hank's rare angry tone, the first thing Anne thought of was that her daughter had told him about Danny's frequent visits. She wasn't sure just how to answer him. Especially if, just in case, Hank was asking her about something else.

Glancing toward the rear of the house to make sure Janie wasn't within hearing range, Anne told him, "I don't know what you—"

"Let me make this easy for you," Hank said angrily. "Janie told me that Daniel's been coming over pretty regularly these days. She says he's been teaching her how to play board games, like chess—"

Anne seized on the last part, trying her best to make Hank see how beneficial these visits were to Janie. "Chess is a very mind-broadening game."

Hank scowled, clearly not in the mood to be played for a fool. "Don't give me that, Anne. This isn't about chess and you know it. It's about him trying to wiggle his way into Janie's life."

"He just wants to get to know her, Hank." She lowered her voice even more, afraid that the sound of raised voices would bring Janie out of her room before she could get Hank to drop the subject. There was too much at stake here. "He's her father—"

"No," Hank retorted forcefully. "*I* am Janie's father."

"Nobody's disputing your place in her life, Hank," Anne stressed, still trying to calm him down. "She loves you. But he's missed so much—"

Hank made a dismissive, disparaging noise. "And whose fault was that?" he demanded. "He wasn't here, remember?" He grabbed hold of Anne's arms, as if doing so would somehow make her see reason. "Tell me, how do we know, after Janie gets all caught up in whatever tales he's spinning to win her over, that he won't just get it into his head to take off again? Have you thought about what that'll do to her?" Hank asked. "I don't want to risk this guy upsetting Janie for no reason." He looked into Anne's eyes. "I can't tell you what to do, Anne. But for the sake of our daughter— *our* daughter," he deliberately stressed, "I want you to think very hard about this."

He let her go and strode toward the door. But before he left, he looked at Anne sharply as he repeated, *"Very* hard."

Anne remained where she was standing long after Hank had closed the front door behind him. His words continued to echo in her head.

She hadn't wanted to admit it while Hank had berated the situation, pointing out what he felt was the obvious, but she was actually harboring the same fears that Hank had raised. And not just concerning Janie's reaction to Danny's possible disappearance from her life.

What if she were to get together with Danny, gave her heart to him the way she had before, and then he suddenly disappeared on her again the way he had twelve years ago? She had barely survived that at the time, but she had had a baby to think of and to take care of.

It was different this time. And she really didn't think her heart would be able to take that sort of abandonment a second time.

*C'mon, Anne, he's not going anywhere. Look at how hard he's working to get Janie to like him, to build a relationship with her. That's not a man who's going to take off in the middle of the night. That's a man who's here to stay.*

It made sense.

And yet…

"C'mon, it'll be fun," Anne coaxed, holding up a pirate costume that was clearly intended for a man to wear.

Dan looked at the costume dubiously. Along with the

ruffled shirt and wide black pantaloons, Annie had a black eye patch attached to the hanger. "I don't know about this."

"The veterinary office is sponsoring a Halloween costume parade—emphasis on the word *costume*," Annie told him as well as her daughter. "That means you can't be in it unless you've got on some kind of a costume."

He saw the excitement on Janie's face, but he was still very reluctant to put on something that, in his judgment, made him look like a fool.

"I can stand on the sidelines and watch the parade," Dan offered, adding, "I'm really good at cheering and clapping."

"I'm going to be in it," Janie told him proudly. "I'm going as Ellie," she added, referring to the superheroine she'd told him about the first afternoon he had been over to her house.

"And I'll be your cheering section," Dan said, still hoping that was good enough. "Everyone needs a cheering section, even a superheroine."

He was weakening, Anne thought. She could see it in his face. He really wanted Janie's approval.

"There'll be lots of people in town who'll be on the sidelines," she told Danny, then emphasized, "This is your time to step up for Janie."

"Where are you going to be?" Dan wanted to know. And then it hit him why she was so adamant about having him dress up. "Wait, don't tell me, let me guess. *You're* going to be on the sidelines, watching us."

"Hardly," Anne countered. "I have to organize and

dress up some of the tamer pets whose owners want them to be in the parade." She paused, then added what she felt was the proper inducement. "Dr. Smith's bulldog is going to be wearing army fatigues."

Dan laughed as he tried to picture that in his mind. He'd seen the animal, a large, squat dog whose expression reminded him of one of the guests at the dude ranch this summer, a disgruntled man who'd found fault with everything during his entire vacation. "I guess that'll be worth the price of admission."

"They're charging admission?" Janie asked, puzzled as she looked at her mother.

"It's an expression, honey. Danny is being funny— or trying to be," Anne told her.

In the last few days, she had relented and allowed her daughter to refer to Danny by his first name. She'd decided the familiarity might make the ultimate transition from family friend to father a little easier in the long run.

At least she could hope that it would.

"I guess that is kind of funny," Janie agreed, glancing in his direction.

"I knew that seeing the bulldog in fatigues would change your mind," Anne told him.

"It didn't change my mind," Danny contradicted. He looked toward Janie before he said, "Actually, the opportunity to walk beside 'Ellie' in the parade was what changed my mind. I've always had a weakness for superheroines," he said, winking at Janie.

Janie giggled, obviously pleased.

It was a sound that she rarely heard of late coming

from her daughter, Anne thought. Hearing it now really heartened her.

Maybe this *was* going to turn out well after all, Anne thought, despite all of her fears.

"We could all really use this diversion," Anne told her daughter and Danny. "It's been an utter madhouse at the lately clinic. I don't *ever* remember it being this busy."

"Why don't you just hire more vets to help you?" Janie asked.

"Out of the mouths of babes," Danny commented with a grin. He saw the indignant look that crossed Janie's face and could guess at what she was thinking. "Just another expression," he quickly said so she wouldn't think he was insulting her. "There's no way that I'm saying you're a baby. No one who can play chess the way you can could possibly be mistaken for a baby."

And he meant what he said. Janie had been getting really good at the game, absorbing everything he taught her like the proverbial sponge. He was in fact rather in awe of the girl's ability to think several moves ahead the way she did, given her age.

Janie looked properly placated. "Okay," she said, graciously accepting his explanation. Turning toward her mother, she asked, "So, are you going to be getting more vets?"

Anne nodded. "Dr. Smith is definitely trying to. He just asked Dr. Hadley Strickland, a friend of his who practices in Bozeman, to fill in at the clinic while she's here visiting over the Thanksgiving holiday," she told them. "He's hoping that might wind up convincing her to stay on."

"But that's just one person," Janie wisely protested. "You need more than one person, right, Mom?"

Dan decided to help Annie out.

"Right," he answered, joining in. "But it's a start," he pointed out. "Maybe if they can get this Dr. Strickland to come work at the clinic, she might know of someone else who Dr. Smith can hire, as well."

Anne said wistfully, "While he's at it, I hope Dr. Smith can see his way clear to hiring an assistant for the reception desk."

"Are you quitting, Mom?" Janie asked in what could only be taken as alarm. The girl had never reacted well to change and having her mother quit her job at the clinic was definitely a major change.

"Oh no, I love my job. How could I leave a bulldog in fatigues?" Anne teased. "But it would be nice to have a little extra help when it gets crazy at the clinic." She slipped her arm around her daughter's shoulders. "I like coming home with some energy to spare for my girl while she still wants to hang around with her old mom."

"You're not old, Mom," Janie said, speaking up quickly. And then she qualified with a mischievous grin, "Not exactly."

"I'll show you who's old," Anne declared. Grabbing her daughter, she pulled the girl closer to her and tickled her.

She let Janie go after a minute, knowing that the girl wanted to retain some of her new "dignity" around Danny.

"In Janie's defense, you did start it by referring to yourself as 'old,'" Danny pointed out.

That earned him a wide smile from Janie.

"Two against one, no fair," Anne cried. And then she suddenly remembered to look at her watch. It was getting late. "C'mon, you two, you have to get into your costumes," she urged. "You don't want to be late for the parade."

Danny gave her a look. "Try me."

"I bet I can get into my costume faster than you can," Janie declared, cheerfully challenging him.

With a resigned sigh, Dan took the pirate costume from Anne, who was holding it out toward him. He made no effort to hide the disdainful look on his face. "Who came up with this whole costume idea anyway?"

"Dr. Smith," Anne reminded him as she went to get her own costume that she'd left hanging in her room.

"No, I mean originally," Dan said, calling after her, "way back in time."

"Probably some very bored people," Anne guessed just before she closed her bedroom door. She regarded her costume for a moment, hoping it would knock Danny's boots off.

He supposed it was worth it, Dan thought as he finished putting on his costume. Wearing this would make his daughter happy, and after all that *was* his ultimate goal—making Janie happy and getting her to accept him into her life. He knew it was still a big leap from there to telling her that he was her father, but he needed all the goodwill he could build up.

And if looking like an idiot, he thought, regarding his reflection in the mirror, helped contribute to that goodwill, so be it.

Damn but he hated Halloween, Dan thought as he walked out of the bathroom. He was carrying his own clothes folded up under his arm.

He encountered Janie first. She was standing in the living room, wearing her blue costume and flowing cape, her hands fisted on her waist. She looked like the very picture of confidence.

Dan pretended to do a double take when he saw her. "Wow, Ellie, have you seen Janie around anywhere? I know that she'd love to get your autograph," he told the girl, doing his best to maintain a straight face.

Her eyes sparkled as she giggled. "Danny, it's me, Janie."

Dan pretended to look around the room as if he were trying to locate the source of the voice.

"Janie? Are you here somewhere?" he said, pretending to be mystified. "I hear your voice, but I don't see you."

Janie tugged on his sleeve. "Right here, silly. It's me. *I'm* Janie. This is just my costume."

"Wow, it looks so realistic," he cried. "I really thought that you were Ellie."

"No, you didn't," Janie told him. But she was fairly beaming over his reaction to her costume.

"Where's your mom?" Dan asked. "She's the one who was trying to get us to hustle and it looks like she's the one who's still getting dressed."

He saw Janie grinning just before he heard the voice coming from behind him.

"No, I'm not. I'm right here. Behind you."

Dan turned around, expecting to see Annie wearing something mundane, like scrubs, which would have been the easiest costume for her. Or maybe some furry costume so she could look like one of the animals that were treated regularly by the vets at the clinic.

He was *not* prepared for the pirate hat with its jaunty feather, the tall black high-heeled boots or the short, willowy skirt topped with a laced-up black velvet vest over a white blouse with wide, flowing sleeves.

"Are you a pirate, too, Mom?" Janie asked.

"Actually, I'm a pirate *queen*. I thought of being a superheroine," she said matter-of-factly, "but I didn't want to steal your thunder. This is better," she told her daughter.

"A lot better," Dan commented, his eyes sweeping over her appreciatively.

All he had seen Annie wearing up until now was her vet clinic uniform, or a pair of jeans with a baggy sweater draped over them. He'd forgotten just how sexy she had looked back when they were going together in high school.

As a matter of fact, she looked even better now than she had back then. So much so that he was having trouble taking his eyes off her.

"Does that make me a pirate king?" he asked her.

"No, you're just a regular pirate," she told him. "That means I get to order you around."

He leveled a questioning look at her. "And this is different how?"

Janie giggled again.

Anne pointed toward the door. "C'mon, you two, let's go. Like I said, we don't want to be late."

"Yes, we do," Danny said as he followed them out the door. In fact, he'd rather not go at all. He would much rather spend the time right here, getting reacquainted with the pirate queen.

But there was Janie to think of, so, with a muted, resigned sigh, he closed the front door behind him and then followed Annie and their daughter to the car.

## Chapter Fifteen

A whole myriad of emotions were vying for top position within Anne when they arrived home, none of them good. There was sadness, disappointment and a feeling of rejection. And all the emotions were centered around her daughter.

It hadn't started out that way.

Janie, Danny and she had had an incredibly wonderful afternoon, joining in the costume parade that had been sponsored by the vet clinic. Afterward they returned to the clinic, where they'd handed out candy to the excited trick-or-treaters who'd come by the downtown businesses.

Since this was Halloween, the day's festivities were to culminate with her taking Janie out trick-or-treating to several of the neighbors' homes the way they had done ever since her daughter was three and had first begged to take part in the sugar-laden holiday.

At least, Anne had assumed that the day would end this way.

But Janie apparently had different ideas.

"Please, Mom," Janie begged. "Why can't I go trick-or-treating with my friends? All the other kids in my class are breaking up into groups and doing it."

Anne hated saying no to Janie, but she was concerned for her daughter's safety. She was also reluctant to give up a much-loved tradition.

"I'm sorry, Janie. But you're just too young to go out after dark with only a few girls with you," Anne said firmly.

Janie was quick to tell her, "Cassie's mother is coming with us."

"Cassie's mother," Anne repeated. She had been replaced by another girl's mother, she thought. That really stung and though she tried not to, she took it personally.

Dan had stayed silent, trying his best to keep out of the exchange between mother and daughter. He heard what was being said and heard, too, what *wasn't* being said. He could hear that Annie was clearly hurt because Janie wanted to go trick-or-treating with another mother acting as a chaperone, not her.

Still, he could see Janie's point. She'd spent the afternoon with her mother and although it had been a lot of fun—she'd clearly looked as if she was having a good time—now she wanted to spend some time with her friends. It was all a part of growing up.

Though he felt for both sides, he still would have

gladly remained on the sidelines, letting this play out without his input.

But then Janie completely surprised him by turning to him and asking him to back her up.

"Tell her to let me go, Danny," she pleaded. "I'll only be gone for a couple of hours."

"A couple of hours?" Anne echoed.

There weren't that many doorbells to ring in the neighborhood. What was her daughter going to be doing with her friends that would last for a couple of hours?

Danny decided to pick a side—kind of.

"You know how it is," he said to Annie. "Kids just want to enjoy themselves."

Anne looked at her daughter. She wanted to put her foot down and veto this, but having Janie angry and upset with her wasn't the way she wanted to end the evening, either.

"How many girls are going?" she finally asked her daughter.

"Eight," Janie said, then promptly named every one of them.

Listening to her, Annie frowned. "I don't know if Cassie's mother is up to handling eight girls on her own."

"Oh, she's up to it," Janie assured her with enthusiasm. "And Cassie's mom is strict," she added, using that as a winning argument. "The only way Cassie could go trick-or-treating with the rest of us was if her mother came along to make sure we behaved."

"I like this woman's style already," Anne commented, although she wished that *she* was the chaperone, not Cassie's mother. Seeing how much this meant to Janie, she sighed. "Okay, you can go—as long as you promise to behave yourself. And if anything goes wrong, anything at all," she emphasized, "I want you to call me immediately, understood?"

Janie looked at her, all eleven-year-old innocence wrapped in fledgling eagerness. "What could go wrong, Mom?"

"You never know," Anne informed her. "Do I have your word?"

Janie rolled her eyes. "Yes, I'll call you if anything goes wrong—but it won't," she added insistently.

"All right," Anne reluctantly agreed. "I'll drop you off at Cassie's house."

"No, you don't have to," Janie protested. "Her mother's coming here to pick me up. She's picking up all the girls."

"See?" Danny said, doing his best to nudge her into coming around. "What could be better?"

*What could be better is if I was the one taking the girls, not this other woman.*

Anne gave him a less-than-happy look, but said nothing.

Just then, the doorbell rang and Janie scrambled to grab the slightly worn plastic pumpkin she used every year to collect her treats.

"That's Cassie's mom now!" she declared, holding onto the pumpkin and rushing toward the door.

"You wait for me," Anne ordered, quickly following in Janie's wake.

But Janie had already thrown open the front door, clearly eager to make her escape.

"Hi," she said brightly, greeting the woman in the doorway. "Mom said I could go!"

Cassie Jackson's mother, a rather big-boned woman with a quick smile, was dressed as Cinderella's fairy godmother.

"Don't worry about a thing. I'll watch each and every one of them as if they were my own," the woman promised, putting an arm around Janie and shepherding the girl out the door.

"Bye," Anne called after her daughter. "Be sure to listen to Mrs. Jackson and have fun."

But Janie didn't seem to hear her. She was already getting into Mrs. Jackson's station wagon, chattering happily with her friends.

Anne sighed as she closed the door.

"And so it begins," she murmured, saying the words more to herself than to Dan.

"So what begins?" he asked her, not sure he understood what she was saying.

Anne turned from the door. "Janie growing up, becoming independent. Once it starts, there's no stopping it," she said sadly.

"She's eleven," Dan reminded her gently. "She's just going trick-or-treating with her friends, she's not going away to college."

"Yet," Anne qualified sadly. "But it'll happen faster than you think." Crossing back to the living room, she sank down on the sofa, the very picture of resigned sadness. "And much faster than I'm ready for," she added quietly.

Dan sat down beside her. She looked so unhappy, it

tore at his heart. He slipped his arm around her shoulders, attempting to offer Annie at least a little comfort.

"It's a long way between trick-or-treating and college, Annie. You'll have time to adjust," he promised her.

Annie said nothing. She just mutely nodded her head. He looked down at her and saw the light glistening on her cheek.

"Are you crying?" he asked, surprised.

Averting her face, she shook her head and managed to get out a small "No" in response.

"Yes, you are," he contradicted. Crooking his index finger beneath her chin, he raised her head and turned it toward him. "You're crying."

Annie jerked her head away. "So what?" she retorted angrily.

"Oh, Annie," he said compassionately, "you can't keep her little forever."

"I didn't want forever," she protested. "I just want a little longer, that's all." She was doing her best to stop the flow of tears. But they insisted on coming.

Danny took her into his arms then and held her closer. She attempted to pull away, then just gave up and sagged against him.

"I know," he said understandingly. "But at least you had more years than I had. You got to see all the things that I missed seeing. You got to make memories," he told her.

Her head on his shoulder, she turned to him then, too overcome with emotion to say a word.

Desperately wanting to comfort her, to somehow absorb her pain, Dan found himself lowering his mouth to hers.

And just like that, the years melted away and they were eighteen again. Eighteen without the restraint of any of the shackles that life had forged for them along the way.

The kiss, beginning slowly and deepening, seemed to unlock all the desire he had kept so carefully locked away. The desire that had been branded with her name on it all these years.

Adrenaline surged through his veins, fueling the passion that was growing and multiplying in every fiber of his being.

He wanted to trace her curves, the contours of her body with his lips. He wanted to make up for all the time that they had lost.

Every kiss just intensified his desire for her, stirring it up to a fever pitch.

He wanted to make love to her as if there was no tomorrow, no consequences to face. Nothing but the raw need and passion that was even now pounding through his veins in sheer anticipation of her and what lay ahead.

As he felt her hands against his chest, it was all he could do not to strip that blood-stirring costume she was wearing from her body.

But it was exactly those hands pressed against his chest that suddenly had him screeching to a halt emotionally and pulling back.

Breathing heavily, her lips all but throbbing from the imprint of his, Anne looked up at him in complete confusion and bewilderment.

"What's wrong?" she cried. "Why did you stop?"

"I can't do this," Danny told her. "I can't force my-self on you like this."

The hurt look on her face faded as she realized that he wasn't rejecting her. Ever noble, he was protecting her.

"You're not forcing yourself on me," she told Danny, her breath all but coming in snatches. "I've been wait-ing for this—for you—for twelve years."

Annie took hold of the front of his shirt and pulled him closer to him. His kiss had instantly triggered the hunger she had struggled to suppress since she had first seen him standing on her doorstep, back in town after all these years.

She had been eagerly anticipating this since that mo-ment.

Yes, she was afraid—with good reason, she felt—but at the same time, now that Danny had rekindled the fire she had been trying so hard to put out, she felt as if she was going to totally self-destruct if he did the noble thing and walked away from her.

She couldn't bear it.

Her eyes held his as she asked, "Are you going to make me beg?"

"No, never that," he told her.

Danny knew that his conscience was still going to bother him. But there was no denying that he wanted Annie so badly, he physically ached. He knew he would have absolutely no peace if he didn't give in to this in-credible craving that threatened to consume him.

Surrendering, Dan began to make love to her then,

softly, gently, reining in the all but insatiable desire to take her quickly, with wild abandonment.

He wanted to make sure that she would have no regrets, no doubts, even for a moment, over what was happening here between them. He didn't want to risk her believing that he was doing this just to satisfy himself, thinking that his first and foremost thought was not of her.

Because it was.

He had always placed her happiness, her fulfillment above his own, and having Annie achieve that fulfillment would make him happy and contribute to his own feeling of satisfaction.

Danny kissed her over and over again, feasting on her lips, on her throat, on the swell of her breasts as he slowly removed each piece of her pirate costume until all of it finally lay on the floor beside the sofa.

He ran his hands lovingly over her body, stroking it as if he were reverently stroking the strings of a priceless instrument, desperate to coax a beautiful melody out of it.

Annie twisted and turned beneath his hands. She loved the way he touched her, loved how he was making her body veritably hum with anticipation.

Unable to restrain herself any longer, she undressed Danny, curbing her eagerness in order not to tear anything. Her eagerness almost got the better of her not once but several times.

The less clothing there was between them, the greater her desire mounted until she felt as if she were on the verge of erupting. Like a wild woman, she raised

her body, pressing up against his, silently urging him
to take her.

And still he went slowly, even though she felt his urgent desire pressed against her body.

Over and over again, she sealed her mouth to his,
her fingertips digging into his shoulders as she silently
offered herself to him.

Dan resisted for as long as he could, wanting to prolong this moment for both of them. Once this lyrical
dance was over and the passion spent, who knew the
next time they would come together as one.

But he could only hold back for so long. And when
Annie opened for him, her silent invitation clear, the
last of his restraint shredded.

He entered her, his mouth sealed to hers just as his
soul had been sealed to hers all these years.

He began slowly but the rhythm sped quickly with
each moment, each thrust, until they were racing breath-
lessly toward the culmination of this union.

Racing toward the top of the mountain and to jour-
ney's end.

As the goal was finally reached, as stars exploded
and rained down all around them, they held tightly onto
one another. Euphoria wrapped itself around them, cur-
taining them in a private world of sensation and ecstasy.

They held reality at bay for as long as they could.
Each was willing to freeze time at this very second
while life-affirming sensations made their blood rush
and their heads whirl.

Dan held Annie to him so tightly he could literally
feel her heart pounding against his. In that moment all

he could think of was that he should have returned to Rust Creek Falls a lot sooner.

Because Annie—and this—was all that made life worth living.

He felt her sighing against him and knew that she was coming back down to earth, same as him. Even so, he wanted to hold her a little longer, pretend a little longer that this was how it was supposed to be—and had been since the beginning.

When she stirred, all he could think of was that he wanted to do it again, wanted to make love with Annie again.

And again.

And again after that, until he expired in her arms. Because right now, he couldn't think of a better way to go than in Annie's arms, making love with her.

## Chapter Sixteen

"**W**e've got to get dressed," Annie cried, suddenly bolting upright and hitting the top of her head against Danny's chin.

Jolted, he shook his head, trying to get his bearings.

Rubbing his chin, he said, "Not exactly the reaction I was hoping for." He'd been kissing her, arousing himself as well as, he'd hoped, Annie.

Annie had already scooped up her clothes from the floor, trying not to panic.

"Why aren't you moving?" she demanded. "Janie could be back any minute," she said, hurrying back into her pirate queen costume. She pushed his costume toward him urgently. "This is *not* the way I want to introduce her to her father."

He stopped dead, surprised. "Then you *do* want to

tell her that I'm her father?" Annie had made it sound as if that revelation was a long way off.

She pulled on her vest. "Yes, of course," she answered.

The prospect of being able to finally tell Janie that he was her father excited him. "When?" Danny wanted to know.

Anne's eyes met his. After the last hour they had just spent together, she didn't think she had to draw him a picture.

"I think that's pretty clear," she told him. When Danny continued looking at her, obviously waiting for an answer as he pulled his boots on, she said, "Now."

He didn't want her to feel pressured. "Are you sure about this?" he asked her.

"Very sure," she told him. And then it occurred to her that *he* might not want to tell Janie yet. "Why, are you having second thoughts about this?"

"Me?" he asked, surprised. "No. I just don't want you to rush into anything you're possibly going to wind up regretting, that's all. I don't want to lose all the ground I've gained with you—and with Janie."

"That's just it," she said as she finished dressing and started straightening up the sofa. "She likes you. Sometimes I think Janie likes you better than she likes me." She smiled at him as she arranged the throw pillows. "And you and I seem to have mended our fences. I don't see any reason to keep this from her any longer. Janie deserves to know the truth," she concluded.

"Well, you won't get any argument from me," Danny told her.

"Good." She raised her head, alert as she listened intently. "Because I think I hear a car pulling up."

Annie's heart was in her throat as she went to the front door and opened it. She was just in time to see Janie coming up the front walk.

The girl paused to wave goodbye to Mrs. Jackson and whatever girls were still in the van. And then, as the van pulled away, Janie ran up to her mother, her face flush with excitement, the plastic pumpkin she'd taken with her utterly stuffed with candy.

"Did you have a good time?" Annie asked her daughter, ushering her in.

"The best!" Janie answered. "I got a ton of candy!" She held up the pumpkin as proof, then she walked into the house ahead of her mother. "Look!" she said to Danny, showing him the pumpkin.

"Looks like a ton all right," he agreed.

"Which you will ration out over the next week or so," Annie instructed.

Two years ago, Janie had gotten sick to her stomach, gorging herself on sweets, and Anne didn't want a repeat of that event, especially not tonight.

Janie sighed. "Yes, Mother, I know the drill." She offered contents of the pumpkin to Danny. "Want some?" she asked.

It was all Dan could do not to hug his daughter. There would be time enough for that later, he promised himself.

"You first," he told her.

Janie grinned. "Okay." Taking a large candy bar near the top of the heap, she then held the pumpkin out to

Danny again. When he took a small piece, she turned toward her mother. "Mom, you want some candy?"

"Maybe later, honey." Her stomach was far too tied up right now. "Janie, I need you to sit down," she told her daughter. "Over here, on the sofa." She patted the seat beside her. Once they were all sitting down, Anne said, "We need to talk."

Janie stopped picking through her newly acquired stash and looked up at her mother. Wariness entered her blue eyes.

"Why?" she asked nervously. "What's wrong?"

"Nothing's wrong. I just— We just," Annie corrected herself, glancing over her daughter's head at Danny, "think it's time that you knew something."

Janie put the overflowing pumpkin on the coffee table and looked from her mother to Danny and then back to her mother.

"You're getting married, aren't you?" she guessed, catching both adults off guard. Janie shrugged carelessly. "I knew there was a reason Danny was here so much." She shrugged again, trying very hard to be blasé. "I guess it's okay."

Annie came very close to losing her nerve. After all, Janie had just given her a way out. It would be easy to accept her daughter's take on this and just let it go for now.

But she knew she couldn't put this off indefinitely, not after getting involved with Danny again, after finding out that the intensity of her feelings for him hadn't lessened. No, she needed to tell her daughter the truth right now.

"That's not the reason that he's been here so much." She raised her eyes to Danny, silently asking him to step in and say something to back up what she was trying to tell Janie.

"I wanted to get to know you, Janie," he told his daughter.

Janie clearly looked confused. "I don't understand. If it's not because you want to marry my mom, then why would you want to get to know me?"

They were back to the same question she had asked the first time he had come over to see her.

Anne drew in a breath and plunged in. "Because he's your father."

Instantly, Janie's expression became a mask of disbelief and anger.

"No, he's not! Hank's my father!" she insisted vehemently. "My father comes to pick me up for sleepovers every week," she cried, as if that was all the proof she needed.

"Hank's your stepfather, honey," Anne told her. She tried to put her hand on Janie's shoulder, but the girl jerked away, furious.

Janie's eyes were blazing as she cried, "Why didn't you tell me?"

"Well, at first there was no reason to," Anne said. "And then, even after the divorce, Hank was so crazy about you, I saw no reason to tell you. But now that your father has come back to Rust Creek Falls—"

"You lied to me!" Janie shouted at her, jumping to her feet. Her fury took in both adults. "You both lied to me!"

"We didn't lie to you, Janie. We just didn't know how to tell you. We were afraid of upsetting you," Danny told her, trying to reason with the girl.

"Well, guess what? I'm upset!" Janie spat out. "I hate you! I hate you both!" she shouted angrily. "And I'm calling Dad and telling him to come get me. I'm going to go live with him!"

Before Anne could stop her, Janie dashed out of the room and ran to her bedroom. She slammed the door. The sound reverberated throughout the house.

Stricken, Anne looked in the direction that her daughter had taken. "Well, that went well," she said, her voice breaking on the last word.

"I'll go talk to her," Danny offered, beginning to head toward Janie's room.

Annie caught his arm, holding him back. "No, don't. It's not going to do any good now," she told him in a hollow voice. She blew out a ragged breath, all but collapsing onto the sofa. "I knew it was going to go like this. That's why I put off telling Janie all this time." There were tears in her eyes as she looked at Danny. "But this is even worse than I imagined. She's going to move in with Hank." She felt as if each word she uttered was cutting up her insides.

"Oh, Annie, I'm so sorry." Danny attempted to take her in his arms, but she shrugged out of his hold, pulling away. He dropped his hands to his sides. "We'd been getting along so well, I really hoped that when she finally knew I was her father, she'd accept it even if she didn't welcome it right away. Please believe me,

I never meant to hurt anyone. I just thought… I thought if I came back…"

He was unable to finish, because he felt that no matter what his intentions had been, it didn't matter. What mattered was that Annie was crushed and their daughter wanted nothing to do with either of them. And it was all his fault.

"I should have just stayed away," Danny said, guilt all but suffocating him because of this latest turn of events.

He looked down at Anne huddled on the sofa in a fetal position. Her heart was clearly broken because her daughter wanted to go live with the man she regarded as her father. He knew Annie well enough to know that she wouldn't stop the girl, wouldn't force Janie to stay with her.

If he hadn't come back, none of this would have happened.

He wanted to apologize again. Wanted to tell her that he would have rather died than caused her this pain.

But nothing he said would change anything. The best thing he could do right now was leave.

Opening the door, he let himself out. Annie was still on the sofa, in shock and staring at the rear of the house as he closed the door behind him.

Hank came to pick Janie up less than an hour later. Janie flew into his arms and held on tightly. "I want to live with you, Dad."

He hugged the girl to him, looking accusingly at Anne over her daughter's head.

He had arrived here so quickly, Anne had no doubt that Janie had filled him in on everything.

She didn't have long to wait before finding out.

"Take your suitcase and wait for me in the truck, Janie," Hank told the girl.

"Sure, Dad," she answered.

Janie left without so much as a backward glance or a single word to her mother.

Anne stared after her, feeling as if her heart had been slashed open with a jagged knife.

"I warned you," Hank said the moment Janie closed the front door behind her. "I told you that no good would come of telling Janie the truth. She didn't need to know that Daniel is her birth father."

"I didn't like lying to her," Anne told him, doing her best not to fall apart.

"You weren't lying to her," he retorted. "You were shielding her from a harsh reality that she was far too young to know. Or to understand."

"And how old should she have been before she found out?" Anne wanted to know, getting defensive.

Except for the last incident—also centered around Dan—she rarely saw Hank get angry, but he was angry now. An angry Papa Bear protecting his cub with un-sheathed claws.

This was about the little girl he loved dearly and Hank intended to keep her safe, emotionally and physically, at all cost.

"With luck, never," Hank answered. "There was no reason for her to know who Daniel was. She was a happy, well-adjusted little girl who had two parents who loved her."

"Now she has three," Annie answered defiantly.

"And she's not all that happy, is she?" Hank countered.

It was obvious that he wanted to say something more, but he sensed it would only denigrate into really angry words that couldn't be taken back. He took a different tone.

"Look, I've got to go. Janie's in the truck, waiting for me," he said, his voice softening. "I'll call you later in the week to let you know how she's doing," he told Anne.

She pressed her lips together to keep back a sob. She could feel it throbbing in her throat. "I love her, Hank."

"I know that," he answered. "And when she calms down, she'll know that, too. But it's going to take a while." Hank was almost at the front door before he doubled back to her. He paused only long enough to kiss the top of Anne's head and then tell her, "It'll be all right."

With that, he walked out.

Feeling as if he had ruined Annie's life for a second time, Danny did the only thing he could for her. He stayed away. He felt he needed to give her time to pick up the shattered pieces of her life and try to put them together again.

To keep busy, he threw himself into working on the ranch with a vengeance. Though he was asked, he refrained from telling Jamie anything that had happened on Halloween. He made a point of denying, whenever Jamie asked him, that anything was wrong.

Jamie knew better, but he bided his time and rather than grilling him, he waited for his brother to volunteer the information on his own. Waited for him to explain why he was suddenly staying on the ranch 24/7 instead of going into town the way he had been doing.

Jamie strongly suspected that this changed behavior had something to do with Anne, but for now, he didn't prod. But it wasn't easy, watching Danny hurting, because he clearly was.

Danny didn't come back. Not that evening, not the following day, nor the day after that. He didn't come back and he didn't try to see her or get in touch with her in any way.

Had he just given up? Anne wondered. Or were those weeks they had spent together just a fluke? Did he really not care about her after all?

She'd been so sure, after they had made love on Halloween night, that they actually *were* meant to be together. But maybe those were just her hormones talking. Maybe she had talked herself into believing that he cared about her after all when he obviously didn't.

Because if he actually *did* care, then where was he? Why wasn't he calling, trying to get her to change her mind? Trying to find a way to help her convince Janie to move back in with her?

Anne continued to go to work at the clinic, continued doing everything that she had been doing, but she was only going through the motions. Inside, she felt as if she had been completely gutted. Her daughter hated her and the only man she had ever loved had abandoned her a second time after he had made her yearn for him.

She felt as if her life was going up in flames and there was absolutely nothing she could do about it.

But even so, she knew that somehow, she just had to.

*Chapter Seventeen*

Anne's natural inclination was to hide. Not physically, but emotionally. To run and to reconstruct those walls that she had so diligently built up over the last twelve years.

The same walls that Danny had so effectively deconstructed like a velvet wrecking ball in one evening of unadulterated passion.

But she sensed that if she continued to do what she had always done, she could expect to get what she had gotten these last dozen years: a life of mind-numbing emptiness. Yes, she'd had Janie, but right now, she didn't even have her.

She knew that she needed to rethink her position as well as her situation. Did she *really* want to continue this way? To live her life without Danny because she wanted to protect Janie? To keep her daughter and herself from possibly being hurt?

In a perfect world, that might have been achievable. But this was far from a perfect world. It was a world where things sometimes got messy, despite the best of efforts and intentions.

Anne really wanted to win back her daughter and, just as important, she wanted to get Danny back in her life, even if that meant risking being vulnerable. Love was worth the risk and she loved Danny with all her heart.

Always had, always would.

It was about time that she grew up and acted like a woman, not like an adolescent, Anne silently upbraided herself.

Danny didn't know if it was the blazing sun that lit up the ranch as he worked next to his brother, but he was finally seeing things clearly. After a great deal of soul-searching he'd reached a conclusion. Leaving wasn't going to solve anything. It wasn't the answer to anything. Whether he was here or in Colorado, he was still Janie's father and now she knew it. What kind of a father would he be, running off again? Moreover, if he did that, just how would that make Janie feel?

Besides, he didn't want to leave. He really loved Annie. Halloween evening had just proved it to him. He loved Annie and if he left Rust Creek Falls, it would mean literally tearing himself apart.

The answer wasn't running back to Colorado or to any other state, even further away. The answer was to dig in and ride out whatever storm might come his way. Ride it out until the storm finally passed and the seas became calm.

Annie was worth anything he had to endure, as was Janie.

Danny sighed, leaning on the shovel he'd been using to dig postholes. But now that he had made up his mind to stay, just how did he go about getting from point A to point B? How did he get Annie to allow him back into her life?

That was the part he needed to figure out.

Next to him, Jamie dropped the sledgehammer he was wielding to pound the new replacement posts into the ground. The hammer hit the ground, falling to the side as he looked at his brother.

He and Danny had been at this, replacing fence posts, for over a day. For the most part, over the course of that time, the sound of the sledgehammer was the *only* sound that was heard. If not for that rhythmic noise, the silence surrounding the two of them would be close to deafening.

Danny realized that his brother had stopped working. "Something wrong?" he wanted to know, looking in Jamie's direction.

"Yes, something's wrong," Jamie answered, doing his best not to sound annoyed. "I've been a good brother and held my peace for as long as I could. I didn't push, I didn't pry, thinking that eventually, you'd open up that sealed tomb of yours that you call a mouth and finally *talk* to me.

"But you obviously like pretending you're a sphinx,"

Jamie complained, "so I'm going to break the silence for you and ask."

Danny looked at him, obviously confused. "Ask me what?"

Jamie bit back a curse. Instead, he just got down to the bare bones of the question haunting him. "What the hell happened?"

"Happened?" Danny repeated as if he wasn't familiar with the word. It was clear that he was stalling, buying himself some time so he'd know how to frame his answer.

Jamie came dangerously close to losing his temper. "Damn it, Danny, you've never been an innocent, so don't try to play one now." Because Danny still wasn't talking, he went over the situation for him step by step. "You came home early Halloween night, dressed like a pirate and as silent as a crypt. Now, what the hell happened that night and why haven't you been to see Annie since then?

"Why have you suddenly become the epitome of a faithful hired hand, shadowing my every move like you don't have a mind of your own or anything else to do? Talk to me, damn it, or the next thing I'm liable to pound with that sledgehammer," he said as he nodded toward where it lay on the ground, "is your head."

Danny took a breath. Jamie was right. He couldn't keep this bottled up inside him any longer. He needed to talk, to get it off his chest so he could finally move forward. "We told her."

"Annie? Told her what?" Jamie asked, confused. "And who's 'we'?"

Dan shook his head. "No, not Annie. Janie. Annie and I told Janie that I'm her father."

"Her *what*?" Jamie cried, stunned. "Hold it, back up," he ordered. "*You're* Janie's father?" Dumbfounded, he stared at his brother. This was the first he'd heard of that. "Are you really sure about that?"

Dan nodded. "Annie told me. She didn't want me to say anything to anyone about it. I couldn't tell you," he began, ready with an apology that didn't make it past his lips.

Jamie waved his hand at his brother, silencing him. "I'm not mad that you didn't tell me. I'm just really surprised, that's all. Annie was away at college and when she finally came back, she was married to Hank. I just assumed that Janie was Hank's. The whole town assumed it."

"Well, she's not, and on Halloween night we told Janie I was her father and she didn't take it very well," he said sadly. "She accused us of lying to her and then she called Hank to come get her. She told Annie she was going to live with 'her father.' It tore Annie up right in front of my eyes. *I* did that to her," Dan said, the sadness audible in his voice.

There was nothing but sympathy in Jamie's eyes as he listened to his brother. "That's a lot for you to be carrying around."

"It's not me I'm thinking about. It's my fault this happened, because I came back," he said, feeling guilt sinking its teeth solidly into his conscience. "And now I have to find a way to fix this."

Jamie looked at him sharply. "Not by leaving again,"

he warned. "Even if I have to hog-tie you, you are *not* going back to Colorado. You belong here. Not just for my sake or Bella's," Jamie told him, mentioning their sister. "Not even for my kids. You owe it to Annie and to Janie to stay."

Dan shook his head ruefully. "Janie hates me."

"Well, then you have to make her unhate you," Jamie said simply.

He was all for that. But there was just one little problem with Jamie's advice. "And how am I supposed to do that?"

"Go talk to her. Not like she's some little kid. Talk to her like she's an adult. Listen to your heart, Danny," Jamie advised. "The time comes, you'll know what to say to her."

"You've got a lot of faith in a guy you haven't seen in twelve years." Frankly he didn't know if he was up to it.

Jamie grinned at him. "Yeah, but don't forget, I've got a lot of memories to work with and I've got a good memory. No matter how rough the calluses are on your hands, you're still the same guy inside that was always there for me when we were growing up. That's what you tap into," Jamie told him. "Be there for her. Be there for your daughter."

And then he stopped as he looked at Danny, trying to absorb the impact of what he'd just been told. "Wow. You a father. Now, there's something that's going to take some getting used to," Jamie told him.

"No more than you being the father of triplets," Dan responded.

Jamie's eyes crinkled as he laughed. "I guess you've

got a point." He stripped off his heavy-duty gloves and stuck them in his back pocket. "C'mon, I'll drive you back to the house. You've got to get cleaned up," he told his brother, adding, "You've got some fancy talking to do."

"What about work?" Danny asked, looking back at the posts that were still on the ground, waiting to be pounded in.

"Work's officially done for the day. Fallon's always after me to take an afternoon off. Looks like this is going to be it," he declared, getting in behind the steering wheel of his truck. "Now, are you going to get in, or are you planning on running alongside the truck until we get back to the house?"

"As appealing as that sounds," Danny said sarcastically, "I think I'll get into the truck." He slid onto the passenger seat.

When Danny looked back on it later, his return to Rust Creek Falls seemed to be fraught with giant bouts of nerves. Nerves had danced throughout his entire body when he'd first stood on Jamie's doorstep, waiting for his brother's first words to him.

The same complete uncertainty had telegraphed itself through his system when he'd stood before Annie's door, wondering what she would say when she finally saw him there.

And now he was going through the exact same thing as he waited for Hank to open his front door.

Dan counted off the seconds. Fifteen went by before the door finally opened. When it did, he found himself looking up at a less-than-friendly face. Hank was all but glaring at him.

"What do you want?" Hank demanded in a voice that was very close to a growl.

Dan silently congratulated himself that at least the other man hadn't slammed the door in his face. He took his victories where he found them.

"I'd like to talk to Janie," he answered.

Hank's eyebrows drew together in a dark, angry scowl. "Well, she doesn't want to talk to you."

Rather than turn around and leave, Dan made an appeal to the girl's stepfather. "Please, Hank. I need to explain some things to her."

Unmoved, Hank retorted, "You've already explained enough."

But Dan wasn't about to be dissuaded. "That's just it. I haven't. I need to make some things clear to her. And after I'm done, I'd like to talk to you, Hank," he said.

Hank looked skeptical, his eyes shrewdly assessing Dan. For a second, Dan thought Janie's stepfather was going to turn him away. But then the rancher blew out an impatient breath and opened the door a little further.

"All right," Hank said. "Come in. But the first second Janie looks like she doesn't want to listen anymore, you're gone, even if I have to hurl you out the door myself. Understood?"

Dan nodded, relieved that Hank was giving him this chance. "Understood."

Resigned, looking far from happy about the situation, Hank turned and led the way into the large, sprawling living room.

Janie was on the sofa, watching TV. The second she saw Dan, she jumped to her feet. "What's *he* doing here?" she wanted to know, glaring angrily at the man next to Hank.

"He says he's here because he wants to talk to you," Hank told her.

"Do I have to?" Janie's voice bordered on whining as she stared defiantly at Dan.

"Hear him out, honey," Hank said, his voice taking on a kind tone when he spoke to the girl. "I raised you to be fair."

Janie sighed, put upon. "All right, if you want me to." She shifted her eyes in Danny's direction as Hank slipped into the background. "Go ahead," she said to Dan. "Talk."

Danny felt as if he was standing before a pint-size judge. Not exactly ideal conditions in his opinion, but they were the only ones he was going to get so he knew he had to make the most of them.

"I just wanted you to know that I didn't know you even existed until just a few weeks ago."

"Mom didn't tell you?" Janie demanded sharply.

He could see she was going to hold that against Annie, too, unless he talked quickly. "No. Your mother had no way to get in touch with me to let me know I had a daughter."

"Were you some kind of bad guy on the run?" Janie asked suspiciously.

"If you're asking me if I was a criminal, no, I wasn't a criminal," he told her. "But you could say that I was on the run." He saw his daughter looking at him quizzically but he didn't want to get into that just yet. "The important part is that your mother was trying to do what she thought was best for you and I don't want you to blame her for any of this, or to hold it against her, agreed?"

The frown on Janie's face told him that the girl wasn't capitulating, at least not yet. She was being defiant and he knew that he needed to convince her. He told her the only thing that he could. "I am never going to try to replace Hank.

"You're right, you know. Your 'real' dad is the one who was there for you, who raised you and encouraged you to do your best even when it wasn't easy. He got to spend the years with you that I couldn't, because I didn't know about you. I can never have that, just like I can never replace him.

"But I would very much like to get to know you, Janie, and get to spend some more time with you if you'll let me. And if you're willing to give me that chance, I think you'll get to see that I'm not really such a bad guy after all."

Dan looked at his daughter for a long moment, then put his hand out to her. "What do you say, Janie? Will you give me another chance?"

Janie frowned and chewed on her lower lip, debating whether or not to believe him. Still debating, she looked down at his hand. And then, finally, she slipped hers into it.

"I guess I can give you one more chance," she told him.

Dan felt as if his very insides had lit up like the candles on a birthday cake.

"I promise I won't disappoint you," he told his daughter, solemnly shaking the small hand.

"We'll see," Janie said, sounding every bit the way her mother did. "But I'm not going back to my mother," she warned.

"I understand. But I'd like you to think about it. She really misses you a lot and she really was trying to do her best for you. You have always been her first priority."

Janie shrugged, trying hard to sound distant. "We'll see."

"That's all anyone can ask," Dan told his daughter. "And it means a lot. To your mom and to me."

"Yeah," was all Janie would say, but from where he was standing, it sounded positive to Dan.

The first step had been taken, he thought. Now all he needed was to get Janie to keep walking.

## *Chapter Eighteen*

The moment it looked as if he and Janie had finished talking for now, Hank seemed to materialize out of the shadows and swooped in, looking extremely solemn.

"I'll see you out," Hank said.

It wasn't an offer. It was a command.

Dan felt like he was given his walking papers. Since he had said what he had come to say to Janie and the situation looked at least somewhat hopeful, he acquiesced to Hank's offer.

"Sure. See you, Janie."

The girl merely nodded, going back to her TV program.

Hank walked beside him in silence until they were at the front door again. Opening it, the stone-faced man surprised him by coming out with him to the front porch.

Once outside, Hank pulled the door closed behind

him. It was obvious that the man wanted to talk, so Dan braced himself.

"I appreciate you not trying to strong-arm Janie into anything," Hank told him.

He'd had a feeling that Hank had been in the background somewhere, listening. It had made him doubly cautious as he'd chosen his words.

"I was serious when I said that all I wanted was a chance to get to know her," he told Hank.

Arms crossed before his chest, Hank stood studying him for a long moment, saying nothing. Dan had almost turned to leave when Hank finally said something further. And what he said *really* surprised him.

"You know she never got over you. Anne," Hank added, although there was no doubt who he was talking about. "I knew that when I married her. But I hoped that in time, she'd learn to love me. Not the way she loved you," he allowed, knowing that wasn't possible. "That kind of thing only comes along once in a lifetime. But there are other kinds of love," he said philosophically. "Gentle, patient kinds of love.

"But I learned that there was never going to be any room in Anne's heart for any other man but you. Eventually, I gave up trying to find a tiny space in that heart for me.

"I'm telling you this," Hank went on, "because if you're not sure about your feelings for her, you should leave now before you do any more damage to Anne— or to Janie. I won't stand for either one of them being hurt," Hank said adamantly. "They don't deserve it."

"No, they don't," Dan agreed quietly. "And I would

die before I was the reason that either one of them wound up being hurt again."

"You did before," Hank pointed out. "You left Anne twelve years ago, vanishing out of her life without a single word."

He knew all that and the act weighed heavily on him now. "The circumstances were different back then."

"Anne was still Anne," Hank reminded him.

It wasn't that he wanted Hank not to blame him. He just felt that the rancher needed to understand why things had happened the way they had.

"And at the time I left, I felt that she deserved to be with someone who was better than me," Dan told him. The words seemed to be coming out of their own accord.

Hank frowned. "What's that supposed to mean?" he wanted to know. He couldn't help thinking that Dan was just attempting to snow him.

Okay, it was time, Dan decided. Time to let the other man know why he had left Rust Creek Falls and why he had stayed away as long as he had.

"It means that at the time I left, I really didn't feel worthy of anybody, least of all someone like Anne." Dan took a breath before he went on. The words hurt. There was no way of getting away from that. "I felt that I was responsible for my parents' deaths."

Hank looked at him, confused. "I heard that your parents died in a car accident."

"They did," Dan said grimly.

Dan blaming himself for something like that didn't make any sense to Hank. Unless… The thought struck him.

"Were you driving the car at the time?" Hank asked.

"No, but I was the reason that they *were* driving."
Dan saw that Hank looked more confused than ever.

He hated this story, hated having to revisit it. But he
felt that Hank needed to hear it so that the rancher could
see Dan wasn't just some self-centered cowboy who
came and went whenever the whim suited him without any thought to the people who mattered. Namely
Annie and Janie.

Wishing he could shield himself somehow, knowing that just wasn't possible, Dan finally launched into
the story that changed his life—and everyone else's.

"My two older brothers, Luke and Bailey, went out
drinking one night. I went with them but at the time I
didn't know that was what they intended to do. It wasn't
too long before they were both much too drunk to drive
home safely. I didn't have the keys to the car and Luke
wouldn't give me his. I was afraid we'd all wind up in
an accident—or worse—so I called my parents to ask
them to come pick us up."

Hank shrugged, not hearing anything out of the or-
dinary. "Sounds like a scene that happens every night
all over the country," he acknowledged. "Parents come
get their inebriated kids all the time."

"Except that those parents all get home in one piece,"
Dan said grimly. "Mine didn't." He looked at Hank. The
rancher was obviously waiting to hear more. "Don't you
see? If I hadn't called them to pick us up, my parents
would still be alive."

Hank didn't quite see it that way. "Maybe yes, maybe
no. When your time comes, you can't outrun your fate,"
the rancher said philosophically. And then he looked at

Dan sharply. "Is this what you've been running from all this time?"

"Yes," Dan said heavily.

"A lot of things to feel guilty about in this world," Hank said. "Not being there for a good woman when she needed you is one. Not being there for your kid when she was growing up is another. But being responsible for your folks' deaths in a car accident when you weren't anywhere near that car? Get over yourself, Stockton," he told Dan. "You're not in charge of everything going on in the universe. Stuff happens and you're just another bystander."

And then he surprised Dan by putting his hand out to him in a show of tentative friendship.

Dan took it, finding himself on the receiving end of a hearty handshake.

"Thanks for trusting me with your story," Hank told him. "Now stop wasting time talking to me and go patch things up with Anne," he ordered.

Relieved, feeling as if a rock had been lifted from his shoulders, Dan murmured a heartfelt "Thanks" as he hurried off to his truck.

"Good luck," Hank called after him.

Dan acknowledged his words with a quick wave just before he got in behind the steering wheel.

The urgent knocking on her door startled Anne. Her first thought was that something had happened to Janie and someone was here to notify her.

Fairly running to the door, she threw it open and was startled to find Danny standing on her doorstep.

A wave of déjà vu passed over her, except that the first time, Danny's knocking hadn't been nearly so urgent as it was now.

She was about to ask what was wrong, but she never got the chance because the very next moment, Dan was scooping her up in his arms and then twirling her around, stealing her breath away, not to mention making her dizzy.

"No more running away," Danny declared, setting her down on her feet inside her house. He held her shoulders in an effort to keep her from losing her balance and falling over. "Even if you decide that you don't want us to be together, I want you to know that I'm not going anywhere anymore, and I'll be here any time you need me for any reason."

Annie looked at him uncertainly. "Then you're staying?"

"I'm staying," he confirmed. "I'm moving back to Rust Creek Falls permanently so I can get to really know our daughter—and be here for her, as well. I want to be a hands-on dad, not just one in name only."

She was afraid to believe him, but she had to admit, she was sorely tempted to. This what she'd been dreaming about all these years: Danny, coming back and wanting to take care of her and their daughter.

"And you're not going to change your mind tomorrow?" Anne asked.

"Not tomorrow, or the day after that, or the day after that times infinity," he replied. "I'm here to stay, Annie. Besides, where else would I go? The only woman I have ever loved lives here, so I can't go anywhere else."

He had never said those words out loud to her, even though she'd hoped and prayed that he would. "You love me?" she asked, wanting to hear him say it again.

"I love you," he repeated. "I loved you twelve years ago. I love you now and I will go on loving you until the day I die. Maybe a little longer than that," he added with a smile.

But Anne felt as if she needed a lot of assurance after what she'd been through. She was not about to begin building castles in the sky on a foundation of sand the way she had before.

"I can't help wondering if you're in love with me, or if you're just in love with the girl I used to be. The girl without a serious thought in her head," she recalled ruefully. Her eyes met his. "Because I'm not that girl anymore."

"I know that," Dan told her. "I know you're not the same person you were then. You've done a lot of growing and maturing over the years. You became a responsible mother and you were even willing to marry someone you weren't in love with just to give your daughter a stable life. And when you realized that you felt Hank deserved someone who loved him for himself, you divorced him even though doing that meant you had to make sacrifices in order to provide for your daughter. That's not something a girl 'without a serious thought in her head' would do. That's something a responsible woman would do," he told her.

"Twelve years ago," he went on, "I promised to protect you and stay by your side and I blew it. Right now, all I want to do is spend the rest of my life making it up to you—if you'll let me." He took her hands in his. "Will you?"

Anne stared at him, wondering if she understood him correctly.

"Are you saying what I think you're saying?" she asked, afraid to let herself believe that. What if she'd somehow misunderstood him? She didn't relish looking like a fool—or having her heart broken a second time.

Danny grinned. "I guess I'm not really any good at this," he confessed. "But in my defense, I've never proposed before."

"Proposed," Anne echoed, her eyes widening as she stared at the man in her living room.

"Proposed," Dan repeated with feeling. Taking her hands again and this time pressing them to his chest right over his heart, he said, "Anne Lattimore, I love you and I want to spend the rest of my life loving you. Will you marry me?"

He saw tears shining in her eyes, threatening to spill down her cheeks. "Tears," he said. "Are they good tears, or bad tears?"

Anne tried to answer, but her throat was completely choked with emotion and for a moment, she couldn't say a word.

Second guessing the reason for her silence, Dan wanted to put her mind at ease and told her, "Hank gave me his approval."

That surprised her.

"He what?" she cried, not really certain she liked the fact that her fate was being hashed out by the men in her life.

"He was trying to protect you, saying that if I wasn't completely committed to you—and to Janie—then I needed to go back to Colorado. That was when I explained to him why I left in the first place. He heard me out and then he came around."

She knew that sharing his reasons with Hank had to have been painful for Danny. "You did that?" she asked. "You told him what happened?"

"I would do anything if it meant that we could be together," he told Anne. "I went to talk to Janie about things. I got her to listen and I think she'll come around." All he wanted to do was show Anne how much he loved her.

And now that he had asked her to marry him, he wanted it to become a reality, but he felt he shouldn't rush her. Dan struggled to rein himself in.

"We don't have to set a date yet," he continued. "I just wanted you to know that I mean business because this time, I'm not planning on letting you get away—not ever again."

"You mean business," she repeated with a trace of amusement.

"Yes."

A wicked smile flirted with her lips. "Well, if you really mean business, then why don't you show me?"

"And how do you suggest I do that?" he asked her, bemused.

"You're a very smart man, Danny Stockton," she told him, lacing her arms around her neck. "I think you can figure it out."

"How many chances do I get?" he teased.

She could feel her heart accelerate as it swelled with joy. "As many as you need," she told him.

"Oh, good," he said just before he lowered his lips to hers. "Because I intend to use them all."

And he very nearly did.

## Epilogue

"I can't believe that we've owned our old ranch this entire time and never realized it," Bella Stockton Jones said to her brothers in amazement.

She, Jamie and Dan moved around the first floor of the old house at Sunshine Farm, trying to avoid cobwebs as they wove their way through an incredible amount of dust and even more old memories.

"We still wouldn't have known about it if Zach Dalton hadn't come to me and asked if I would consider selling the old ranch to him," Jamie said, tugging back a drape and unleashing a swirl of dust.

"I told him I didn't know what he was talking about," Jamie continued. "That the ranch didn't belong to us. But Zach insisted that it did. He said that he'd looked it up in county records and according to them, the property was still ours."

"If it belonged to you, why didn't your grandparents tell you?" Annie asked, puzzled. She'd insisted on coming along for this walk-through in case Danny needed a little moral support for his return to his old family homestead.

"You're asking the wrong person," Dan told her. "I have no idea why those two old people did anything." He wasn't bitter toward his grandparents at this point— he was just sad.

"Maybe they felt too put-upon just taking care of us and didn't want to be bothered looking into anything else. They did take in two of us," Bella said, adding, "Grudgingly."

"Those days are best left behind us," Dan told his siblings. He had no desire to dig up any more painful memories. They had all had enough of those to last them a lifetime and a half and it was time to move forward.

"I guess we have a lot to thank the Daltons for," Jamie said, crossing to the other end of the room and pulling back more drapes.

"You mean for telling us about the old Sunshine Farm?" Dan asked.

"That and airing that program of the triplets and me that Travis had documented. If it hadn't been for that— and for him—you would have never come back to Rust Creek Falls," Jamie pointed out.

Dan's hand tightened around Annie's. "Oh, I'd like to think that I would have come back eventually. But you're right," he agreed, looking at Jamie. "Travis was instru-mental in making me finally decide that it was time to at least come back to see how everyone was doing."

"So now that you've taken a look around, what are you going to do with this place?" Anne asked, directing her question to all three Stocktons.

Jamie was the first to speak up. "I think we should try to fix it up." He looked at Dan and Bella. "What do you think?"

"Sounds good to me," Bella answered, nodding her head.

"I'm in," Dan told Jamie. "After helping you out at your place, I've gotten pretty good at fixing things up."

"I don't know about 'good.' I'd say that you're a work in progress at the moment," Jamie said with a laugh. "But sure, we could all pitch in to get this place looking livable again."

"Mom and Dad would have liked that," Bella told her brothers.

"Do you think you could have the ranch ready for a Christmastime wedding?" Anne asked quietly.

Dan whirled toward her. "Christmastime?" he repeated. "Is that when you want it?"

Her smile was almost shy as she answered, "Yes."

"Wait, hold it," Jamie spoke up, looking at Dan and Anne. "What wedding?"

"Are you two getting married?" Bella asked, excitement echoing in her voice before Dan could answer their brother's question.

"Yes. Yes, we are. And it looks like it's going to be a Christmas wedding," Dan said, pulling Annie close to him.

"Well, congratulations!" Jamie cried. "Let me be the first to kiss the bride-to-be."

"That's my job," Dan told him, elbowing Jamie out of the way. "You can be the second." With that, he kissed Annie. Under the circumstances, it was a quick kiss, but it expressed all the love he felt for her. "I just wish that the rest our siblings could be here for the wedding," he said wistfully.

"Don't worry," Jamie promised with determination. "They might not be here for the wedding, but we'll find them. I won't rest until we do."

"Neither will I," Bella added.

"That would be the very best wedding present of all," Anne told them, smiling up at Dan.

"See why I love her?" Dan asked his siblings. Looking at Annie, he said, "Yes, I totally agree, it would," just before he kissed her again.

It was the most happiness that the old homestead had seen in a decade—with more to come.

\* \* \* \* \*

*Don't miss the next instalment of the new*
*Montana Mavericks continuity*

## MONTANA MAVERICKS:
## THE GREAT FAMILY ROUNDUP

*Rancher Eli Dalton feels like the last single man*
*in Rust Creek Falls. Could visiting veterinarian*
*Hadley Strickland be the wife he's been looking for?*
*He vows to give her the best Christmas ever—*
*but first he'll have to heal her broken heart...*

*Look for*
*THE MAVERICK'S SNOWBOUND CHRISTMAS*
*by* USA TODAY *Bestselling Author*
*Karen Rose Smith*

*On sale November 2017, wherever Mills & Boon books*
*and ebooks are sold.*

# MILLS & BOON®

## *Cherish*™

**EXPERIENCE THE ULTIMATE RUSH OF FALLING IN LOVE**

## A sneak peek at next month's titles...

**In stores from 19th October 2017:**

- **Newborn Under the Christmas Tree** – Sophie Pembroke *and* **The Rancher's Christmas Song** – RaeAnne Thayne
- **Snowbound with an Heiress** – Jennifer Faye *and* **The Maverick's Snowbound Christmas** – Karen Rose Smith

**In stores from 2nd November 2017:**

- **Christmas with Her Millionaire Boss** – Barbara Wallace *and* **A Cowboy Family Christmas** – Judy Duarte
- **His Mistletoe Proposal** – Christy McKellen *and* **His by Christmas** – Teresa Southwick

*Just can't wait?*
Buy our books online before they hit the shops!
**www.millsandboon.co.uk**

**Also available as eBooks.**

# MILLS & BOON®

## EXCLUSIVE EXTRACT

Beautiful, young widow Noelle Fryberg is determined to
show her Christmas-hating boss, millionaire James
Hammond, just how magical Christmas can be…Could she
be the one to melt his heart?

*Read on for a sneak preview of*
**CHRISTMAS WITH HER MILLIONAIRE BOSS**
*the first book in the magical* **THE MEN WHO MAKE
CHRISTMAS** *duet*

He'd lost his train of thought when she looked up at him,
distracted by the sheen left by the snow on her dampened
skin. Satiny smooth, it put tempting ideas in his head.

Like kissing her.

"Don't be silly," she replied. For a second, James thought
she'd read his mind and meant the kiss, especially after she
pulled her arm free from his. "It's a few inches of snow, not
the frozen tundra. I think I can handle walking, crowd or no
crowd. Now, I don't know about you, but I want my hot cocoa."

She marched toward the end of the aisle, the pom-pom
on her hat bobbing in time with her steps. James stood and
watched until the crowd threatened to swallow her up before
following.

What the hell was wrong with him? Since when did he
think about kissing the people he did business with? Worse,
Noelle was an employee. Granted, a very attractive, enticing
one, but there were a lot of beautiful women working in the
Boston office and never once had he contemplated pulling one
of them against him and kissing her senseless.

Then again, none of them ever challenged him either. Nor did they walk like the majorette in a fairy band.

It had to be the drone. He'd read that concussions could cause personality changes. Lord knows, he'd been acting out of character for days now starting with agreeing to stay for Thanksgiving.

It certainly explained why he was standing in the middle of this oversized flea market when he could—should—be working. Honestly, did the people in this town ever do anything at a normal scale? Everywhere he looked, someone was pushing Christmas. Holiday sweaters. Gingerbread cookies. One vendor was literally making hand-blown Christmas ornaments on the spot. Further proof he wasn't himself, James almost paused because there was one particularly incandescent blue ornament that was a similar shade to Noelle's eyes.

The lady herself had stopped. At a booth selling scented lotions and soaps wrapped in green and gold cellophane. "Smell this," she said, when he caught up with her. She held an open bottle of skin cream under his nose, and he caught the sweet smell of vanilla. "It's supposed to smell like a Christmas cookie," she said. "What do you think?"

"I like the way your skin smells better."

Don't miss
THE MEN WHO MAKE CHRISTMAS:

*CHRISTMAS WITH HER MILLIONAIRE BOSS*
by Barbara Wallace
*Available November 2017*

*SNOWED IN WITH THE RELUCTANT TYCOON*
by Nina Singh
*Available December 2017*

www.millsandboon.co.uk

# MILLS & BOON®

## Why shop at millsandboon.co.uk?

Each year, thousands of romance readers find their perfect read at millsandboon.co.uk. That's because we're passionate about bringing you the very best romantic fiction. Here are some of the advantages of shopping at www.millsandboon.co.uk:

* **Get new books first**—you'll be able to buy your favourite books one month before they hit the shops

* **Get exclusive discounts**—you'll also be able to buy our specially created monthly collections, with up to 50% off the RRP

* **Find your favourite authors**—latest news, interviews and new releases for all your favourite authors and series on our website, plus ideas for what to try next

* **Join in**—once you've bought your favourite books, don't forget to register with us to rate, review and join in the discussions

Visit **www.millsandboon.co.uk**
for all this and more today!